TALES OF TUCSON

By

ANTHONY RANDALL

First published in Great Britain 2020
Jemmett Affection

Paperback version worldwide 2021
Koala T Publishing
1 West Lodge
Dorchester
Dorset
DT2 8JA

Cover design by Anthony Randall.

1st draft edit: Vanessa Gottesman.

2nd draft edit: Tom Benson

A special thank you goes to authors John Hennessey,
Sylva Fae, Ceri Bladen
and Katerina Sestakova Novotna
Your input and advice was invaluable

For my fellow explorer and oldest friend
Shane Lamont
Without you, adventures would not be so.

Thank you for your companionship
The fun, the music
Your eccentricity, your quirks, your skills
And your unbound sense of fun.
But most of all, your audacity,
It took us places we might never have gone.

Contents

Introduction

This is volume one of a two book series, a work of fiction based on true events played out long ago, in a very different time. I'll leave it to the reader's discretion to cipher the make-believe from the real.

These pages mostly cover year one of the tales, 1988, although it starts with a flash forward, to provide a flavour of what is to come. Enjoy. A.R.

1
The Hearse

July 1989.
Mid-morning Tuesday, I think.

The car rounded the corner of East Glen and Alvernon and came to a halt curb-side on familiar oil-stained dusty ground. It rocked like a nudged cradle, with a final touch of the accelerator, before all life was extinguished by a quarter turn of the key.

Despite its years, it had driven like a silk scarf wafted over enamel. Hidden beneath a gossamer veil of baked-on desert grime, harboured an iconic gothic masterpiece, craftsmanship that no longer extended in the making of American automobiles.

Tom and Seamus sat either side of their cynical boss, on the black leather bench seat, at the front of an enormous 1970 Cadillac Superior Royale hearse. Saul Berns slouched in between them nonchalantly chewing gum, smacking out a rhythm with his tuberous lips.

"I want you to take this fuckin' thing up to Ron Ruby's. Leave a fuckin' note on the windshield saying your car has arrived!"

The boys laughed, despite the ludicrous, acidic instruction inciting gurgling bile to secrete and boil in their stomachs.

What kind of situation had they slipped into? This wasn't what they had signed up for, doing leg work for a gangster, five-thousand miles outside of their comfort zone.

But like it or not, ultimately he was their boss; he paid them to sit here in the sunshine, he put beer in their bellies, girls in their arms and fundamentally provided them their liberty in the United States. It was an unpalatable dilemma; do as requested or go home.

The leviathan had sat there for several years unloved, sinister, Munster-like, with a touch of 'Christine' about it. And happened to be exactly what Saul Berns was looking for.

Now as they wilted under blistering Arizona heat, following a test drive with the AC turned off, Saul had revealed his intentions.

Tom was at the wheel. "That'll wind 'im up!"

"Uh?" Saul found these two Brits hard to comprehend at the best of times.

"Make 'im mad," said Seamus interpreting Tom's colloquialism.

"That's the least that cocksucker's gonna get when I'm through," replied the boss. "Now let's pay for this piece of shit and then take me home. You can wash it when we get back, and then drive this fucker up tonight … it'll be a nice supplement with the fuckin' morning papers."

Seamus was cautious in his response. "Aha," he murmured; the task was becoming increasingly more daunting.

Fifteen hundred dollars was a cheap price to pay for a vindictive little poke at your enemy and besides it wasn't Saul's money he was paying with—it was never Saul's money that he squandered.

Ron Ruby was Saul Berns' nemesis; they had hated each other for the past 15 years. Like Saul, Ron was an associated mobster with a caustic history, who now dealt in the murky grey areas of land acquisition and development.

Ron wanted parcels of land that Saul had obtained and was vehemently hanging on to.

Ron's grand scheme was to build a satellite city consisting of 21,000 homes and 2 resorts on fragile conservation land centred on a ranch in the south east corridor adjacent to the Saguaro National park, in Tucson. The project was causing uproar amongst the town's 'green' fraternity and naturalists who had formed a coalition to halt the rape of their land and had enlisted the leadership of one Dr Kevin Launcher, an eminent conservationist and professor from the University of Arizona.

Ron required this land to complete his multi-million dollar investment and would pay massively over the odds for it. Saul Berns would rather slit his own throat before selling to "that fuckin' big-shot sonofabitch."

The feud between the opposing parties was festering into a political storm, with the town planning and zoning departments caught in the middle.

What started out as just another Rancho Vistoso or Green Valley project, had turned into a fiery referendum on the future of the city. A juggernaut that had solidified both sides of the spectrum and threatened to gather a few scalps before the final outcome was resolved.

Saul had sided firmly with the alliance, but he cared little about conservation, he just wanted to turn over his adversary, Ron Ruby.

Later that evening with the setting sun creating another spectacular trifle-layered sky, the boys were busy preparing for Saul's latest skulduggery.

Tom was perturbed and fidgety. "What if we get tugged by the 'Old Bill'?"

"We'll be alright," assured Seamus, "we'll take it easy."

"It's gonna look pretty conspicuous driving around in that fuckin' thing in the middle of the night." Tom was peeping through a crack in the curtains towards the parking lot below their apartment. Some of the local kids had mustered up the courage to go peer inside the monster car, probably hoping that Vampira wasn't laid out in the back.

"It's got no tags 'n no insurance; let's 'ope you don't get a squad car up ya' arse."

"They'll just think it's students 'aving a laugh," replied Seamus.

"They'd better be blind, I don't think you could survive another appearance in front of a judge!"

Seamus gave a short "ha", in return.

Some months previously, Seamus had been pulled over on his way to work by a police officer, for speeding in their Chevrolet El Camino. The inspection revealed that he had out of date tags on the number plate, lacked insurance, had no valid driving licence and had outstayed his visa in the USA. It was a dead cert that Seamus would be deported; absolutely no doubt about it and Tom had started to entertain plans to go it alone.

But once the judge had deduced that this engrossing defendant was an Englishman, they got into a lengthy rapport about London, the weather and English actors, particularly Rex Harrison (Dr Dolittle) the judge's favourite. And after charming his 'Honour' with disingenuous wit, Seamus was dismissed with nothing more than a $100 fine and a 2 day 'step course' on speeding to attend at a police station.

Of course Seamus, being Seamus, only went for one day.

After this brush with expulsion, the boys had decided to at least make their car legal. They got insured via Caitlyn Bern's brother, Charles, who insured the car for himself, and then put them down as named drivers. They ran the El Camino through an emissions test to get the tags up to date and then they both took their driving test, a simple affair compared to the UK equivalent. It consisted of driving their Chevrolet once around the block with a police officer beside them, who was more interested in their accent than paying attention to their driving skills, reverse parking between two traffic cones, simple, and sitting a written multiple-choice Q&A paper.

Twenty-six questions on road awareness of which 21 was the pass mark. Tom and Seamus sat one in front of the other at a desk along with 30 or more other hopefuls in a deathly silent sterile station room headed by one officer. It was like re-sitting a school exam but without the smell of pubescent teenagers.

Two questions into the test and Seamus was whispering back to Tom. "What's the answer to number three?"

"A," replied his buddy.

"What's the answer to number four?"

"C," Tom hissed.

This went on incessantly throughout the whole exam, with Tom getting more and more agitated, and spotlighted by the ripple of giggles from those around them. The examiner uncomfortably frustrated, burned a hard stare into Tom, but it had no effect on his mischievous friend in front.

After half an hour the papers were collected and marked while the gathering awaited their fate.

"I thought we were gonna get thrown out then, you bloody nuisance," Tom frowned.

Seamus laughed. "I knew the answers really, I was just winding you up," He grinned.

"You fucker," replied Tom.

The test papers came back and they'd both passed, but to Tom's amazement Seamus had scored one more correct answer than him.

"'ow the fuck did that 'appen?" he said astounded.

Seamus shrugged nonchalantly. "Dunno, luck I s'pose."

They lined up for their photos to be taken, smiled for the camera and had their licenses processed there and then, laminated and handed over.

Out in the car park the lads were stunned by how little time it had taken. They stared at their licenses. "Arizona driver license, expires 2021," read Tom, "I'll have to do a retake when I'm sixty or I'll have trouble getting into bars!"

"Mate," said Seamus "I think you should do a retake now, that photo's gonna make doormen think it's a fake. You look about fifteen!"

"Ha," barked Tom, "it's me' genes."

"You're wearing shorts," cracked Seamus.

"This is true, let's go tell Caitlyn the good news."

The boys slipped into their car and for the first time in the USA, drove legally back to their illegal place of work.

"So what's the plan then?" asked Tom, "you gonna wear gloves?"

"I'm gonna wear that Frankenstein mask that I got for Halloween last year. That'll crack people up when I pull up beside 'em at traffic lights."

Tom chuckled. "Na, seriously you've to wear gloves, you don't wanna leave any prints."

"Got it sorted mucker," said Seamus pulling on some huge fake gorilla hands. The boys almost pissed themselves laughing as Seamus ballet danced around the living room in nothing but his Y-fronts, gorilla hands and Frankenstein mask.

***

Tom had been in Tucson the longest. He originally came over for three months to visit his sister Keira, who was living at Bear Paw Nature Reserve near Colossal Cave with her husband Tom Price and their three-year-old daughter, Amber.

The Prices' worked for the park's wardens; Keira cleaned their huge Adobe house, which sat secluded in the middle of the reserve on a mound of rocky scrub surrounded by towering Saguaro cactus and outcrops of Mesquite trees and Brittlebush. Tom Price was caretaker of the numerous picnic areas that scattered the park.

Tom Reynolds had arrived one March morning bleary-eyed, translucent-skinned and broken-hearted. Three months R&R with his sister was going to do him the world of good. His dad however, who had driven him to Heathrow airport in freezing rain, thought this was the last he'd see of his son. He was convinced Tom would be stabbed to death or something equally as cheery. Tom's dad had given him £500 to spend and a handshake. A paltry payment for a last goodbye.

His brother-in-law was exuberant and giggling like a loon when Tom appeared through the arrivals gate at Tucson International. Wearing the obligatory brand new clothes for a trip abroad, the traveller, being British of course, bizarrely carried a warm coat hooked over his arm.

Tom P greeted Tom R with a hug saying, "pinch y'self, y'dreaming, you're in America now, son! Ha, ha, ha."

"Alright Tom, thanks for meeting me mate, 'ow's things?" he replied drowsily.

"You won't believe it son; you'll think you're dreaming! 'Ow was the flight?"

"Long and annoying, I couldn't wait to get off the plane at LAX. I felt like I was gonna explode. But I was sat next to a beautiful bird, only 18 and gorgeous, which was pleasant; shame she 'ad a bloke waiting for 'er at the airport."

"Don't you worry about that, son," said Pricey. "The birds will be falling all over ya 'ere, they just love that English accent," he reasoned with a poor American twang.

The Toms had known each other since they were ten years old. They were the same age within a month and their parents knew each other well. Other than that, they couldn't have been more polar opposite.

Pricey was loud, a leery rogue, a brigand who wouldn't think twice about stealing from his own mother and often had. He was a master liar, a con artist, someone who wormed his way into your business whatever you were doing and then claimed it to be his own, a wife beater and a complete nuisance. Mind you Keira gave as good as she got, they used to fight like cat and dog at times, Tom had to get between them on several occasions. Pricey was however keenly generous, which was probably out of a need to be liked. He had a mop of rigid orange hair, (Keira called him ginger chicken-bollocks), piercing green eyes and freckles. He was of average height, solid in stature and loved to smoke weed, copious amounts of weed, to the point of incoherence.

Tom Reynolds was kind, thoughtful, softly spoken and methodical; worth a second glance, but not always a third, he thought. He'd been paid many a compliment in the past, but whenever he looked in the mirror all he would see was disappointment. The reflections stifled his confidence.

"You won't need that any more," referred Pricey to Tom's coat. He was right; the warm night air outside the terminal was magical, a soft fuzzy reverie, a land with its own unique smell, a signature that would ingratiate Tom forever.

He drenched in the atmosphere "Nice 'ere innit!"

"You're in America now son," repeated Pricey again.

***

When darkness fell, the boys left their air-conditioned little pad and were once again engulfed in hot dry air, stepping out of the front door felt like walking into a baker's oven. They'd been here for more than a year but still hadn't acclimatised to the brutal taxing heat.

They meandered down the steps and out to the car park wearing long shorts, vest tops and Airwear boots, just the 'clobber' for an evening's tomfoolery.

Tom was going to follow Seamus in the Super Sport until they made the delivery, then they would hightail it to the Uni campus for a few beers and a bite to eat, maybe at 'Gracious Bob's'.

The journey to Ron Ruby's house in the foothills of the Catalonian Mountains was thankfully uneventful. They cruised along the sand-coloured stucco boundary wall and passed the electronic entry gates that had been advantageously left wide open.

Quietly rolling to a stop on the street they extinguished their headlights and turned off the engines. Tom got out and walked on to Seamus who sat nervously tapping his black ape fingers on the steering wheel.

"That's a result," whispered Tom, "leaving those peeled back."

"We better get this done before anyone sees us. I'll wait here in the motor, you drive up slowly with y'lights off, then leg it. Maybe they're out for the night. Don't forget the note on the dash!"

Seamus was pensive. "What if someone pulls a gun on me?"

"Zig zag!"

"What?"

"Run in a zig zag, it'll be 'arder for 'im to 'it ya!" certified Tom.

"For fuck's sake," laughed Seamus nervously, He took a long draw from a one skinner spliff, flicked it to the ground and said, "D'ya wanna swap?"

"Do I fuck! We tossed a coin—you lost. I'm waiting 'ere."

"Mate," said Seamus throwing back his head.

Tom just stared back at him *nonplussed.*

"'urry up or we're gonna get fuckin' caught."

Behind, the sound of an oncoming car caused them to swivel round to see what was arriving. An open-topped Porsche Carrera with two college jocks inside slowed down as they approached the hearse and rubbernecked as they passed.

"Nice wheels Herman!" They shouted before speeding off.

Tom just nodded; they couldn't afford a scene.

With that, Seamus started the big beast up, took her down the road, performed a u-turn and headed back to Ron Ruby's drive. He extinguished the lights and swung the Cadillac in through the gates and very cautiously rolled her up the sloping drive in pitch darkness on tick-over.

Ruby's house was huge, a two-storied modern villa with sand-faced walls, expanses of glass, turrets and circular terracotta tiled roof sections that splayed forward like open fans. The paved driveway swooped around the manicured dry-zone garden which smelt of damp earth and cactus blossom, and arced into a turnaround in front of the main entrance centred by a garish stone fountain in full spume. Seamus didn't want to wake the dead, so he opted to abandon the hearse across the face of the triple garage doors to the right of the house.

Positioning the calling card on the dashboard, he stealthily extracted himself and closed the door with a gentle click.

His heart was pounding in his chest as he made for a quick tiptoe walk back down the drive, as best he could do in Airwear boots. Not a sound escaped the house, no sudden illumination, no dogs barking, nothing. Piece of piss, he thought.

He neared the entrance gates hoping to step out of entrapment and into street light, but suddenly bright headlights of an incoming car flared against the surface of the open gate.

Seamus sprang sideways like an elk on coiled feet, avoiding a mass of agave plants and managed to crouch behind a fair sized boulder, one of several that adorned the landscape, cutting his knee in the process. "Fuckin' 'ell … fuckin' 'ell," he whispered, followed by "bollocks," as he saw the electronic gate come to life and slowly start to close. He knew that Ruby would soon see the new mode of transport awaiting approval and blow his top at the sight of it. Seamus had to make a run for it before he was caged in the grounds and surely tortured to death when captured.

Up like a sprinter leaving his blocks, he straggled and stumbled his way across lethal terrain, negotiating dangerous projectiles as best he could in the dark. He made it to the boundary wall just as the gate maliciously smashed into its locking mechanism, barring his escape and filling him with dread. From behind him he could hear a commotion brewing near the house; he had to get out sharpish.

Edging along the rough surface of the wall, gingerly probing for salvation, his leading leg abruptly stopped in mid-motion, halted by something hitherto unseen, something prickly, hairy, warm and smelling like the large mammal enclosure at London Zoo. The beast let out a guttural resonant grunt before leaping to its feet and turning to face the poor bastard that had woken it from slumber.

Javelina? thought Seamus, *shit*. The collared peccary weighed around 60 lbs, had two huge razor-sharp yellow tusks jutting out of its mouth and although a vegetarian, fancied a chunk of Englishman on this night. It forced a couple of short breathy snorts through its nose and flexed itself ready to charge. Seamus, frozen with fear momentarily, had no time to think before instinct took over.

Jumping upwards, he used the dynamics of the sprinting pig to his advantage by stepping on its back to reach the top of the eight-foot-high wall. The pig squealed as Seamus' 14 st bore down on his spine using it like a springboard, hurling him up and over before the pig shot off terrified into the darkness.

"Hey!" boomed a voice from the direction of the house.

For once Seamus declined to answer.

Crashing down on the other side of the wall in a heap of sweet, blood and prickly pear, he lost no time dashing for the El Camino.

Tom, expecting his friend to pop out of that garden in rather a hurry, had started the engine and opened the passenger door in anticipation.

"Drive!" shouted Seamus throwing himself into the car.

Tom floored the Chevy and they wheel spun their way up the street, lights off for a couple of blocks and as quick as they dared. Taking many turns, Tom slowed the vehicle and negotiated his way down the foothills and back into Tucson, all the while checking his rear-view mirror for any vengeful gangsters that might have kept pace. Luck was with them, there were none.

"That was close," gasped Seamus. "I ain't doin' that again… A fuckin' Javelina attacked me."

"They've got pigs as guard dogs?"

"It was a fuckin' wild one kipping in the garden… I ran into the fucker by the wall."

"You tellin' porkies … did you give it a karate chop?" Tom grinned.

"It ain't a laughing matter … look at the state of me' legs." Seamus raised a foot up onto the dashboard so that Tom could see the extent of his injuries.

He gave them a quick glance. "Shit, did the pig do that?"

"And the cactus and the agave and every other fuckin' thing with spikes and prickles in that fuckin' garden." Seamus appeared rather tense.

Tom was quiet for a few minutes. "Did you leave the note?"

"'course I fuckin' did … wos' the point in deliverin' the joke without the punchline?" Seamus was picking bits of thorn and gravel out of his wounds and feeling hard done by. He had a particularly nasty gash on his right shin and razor cuts all over his legs and hands.

Tom thought it a good idea to lighten the mood. "Wos' the difference between a pig and a stepladder?"

"Fuck knows."

"See, that's ya' problem right there."

Seamus was wide eyed. "It's not fuckin' funny, if it wasn't for that Javelina's assistance I'd be pleading for me' life right now."

Sidestepping the seriousness of Seamus' disposition, Tom made light of it again. "Imagine Ron Ruby's face when he saw that 'earse, 'e'll know it was from Saul."

"Uh ha." Seamus concentrated on a cactus thorn embedded in his left knee.

"Saul's gonna laugh his bollocks off in the morning—" Tom paused and took another look at Seamus' legs. "I better take ya' to Julie's house so ya' can get cleaned up, we can't go out with ya' lookin' like that."

Julie was a sweet-natured girl, smart, pretty and independent. She lived in the middle of town close to the university and had been Seamus' confidante and lover for several months. He relished her company, yet he treated her apartment as a kind of motorway service station, in for a top-up of affection and out after a short stop.

Tom held the girl in high regard, she was amusing and kind, but he didn't personally find her attractive; she had the misfortune of having a vertebrae missing from her neck which restricted her movement, so that she had to turn her whole body in order to look over her shoulder and it made her head seem like it was sitting on her shoulders. This never bothered Seamus who reported her to be a revelation in the bedroom, where they would often spend days wallowing in their own dirt.

"Okay," she said upon opening her door, "what have you done this time?"

Seamus related his story whilst she retrieved various fluids and ointments from a cupboard. "Help yourself to beer Tom," she said in mid flow.

Tom gravitated to the enormous fridge, opened the door and wallowed in its golden light. The ancient monster was brimming with goodies, best of which was a twelve pack of Miller genuine draft. "Draft in a bottle," the contradiction tickled him. "You two want one?" he hollered.

"Be rude not to," replied Julie.

"Yowza … phwoar … Jesus Christ that 'urt." Seamus winced as iodine was dabbed on his cuts.

"You big baby, it's only a scratch," insisted Julie with a hint of sadism.

"That big bugger's not, I think it needs stitching," he whined.

"Stick a plaster on it, it'll soon heal up," interjected Tom.

"Stick a what on it?" said Julie bemused.

"Sorry, a Band-Aid, I keep forgetting that you don't speak English."

Julie laughed; she loved the boys' satirical sense of humour. Her face then changed to pensive, and then concerned. "You really shouldn't do Saul Berns' dirty work you know, you'll get yourselves hurt or arrested or something."

"I am hurt!" protested Seamus.

"No I mean *really* hurt; these are hard-nosed criminals that you're messing with."

"We'll be alright we're just havin' a laugh," Tom masked the fact that he was really crapping his pants. "Besides, no one knows who we are; we're on 'oliday if anyone asks."

"Just be careful is all that I'm saying," remonstrated Julie.

Tom leant back on the sink unit. "Yes Mum." He took a swig from his bottle.

"I'm peccary-proof," assured Seamus from his seat on the kitchen table. "I just have an issue with cactus."

***

Eight months into their stay in the United States the boys had decided to write, direct and star in their own home movie, on a camera that they had borrowed from Caitlyn Berns. They entitled it *'And for desert'*. It featured some local TV footage that they'd appeared on, some comedy sketches that they had improvised, a trip to the Grand Canyon and a heartfelt hello message to the folks back home.

On November 5th 1988 they went out into the Rincon Mountains to capture the rugged beauty of their desert surroundings. Tom was setting up the camera, focusing on Seamus who plonked himself down on a rocky outcrop right next to a teddybear cactus; so called due to the shape of the plants limbs and fuzzy fur-like appearance of their close-knit spines being reminiscent of a toy bear.

These small Cholla cacti have an intriguing way of propagation. A small joint will attach itself to anything that passes too close and break off, with the prospect that they'll be carried into the yonder and later discarded onto the ground, set down roots and become a new plant that is genetically identical to the mother from which it came. Each spine on the joint is covered by a paper-like sheaf that falls off at the slightest touch to reveal a lethal barbed spine that once in your skin, is excruciatingly painful and extremely difficult to remove.

The boys had a British Union flag on a short pole that they had wedged in between some boulders behind where Seamus was sitting, to give the scene a sense of the 'Brits abroad'. This was to be the opening shot of the movie, the British flag fluttering in the breeze against a perfect blue sky, tall green cactus imperious in the background and two ridiculously dressed home boys introducing their families to their adopted country.

The camera was static on a rock, looking up to where Seamus sat. Tom clambered to perch beside him at the exact moment the flagpole decided acting wasn't for him. It keeled over, slamming into the teddybear cactus, pushing it forward and into Seamus' shoulder.

"Aahh … fuckin' 'ell … aahh … what the fuck is it?" cried Seamus, "aahh!"

Tom straightened up, saw the cactus joint in Seamus' bare flesh and scrambled to his feet panicking, involuntarily laughing at his friends' plight. The limb of the beast had embedded into Seamus' skin in several places and was searing him like tiny red hot branding irons.

"Get it out, get it out, get it out!" Seamus hollered.

What could Tom do? He couldn't touch it for it would surely stick into him. All they had to hand in the way of tools was a pair of sunglasses and a notebook.

At first Tom tried to prise the thing off with an arm of the Ray Bans, but all this achieved was to roll it on to a fresh part of skin and further attach itself. Seamus continued to scream with every attempt at extraction, which made Tom laugh even more, the camera kept on recording.

Having had the brainwave to use the notebook as a shield on Seamus' shoulder, Tom painstakingly managed to remove the limb after exerting some effort under the still scorching autumn sun that was peaking at 86°F; hot enough to fry an egg on a boulder.

Each spine had held on like grim death, pulling Seamus' skin outwards forming a tiny pink cone at least a half inch long before finally yielding to pressure, each extraction causing severe pain to the victim.

The process took at least an hour and truly disturbed Seamus for weeks after, who insisted it wasn't the flagpoles fault, but the cactus', which had actually jumped at him.

Tom apologized for laughing at the time, but when watched back on video, the scene had both of them in fits of laughter.

***

Julie, Seamus and Tom drove to Gracious Bob's, a venue in the centre of the campus. They could have walked, it was so close, but Seamus was having trouble in that department.

The night was balmy and the soft reggae tones from Mystic Lights wafted into the car park a familiar tune. The band had a residency here and the boys knew them well. David the singer and Jamie the bass player nodded to the trio as they sashayed and hobbled up to the bar, 'plonking' themselves down on heavy wooden bar stools facing the stage.

Gracious Bob's was typical 80s design, walls of glass and acres of stained timber. It had a sunken dance-floor in the centre of the room, circled by elevated, balustrade dining areas, sandwiched between the stage riser at one end against the front wall, and the tri-sided bar at the other. The kitchen was out the back.

"When's your next gig here?" asked Julie raising her voice over the music.

"A week next Friday, we're trying out a new keyboard player, 'e's blind and deaf!" quipped Seamus.

Julie gave a look of bewilderment, "Sounds interesting."

"Yeah 'e's a cross between Ray Charles and Beethoven, he can't see or hear what 'e's playin', but it feels great," enlightened Tom. "One day we might even plug 'im in."

"You're kidding right?" Julie was aghast.

"Na'," said Tom straight-faced.

Seamus had his head buried in the menu.

"What happened to your last keyboard player, wasn't he blind as well?"

"And arrogant; 'e once shut my foot in the car door as I was getting out behind 'im. It hurt like fuck an' 'e didn't apologise … didn't even say gee or anything, 'e just stood there waiting to be led into the gig. I think 'e thought the world owed 'im a favour."

The band finished their song to enthusiastic applause and then dedicated the next song to their English friends at the bar, Seamus and Tom saluted as the 'Lights' struck up a reggae version of *'The Boys are Back in Town'*.

"I'm havin' the Sonoran chicken tacos; two soft flour tacos stuffed with pulled Sonoran chicken breast, topped with cabbage and a fresh Pico de Gallo, served with Spanish rice and authentic charro beans," read Seamus quoting from the list. "What you guys 'avin'?"

"A beer to start with I think," said Tom, "pitcher of honey beer alright for everyone … Julie … yeah? Alright then order up Seamus, let me look at the menu."

"Why don't you have the Carne Asada, the marinated steak, it's really good here," advised Julie.

"We're off the red meat now love, if I can't kill it then I won't eat it," proclaimed Tom.

"Could you kill a chicken?" she asked.

"He's always wringing 'is chicken's neck," ribbed Seamus.

"What?" said the confused American.

"Bashin' the Bishop … Shakin' 'ands with the unemployed … 'Avin' one off the wrist," Seamus continued.

Julie was now totally dumbfounded.

"It's the Southern Border Stromboli for me old chap," Tom concluded.

Julie was swivelling on her stool left and right, not knowing what to make of these guys. "I'll have … the Lizzy salad," she said at length.

"Thin Lizzy is it?" asked Seamus nodding towards the band.

Julie laughed. "That's right," she said, patting Seamus' good knee.

"Mixed greens tossed with lightly-grilled chicken, sliced thin, smoked bacon, chunky gorgonzola, red onion, sweet bell peppers, spiky croutons tossed in the very best basil, olive oil, rice and vinegar dressing you've ever had."

"You've sold it to me," said Seamus "'ook me up one of those; I'll go back to just white meat tomorrow."

Tom rolled his eyes. He knew that his mate was only appeasing him on this slope towards vegetarianism; it was just easier when cooking at home for them both to have the same thing.

They left the bar at midnight fully sated and merry but with a sensible head on, for it were mid week and they had work the next day. Seamus stayed at Julie's apartment while Tom drove home, carefully within the speed limit and on the look out for any hoods who might be tailing him. There were none.

After a full night's sleep, dreaming of frosty mornings and running around the countryside exhaling vaporised breath, Tom awoke to another sun-blinding roasting morning. He lay there, motionless for a while cringing from the thought of what might have happened to them the night before.

Ron Ruby turning up like that was too close for comfort and he shuddered before rising from the bed. He washed, dressed and had a cup of tea, gathered some work clothes for Seamus, then left the apartment. "Let's see what today brings," he said aloud, wondering about the reprisals.

Outside Julie's house Tom honked the El Camino's horn to little affect, Seamus was still in 'the land of nod'. He was never, ever, ready on time. "I've spent 'alf my life waitin' for this bloke," Tom conceded before pursing his lips.

Julie's door bell was eventually answered by a puffy-faced, bloodshot excuse of a best mate, shrouded in an ill fitting peppermint dressing gown.

"Come on we're gonna be late," thundered Tom.

"Two minutes … I'll be two minutes," assured Seamus.

Tom threw Seamus' clothes at him, "'urry up, I'll wait in the car." He caught a glimpse of Julie's naked back through the open bedroom door as she lay entangled in the bed sheets, like an alabaster nude statue. She never stirred.

On the way up to Orange Grove, Seamus pleaded for Tom to stop at a Seven-Eleven to buy some apple juice. "I'm dyin' of thirst mate," he proclaimed.

Stopping made them even later and added to Tom's frustration; he hated to be late for anything.

By the time they reached the Berns' house it was 9:10 a.m. They parked the car at the bottom of the drive and marched up to the house through the shaded approach of date palms. They entered the building via the open double garage doors to the right, on through the utility room and into the kitchen where they greeted the Berns' with a "Good morning."

Caitlyn was fixing some breakfast by the stove while Saul reclined in one of the cushioned wicker chairs facing the patio doors which led to the garden.

The mingled aromas of fresh percolated coffee, toast and scrambled eggs relaxed the boys into a false state of symmetry.

Caitlyn flicked her eyes at them briefly and smiled.

"You gotta watch?" Saul demanded without turning around.

"Yes Saul," replied Tom.

"It's broken," Saul said sarcastically.

"Sorry we're late Saul," said Seamus, "the traffic's a nightmare today."

"Bullshit," snapped Saul, "you're always fuckin' late."

"That rat bastard's been calling here this morning, thanking me for the present. Says he'll loan it to Caitlyn in the not too distant future, that sonofabitch, cock-sucking piece of shit. I'm gonna shove that car so far up his fuckin' ass they have to open his mouth to change the fuckin' oil."

"I nearly got caught in 'is garden," offered up Seamus in an attempt to calm his boss.

"What?" snapped Saul looking over his spectacles.

"Ruby come home mid-delivery, I had to 'leg it' through the garden and leap over the wall to escape, 'ad a fight with a Javelina on the way as well."

Saul looked his employee up and down and barked out "Ha, work-related injury, there's no fuckin' insurance gonna cover this event." Saul's crooked smile meant his mood was lightening. "Did he get a look attcha?"

"No Saul it was too dark, we shot off pretty sharpish."

"Good, I don't want your asses nailed to a fuckin' cross."

"Saul honey, your eggs are done," interrupted Caitlyn.

"Ok, ok, you guys go pick some fruit while I eat my fuckin' breakfast, then one of ya can take me to the office. I want four orange, three tangerine and one grapefruit each, you got that?"

"Yes Saul," they said, and then left to retrieve some white plastic carrier bags from the garage.

"Bit tetchy," whispered Tom.

"'e'll be alright after a coffee and a stick o' gum," managed Seamus through a yawn.

"'ow many packets o' gum d'ya reckon 'e gets through in a day?"

"D'no, but 'e must be keeping Wrigley's in business."

The boys separated and got to work in the orange grove, climbing the trees and picking the fragrant ripe fruit. The climb was tricky because of a thick mass of interwoven, sharp twigged branches on some of the trees, in need of a prune. But the fruit were the best oranges the boys had ever had in their lives. They were intoxicating and tasted exactly how orange blossom smelled. You couldn't just eat one, you had to have two or three; they were that delicious.

Tom had managed to fill one bag of oranges when he heard Saul seething again, from the garage.

"What the fuck's this? I said four orange, three tangerine and one grapefruit, you dumb shit. Not one fuckin' mixed bag. Four bags of oranges, three bags of tangerines and one bag of grapefruit, like you always fuckin' do. Jesus H Christ!"

Seamus, still half asleep, had picked just one grapefruit, three tangerines and four oranges and was now being berated by a raging maniac for his blunder.

Tom giggled behind the camouflage of a tree canopy as Seamus, red-faced, was sent back to, "Do it right this time."

Saul had mellowed with the boys just lately, treating them better than he had his adopted son; Caitlyn's 23-year-old, Jamie, who in Saul's eyes was just a waste-of-space drug addict and something to ignore.

Jamie had tolerated living with his menacing stepfather and doting mum for 5 years but had finally been shipped off to college after some extremely wild behavior.

"That spoilt brat's gonna fuckin' kill himself one day, he ain't gonna fuckin' do it under my roof," he had said to Caitlyn as he slammed the front door shut on his stepson.

Jamie had left Tucson on an Amtrak train with a bag of clothes and a hand gun.

Saul Berns was born Saul Bernstein, in New York City in 1907; his parents were Jewish Russian immigrants from Odessa. He westernised his name in later life because he shared it with an infamous double agent spy who was unearthed by the CIA and tried for crimes against the state. Saul quickly reeled from any unnecessary attention, changed his name and became less prominent—less conspicuous.

He got involved with gangs and crime at an early age; in what was to become known as the Jewish Mafia, and at the age of 21 had apparently amassed enough fraudulent money to buy an island in the East River, hoping to develop it into a residential area. This didn't come to pass, so he sold it on for a huge profit. Hundreds of murky deals followed including one time using the classic sting of exchanging property deeds for a million dollars in cash, by switching identical briefcases with a sucker, in a crowded railway station, one carrying the deeds, the other a couple of telephone directories.

Saul thought this was highly amusing, but having the balls to actually do such a thing was a part of his success.

In the 1950's he married a world famous opera singer and although turbulent, they enjoyed a lavish lifestyle, one time spending a whole year on a cruise ship with his pal, movie legend, Anthony Quinn.

In the 50s, New York was a place of opportunity, the skyline was comparatively tame compared to the reaching spires of concrete and glass there today, and there were still many plots of un-urbanised land for sale. Saul formed a syndicate of 20 Jewish business associates who bid for these plots of land at auction. Keeping their bids pathetically low, they were able to buy the land at ridiculous prices, develop it and sell it on, making a fortune in the process.

Inevitably, greed took over in the dog-eat-dog underworld and one by one the syndicate members were squeezed out and ripped off. When finally the balance tipped in favour of the aggrieved, despite being a powerful and feared man in the city,

Saul Berns received numerous death threats. The heat became too hot to handle and he fled town, taking refuge first in Las Vegas, where the big shot New Yorker lavished his cash, hanging out with movie stars and singers like Sammy Davis Jr and Nat King Cole.

This was playtime for Saul, but it ruined his marriage and in the 70s he divorced his wife, leaving a sizeable pension for his two sons and a lump of property in New York.

He headed for even more ambiguity down in Tucson Arizona, like a snow bird on permanent vacation, where he set up a real estate company, acquiring land through dubious circumstances and selling it on. He employed pretty, blonde, Baton Rouge girl Caitlyn Emberg as his secretary who at the time was in her mid-20s, married and had a young son. Saul was 65, 30 years her senior. He was rude, arrogant, bad-tempered, foul-mouthed and had a typical dry New York sense of humour. He could assassinate your character in one flippant sentence, but over time Caitlyn came to think of him as powerful, generous and endearing; a provider, and a protector.

Somewhere along the line they fell in love, which struck the boys as pretty amazing, since he had told them that one time a girl had come for a job interview with her baby in a stroller, and Saul had held the infant out of a multi-storey window, threatening to drop it if the girl didn't give him a blow job. This may well have been Caitlyn.

But apparently it was love and during the early 80s Caitlyn left her husband and moved in with Saul. Within a few years they were married, had bought a decent property on Orange Grove Road, remodelled it, filled it with fine art and shipped in Jamie, a troubled but now spoilt teenager.

All was swell in the Berns' household; Saul was now 71, he had an office downtown, a dutiful blonde token wife, crooked lawyers, accountants and notaries under his command and 17 bank accounts lending him money on the deeds of land that he didn't actually own.

The scam worked thus; he would view an area of land with the prospect of buying it, acquire the deeds for approval, forge a sales agreement, have the document notarised, register it with county hall as his property, then split the land up into smaller parcels and sell individual lots to his various companies that were scattered around the United States and some others that were offshore. All unbeknown to the true owner who would only realise that he no longer had possession once a real buyer came along. Saul would then take the deeds to his banks and borrow money on the equity. This activity was now his sole income.

The original duped landowners would face a near impossible task of fighting for ownership in many different state courts. So enormous was the battle that few would persist, giving it up as far too costly an exercise. Saul was a clever ruthless bastard and everybody knew it.

After the fruit had been gathered, Saul took the boys to the back-lot to show them what he'd like done today. The garden was typically landscaped for this part of the world, lots of raised planters containing large boulders, yucca, cactus and palo verde, with a scattering of citrus trees, remnants from the orange grove that once sprawled along this old road. Most of the ground here was paved in something akin to York stone and there were steps at various levels leading from an expansive arcaded patio up to the pool area, all of which was walled off from the neighbouring properties with a 5 ft, cream-painted, block and stucco perimeter. Beyond this, in the 'back-40' was a brick pathway that meandered through a tall line of cypress trees and a border of mature palo verde. This lot was fenced off with seven-foot chainlink mesh.

Saul pointed to some wilting fronds on an infant desert fan palm, "You can cut bullshit out," he said with a cursory swathe of his hand. "Cut that bullshit," he said indicating the lower limbs of perfectly healthy agave plant. "Clear up the dog crap, water everything, rake the fuckin' leaves and clean the fuckin' pool. When you've done that you can wash the fuckin' dogs especially Reina … she stinks."

"Right, Seamus, you can take me to the office, get those bags of fuckin' fruit and put 'em in the Elegance; I'll be out front in five minutes."

It was 9:30 and the temperature was climbing rapidly, Tom stripped down to just his shorts and boots revealing a firm teak brown torso glistening with beads of sweat that had formed along his spine. They would not run or form pools on his waist band, it was far too hot, the water sapping from his body would evaporate without a trace. He gathered some tools from the shed and set to work pruning the plants as instructed, oblivious that he was under surveillance.

Forty-five minutes later the iron-gate that divided the front and back yards creaked into life and slammed shut again. Seamus had returned.

"How was 'e on the way in?" Tom was on his knees in the dirt.

"Never said a word, just sat there chewing and tapping on his briefcase."

"Seamus! Tom!" A shrill melody pierced the morning air from the open patio doors. Caitlyn Berns was calling them in for breakfast, a ritual that had become a regular occurrence since they were now a part of the family. But it was something secret, something mischievous, and something that Saul had no idea about.

Caitlyn had made scrambled eggs, Louisiana-style with shrimps, tomatoes, onions and peppers, toasted English muffins and coffee with a shot of Bailey's liqueur.

The boys wandered into the kitchen, then sat in the wicker chairs with their plates, while Caitlyn flitted around them clumsily spilling things and apologising for being such a 'klutz'. One time, while showing the boys her new camera she stepped into the dog's giant water dish, a stainless steel bowl that was always in the same place and always filled with water. How she could not know it was there was amazing. She plopped straight in it, with a look of sad disappointment on her rosy-cheeked face.

Seamus loved the breakfasts, the escape from work, the titillating flirting with the boss's wife; he would pull her leg all day long if he had the chance.

Caitlyn loved playing the overzealous host; it was her pleasure, her playground when her husband was out of the house; she spoilt the boys as much as she dared.

Tom enjoyed the freebies but felt guilty for getting paid to do so little and a bit apprehensive that they might get caught at any given moment. So he was on ten-percent guard all of the time and couldn't bring himself to enjoy it as much as Seamus did. Besides these morning breaks were getting longer and longer and starting to seem like a chore.

Caitlyn was still attractive for what the boys considered a mature woman, even though she had piled on a few unwanted pounds. She kept herself pristine by taking more than necessary showers during the day and there were dubious moments when she couldn't be raised at all.

Seamus had quipped that she was, 'probably playing with her twat'.

This amused Tom but he disregarded it considering the amount of times she went missing in eight hours!

"I'm going over to Macy's for the rest of the day," she said while piercing yet another can of decaffeinated diet Coke. "I'll leave the door open. Help yourselves to anything, but make sure you clean the dogs; Saul's most upset with Reina. I don't know why she smells so much. I'll take her to the vets next week; see if there's anything wrong."

Macy Moore was a multi-million-dollar heiress friend of Caitlyn's who also had an eye for Tom, and the competition of who could best win the boys' favour, was hotting up.

"No probs' Caitlyn, we'll get it all done," assured Seamus.

"Thanks for 'brekky'," said Tom, "we'd better crack on Monty, time's getting on."

They left the coolness of the house and went back to work, Seamus reluctantly, hanging back as much as he could.

Tom finished the pruning and then got the hoses out to run water to all the large plants. A ring of earth walled up each specimen like tiny hill forts, creating a perfect reservoir so as not to waste a precious drop.

Seamus cleaned the pool while the two golden retrievers swam in it, which seemed like a pointless task. Fonda, the sleeker, more active dog rejoiced in diving for a rubber ball that Seamus repeatedly threw back in, while overweight Reina just lolloped in the shallows.

"That's them washed," said Seamus triumphantly.

"You'd better soap 'em up mate, 'e'll know you ain't washed 'em properly if you don't," advised Tom, "an' the other two beasts."

The Berns' had four dogs; the other two being Miko and Tres Jolie, a pair of Japanese Akitas that were Saul's pride and joy, especially the boy Miko. He loved that dog more than any living creature. Woe betide if anything should happen to him.

Japanese Akitas were bred for hunting bears and other large game in ancient times, ferociously cornering and containing the prey until the hunters arrived. They are huge dogs, the males in particular, with massive heads, paws and powerful jaws. Two males in a face off could rip each other to shreds if riled. But these two were good-natured with fur as soft as silk. Jolie was pure black with a wisp of white on her chest, while Miko was a traditional Black-Masked Pinto.

"Alright, but I need a pony first, I'm burstin'," said Seamus.

"Caitlyn won't mind; use the lav' in Jamie's room."

"I can't mate, I'll 'ave to go *au naturel.*"

"What … what's wrong with the bog?" asked Tom puzzled.

"I just can't use someone else's … for that," explained Seamus with a lopsided grin, as he tip toed up to the back-40 to find a comfortable perch behind the Oleander hedge.

Tom shook his head in disbelief, "'e's got some strange habits," he said to himself.

Within five minutes Seamus was back. "I 'ope you've wiped your arse," quarried Tom.

"Oleander leaf, old boy, very absorbent," Seamus laughed.

The day wore on; Seamus captured and washed Miko who proceeded to dry himself on the living room furniture and rugs.

But he couldn't find Jolie. They searched the house and the grounds, calling her name to no avail, for half-an-hour. Suddenly she appeared, trotting down the yard, pink tongue lolling out of her gaping jaws, as happy as Larry and eminently proud.

"Oh, for fucks sake," said Seamus, "she's only rolled in me' poo."

Tom burst out laughing and ran away from the reeking animal. "You dirty bitch!" he shouted. "I'll be over 'ere, rakin' leaves," he called from afar, still sniggering.

Seamus grabbed Jolie by the collar. "Eurgh … I never thought I'd 'ave to clean me' own turd off a dog," he said with disgust.

Jolie got the full treatment with a hose before being doused with pet shampoo and thoroughly 'sudded'. The muck took an age to clean off, hampered by the dog struggling to get away all the while. When she was finally cleansed she went berserk around the garden drying herself. The boys wouldn't let her in the house till Caitlyn came home and even then they were convinced that she still smelled like Seamus' arse, but they didn't mention it.

2
Dawn of the Dread

Tom entered the United States on the first day of March 1988 following the break- up of his relationship with the mother of his eight-month-old son Kit.

His ex, Lela, was strong-willed, vehemently independent and anomalous. She made it quite clear that Tom was now surplus to requirements. He'd had his uses when he was new. He taught her how to drive, moved her belongings back to her mum's house because she couldn't bear to live in self-made squalor any longer, and he gave her the child she had so longed for.

Tom was supportive and kind, but in Lela's opinion he fell in love too easily, and he tortured himself by falsely believing he wasn't dynamic enough for her. The truth was, they just weren't compatible. Heartbreaking though it was; he was yet to learn that no matter how hard he tried, he could not mould himself into the object of her desire. The harmonics were completely wrong, and Lela felt it, like loaning somebody else's clothes; it's inexplicably disconcerting. You can't make somebody love you through pure aspiration.

She was artistic, avant-garde, and practical; played the saxophone, sang, and made her own clothes and furnishings. She was gorgeous, had wild raven hair and capricious blue-green eyes; the colour varied depending on her mood.

Contrarily, Tom was straight down the middle, conventional, un-extraordinary perhaps, but he had poetry on his side, a knack for a lyric, drive and ambition; not a natural musician. He had a desire to break out and be somebody, to do something of note. He also loved Lela more than life itself; she represented an alternative life, a life he wanted.

She was enigmatic and mysterious, an untouchable urban sprite, impossible to lure, yet somehow he had caught her.

After they'd split, he became yesterday's news, an abandoned sunlight-faded newspaper, attracting nothing but dust on a forgotten basement shelf.

Devastated by the separation, he felt worthless, spent, dizzyingly confused and bereft of air. Finally, after eight months of anguish, and at the invitation of his sister, he packed a suitcase, quit the garden-centre job he adored and crossed the Atlantic in an attempt to patch up his tattered soul.

From the comfort of Keira's Adobe house, Tom wrote many letters and sent parcels of clothing back for Kit, to help Lela out. She was jobless and relied on welfare handouts to get by. Apart from the huge responsibility Tom felt for his child, he was still clinging to the hope by his keratin, that one day she might want him back.

In one reply to his letters, Lela agreed to fly over with Kit for a holiday if Tom could send her the air fare. He was energised, and arranged for his mum to post £350 to her straight away. But Lela spent the money on a car, giving him the excuse that the weather in the UK was freezing and public transport was impossible for her and poor little Kit. Tom wrote back that he understood, but inside he was deflated, once again used and fobbed off.

A dark image resurfaced in Tom's mind, a black pearl of a thought seeded there by his friend William back in England.

Lela had recently been allocated a one-bedroom council flat in Little Chalfont, Buckinghamshire. William was convinced Lela only got herself pregnant to secure council accommodation. At the time, Tom found that idea abhorrent, but as everyone knows, love only blinds the affected.

***

Being fresh to this part of the world and relatively naive, Tom was shaken to the core within three days of his arrival in the US, to hear on a local news channel, that a boy of 13 had slaughtered his entire family with a revolver, because his dad wouldn't let him play a cassette tape of his favourite band.

Mum, dad, brothers and sister wiped out in a temper tantrum. A British kid would have slammed some doors, wrecked his room maybe, and that would have been the end of it. What kind of a country was he in that allowed children to have access to lethal weapons?

A week later Tom was watching the TV while Keira and Pricey were at work and Amber was at pre-school. Intently absorbed in some ridiculous daytime soap opera, it gradually dawned on him that helicopters were circling up above the house. The drone oscillated in the rocky valley, growing stronger and forcing Tom to investigate.

He went to the window and looked up at a matchless blue sky where two black, and a blue and one white helicopter were hovering above a scrubby mound, halfway between Keira's house and the park warden's large Adobe.

Tom fetched a pair of binoculars from a drawer and scrutinized the hillside. There on the ground flanked by several enormous saguaro sentinels, sat a silhouetted menacing figure, cross legged and hunched forward as if protecting something.

Suddenly a KOLD TV news flash interrupted the dull narrative on the telly.

"Breaking news, Pima County Sheriff's Department has cornered escaped fugitive Conrad Batty in the desert near Colossal Cave. We understand SWAT teams have been deployed in the area to contain the situation and convince Batty, who has been on the run now for two days, to give himself up. Kidnap negotiators have also been brought in because Batty has abducted his three-year-old son and at this moment in time the child's whereabouts is unknown. A police spokesperson has said that Batty has threatened to kill the boy and himself if he is not allowed to go free. It is believed Batty is holding what appears to be a large hunting or Bowie knife to his stomach and is sitting on the ground. Our news team is on the scene with these pictures."

The television showed shaky aerial shots of the reclining Batty, with footage that zoomed in and out in a futile attempt at focusing on the knife.

Tom looked back through the binoculars, then back at the screen, enthralled that he was witnessing the stand-off live outside the house and viewing the same pictures on the TV. He looked again through the binoculars; this time he could make out the knife, it was maybe a 1 ft long, the guy held it in both hands pressing the point into his belly.

Men in black jumpsuits were now streaming down ropes thrown out of the black helicopters, clustered with weapons and equipment. They wore sunglasses and black helmets and once on the ground, melded into the desert floor. It looked like a scene from a movie but it was happening right there in front of him, he was riveted to the window.

The telephone jerked into life like the final buzzer in a quiz show and made him jump. "Fuck," he muttered.

It was Keira, wanting to know if he was watching the action. "Stay in the house," she advised. "I'm gonna wait up here 'til it's all over."

"Alright … I can't believe this is 'appenin'. I'm watching it on the telly and outside at the same time."

"There're some nutters over 'ere," she said. "You read about this sort of thing everyday. Look I'm on me' boss's phone, I'll call you later, stay indoors, bye." She hung up.

Once again Tom surveyed the hill. Somehow the men in black had managed to creep up on Conrad Batty unnoticed, and there was now a cop and a plain-clothes man just a few feet away from the escapee, trying to appeal to him. At least two dozen SWAT guys were poised in the scrub, weapons raised, ready to bring the man down.

The stand off went on for four hours, well into the afternoon with the police continuing to inch nearer to the fugitive. Pricey called; he had picked up Amber and was at the entrance to the reserve, but the Sheriff's Department wouldn't let him through and Amber was throwing a strop.

Tom kept glued to the action; it was warm out there, so Conrad Batty must have been delirious with thirst. The news loop kept running the same bulletin because nothing was happening out on the hill.

All at once, a flurry of activity brought the binos back to Tom's eyes. The cops had jumped Batty and a tangle of dust and limbs flayed in the dirt, before the convict was finally pinned face down and handcuffed. An ambulance hurtled up the track and medics swarmed all over the prostrate captive. In the melee Batty had indeed stabbed himself and ripped open his intestines; he bled out in the ambulance and was pronounced dead when he reached the hospital. His son however was found safe and well at his grandma's house, where he had been all along.

The Price family came home and very little else of the story appeared in the news over the following days; it was just another occurrence in Tucson and nobody thought it much of a trial, except for Tom. He felt melancholy over the ordeal and deeply saddened that the boy had lost his father, when surely it could have been handled in a less violent manner.

"This is the wild west, son," stated Pricey, "not Garston Park." It was indeed.

***

Keira and Pricey decided it was high time that Tom had a night out. Persuading a female member of staff at the cave with a $20 bill to babysit Amber, the three of them launched into town for a knees-up at The Wildcat House on N. Stone Ave, a big block of a building that had an illuminated cartoon cat wearing a Stetson ringed by a doughnut of red and blue neon high on the entrance wall.

It being a Friday, the place was rammed to the gills with a mixture of college kids and rednecks intent on getting smashed. There wasn't a band playing tonight, but the DJ was doing a decent job of keeping the dance floor busy.

The three Brits squeezed against the bar and over time managed to secure a couple of stools. An hour of talent-watching produced a spark in Pricey's brain, he thought it a jolly wheeze to inform the bar staff that Tom was in fact Andrew Ridgley, of the duo Wham.

Much to Tom's protests, for although they heralded from the same town, and Tom's brother claimed to have broken Andrew Ridgley's nose one Sunday afternoon, he bore no likeness to the guitarist whatsoever. Miraculously the ruse worked and soon there were three or four female bar staff hovering in Tom's vicinity, asking him questions, giving him free drinks and flirting.

Pricey was illustrious with his fruitful prank and stoking the fire, sensing that there might be a free meal in it as well, he went and told the DJ who was in.

Tom was dying inside, he knew this wouldn't last, and it didn't.

The Disc Jockey put on the video to *Wake Me Up Before You Go Go*, which appeared on the multi-screens around the bar. Tom's cover was blown.

"That's not you … that's not you," mocked the entire bar staff before dissipating like steam out of a window.

Tom sank onto his bar stool embarrassed as hell.

He thanked Mr Price.

***

A month slid by and with it a rise in temperature. Tom had bought some new Levi 501s from a mall, excited by how cheap they were compared to the UK's prices, but the only thing he wore during the day now were shorts and polo shirts. He took his Minolta 35mm camera everywhere he went and was amassing quite a pile of undeveloped film. He snapped at everything that moved and some things that didn't, spending many hours out on the reserve alone, exploring its rugged interior.

The Sonoran desert has a jagged harsh beauty, stunning and cruel, intent on protecting its own. Every inanimate object possesses thorns and prickles and spikes and razor sharp edges, and hidden beneath the rocks or in dark nooks and crannies lurk venomous nasties primed to take chunks out of you. After several cuts and lacerations Tom became guarded when meandering through the bush at Bear Paw, but it didn't dampen his wanderlust. He was amused by the little ground squirrels darting in and out of their burrows as quick as a Chameleon's tongue on a cricket. The squirrels fed on fallen seeds, cactus fruits, insects and mesquite beans, spending long periods of time sitting upright on their hind legs, holding food in their tiny paws, constantly attentive for predators. They happen to be top of the menu for rattlesnakes.

Coyotes would come around to the back of the house at dusk looking for scraps of food or the occasional squirrel. Tom Price would sometimes put out leftovers for them, encouraging a pack of three or four animals at a time. Their reflective green eyes bore into the watchers, ever alert, ever vigilant, ready to flee. Despite common belief that they might attack, they posed very little threat at all to an adult human, although if starving they would strike at a toddler or domestic pet.

Tom thought them to be beautiful, elegant and stealthy, not at all like the scrawny treacherous villain portrayed in the Roadrunner cartoon.

He once followed a pale pink Gila monster up the dirt track road, it preferred the accessible tyre ruts to open scrub as a form of highway. A two foot long dinosaur that clawed its way through the dust at some considerable pace, followed by bouts of motionless respite. Tom got as close with the camera lens as he dared, just out of striking distance from its huge powerful jaws that could rip a finger off if provoked.

Standing on a bare hillock adjacent to the Adobe house one time, he was suddenly dive-bombed by something so fast that it appeared invisible. At first he took it for an insect because of the whirring, buzzing sonic sound that it made during its fantastic flypast, a pendulum motion from high in the sky directly above him, down and around past his chest and then up again and out of sight.

Only after several attempts at locking a visual onto the attacking critter by following its flightpath, did he in fact catch sight of the perpetrator, a tiny red and green fluorescent humming bird whiplashing the air at tremendous speed. He found out later from a local resident that the bird, Anna's Hummingbird, was simply performing a mating ritual, showing off to a nearby female with 100 ft vertical dives, a performance that Tom had probably, inadvertently ruined.

Once or twice Tom went to work with Pricey and helped clear the picnic areas free from barbeque remains and beer cans, and then raked the ground ready for the next party. He noticed the dry river beds winding throughout the park, almost obscured from view by ranks of mesquite and ocotillo trees.

Wondering what happened to the water, he asked Pricey if they ever flowed.

"Yeah, they're *Washes*."

Tom puzzled over the word.

"During the rainy season these fill up like you wouldn't believe," said Pricey. "People and cars get washed away; it's fuckin' nuts."

"Where does the water come from?"

"The sky."

"Yeah but, how comes it ends up as a river?"

"It runs off the mountains. 'Cause the ground's so dry it don't sink in an' it funnels into these washes. They only last about a month, then they're gone. You wouldn't know they'd been 'ere."

"So where does the water go?"

"Downhill," smiled Pricey.

Tom sat in silence for a while thinking of the hundreds of cars that must be bobbing about in a large reservoir somewhere, like rusting apples in a barrel, their skeletal drivers still clutching at steering wheels.

Pricey broke his daydream. "Let's fuck off 'ome. I've got some friends coming 'round this afternoon for a drink. There's a bird that's got a management company, might be interested in your songs."

"Really? 'Ow did you meet her?"

Pricey replied in a comedic German accent. "I have vays of making new acquaintances … she also sells dope."

Forever apprehensive when meeting new people, Tom settled for being reserved when the guests arrived, he subconsciously revealed little of himself until he got to know the lie of the land, preferring to observe rather than be scrutinised. This is to the detriment of anyone pursuing a career on stage, and something Tom had had to address. He had been a seasoned singer for the past eight years and although he had overcome a chronic pre-stage nervous stomach, he still didn't project any hint of charisma until well into a first set. Adrenalin usually brought out the best in him.

First to arrive was Katie Pirelli, a petite blonde elfin, ex-pat, 60s rocker, who owned a music club, the aforementioned management company, and a fetish latex and leather clothing store. She also had a VJ spot on a local TV music channel, a passion for local bands and keeping music live. She was laid-back, softly-spoken and oozed endearing humility. Everyone called her KP.

Katie's boyfriend, Glen Healy, was a movie lighting engineer 20 years her junior, gentile and utterly smitten with his entrepreneurial lady. He was quiet, considerate and erudite. The pair of them loved their weed.

By comparison, their friend Jennifer Floral-Peak was a gushing aristocratic good-time girl, a magnanimous existentialist with fervour for Earl Grey tea in the afternoon, and champagne for all other occasions. She bubbled around everyone, drawing as much fun as she could possibly extract from any situation. Her long flowing brunette locks swished wildly in abandonment and complemented her full figure. She had an ample bosom and promoted it in a low-cut summer frock.

The other lady was KP's best friend, Kate Norton or, Tucson Kate as she was sometimes called. They had once shared a house in LA and both being called Kate caused obvious confusion, so nicknames soon surfaced for convenience sake.

Tucson Kate was a generously proportioned lady in her late thirties; she was kind, subtle, free-spirited and wise, a divorcee who lived with her two teenage children and a menagerie of pets.

The quartet cascaded out of Jennifer's huge burgundy Plymouth Gran Fury that had crunched to a halt amidst a cloud of dust. The passengers emerged like floral-patterned spectators at a high society polo match, all teeth and laughter with magnums under arms and spliffs on the go, raring to party.

Hello and kisses abounded as Tom was introduced as the new pedigree on the block. While Keira slaved at the barbeque, Pricey 'gave it large' about the talents of his brother-in-law, selling Tom like he was the new messiah of rock which Pricey had somehow managed to spawn.

Tom was embarrassed once more, so diverted the attention by enquiring after Katie Pirelli's management company. "So 'ow long 'ave you been managing bands KP?"

"Oh about twenty years. I once signed Van Halen when I was in LA."

"Really, what, you were their manager?"

"No," she laughed, "I booked them for one gig, Eddie's such a sweetheart and he sure knows how to par-dee."

She'd obviously been in the states for a long time; her accent had fused into that mid-Atlantic hybrid where all the T's became D's and sentences ended with an upper inflection.

Jennifer, on the other hand, refused point blank to be Anglo-American, preferring instead to retain her identity because it was more "distinguished".

"Oh," said Tom, "before they were big time?"

"Yeah, this was in the 70s when the west coast was very psychedelic man." She made quotation marks with her fingers and laughed unreservedly. "I've done a lot of rock and roll since then; but things are a bit calmer these days."

"Who 'ave you got on your books now?"

"I've just taken on a really good reggae artist by the name of Natty Dread. He's a Jamaican DJ, dancehall-style singer, and he's over here looking for a band. He wants to cut a new album. I should get you guys to hook up; he's really nice."

"Okay, sounds good. Can I give you a tape of mine, see what ya' think? It's a demo that I made in me' studio just before I came out."

"You have a studio?"

"Well, I share studio equipment; it's in me' mate's dining room."

"Oh, are you in a band at the moment?"

"No, I'm on me' 'Todd' right now."

The lady laughed once more, she hadn't heard that phrase in a long time. "You ought to form a band, I can give you some gigs at The Haze and you could rehearse there during the day if you like. Have you met any musicians yet?"

"I'm only 'ere for three months. KP and I 'aven't ventured out much really."

"Oh that's a shame, hasn't Tom-one taken you down 4th Avenue yet; it's the centre of bohemia you know."

"Tom-one?"

"He's *Tom-one* 'cause I knew him first, you're *Tom-two*," she giggled.

"Tom!" she shouted at Pricey, "you have to take Tom-two into town more, he needs culturing!"

"Some of us 'ave to work for a livin' love," Pricey chuckled whilst rolling a joint.

"Bloody cheek." KP winked at Tom.

Jennifer and Tucson Kate had moved over to help Keira with the food; Amber was watching her favourite Disney movie Lady and the Tramp, or 'Tamp' as she called it, inside the house. Glen was in deep mumble with Pricey about the quality of the Sensimella they were scoring these days, when another car bounced up the track and arrested close to the Plymouth.

Out jumped a white Rastafarian named Dubwise, whose dreadlocks bounced like coils upon his tie-dyed vest, and a black Rasta called Hal wearing a red, black, green and gold woolly Tam and a black t-shirt sporting a large cannabis leaf motif.

Pricey rushed over to receive them. "Hal, Dubwise, come me' 'bredren'," he said using a language alien to Tom's ears. "Eh me' love yer' na'."

Tom was baffled; Pricey had changed personality to embrace another culture like an octopus on a new reef. "Wouldn't think 'e was from Watford would ya'?" he said to KP.

Hal and Dubwise were in a band called Jah Vibes, a fledgling four piece from Tucson with an imminent gig. Pricey was heavily into reggae music, the culture, of course, often infused with marijuana was his natural mania, a leaning that would one day almost cost him his life.

Tom was cordially invited to the gig, it was in a school hall in Casa Grande, a hundred miles away from Bear Paw and he eagerly agreed to go, even though he had never driven in the States before, had no insurance to drive Pricey's truck and had no idea where Casa Grande was on a map.

It was a massive leap of faith for him to make. He was to follow Dubwise up interstate 10, but he had to make his own way back in the middle of the night on unfamiliar roads without an established sense of direction. A pang of anticipation burned in his chest but he gulped in air and quelled it.

"When is it Hal?"

"Saturday, man. It'll be bad, man, bad."

Why was he subjecting himself to something bad? But hey, he thought, nothing ventured.

The party filtered into the early evening and petered out, the guests had other places to be and as easily as they had flowed into the wilderness, they ebbed away to suburbia, suitably inebriated.

Tom didn't smoke cigarettes, but had smoked a little weed in the past. Being in bands, it was inevitable that drugs would surface to enhance the flavour of a rehearsal session, or induce a performance. In the right company, at the right time, he had enjoyed being stoned or 'shroomed. Nothing artificial though, he would never touch anything manmade. It was natural or nothing; apart from lager and spirits, and headache pills, and antibiotics and hayfever tablets, oh, and his asthma inhaler—that stands to reason.

A couple of tugs on a sensi' spliff however were enough to leave him cotton mouthed and giddy, so he took to his bed and stayed there 'til morning.

The next day Pricey thought it a good plan for Tom to have some driving experience. He was to take Amber to pre-school and then do some grocery shopping. He would take the car because Amber had to be bolted into her child seat, in the back.

The most trying half hour of his life so far was now about to take place, an experience that would be enough to piss off Saint Nicholas.

Amber detested being strapped into the seat, she would scratch and bite and kick whoever had the unfortunate task of forcing her in. Once constrained she would scream her lungs out for the entire journey, relentlessly, without pause, and nothing would placate her until she reached the destination and the button-on cross-ply webbing was released. Then, instant quiet, like the trauma hadn't existed at all.

It defied all logic, Tom was an exceedingly patient man, calm in most situations, tolerant, compromising, but this intolerable test on the journey in, almost made him stop the car and launch the child into the wilderness. Salvation came in the form of a Kinder Care car park and once in the hands of a nursery worker the little devil couldn't have been happier, neither could Tom.

"Keira can pick that up," he said to himself re-entering the car. He sped off to a supermarket on 22nd street.

Fry's was a massive store, far bigger than any he had witnessed in England and strikingly air conditioned. Slicing through the invisible wall of super cold ventilation expressed from units above the expansive entrance brought blissful relief from the heat. It was a chill that he soon acclimatized to, only to be assaulted by a torrent of delectable smells. Fresh bread baking, roast and fried chicken ready to go, donuts galore, coffee brewing, pizza being cooked, soda fountains, fruit mountains and pick and mix buckets of sweets like dustbins. Tom's eyes were on stalks; it was an exaggerated shopping extravaganza, the likes of which he had never experienced.

Everything was so big, big trolleys, big packages, big fridges, hmm, big people.

He caught sight of one of the grossest apparitions that had ever come to pass. A huge individual weighing in the region of 560 lbs wearing shorts, long socks and sneakers. He had on a t-shirt that only covered half of his belly; a glutinous mass, rivered with blue and purple veins which was so huge it flopped inside the trolley doubling up as a belly buggy. The pony-tailed, obese freak was taking its own carcass shopping. It was obscene, but being British, Tom just pretended the thing wasn't there.

After half an hour, and having completed his shopping list, he noticed an express photo lab. He had 6 rolls of film to process with him, so he handed them over to the female assistant and asked how long they would take to develop.

"Excuse me?" she replied.

"When shall I come back to collect the pictures?"

"Oh my god, where are you from?" she looked like a surprised turkey on December 24th.

Tom bemused by her excitement simply said, "London" using the capital as a reasonable approximation.

"London, that's in England right, oh I just love your accent, I could listen to it all day," she sang.

He stared at her gormless expression.

"I'll make you a tape; you can put it on loop and listen 'til your heart's content."

"I don't know what you're saying, but it sure sounds good," she drawled.

Tom thought it best to speak slower, in a staggered manner. "How long for the photographs?"

She mimicked his method like he was the simple one. "Oh, they will be ready in an hour."

"Thank you, I'll be back," he replied with a quick smile, and then he wondered off to the CD aisle to check out some new albums. The assistant watched him leave, starry-eyed, as if she'd just met royalty.

After perusing the plastic for five minutes he recalled that he didn't have a CD player, so he picked up a music magazine instead and headed for the cooked-chicken counter, choosing two pieces of southern fried, some French fries and a large Coke. He sat at a Formica table/chair composite, devoured the delicious greasy food and studied the magazine closely, coming to the conclusion that he couldn't afford to buy a new guitar.

The allotted hour passed, so it was time to pick up the photos. Back at the counter the docile lab technician was pleased to see him return and in a practiced overused monologue asked him if he would like to pay for them here, or at the checkout. Tom thought it made more sense to pay for everything at the checkout, so he took that option.

"There you go sir, and you get a free roll of film with every processed reel, have a nice day," she sang.

"Oh thank you—you too," he said, surprised.

Tom gave her another benevolent smile and sauntered off to the tills, 35 cash registers, each staffed with a teller and a bag operative.

Tom picked a half empty conveyer belt so that when he had finished unloading, the cashier would be ready for him. Whilst unloading he read a headline on an Enquirer magazine, *'Mother gives birth to baby with wooden leg'*. That's hilarious he thought, then read another, *'Lancaster bomber found on the Moon'*. He laughed out loud; some publisher was having a right giggle. And people buy this shit?

The teller bid him good morning and ran his goods past the bar code scanner. When she came to his photographs she asked him if he had paid for them already. A second's pause, then he heard himself saying yes. The teller handed them to him and carried on nonchalantly scanning his goods.

"Paper or plastic?" said the bag man.

"Oh, paper please," he responded, feeling his cheeks redden with guilt. Suppressing his dishonesty, he remained calm.

Pushing his trolley past a security guard on the door who took not the slightest notice of him, Tom was amazed how trustworthy Americans were. He'd just saved himself $36 on development and received 6 new rolls of film thrown in for free. Not only that, he forgot to pay for the chicken dinner as well. How unfortunate, he thought; that was way too easy.

Saturday came and Tom found himself following Dubwise up the interstate towards Casa Grande, the truck's stick shift took some getting used to, having to change gear with the right hand felt completely alien. The journey took around two hours. Dubwise had a small clapped out Japanese hatchback which would probably run quicker with the engine turned off and Tom was doubly frustrated by the speed limit on the motorway, a paltry 55mph, which seemed agonisingly slow and after a while made his accelerator foot ache from being held in one position.

The gig was in a small scruffy hall, poorly attended, and the band weren't very impressive. Tom felt like a peanut in a box of Liquorice Allsorts. He didn't belong here and after two hours of monotony, he decided it was time to bugger off, so he slipped out the front door without saying goodbye to the band.

Darkness had descended on hazy Casa Grande, making the route home an inky blank canvas. But Tom persevered and managed to stumble across the interstate and once upon it he took comfort in the fact that it was just one long schlep back to Tucson. He would be okay from here on in.

Pricey's 1970s Ford truck was a bit of a beast, but smooth enough once cruising. Rock and Country tunes were bleeding out of the radio, the unfamiliar concrete slab rolled on with just a smattering of cars on the road that night, the centre meridian was wide and road markers zipped by at regular intervals. A mesmerising hour passed before Tom had a slight notion the dashboard lights were getting dimmer. Ten minutes later he was sure; they were definitely losing luminescence. The headlights were also fading, the radio crackled out and the engine started to lose power.

Tom's heart sank into the bench seat. "Don't break down in the middle of nowhere," he pleaded out loud.

He accelerated hoping to somehow cure the ailing motor vehicle with mere thrust, "Nurse it, nurse it, come on baby," he whispered, "don't let me down." Mobile phones were still a thing of science fiction, he had very little money on him and now he doubted that he was even on the right road. Nothing seemed familiar; no town lights, no motorway lights, just dirt and desert and highway. The truck started lurching and spluttering, gasping for fuel, obviously about to die when suddenly an orange sulphur glow beckoned like a beacon of salvation up ahead; if he could just keep it rolling another half mile.

"Come on, Bessie," he begged. An exit ramp appeared, and the refuge of a truck stop. It was bleak, decrepit and deserted but deliverance for Tom, who thanked whatever deity was looking out for him that night. Now does it have a pay phone, he thought. Yes! He spotted one next to the darkened shop.

Rolling under the canopy, he resisted the instinct to turn off the engine. She was labouring to keep going, but Tom couldn't chance it. He made a call to Pricey, it was 2:00 a.m. and he'd be asleep, but surely he would come out to rescue his brother-in-law—wouldn't he?

To Tom's surprise Pricey thought the predicament was hilarious, he wasn't mad at all. "Where are ya' exactly?" he asked.

Tom looked around searching for a name plaque of some description; there weren't any. "Err … I 'dunno'. There's no one 'ere to ask either."

"Look on the phone box by the number."

"Oh yeah, Marana, I'm in Marana, just off the I-10."

"All right, I'll be about forty minutes. Don't take sweets from any strangers."

"Chance'll be a fine thing, the place is desolate."

Waiting in the faltering cab under the phosphorescence of a single bulb, time diminished. Frequent glances at his watch didn't shorten the distance between being marooned and liberation. Tom shut his eyes and flopped his head back against the rear panel. Within moments he was sinking into oblivion, falling into a welcoming black hole.

A tap of metal on glass startled him back into the here and now. Spinning his head sideways, he was greeted by a figure in a grubby Diamond Backs baseball cap, and a filthy blue and black lumberjack fleece jacket. Greasy hair poked out of the cap, oiling the vagrant's upturned collar.

Tom's heart raced, this was exactly the situation he'd hoped to avoid.

"Wos up?" croaked the tramp.

Tom wondered what this guy had tapped the window with, maybe he had a knife, or maybe it was just a ring on his finger. "Just waiting for me' mate," he replied, searching his mind's eye for any weapons that may be at hand.

The guy curled his lip, uncomprehending Tom's accent, he spat to the ground. "You got a cigarette?" he snarled.

"Sorry mate, don't smoke." Groping around behind his seat with his right hand, Tom felt his fingers curl around a large monkey wrench. If this guy opened the door he was going to smash him straight in the face with it.

"Ya'll got cash?"

The request was menacingly provocative, and followed by a lopsided grimace, reminiscent of a dragon with toothache.

Tom could see where this was heading and it made his blood run cold. The hobo's deep set eyes tunnelled into him like angry dark matter that could slice straight through glass, flesh and bone, and rip out Tom's pounding heart like he was plucking a flower. Tom's nerves on high alert shuddered in anticipation of the impending violence.

A spangled glint from an abruptly visible switchblade in the vagrant's right hand, reflected from the headlights of an approaching vehicle, disturbed the would-be assailant. He twitched anxiously, his eyes darting from the headlights to Tom and back again. The penny dropped, he was outgunned, he lost his bottle, turned on his toes and fled into the pitch black wilderness, his fleece flapping behind him like some kind of anti-hero's fouled cape.

Pricey was giggling to himself as he skidded to a halt in a cloud of dust, in his boss's Jeep, 'toking' on a spliff, 'Steel Pulse' blaring out of the cab.

Tom was tired and anxious, but wholly grateful the cavalry had arrived. "Did you see that bloke run off into the bushes?" he spluttered.

"Nope," said Pricey looking quizzical.

"'e was gonna mug me. Thank fuck you turned up just then."

Pricey scanned the darkness. "We better fuck off fast then."

Laying in the dirt under each motor, he hooked a tow rope between the trucks, then after giving himself a good brush-down, he pulled Tom back to Vale, which in itself was a hair-raising journey, with no lights, no power assisted steering and little in the way of brakes. After Tom nearly ramming the Jeep a couple of times, they finally made it home at 3:30. Tom was exhausted from sleep deprivation and faint from concentration.

In the light of day the breakdown turned out to be nothing more than a broken alternator belt and simple to fix, but the night before had been a harrowing episode for the young Brit.

***

Two months in, the brother-in-law was spending less time at work, shunning his duties to take Tom to different places.

Tom felt uneasy in their home. Keira and Pricey had always shared an ugly, estranged, often violent, on-off sort of marriage, and Tom's sister had confided in him that she wanted to leave Pricey and go back to England.

She hadn't made any plans as yet, but the outcome was inevitable. For now, living at Bear Paw was stretching borrowed time.

The Toms went to visit KP at her club, 'The Purple Haze'. It was on the west side of North 4ᵗʰ Ave, a busy dishevelled little thoroughfare, rammed with alternative clothing boutiques, crystal shops, herbal accessory outlets, galleries and restaurants.

KP occupied a double fronted building that ambled back to a yard and outbuildings. The club's entrance sported blacked-out glass with a big purple neon tube sign above the window highlighting its existence. Inside the décor was typical of a live venue; minimalistic, bare, sticky floorboards, black walls, limited tables screwed to the floor and bench seating. A large stage was situated at the back of the room, a lighting gantry, PA system and a complete half of a 1950s Purple Buick Riviera, magically affixed to the wall. The place smelt of cigarettes and stale cola.

Tom felt in residence instantly, he'd played many venues like this.

They went into the office and were greeted enthusiastically by KP and Glen, who proceeded to roll a welcoming joint. The place was buzzing with bodies, Tom got introduced to some colourful characters; there was Arty, KP's business partner and co-owner of the Haze. He was tall and sinewy, had long black, dead straight, lifeless hair and rather pronounced buck teeth. He reminded Tom a bit of Alice Cooper and seemed to be a tad preoccupied to embrace a new foundling.

Arty was flitting around discussing PA problems with his wingman, a black-leather clad, grunge metal drummer and resident DJ named Scorpion, whose beautiful girlfriend Sasha floated around the place like a gothic ghost, never speaking, fashionably sullen and demure. The rumour had it that Scorpion had given her herpes, no wonder she was miserable.

Sean Adams, the club's caretaker/janitor was larger than life, 6-6 tall, rotund, with long white hair and flowing white beard. He was the epitome of Santa Claus and indeed donned the red outfit every Christmas; hired out to one of the malls, the star of an incredibly realistic Santa's grotto. Although Sean came from Michigan, he spoke with a deep cowboy timbre, was rosy-cheeked and always had a smile on his face. He came across as highly intellectual, and ultra non-conformist, like he had been damaged somewhere along the line, maybe a veteran of Vietnam or Korea.

Tom never asked.

KP showed the boys around. Next door was her clothing store, 'Misinformed'. It stocked the kind of regalia a New York dominatrix might don, although the shop held fast to the premise of a rock clothing outlet. There were whips and gimp masks and various other contraptions the likes of which were from another dimension; most of it of a sexual nature.

Tom wasn't a prude, he just found this sort of garb to be a bit comedic and unnecessary.

The girl manning the till was Jennifer's 19-year-old daughter Selena; blonde, bold and bubbly, born in the USA but managed a perfect English accent when prompted. She was street savvy, erudite, cool and moderately flirting with the goth scene.

"Would you like a drink?" asked KP. "We don't sell alcohol here but we do have ice cold soft drinks on tap."

"Why don't you sell alcohol?" asked Tom.

"Oh, we're an under 21 club. We don't have a liquor license, thank God, so the little darlings can't get pissed and trash the place."

"You can't drink until you're twenty-one, is that right?" enquired Tom.

"That's right, not in a bar, no, and nobody can drink in the street either, that's why you see winos drinking from paper bags. It's an immediate arrest if you're caught displaying liquor on the street, so be warned. Would you like a Jolt, It's kind of like Coke but with twice the caffeine?"

"Will it stiffen my resolve?"

KP laughed, "It'll stiffen something."

"I'll have a pint then."

It was twice as sweet as Coke and rather lively.

The tour carried on through a small recording studio, past the washrooms, through a large storage room and out into the 'back-lot'. The rear yard could accommodate 15cars at a push, and terminated with a large chain linked gate on North Herbert Ave.

Glen came out to tell KP that Natty Dread had arrived.

"You must come and meet the Lion of Zion; I've hooked him up with Sonny Ensenada, a local keyboard player. Natty will be lodging with Sonny and Bonita until I can rent him a house."

Back in the office the Dread was sitting on a corner of the table looking apprehensive. His eyes flicked around the room weighing up the mob that had flooded into his space. He wore a substantial green, black and gold Tam, clenched to the back of his head, atop a mass of thick dreadlocks which tailed half way down his back.

KP introduced everybody. They shook hands.

Pricey said something incomprehensible to the Rastafarian, to which Natty just slowly nodded.

Katie Pirelli made it clear that she wanted to talk business to her new artist, so before they took their leave, Pricey invited Natty to come over for Sunday lunch sometime soon, then the boys bade everyone goodbye.

Natty gratefully accepted the invitation. He had lived in Brixton for some years and enjoyed a good Sunday roast.

"You should get in with 'im, son," said Pricey wrapping an arm around Tom's shoulders as they walked out of the club. "'e'll make us rich."

"Err, let's just 'ave lunch with him first … see if we get on," replied Captain cautious.

3
Transition

By the end of March the temperature was hitting 80°F. Triggered by the first spring rains, the desert burst into bloom. Around Bear Paw the prevailing blossom seemed to be the yellow flowered brittle bushes, whose luminous heads were like miniature sunflowers emblazoned on a blanket of grey-green fuzz. Interspersed were brilliant splashes of purple from the flower of the beavertail cactus, or the red globemallows and delicate white desert poppies. Clumps of pink flowering mohave thistles contrasted brilliantly against the rusty orange soil and everywhere, in abundance, the green old men of the desert, the majestic saguaro's.

Mesquite trees were in full leaf now, contrasting massively against the big blue sky, an endless azure canopy that arced uninterrupted from horizon to horizon. From high vantage points you could literally see the Earth's curve, and contrails from distant jets looked like they were missiles being fired heaven-wards from the ground. The first time Tom witnessed this he thought that he was watching a rocket launch, or maybe something less than terrestrial until, after watching it for a time, the aeroplane levelled out overhead and its profile could be disappointingly discerned.

The airspace here got busy at times, not just from international passenger flights, but because Tucson also has a substantial Air Force base, a National Guard air base and of course a plentiful supply of police and civilian helicopters that were almost a constant sight.

Davis Monthan Air Force Base is the home of the 335th Air Wing and primarily trained A10 'Thunderbolt' pilots. These pig ugly tank-busting black aircraft scream around in pairs at irregular intervals, often upsetting the tranquillity of one's day.

Their manoeuvres sometimes include low level attack patterns that are bone-jarringly menacing when you are least expecting it.

The base is also famous for its aircraft boneyard, a phenomenally large expanse stockpiled with some 5,000 mothballed, maintained, aircraft. Preserved, their engine vents and windows are wrapped in paper and ready to fly if necessary. Some of the planes were for sale to friendly foreign governments who might be in need of out-dated war machines; others were held in reserve—just in case.

Tom was driven past the boneyard along Kolb Rd with Bob Alverez, Pricey's step-father, a Mexican-American who had married Ellen, Pricey's mum.

Rank after rank after rank of identical aircraft employed the airfields on both sides of the road. Bombers, fighters, helicopters, transports, spy planes, airliners, each one precision parked; a clone robot army patiently waiting for the command to go. The spectacle was fascinating, enchanting almost, yet apocalyptically foreboding. The sight of so much awesome fire power in one place implied something sinister, and far too surreal to absorb entirely.

Bob was quite knowledgeable on the history of the place and enjoyed showing Tom around in his gold 1975 Pontiac Grandville Brougham convertible.

"The dry climate and alkaline soil down here make perfect conditions to store these planes," informed Bob, "and you'll never see a rusting car in these parts either." He patted the top of the door of his pristine beloved car where his arm rested.

Bob wore a straw Fedora hat, a red bandana around his neck and police motor cycle shades. Slightly resembling Carlos Santana with his thin moustache and open, button-neck T-shirt, he looked really cool cruising the streets at a snail's pace.

Bob was a recovering alcoholic and attended regular AA meetings. Even though he'd been dry for 12-years, he still considered himself to be a drunk.

He had a 14-year-old daughter called Nicole, she meant the world to Bob; she was sweet, pretty, and a lovely person, but for some reason Ellen detested her.

Perhaps Nicole received more attention than Ellen; Tom would never know, but he did know Ellen. She was a vicious, evil, vile creature and a money-grabbing, thieving piece-of-work, who had lied and deceived her way through life, leaving an aftermath of devastation wherever she trod. Tom couldn't trust the woman one bit and avoided her company as much as possible. He learned much later from Keira that Ellen used to spit in Nicole's dinners, which affirmed his detest for the loathsome woman.

Bob invited Tom on a trip down to the border town of Nogales, Mexico and, of course, Tom jumped at the chance to visit another country. Nicole went along for the ride. The journey south on the I-19 took just over an hour-and-a-half and was full of questions about Bob's upbringing.

Tom got the low down on how Bob had entered the USA illegally before he obtained citizenship. When Bob was a boy, he and his friends tunnelled under the border fence and walked in the cover of darkness over several nights before finally reaching Tucson. He stayed with an uncle in a trailer park cleaning cars and washing dishes in a Mexican restaurant to earn his keep. He'd do anything just to stay in America; even sacrificing both funerals of his parents back in Heroica Nogales, which, of course, had long-term devastating effects.

In the 60s an amnesty was declared for any 'illegals' that had been in the states for more than ten-years. Bob qualified and got his green card, this meant that not only could he now go to college, he could also go to and fro from the USA, which prompted a career in drug smuggling.

He told Tom that as a young man he used to visit a dealer in Nogales who had so much marijuana stacked in bales in his house that you had to walk through thin corridors of the stuff to negotiate passage. The 'puff' was piled to the ceilings. Bob and his four friends would buy a suitcase full of grass and stash it in the boot, or trunk of a car that belonged to a couple of wholesome looking, young, blonde, American girls. They would then all drive to the border, with the boys in front trying to act as suspicious as possible inevitably getting stopped by the guards, while the girls would pass through without question as Bob's car was being pointlessly searched. Apparently this worked every time and they never got caught.

Intrepid, thought Tom.

"Do ya' still bring a little back?" he asked tentatively.

"No, no, those days are long gone my friend; I'm strictly just cigarettes now, man."

"You must 'ave made a packet runnin' that much stuff at a time."

"Oh we used to smoke a lot of it back then; I'd be stoned most of my days and drunk most of my nights. Hell, I never did make it to college and I stayed drunk until I met Nicole's mom, when I was twenty-four, she helped to straighten me out, along with the AA."

"Where's Nicole's mum now?"

"Oh, she died when Nicole was five, she caught meningitis; there was nothing we could do."

Tom became pensive for a while, the wind ruffled his hair and the sun burned down on his forehead and arms. He looked back at Nicole; she had her feet up on the rear seat, her head angled between the back-rest and the side panel. She looked asleep, but behind her dark glasses who could tell; her long black hair danced wildly in the slipstream and perspiration glistened above her top lip. He couldn't imagine growing up without a mum, but it seemed that Bob had done a decent job despite a shed load of obstacles.

"Mexico," proclaimed Bob, snapping Tom back to the present.

They were entering a town that was not unlike any other part of Arizona, same clean streets, same building types and the same shops.

Disappointed, Tom asked, "What ... we're in Mexico now?"

"No, no, we have to cross the border first; we're still on American soil."

They rounded a curve and joined a queue of traffic. Ahead, around 20 cars waited in line, pointed towards the border gates, an impressive grey metal structure that bridged the freeway, resembling an over-exuberant animal park entrance. The words 'Welcome to Mexico' arced across its pinnacle, flanked by the national flags of both countries.

A quick uninterested flick through their passports by a sweaty border patrolman was all that was deemed necessary to enter the country, a length of a car later they rolled into the third world.

Tom straightened in his seat, the contrast was startling. The potholed road was strewn with litter, the houses in disrepair, unpainted and unkempt. Some were nothing more than wooden shacks nailed up with mismatched timber, rusty corrugated iron, chicken wire and cardboard; an indication of downcast people building with whatever came to hand. The makeshift gardens were like gypsy camps scattered with fly tipped household waste and broken fridges. Chickens ran amok in the streets and stray dogs were rife.

For the first time in Tom's life he encountered beggars, children as young as five, filthy dirty, swaddled in rags poised in shop doorways holding out their grubby little hands. He wondered if it was just theatrics, after all this was also a tourist town.

"Are those children for real?" he asked Bob.

"Oh yes, they're the poorest of the poor; their parents send them out every day. They know that flush Americans will pour pity on them, and they'll get beaten if they go home with empty bowls."

"Jesus—"

"He'll look out for them," preached Bob.

It slipped Tom's mind that Bob was a man of faith.

Finding a place to park on a street lined with shops and restaurants, they got out; fixed the vinyl roof over the car, then took off for a tour.

The shops were typically geared for tourism, not the full flavour of Mexico Tom was hoping for. But they stopped outside a restaurant that Bob was familiar with to peruse the menu

"Can we eat now, Dad?" pleaded Nicole, "I'm real hungry."

"They do excellent burritos here, would you like to try some Tom?"

"Certainly would, Bob, I'm hankerin' for a bit of authenticity."

"Then you're in for some validity my friend. Step this way."

Tom went for a Cabo san Lucas burrito with cooked shrimp and lobster mixed with cream, vinegar and mayo, jack cheese and cilantro leaves, with a side of refried beans. While Bob plumped for a Carne Asada, with black beans, cilantro, diced onions, and a side of Spanish rice. Nicole opted for mini pork Tamale's and a chilli pasta salad.

The food was exquisite, astonishingly cheap, and far superior to the pseudo-Mexican crap they dished up in chain restaurants over the border.

Tom washed his meal down with a large coke, out of respect for Bob. The Brit was so full he thought his stomach might burst. His host would not let him pay for a thing, even though Bob was by no means a wealthy man, Tom was his guest in the place of his birth and he would hear none of the lad's protests.

"How would you like to visit a professional recording studio my friend?" Bob asked as they strolled back to the car.

"What … 'ere in town, you know someone?"

"Yes my cousin has one at his house, I haven't seen him in a while; would you like to see Uncle Tito, Nicole?"

"Uh ha," she replied earnestly.

Tito's villa stood in a more lucrative part of town, it wasn't vast but modest and you could tell that the guy had made a decent living from his craft. Tito was a big guy with close-cropped hair, a stylized beard and massive hands. Tom couldn't imagine how he managed to play a musical instrument with mitts like those.

The welcome, as usual, was warm and exuberant and somewhat more intimate than is the custom in England. Within five minutes Tom felt like he had known the guy for years. Nicole disappeared into the house to see her auntie and cousins while Tom got an exclusive tour of the studio.

It was bigger than any he had ever recorded in, spotlessly clean and acoustically perfect. Tito had a grand piano in the 'live' room, a Hammond organ, a Rhodes electric piano set up, and a choice of Yamaha and Korg synthesizers along one wall. There was also an array of electric, acoustic and bass guitars hanging in a long rack against another wall. In the substantial engineers booth sprawled a 36 channel Allen and Heath mixing console, a 24 track, 2-inch tape recorder, stacks of outboard effects, processors and the best studio monitors that money could buy.

Humbled by the quality in the room, Tom felt like a little fish in a huge pond.

"'ave you recorded name artists in 'ere Tito?" he asked sheepishly.

Tito smiled "Oh, none that you would have heard of, amigo. Mostly Mexican and Latin American artists, the American musicians all wanna record in LA or Nashville … Jose Moran, Lucero Leon, Tamberiche, Sasha Barroso; you heard of any of them?"

"No I'm afraid not." Tom would have loved the chance to record in somewhere like this, but he felt himself far too insignificant to even consider it. "Do you play an instrument, Tito?"

"Keyboards, yes, and a bit of guitar; mainly Spanish traditional. If you want to play with anything go ahead. I need to talk to Bob for a while anyway; help yourself." He indicated towards the 'live' room.

Tom fancied a tinkle on the grand piano so he slipped off and left the men to it.

Twenty-minutes later, after Tom had exhausted his repertoire of piano chords, Bob peered around the door jamb.

"We are going to leave now buddy, if you are ready."

"Sure," he said. "Lovely bit a' kit this."

They ventured outside; Bob was talking Spanish to Tito and his wife, and carried a gift wrapped package under his arm the size of an average stereo speaker.

Suspicious, Tom passed close to Bob, sniffing the air for anything vaguely narcotic. What he received was surprising—a whiff of fresh laundry.

Pricey had told him that a foolproof way to deter sniffer dogs was to wrap drugs up in tumble dryer sheets. The fragrance from them is so strong that the marijuana smell can't be detected. Fuck, he thought, he's gonna smuggle in some dope.

Bob put the gift in the boot of his car and closed the lid.

Tom camouflaged his anxiety, he thanked Tito for his hospitality and wished him well.

Nicole kissed her cousins goodbye and they set off back to Tucson.

In the queue for the border, with thoughts of rotting in a filthy dark prison cell, forgotten and potentially bum-raped by vicious giant inmates, Tom had to come up with a plan to distance himself from the consignment while passing through immigration.

He told Bob that he wanted to get his passport stamped with a big Mexican crest, and that he'd walk through the border gate and meet them on the other side. Bob didn't seem fazed, so Tom hopped out of the Pontiac and headed for the pedestrian line.

At the gate his passport received the usual nonchalant flick through, but no rubber stamp appeared. Tom gesticulated he wanted a stamp, at which, the lethargic guard pointed towards an office in the main building. Comprehending the directive Tom wandered over and went in. After three unsuccessful attempts at trying to make himself understood, he finally found someone willing to give him a stamp.

"Here we go," he said to himself smugly excited to be getting another country's insignia in his passport. The stamp that he received however was a smudged single line date stamp that was barely readable.

Downhearted, but certain he'd wasted enough time for Bob and Nicole to have crossed the border, he mooched off towards the American line once more.

To his utter horror, he could see the convertible had been singled out and was having its boot searched. Bob was standing with his back to Tom, hands on hips and watching two border police examining the dubious package. Nicole stayed in the vehicle, unperturbed.

Keeping his eyes forward Tom willed himself not to notice what was going on. He shielded his nervousness and pretended nothing was awry. As much as he hated to abandon his Hispanic friends, an orange jumpsuit with steel cufflinks weren't *en Vogue* this spring either.

Passing through the gate with ease, he decided to walk on for a block and wait in plain view. Looking over his shoulder constantly, hoping that he had got the situation all wrong and that they would be through the entry point at any second.

He waited and waited, whilst considering his options for travelling back to Tucson. He sat on a bench and stared at the ground.

A greyhound bus would be novel, uncomfortable, but cheap. There was hitchhiking, although that idea seemed fraught with peril; or maybe he could call on Pricey again to bail him out.

Two honks from a loud car horn broke his considerations.

"Hey Buddy, do you wanna ride?"

Tom looked up to see a shining gold Pontiac with Carlos Santana at the wheel.

He was so relieved that he almost jumped in the air, but he reserved the temptation. "You going my way?"

"If it's north, hop in," said Bob blithely.

Nicole was in her usual repose in the back, and it appeared that they hadn't been caught redhanded with a large shipment of illegal herbs after all.

"I thought that you'd be through way before me, what took you so long?" asked Tom disingenuously.

"Ah, we got searched by the guards, wanted to know what the gift was in the trunk."

"And what is it?" Tom was just as curious as the guards.

"It's a joke for Tito's brother Teo. A box of laundry powder. Tito says that he should wash his pants more often. Did you get the Mexicano stamp?"

"For what it's worth." He flashed the pathetic blue smear in front of Bob.

"Hey they did you proud there, buddy … next time, huh?"

They headed home.

***

April rolled in like a returning tide and before they knew it they were ankle deep. Pricey decided he needed a holiday and asked Tom if he fancied going to Disneyland. Of course, he did, what kid didn't? So, they rented a 6-berth Winnebago for a week and set off for California.

The route to the west coast along the I-10 and then the I-8 was tedious, monotonous and took the best part of a day. Pricey thought it hilarious to side up to gigantic haulage trucks and entice them to sound their impressive air horns, by giving the drivers the internationally recognised hand signal of a fist pulling down on a chain. The truckers always complied and it was funny for the first couple of times, but became annoying after a short while, yet banally he kept on doing it.

Skirting around America's finest city, they picked up the I-5, the San Diego freeway where the scenery at last livened up. On through Del Mar, Carlsbad and Oceanside, they were still on the interstate. But now, at least, they had communities and different fauna to look at; banks of woodland populated with spruce, cedar and pine mixed with broadleaf hardwoods. They passed over several lagoons and a place called Cardiff-by-the-Sea.

"Cymriff biff," said Tom in a Welsh accent.

"Lechyd-da," replied the Price.

Occasionally now, they got exciting glimpses of the sea through breaks and troughs in the land to their left, it was a deeper blue than the sky, but hard to define between the two, for they smudged together seamlessly on the distant horizon.

By the time they reached San Onofre State Beach they were parallel to the Old Pacific highway and the endless ocean stretched out uninterrupted for miles.

Rolling scrubby hills defined the land to their right, framed vividly by the wispy clouded blue slab that enclosed the west coast like an azure crystal cloche. At Capistrano Beach they exited the freeway and picked up Route 1, the Pacific Coast Highway. The traffic here congested amidst a noticeably more condensed suburbia, with condominiums and apartment blocks encroaching on the road.

Further along they came to a hamlet called Laguna Beach, an idyllic little artist's community, quintessentially American, Tom thought; lovely, he made a note to retire here. It had a perfect spotless sandy cove, timber constructed houses and bungalows, a seafront of galleries and restaurants, and an ambience of sun-drenched tranquillity.

The family decided to stop here and have a walkabout. They bought groceries at a wholefood store and perused a few gift shops.

Tom loved the relaxed attitude of the community, it suited his personality.

Passing an open-fronted, white timber clad restaurant that backed onto the beach, Tom locked eyes with a recognised face. Frank Gorshin, the original Riddler in the Batman TV series. Gorshin knew he'd been spotted and so gifted Tom a knowing Hollywood smile. There was a moment's connection between the two, before Tom nodded and walked on, chuffed to bits he'd met nobility.

Pricey wanted to get on down the road, so egged them all reluctantly back onto the RV.

The destination for the night was Newport Beach. Pricey parked on West Oceanfront in a large public car park, with a clear view of the Pacific. They trooped out and bounded barefoot to the shore, hell-bent on an inaugural dip in the world's largest ocean. The sand on the vast beach was ultra-soft, ambrosia to walk on after a long sweaty journey. If he lived here, Tom would never wear shoes again.

Amber went in up to her knees and squealed with delight as tiny waves crashed around her legs. Pricey turned into a ten-year-old and ran amok in the surf, kicking water over everybody and doing handstands fully clothed, until all his money fell out of his pockets, inducing a panicked scramble for soggy notes.

Tom and Keira ambled along the shoreline admiring the diversity of the beach-houses, and day-dreaming.

"Wouldn't it be lovely to live in one of these bungalows?" she said. "I'd be on the beach every day."

"'andy for a drop of sand if you 'ave a wall to build," he said, pulling her leg.

Keira laughed, "Trust you to think of that."

The day was nearing its end; they returned to the Winnebago, made dinner and watched the sun set fire to the sea as it disappeared over the boundless horizon.

With a decent meal and a couple of bottles of Bud inside him, Tom was more than content. Keira put the food-stained, unconscious Amber to bed and the three of them sat out in the temperate evening air contemplating their next move amid talk of quality past times.

Morning broke grey, damp and misty; the climate had cooled to a chilly 55°F. Tom drew back the curtains and was stunned by a spectacle. Three black dorsal fins of migrating Minke whales, a family pod perhaps, heading south, cut through the dull surf, rising and diving in perfect unison like upturned boats, the keels of the underworld. He watched through condensation-obscured windows until they faded into the murk, quite unable to move.

Pricey stirred next, stumbling into the kitchen.

"Morning," he said ambling for the toilet. "Must visit the vicar."

"You missed that," said Tom passively.

"Missed what?"

"Three whales just passed by about a hundred yards off shore; it was mesmerising."

"They must be mad; it's freezing in that sea. Gotta 'ave a piss I'm burstin'."

When Pricey came out he shouted down to Keira, "What's for breakfast, Keir?"

"Shut up and get back in the frying pan," she hollered from the bedroom.

"I see," scrutinised Pricey. "It's like that is it?"

From the car park they headed inland and onto the Santa Ana Freeway, then north into Anaheim, exiting on Disney Way and skirting the palm treelined perimeter of Walt's famous theme park.

With the RV moored, they traversed the extravagant brick-paved esplanade, through the giant gold letters spelling California and up to the turnstiles of the Magic Kingdom.

After high expectations of the corporation's flagship, Tom was positively disappointed. It was much smaller than he'd imagined, the rides were un-extraordinary and it was plonked right in the middle of suburbia. He'd always supposed that the park would be surrounded by lush rolling hills and fragrant meadows, not Travelodge's and Denny's restaurants. The whole attraction was nothing more than an over-contrived artificial cash cow and certainly not what dreams were made of. Tom wandered thoroughfare trying to look excited for Amber's sake, but feeling swindled by a supercilious conglomerate.

The family wanted to ride on the ghost train. It looked pathetic, a carriage ride through a concrete mountain with plastic skeletons on strings and piped maniacal laughter.

Half-heartedly Tom climbed aboard and slunk into the plastic moulded caboose next to his neice. Midway through the dismal jaunt, he was about as frightened as the Terminator in a pillow fight, when suddenly something whispered in his ear, "Are you scared yet?" its ghostly breath hissed on his skin, Tom swiveled back sharply, but there was nobody there, just pitiful scenery, darkness and distant screaming. He was bloody scared now! He tried to apply logic to the source of the words; the next car back was too far away for anyone to have leaned forward for a prank and only a four-year-old sat beside him. He clung on to the rail in front uncertain if he had just imagined the voice, or if it had been a trick of the ride. He shivered; no, it had definitely been real.

Pricey thought it was hysterical, Keira believed it to be part of the show. Tom found it incredible neither of them empathised or shared his anguish; he was left traumatized by it for the rest of the day.

The only compensation that he received for his disenchanting visit was having his photograph taken next to Tigger, because Tigger was his favourite lunatic.

After being fleeced by Mr Disney, they set off into Los Angeles along the I-5. The districts here, like London, bled into one giant uninterrupted metropolis, and by the time they reached the outskirts of LA proper, the road was dreadfully congested and high rise buildings threatened to herd the traffic into a bottle neck of no return.

The sunlight was diffused by a permanent suffocating exhaust haze and the Winnebago appeared terribly conspicuous amongst the commercial traffic on the interstate, making its occupants a little paranoid.

Santa Ana turned into the Hollywood Freeway and they exited near the 101 to pick up Sunset Boulevard. Still unimpressed, until they reached Hollywood where the difference in wealth immediately became apparent. It was like Knightsbridge only with fan palms, blue sky and double the opulence.

"There's some fuckin' money round 'ere boy," Pricey announced enthusiastically.

Tom smiled. He was quietly enjoying the vista. The scene of so many movies and TV shows for a lad from a small town in Hertfordshire this was an eye candy overload.

They reached Beverly Hills where the properties turned into mansions and the streets were greener and lined with lush tall trees; and every vehicle was a limousine or a super car. Turning into North Beverly Drive they climbed further into the hills. The higher they climbed the more expensive the property became, the grander the house, the more illustrious the security, the more magnificent the panorama, the greater the feeling that they were trespassing.

Two days into their trip had resulted in a rather full waste tank, and now the smell woofing up on every bend of the road had become unbearable, like driving around in an open slurry spreader.

Pricey expressed the obvious. "We're gonna 'ave t' empty that tank."

"It fuckin' stinks," piped in Keira eloquently.

"Not up here, surely?" said Tom horrified at Pricey's gall. "What if we're caught, I'll die of embarrassment?"

"Trust me, I'm not a doctor," ribbed Pricey.

He turned the RV around at the end of a vacant, pristine white smooth concrete cul-de-sac and parked it next to a deep open-mouthed storm drain.

Acting out the scenario of a man stretching his legs, he uncoiled the waste pipe and flopped it down into the gaping gully. He released the valve, letting out the sewerage in a great torrent of effluent gurgle.

Two minutes later they were rolling again, fresher than a wiped bum.

"I don't believe you did that," said Tom in a daze. "We've just shat on Beverly Hills."

Coming back down the hill, they crossed West Sunset Boulevard again into North Rodeo Drive, a lush lane of neat shady trees, a clipped shrub meridian, fabulous modest houses and manicured gardens. No 725 had been the home of movie star Gene Kelly. They passed his place unknowingly.

Over Santa Monica Boulevard the road took on a profoundly different aspect. The most ostentatious lavish shops in the whole world presided along this little strip, just three blocks long; including the most expensive shop on the Globe, 'Bijan'.

"Pretty Woman," said Tom suddenly.

"I've spotted quite a few," said the Price.

"No, some of the film was made along 'ere, I recognise the shops."

"Shall we get out and 'ave a look round?" said Keira, itching to do a bit of retail therapy.

"Why not?" said her husband in rhetorical fashion.

As luck would have it, he found a free parking space on the corner of North Rodeo and Santa Monica.

The sun was waning on a warm beautiful fragrant afternoon; the temperature was hovering around 65°F, perfect for a stroll. They ogled and smeared the glass fronts of luxurious stores such as Tiffany's and Cartier, open-jawed at the price tags. The Beverly Hillbillies had come to town, very much the uninvited party guests.

After an hour of yearning for the unobtainable, hunger took control and not having the where-with-all for Rodeo's fine food emporiums, they tramped away, back to the motorhome. Instead of leaving to find a suitable campsite, they decided it would be quite reasonable to cook a meal here, where they had parked.

The aroma of fresh grilled fish billowed out of the extractor funnel atop of the Winnebago and wafted up the lavish avenue like an unrefined spirit. Brazenly the RV's occupants shamelessly enjoyed a delicious meal of rainbow trout, buttered new potatoes and a tossed salad, on the most sumptuous street in the world; at a faction of the price it would have cost in any of the close proximity restaurants.

Spending that night on Huntingdon Beach, it was determined the next day should involve a trip to Universal Studios out in the Hollywood hills. They took route 101 out past the iconic landmark sign above the city on Mount Lee, on to Buddy Holly Drive and into the massive complex. This was much more like the experience Tom was after. Truly set amongst open rolling hills, the enormous attractions could be seen from outside the perimeter. At the gate however, the entrance fees were extortionate and far more than the family could afford. Despondent, they turned away and headed back toward their transport.

To the left of the entrance gate were the exit gates, they were partially open and unguarded. Inside on the tarmac, waiting to leave, was a tour train with empty seats in the last carriage. As quick as blinking, Pricey was through the gate opening and sitting on the bus, swiftly followed by the rest of the clan. It was as much as Keira and Tom could do to stop laughing, but they held their nerve and soon the tour got underway. Unbelievably nobody said a word.

"That was 'andy," said Pricey after a moment. Tom raised his eyebrows in response, concealing the chicanery.

First stop was the harbour for the TV series Murder She Wrote; it looked real enough, if somewhat compact. The bus crossed a bridge at the far end of what was actually a lake not a harbour, which suddenly collapsed on one side, tipping the passengers in a controlled lurch, towards the ferocious yawning mouth of an outlandish plastic replica of the shark from Jaws. The squealing tourists reeled from the cheaply reproduced upper body of a monster, which would have been 30ft-long if whole, its gnashing, chipped painted cakehole about as frightening as a Halloween pumpkin.

The tour carried on through a King Kong animatronics set, a burning building affair, an A-team car-chase scene and past a cowboy gun fight in a western street. All of which gave a slight insight into the making of movies, however pastiche. But the thing that really grabbed Tom's imagination were the convincing mock streets, a Tudor England village, a New York city block, and best of all the town square from Back to the Future. The square was complete with the clock tower, cinema façade and the ice cream parlour on the corner of the block, where Marty McFly stands up to Biff for picking on his young father. It dawned on Tom that the set had been used in many movies, but he loved Back To The Future, and just being there was indescribably connecting some dots.

At lunchtime they dined in a convenient restaurant on the complex and then drove to Santa Monica for the afternoon. Here, the white sandy beach was as deep as a football field and gave the impression of being infinitely wide. The Cirque De Soleil had pitched on the shore, its impressive Grand Chapiteau ruling the sand.

Alas, a lack of funds prevented them from going to the circus so they contented themselves with a walk along the front, up to the end of the pier beyond Maria Sol where the ocean lapped at the pier legs in great gulps, forcing powerful sea spray to rattle the planks beneath their feet.

Turning their backs on the sea, presented the entire palm tree-studded, apartment-strewn Santa Monica coastline, all the way from East Malibu to Redondo. The warm sun on their skin and the fresh onshore breeze invigorated and energised the posse to walk on further, down to Venice Beach past all the surf shops and psychedelic boutiques, on to Muscle Beach where they could eyeball the posers and body-builders. This stretch was beguiling, engrossing; they sat down on a bench and watched the entertainment for a while until Amber became restless and complained continuously. Walking back past street performers and buskers, they came to a guy who appeared to be naked behind a huge piece of cardboard held between his hands, on which he had written the words 'Need money for a penis reduction', he was getting ample attention, and his cap was filling up, a clever ploy; easy money just for being audacious.

This night they opted for a car park in the grounds of Ocean House, just up from Palisades Park. They woke to another beautiful day, their last in LA, and after a fried breakfast, regrettably, they drove back along route 1, stopping at Redondo Beach for a look-see and once more to Laguna Beach for a final envious farewell.

From Capistrano Beach, Pricey picked up the I-5 again and began the long haul through southern California to Arizona and back to Tucson. They'd had a laugh and seen some unforgettable sights, but the trip felt a little superficial because Tom didn't really relish the company of his brother-in-law.

Pricey had been on his most cordial behaviour; but a lot of damage had been done in the past and although he was willing to be affable for his sister's sake, his appreciation for Pricey's generosity was always tainted with suspicion.

***

Sunday lunch didn't necessarily incorporate a roast dinner, but today Keira had rustled up a fabulous roast beef banquet complete with Yorkshire pudding, roast potatoes, runner beans, carrots and Bisto gravy, followed by a fresh fruit salad and cream. The guest of honour was Natty Dread, who Pricey had picked up from town and brought over to the house. The Dread was smartly dressed in black trousers and a long, slender open-necked, white cotton shirt; his locks contrasting the fabric down his skinny back. He spoke with a thick Jamaican accent in measured sentences, often terminating with the phrase "Sim say" or just "Sim?" Short for "see what I am saying." He seemed relaxed, if a little wary of Pricey's intentions, but they shared a common language that Pricey had picked up from his dealings with Rastafarian drug dealers back in London. Most of the spiel flew over Tom's head.

"You hungry boys?" Keira asked with an expectant smile.

"I could eat a scabby 'orse between two piss-stained mattresses and chase the jockey for afters," replied Mr Price.

Natty wet himself laughing; Tom had heard that slice of doggerel more times than he cared to remember.

After a superb lunch Natty rolled the most enormous joint the world had ever seen, it resembled a king sized tampon. He drew long exaggerated tugs on the thing, quite comfortable now, dangling one tentacle leg over the arm of the chair, legs splayed, head back, and eyes closed, whilst listening to the cassette player filtering Tom's songs into the living room.

The last tune, a slow number in a 3/4 signature, Natty listened to three times. It appeared that he was having trouble incorporating the rhythm.

"Dem' good tunes y'na," he said at length. "Maybe we c'write some ting together, sim?"

"Yeah, sure, when do you want to hook up?" Tom was somewhat astonished; surprised that Natty would want to work with small fry like him. This was an established recording artist and he appeared to want to co-write some songs with a bloke who'd never made it past an A&R man at a record label.

"You come over to Sonny's house tomorrow sim. We bin' working on sum' tunes and tings, but me' need a guitarist; you play?"

"I can play rhythm, that's 'ow I write, but I don't 'ave a guitar 'ere."

"I can get guitar, Arty … 'im as guitar."

"Ah, cool, what time do you want me to come over?"

"In de' afternoon … me' don't do early sim?"

Tom nodded. "Okay, we'll come over at one o'clock, and get to know everybody."

So it was agreed.

That evening while Pricey was taking Natty home, Keira told Tom that she was leaving her husband for good; she had put up with his nonsense for long enough and had come to the conclusion that he was a waste of space. He didn't want to work any more, just sit around and get stoned, and now that Natty had come onto the scene, he was going to be up the Rastafarian's arse all the way. She was going to pretend to visit their mum in England with Amber for three weeks but never return, Pricey would be losing his job soon anyway, so they'd be homeless again and she couldn't do that to her daughter any more.

"Why don't you stay on 'ere in America, Tom? You 'ave nothing to go 'ome for, mum's selling the 'ouse and moving in with Don anyway, and you don't 'ave a job or a band. Can't you get Seamus to come out; you could form a band 'ere?"

It was all a bit too much to digest in one helping. Maybe Seamus would come out; he was only job hopping at the moment and at 25, was still living with his parents. Tom's mind went into overdrive. Could he stay out here? What of the legal consequences? What would he do for money? Where would he live?

"I'll 'ave to think about that one Keir, that's a lot to take in. I do love it 'ere, so would Seamus, but 'e ain't got a pot to piss in. 'ow's 'e gonna find the airfare?"

"Ring mum up tomorrow; see if she can 'elp, maybe Don'll lend you the money or something."

"If Seamus does come out, I'll stay, but only if; 'cause I ain't gonna live with your husband, not without you 'ere."

When Pricey returned, Tom told him that he was thinking of asking Seamus to come over and the possibility of him staying on.

"Fuckin' great," he boomed. "Get on the blower tomorra' … tell 'im 'e's gotta come." Pricey went off to bed already planning a nationwide tour in his head, with himself as tour manager.

The next morning Tom phoned his best friend and put the opportunity to him.

Seamus was caught off guard and didn't know how to respond, but he said he would mull it over. Seamus reliably agreed to do far too many things, with far too many people, at any one given time, and invariably let most of them down.

From experience Tom had found that the best way to be in the same place at the same time as Seamus was to actually go round to his house and capture him. Asking Seamus to arrive under his own steam was as good as asking a cat. He wasn't holding his breath.

Tom's mum already knew of Keira's plans and was pleased to be getting at least one of her children back. Although she missed her son terribly; she knew this experience would vastly broaden his horizons. If Seamus made up his mind to go to the States, she was going to sell Tom's Transit van which he'd left at home, along with a few ladders and tools. The cash would buy Seamus a flight.

Tom still wasn't sure if he was doing the right thing, but he decided to toss a coin in the air and see what it dented.

4
Musical Beds

Sonny and Bonita's apartment was situated on the east side of town, on the middle floor of a three-storey block. The type of development was commonplace; large, cream-coloured stucco buildings bordered by a car park and a low wall encompassing a laundrette and a central swimming pool. Their apartment overlooked the pool at the rear.

Sonny was American, slight in stature, in his mid-30s and was never without a hat. Tom supposed that he must be balding, but didn't want the world to know. His wife was petite and pretty, they were both of mixed-race and had a couple of young boys.

They welcomed their English guests warmly, perhaps a touch sceptically, and beers were handed out liberally. Tom got the impression that Sonny might have wondered why the 'Honkies' were on board.

Natty informed Pricey that they had to go over to Arty's house, because that's where the guitar lived. They were welcome to use it for songwriting, but Arty would like the instrument to stay at his house.

The guys all ventured out to the balcony; the afternoon was hot but not oppressive, a cooling breeze ruffled the palm fronds just enough to be noticed. Down by the pool a young lady was topping up her tan.

With a strange display of primal sexual desire, Natty's testosterone levels went into meltdown, he jigged feverishly behind the metal railings like a caged beast.

Pricey pursed his lips and kissed his teeth, the kind of noise we make when calling a cat, followed by his standard "eh, me' love yer' na'."

Tom waited in the wings, his esteem far too low to contemplate approaching pretty girls.

The target of their overture stirred just enough to casually incline her head towards the troop of knuckle dragging hominids, jittering on the balcony above.

She coolly lifted her sunglasses for a clearer view, rose up onto one elbow and turned onto her side. A tiny pastel pink bikini hid the modesty of her perfectly formed frame, which was paler than a body should be living in this part of the world.

Shading her eyes like a salute, she perused the four gentlemen as if she was studying a menu.

"Me' wanna' marry ya' nah'," Natty hollered down.

The girl swung her legs round and perched on the edge of the sun-lounger.

"You're kinda cute," she said.

Natty bounced up and down like he'd won the lottery.

"Not you," she said, "you," pointing at Tom.

Tom was taken aback; he hadn't had any intimacy with a girl for three months and hardly considered himself worthy of this bundle of joy.

"Me?" he said with his hand on his chest, still unsure if he had heard right.

"Yes, you," she said, "come down here," and she beckoned Tom with an enticing crooked finger.

Pricey and Sonny mocked Natty for being so confident and teased him over his chat-up lines, while Tom apprehensively descended the stairs.

Her name was Cindy, she wasn't stunning, but highly provocative, and she lived just across the lawn from Sonny, on the ground floor. She asked Tom what he was doing here and who his friends were. He sat on the next lounge chair along, the sun on his back, and gave an abrupt version of events. She drooled over his accent and produced her phone number saying, "Call me tonight; we'll go on a date." More than surprised, Tom was bolstered by her interest in him. He coyly promised to phone her later, said goodbye, and then sauntered back upstairs to his intrigued mates. Cindy returned to worshipping the sun.

Arty's leased house idled on a quiet block further east, overawed by the splendour of Mount Lemon, the highest point of the Santa Catalina mountain range, in a road called East Calle Kuehn. It was a shingle roofed bungalow situated on a swooping corner at the end of the street; it had a tidy kidney shaped swimming pool in the back garden and a double garage on the side that had been converted into accommodation for touring bands, hosting a timber jungle of bunk-beds, tables and chairs. The house itself had three bedrooms, a large sprawling lounge, brandishing a massive TV that was tuned to MTV, and an open kitchen/diner. It was sparsely furnished and desperately in need of someone who gave a shit.

Arty shared his house with his girlfriend Rene, a housemate called Kelly and his dog, a basset hound named Huckleberry who wore a dirty red Paisley bandana round his neck and smelt of smegma.

The master bedroom had its windows blacked out with aluminium foil, so that the master could sleep during the day and work all night, which Arty tended to do more often than not.

Tom was introduced to the guitar, a pink replica Fender Stratocaster; more an ornament than an instrument. It hadn't been played in years and badly needed re-stringing. He sat on a bunk-bed in the dimly lit band room and picked the thing up; it weighed a ton. Tuning it as best he could with out a guitar tuner, he began strumming some chords.

Natty pulled up a chair and immediately began to direct some reggae rhythm and chord shapes that he liked the sound of, hastily followed by some thrown-together lyrics, in a very loose scat style.

"Life is strange … but people are d' same … all over dis' ol' world …."

Pricey danced like a stiff puppet in the background and Sonny bubbled on a little Casio keyboard that he had brought along. Within an hour they had their first song structured, and were working on a second.

By the early evening they had the bones of half a dozen tunes cobbled together and decided that would be enough for today. They ventured into the kitchen where Kelly was fixing herself some dinner. Natty went into the garden and spread himself out in a hammock between two shady eucalyptus trees, one leg dangling limply over the side like a lazy tail. Sonny sat down in front of the TV, while the two Brits perched on bar stools in the kitchen and cracked a couple of bottles of Rollin Rock.

"So what do you do for a living, Kelly?" probed Tom.

Kelly was 30-something, had a toned athletic body, a large mouth full of perfect pearls and straight bottle-blonde hair to the middle of her back. She wasn't the tastiest chocolate in the box, but she was overtly cheery and suitably sociable.

"I'm a dancer," she replied.

"Oh, what sort of dancing do you do?"

Kelly laughed. "Ah you'll see." she said through a smile, and carried on preparing her meal.

Tom was mystified why she didn't go into more detail, but pondered it little.

Pricey was occupied skinning up a large spliff with the dexterity of an embroiderer wearing kitchen gloves, when above the din of the TV blaring out Poison's *Every Rose has Its Thorn*, they heard a low distant woof. Kelly unfaltering, said "Oh that'll be Huck; he's taken himself for a walk again. Could you let him in for me please, Tom?"

"Yeah sure," said Tom. "'ow did he get out?"

"He lets himself out, stands up on his hind legs and opens the door, it's some trick."

It certainly was; the door handle was a round polished steel knob that was slippery for a human to grip, so it was baffling how a dog's paws could manage it.

Tom let the hound in; Huck looked up at the stranger with his doleful droopy eyes and woofed once more, as if to say, thanks man, then trotted off to the kitchen and stuck his nose in a water bowl.

Five minutes later the doorbell rang, this time Kelly went to answer it herself. It was her friend 'Animal'.

This girl was tall and skinny with shoulder length corkscrew blonde hair, not a beauty, but sassy and carefree. She spoke with a southern accent and seemed undaunted by having a houseful of strange men to talk to.

"Animal's a dancer too," said Kelly.

"Oh yeah, we dance *all* the time," said Animal, pirouetting on one leg.

"Where do you work?" asked Pricey.

"At TD's on 22nd Street, ya'll should come one night."

"I think we shall," said Pricey with intrigue. "What nights do you work?"

"We get Sundays off, a girl needs her rest," said Kelly.

Pricey laughed, he knew the score, but Tom really didn't.

"Alright, we'll bring Natty along, he'll love it," said the Price.

Three nights later, after the sun had gone to bed; the two Toms, Natty and Arty got out of Pricey's Nissan in a shabby car park at the front of a bar on 22nd Street.

The rose pink walls supported a massive, illuminated, day-glo pink and black sign depicting the letters TD's. Still Tom was none the wiser as to the nature of the establishment, but once they had paid the cashier and passed through the inner doors all became quite clear; it was a strip joint and out on the floor wearing nothing but a gold-sequined G-string was Kelly, wrapping her self around a pole and contorting her body like a bendy toy.

Tom was astonished and slightly embarrassed because he knew the girl, and she may not have been the hottest chick in the building, but she did have the most amazing breasts.

Arty and Pricey were giggling wildly at Natty's eyes popping out of his head; he didn't know which pair of boobs to look at next.

"Do you get it now Tom?" said Pricey "TD's … titties."

Kelly must have seen the boys, but she chose not to mix business with pleasure and carried on cavorting professionally. The lads grabbed a table near the stage and ordered a pitcher of beer from a fantastic looking topless waitress, who accepted the money in her bikini bottoms. This was another world for Tom, he'd never even seen strippers in a pub before, it was both fascinating and erotic, but he wasn't frothing like a schoolboy, unlike Natty who couldn't keep still.

"Me' gonna find a new wife tonigh'," he chanted, "sim?"

Animal appeared next on stage, like her friend, ignored the boys, and after discarding her little white negligee, proceeded to perform the crab position, hoisting high her Morris Minor bonnet right in front of the lads faces.

"That's 'andy," said Pricey.

Animal had small tits, but she made up for her lack of protuberance by being an extraordinarily supple contortionist, as were the majority of the girls, who earned a tidy sum from the fat, sweaty types who stuffed dollar bills into thongs and panties. The lads stayed long enough for a few pitchers of draft, and then when it all became a bit samey they decided to go to The Purple Haze, where some local bands were performing. Tom left the club pleasantly enlightened; Natty left there in love.

***

Seamus called at the end of the week; he had handed in his notice at the double-glazing company and would be flying out in a week's time, with a month's salary in his pocket. Tom's mum had sold the Transit van and had bought Seamus the cheapest flight available; he was going to test the water for a month; create a few splashes.

This development, however, led to a dilemma. Keira had booked her flight home to coincide with Seamus coming out; they would be in the air at the same time, flying in opposite directions. The adobe house and Pricey's job were to be abandoned, so the three boys would have nowhere to live, plus

Tom's visa would run out in two weeks time, leading him to worry about the consequences of remaining in the States. Would men in suits pull up in a car one day and whip him away for out-staying his welcome? He could no longer travel outside the USA without keeping away for three months before re-entering. And then there was money. He only had a couple of hundred dollars left and no credit cards to fall back on. He was going to have to put his faith in luck and a spot of charity to see him through. This was nuts.

Benevolence emanated first from Arty, who promised the two Toms a bedroom in his house until they could get themselves sorted. An absolute godsend, but, being afraid of a refusal, they opted to retain a crucial piece of information; the little matter of Seamus, an unknown Brit', infiltrating the household. They would cross that narrow bridge later on.

Meanwhile Tom plucked up the courage to call Cindy, who was delighted and wanted to go out on a date that very night. The trouble was it clashed with a recording session with Natty in the studio at The Purple Haze.

Natty said he didn't mind if Tom rocked up later, as it would be an all-nighter any way. Tom should "go out and get de' pom-pom."

He arrived at her apartment around 7:30 p.m. She had scrubbed up delightfully; applied some make-up, volumised her hair and squeezed into a tiny peach-coloured mini dress and some strappy sandals. The figure hugging skirt was a massive turn on.

She offered to drive them in her newish Pontiac Firebird, but Tom being a gentleman, insisted on taking Pricey's dirty truck, an unimpressive move he lamented immediately.

They went to a Hawaiian bar just off Speedway, fortuitously in the midst of happy hour, and so indulged in two-for-one Pina Coladas, some Mahi Mahi fish and a Chicken Adobo, which was superb.

During dinner Tom explained his presence in the USA in more detail, pointing out he would be in the studio later that night. Cindy sat with confident poise listening to every word, relishing the Englishman's voice. She worked in an office that dealt with corporate insurance with a floor full of other women, whom she rapturously bitched about. Tom got the impression that she didn't enjoy her working environment much at all.

Somehow the conversation tilted towards the erogenous.

"I masturbate a lot," said Cindy quite matter-of-factly.

On the outside Tom reflected a calm nonchalance, but inside his pulse was racing, sending his blood in a southerly direction. He had never heard a girl talk openly about fumbling in the cupboard before, especially in the middle of a restaurant on a first date.

"What … every day?" he enquired as sedately as a man filling out a questionnaire.

"Yeah, maybe five or six times a day, often in the bathroom at work … all girls do it, don't let them tell you otherwise, because they're liars."

Tom was seduced by her revelation, but also a little disturbed. A filament of an unstable personality glinted across the table.

She was vivaciously wild-eyed. "Do you do it too?" she gushed,

"Oh yes," he said acting cool, "but not as much as you, I'd wear the poor thing ragged."

With this correlation, Cindy became effervescent; she insisted on paying for the meal, grabbed hold of Tom's hand and led him to the car park. Her evocative behaviour escalated in the truck on the way back to her apartment, leaning over and fondling Tom's swollen goods while he drove.

"Hmm," she squirmed.

Tom played it down like it was an everyday occurrence, but beneath his frosty veil he was desperate for a shag; and this was definitely game-on.

Once inside her apartment Cindy went straight to the music centre, put on a CD of American rock anthem's and started gyrating like she was the focus of a raunchy music video, rubbing her body and grinding her posterior his way.

Absolutely indicative to a bit of how's ya' father, he concurred.

Walking over to her, he caressed her hips with both hands, pulling her backside close to his aching groin. She smiled, turned and gently pushed him away, continuing to dance.

Little tease, he thought.

He moved in on her again, again she pushed him away, and then a third time.

Disenchanted by her game, he sat down on the sofa and scrutinized her writhing to the rhythm of the music. This dance was obviously meant to be a solo performance, but it was frustrating. He tried once more to join in, and received the same treatment.

It was a bizarre situation, contra signals, annoying and confusing.

"Do ya' wanna fuck or not?" he asked plainly.

She looked pained, as if all this innuendo hadn't meant to be a turn-on.

"Oh I just want to dance," she said innocently, running her fingers through her tousled hair, simultaneously continuing to wind and grind, which only served to wind him up.

He may as well just piss off, this was a waste of his time, but before he did, he decided on some decadence.

"Mind if I jerk-off in the bathroom then?"

Staggered, she stopped dancing and stared as he strode into the connecting room.

In the midst of bashing one out over the toilet basin, Tom glanced over his shoulder to find that Cindy had snuck in behind him. Her hand was up her hoisted dress and into her orange panties enthusiastically flicking her bean. She was whimpering and rubbing her back against the wall in ecstasy, clearly this was her forte.

Reaching the vinegar stroke, Tom did an about turn and let her have the full force of his ejaculation. The shock of having hot cum splattered across her dress and arm broke her from her fantasy, she inhaled a short sharp breath and ceased fingering herself.

Flushed with relief Tom arrogantly cleaned himself up with toilet paper, while Cindy remained motionless against the wall, hand still in her knickers. He told her that he would call her tomorrow and walked out, leaving her literally plastered to the wall.

"What the fuck 'appened there?" he wondered, striding for the truck, his head full of conflicting emotions. He was equally ashamed, annoyed, embarrassed and amused. Did she want him to be more assertive and rip her clothes off, or should he have been cooler and waited for her come to him. Either way, he had played it wrong and was beating himself up over it. He just didn't get the prick-teasing, she must have wanted sex or she wouldn't have joined in with the final act, he thought. Too weird for his tiny mind; he drove off to the studio.

All was quiet on 4th Avenue; it was 10:00 p.m. and walking through the still, balmy night air, felt like sifting through shrouds of warm silk, protected by an ultra-soft fleecy blanket from the cold nights that he was accustomed to.

He found Natty inside a sound booth laying down some guide vocals. Natty nodded at Tom as he passed, heading for the control room.

Sonny was there, and a stout, short engineer called Simon, who was grumpy and a bit anal, hardly acknowledging Tom's existence. Another Rasta had joined the party, a jolly round faced man with a scrappy beard and a gap between his long front teeth. His name was Denny Kirk, a guitarist and singer of some repute, who had had moderate success with his Roots band, The Reflections.

"'ire?" posed Sonny.

"Yeah, 'ad a good time." responded Tom keeping it simple.

"Hello I'm Tom." he held his hand out towards Denny.

"Nice to meet you man, ire, ire," replied Denny humbly.

He was from the Caribbean but had been an American citizen for so long his accent had softened.

It was soon established that Denny was by far the better guitarist and would be providing the majority of the guitar tracks on tonight's session, although Tom laid down a rhythm track for every song, ten in total, they were kept low in the mix.

This was fine with Tom, who didn't consider himself much of a player anyway; he was content just to be a part of the songwriting process for the album.

At around 2:00 a.m. the strains of being up all night were taking their toll. Yawning persistently, Tom wandered off to the bar and poured himself a pint of Jolt, to caffeinate his slowing heart rate; this didn't improve things much at all, and by 4:00 a.m. he was lying on the well trodden carpet in the control room, slipping in and out of consciousness.

Natty however didn't seem to be affected by sleep deprivation in the least, and was strangely just as bouncy as he was when Tom had come into the studio. Perhaps he had a cold, because every few seconds he was rubbing his nostrils and sniffing quite a lot.

Tom had scant idea that the Lion of Zion was shovelling spoonfuls of Columbian marching powder up his nose. He'd never even seen the stuff before.

By 6:00 a.m. they were done, 10 new tracks in the bag. The ashtray was an erupting cigarette and spliff volcano, empty cups and takeaway boxes littered the floor and five red-eyed people emerged from the session desperate for a bed.

Tom wearily followed the Dread back to Sonny's house for a kip on the couch, half delirious; he couldn't face the tedious journey back to Bear Paw without the threat of a major accident, so a few hours in Sonny's living room appealed to his grey mush.

The hushed tones of small children, and the low rumble of a television set, brought Tom round from a frustrating dream, in which he was trying to have a bath, but each time he got into the tub he would have an item of clothing on, so he'd get out and take the dripping garment off, get back into the water only to find that he was wearing something else instead, and so it went on until he woke.

Sonny's kids were playing with their toys and being remarkably sensitive towards a stranger sleeping on their settee.

Tom's eyes ached, and when he sat up his brain seemed to be independent from his skull, moving a split second after the rest of him. He needed a drink, so swayed to the kitchen in search of something cold. Thankfully there was a 12 oz plastic bottle of water in the refrigerator, which he claimed with vigour.

Bonita got up to fix the kids some breakfast.

Tom greeted her, and then went out to the balcony to get some air, and maybe a glimpse of Cindy; she didn't appear.

The day had turned cloudy; the dark threatening sky spoke of imminent rain. Tom felt flat, he yawned in an attempt to replenish his brain with much needed oxygen. He longed for sleep, but had to get back to the reserve. Natty wanted to come with him for dinner that evening, but was still asleep. He waited another distressing hour making small talk with Bonita about the recording session and the weather back home in England. She hadn't ventured out of the country before and now that the children had arrived, didn't think it likely for a while.

At around 11:00, he could stand it no more, rain was falling heavily and distant thunder resounded off the valley floor like long range ordnance. It was going to get worse before it got better. He woke Natty, urging him to hurry and get ready. Tom's temples palpitated; sending a searing pain across his eyes, ruining his senses, all he could imagine was his single bed in the cool quiet of his room.

Half-an-hour later they were out the door. The rain was so excessive now, the trucks wipers couldn't cope with the volume of water being thrown at them; it was an arduous task just trying to keep within the traffic lane, let alone perceive the other cars around them. The road was brimming like a river, and passing vehicles doused the truck with tank loads of cold grey splash that were so bad they may as well have been submerged.

Keeping his speed down to a minimum, he had no choice but to go with flow. The junction of E. Broadway Blvd and E.

Harrison Rd came up suddenly, sooner than expected, and Tom found himself in the outside lane, and travelling too fast for the turn. He indicated, looked over his shoulder then cut across all three lanes pulling sharply right into Harrison. The force of the move on the slippery surface sent them aquaplaning sideways, across the head of the opposing lane and into the open mouth corner entrance of a 76 filling station.

Tom instinctively reacted by counter steering the truck, causing it to snake abruptly left then right before coming to a jarring halt on the sodden rain-pelted forecourt. Shaken but miraculously unscathed, with steam from their overanxious bodies having fogged up the windows; Tom inhaled sharply and turned towards Natty who was gripping the dashboard with tension-bent fingers, and had turned ashen with fear.

"Don't do 'dat again man," said the Jamaican, graver than any human being had ever uttered.

"Sorry mate … that shit me up just as much as you. We're lucky we never 'it anything; fuckin' 'ell … you alright?"

Natty fell gently back into his seat and nodded, but didn't say another word for the entire journey.

Tom drove with intense caution and gradually the colour returned to Natty's face. His driver, nerves frayed, felt irresponsible and foolish, but extremely fortunate to have come through unharmed. Perhaps another one of his nine lives had just spirited away.

***

The day that Seamus arrived was a hectic one. Keira and Amber flew out in the morning, it was an emotional farewell. Tom said things like, "I'll see ya' in three weeks," and, "'ave a lovely time," knowing full well it was just a ruse for her husband, and he thought that deep down Pricey must have known she was never coming back.

Pricey kissed his daughter goodbye; it would be the last he would see of her for three years. For him, this freedom was akin to a bolt-cropper cutting through his ball and chain. He had been let loose and boy was he going to enjoy it.

The Toms packed their suitcases, and just like that, bid goodbye to their desert home, not looking back, but ambling off to Arty's house in Pricey's beaten up white Nissan.

The spare bedroom contained just one double waterbed, but from somewhere Arty had acquisitioned a double bed and a single. If the lads could disassemble the waterbed, they could fit in the other two with room to spare. Tom volunteered to stay at home and dismantle the waterbed, while Pricey, Glen and Natty shot off to get the new ones.

The foe that Tom now faced had four wooden panels around the outside, housing the plastic inner bladder like a bubble in a box. He dragged in the garden hose, located the drain plug on the underside of the mattress, unscrewed it and with a little spillage connected the two together.

Draining off would take a few hours so rather than just sit there and watch, he'd do something constructive by taking apart the sides of the bed using a Phillips head screwdriver he found in a drawer. They came away easily enough and he stacked them up neatly against one wall, keeping all the screws in a tidy little pile.

When it came to removing the last leaf, the bladder, which was now half empty, decided on a bit of exploration at ground level. In one almighty gelatinous revolution, it flopped down onto the tiles like a giant shaved scrotum. The hose broke loose and water began gushing forth like a breached dam, flooding the bedroom and heading down the hall. Tom grappled with the venting monster and replaced the plug before the entire contents came out, cursing his foolhardy idea. Of course if he had been more patient and waited for the water to drain completely; this would not be his predicament.

After mopping up the water with some towels, he then tried in vain to drag the depleted hulk out of the bedroom, but of course it still weighed a ton and wasn't to be moved. The lads returned to find a sweaty, wet, panting fella, who felt reasonably idiotic for attempting to shift the thing on his own.

"'e are," said Pricey, "Lets drag it outside and empty it in the pool."

All four of them gripped onto the monster and tried to lift it, but it was still ludicrously too heavy.

"Why don't we roll it down the hall?" suggested Glen.

"I'm glad I thought of that," said Pricey laughing.

With great effort and farcical employment, they turned and pushed and rolled it all the way out to the garden before extracting the plug, at last draining it into the pool.

Standing there admiring their handiwork, their ripped and torn adversary now beaten and surrendered, they were surprised by Arty who had just crept in with Rene.

"How did ya'll get that outside?" he asked in his Tennessee accent.

"We picked it up and carried it," said Tom innocently.

Arty burst out laughing. The thought of the enormous weight in water and the awkwardness of carrying the thing full, up through the house was preposterous. But the lads backed up Tom's story, and somewhat suspiciously he half believed them, making the obvious remark that they should have emptied it first.

But still, he must have thought that they were inhumanly strong to have pulled that stunt off.

Rene looked like she was off her face, she wondered into the living room to stare at MTV.

Within an hour the new beds were in place and made up with linen from Pricey's house. The Toms had moved in.

Natty made a red snapper curry for dinner; it was superb, washed down with copious bottles of Corona. They sat by the pool, soaking up the early evening sun while Glen rolled a couple of spliffs.

Arty left for work giving the guys a front door key, Kelly went off to dance for her supper, whilst Rene stayed transfixed to the TV screen.

"Ya' fren' can play guitar?" Natty asked Tom.

"Yeah, 'e's really good, 'n sings too."

"'e's the bollocks," added Pricey, 'bigging' Seamus up.

"Sa' maybe ya' can both join de' band, sim."

"Sure," said Tom. "It'll sound great; who else ya' got in mind?"

"Me' d'no yet 'bout bass 'n drum, but me' gotta fren' in LA who play de' trombone, 'im come along sim, come an' play wid' me' ya' na'."

"Sounds good … we're picking Seamus up tonight from the airport."

"Him gonna stay 'ere?"

"Yeah man, but Arty don't know yet."

Natty laughed. "'im gonna be mighty unimpress' ya' na'."

"'e'll be alright when 'e meets Seamus, everyone loves Seamus," said Pricey.

"Seamus loves everybody," added Tom.

"Trus' in Jah," affirmed Natty.

Tom went inside the house to get another beer and saw Rene crying on the sofa. He went over and asked what the matter was; she was definitely high on something.

"I don't love Arty any more," she snivelled; her nose was a rather unattractive red.

Tom felt sorry for her and draped his arm around her shoulders.

Her dirty blonde, dishevelled hair looked like it was afraid of hairbrushes and her mascara had run, giving her Panda eyes.

"Ah, you've just 'ad a little too much to drink, why don't ya' go to bed and sleep it off?" he said.

"If you come with me," she slurred.

Tempted, Tom said, "I don't think that's a good idea is it … come on I'll take ya' to your room."

He took her hand and led her into Arty's where she put her arms round his neck and attempted to kiss him. He avoided her lips and instead gave her a big cuddle, hoisted her to the bed and laid her down.

"I'll see ya' tomorrow," he said, leaving her curled up and crumpled, as he closed the door. Out on the patio he never breathed a word of what just occurred, it was best left unsaid.

***

The Arrivals lounge at Tucson International Airport is small in comparison to other global destinations; just one room decorated in standard airport trappings where people enter straight off the plane down a stainless steel corridor, bewildered and bedraggled after a beast of a journey, which from England takes a minimum of 24 hrs, door to door. There is no immigration control, because Tucson just deals with internal flights, even though it's termed international. So once your bags have been collected from the carousel, you are free to assault America in any which way you choose.

It's a feeling of release you get when you finally step into the outside world after being hermetically contained in transit for the best part of a day and for Seamus it was no exception.

He sauntered into Arizona pasty-faced, bloated and desperate for a cigarette, the picture of unhealthiness.

Tom and Pricey watched him with jubilant smiles, Tom especially glad to see his best friend.

"Mate," said Seamus taking Tom's hand, "that was some fuckin' expedition."

"Good to see ya' mate, ya' look knackered."

"I fell asleep between Chicago and 'ere with me' 'ead dangling in the aisle, the stewardess 'ad to wake me up coz she couldn't get 'er trolley passed. What time is it?"

"Two-thirty, mush," said Pricey. "Bet ya' got jet lag."

"I need a lag, where's the bog?"

"Round the front, son, throw some shape into ya' self, you're in America now," said Pricey getting all excited.

The three of them laughed, it was an odd circumstance that these Garston Herberts should wind up co-habituating in the Sonoran desert; three quite different souls at that.

"I flew Kuwaiti Air," said Seamus. "They 'ad a map on a wall in the middle of the plane and every now and then an air 'ostess would come along and move a cut-out shape of a plane on a bit, to show our position across the Atlantic … it was 'ilarious."

"Did ya' 'ave to pray to Allah before you took off?" asked Pricey.

"On our fuckin' hands and knees mate, in the aisle," said Seamus. "Ha, ha, ha. I didn't mind that … it was the chickens and goats running loose that bothered me, there was shit and straw everywhere." He made chicken and sheep noises.

They laughed some more. "Must 'ave been chaos. What sorta grub did you 'ave?" asked Tom.

"Well let's put it this way. We were a goat and a couple of chickens short when we landed at O'Hare."

They roared. "Come on let's get ya' back to Arty's 'ouse," said Tom, "I'm afraid you've gotta share a double bed with Mr Price, but I understand 'e's a gentle lover."

Seamus barked another laugh, "As long as I can sleep in the X-posish', I'll kip anywhere."

5
Cornerstones

A trio of grown men in a sealed box tends to build up a stifling excess of gas. Tom woke first, hot and sticky, deprived of clean air; he had to get out. Seamus was still on his back snoring efficiently and Pricey was unconscious.

Tom put on some shorts and slopped off to the bathroom to vent his aching bladder. Relieved, he padded out onto the patio and slumped into a white plastic pool chair. He was still tired; he rested his neck on the curved smooth rim of the back rest and closed his eyes. The temperature at this time in the morning was around 70°, but in the shade it was very pleasant, just right to be partially naked. He pondered the predicament they were in, the thin mooring line they had securing them to the bank; it was tenuous to say the least.

Pricey and Seamus emerged a short time after, and all three of them hunched around the breakfast bar for a chin-wag.

Over a mug of tea and some cereals they bantered in lowered voices, before creeping out of the house in an action to evade Arty and Rene; they succeeded, the vampires never stirred.

It was a beautiful morning, a crystal clear sky, the air laced with a hint of Acacia blossom. The lads opened the doors of Pricey's Japanese mobile oven; Tom and Pricey instinctively wound down the windows before getting in, Seamus however, naively sat straight down on the back seat of the searing hot plastic upholstery, literally burning his bare legs.

"Yowza, these seats are fuckin' scorchin'!"

"Yep … it can get up to two hundred degrees in 'ere during the day," said Pricey, "enough to melt the fuckin' steering wheel. Pull ya' shorts down a bit."

Seamus complied, thinking it would be a good idea in future to bring a towel along. The boys were off to The Purple Haze to introduce Seamus to KP in an attempt to beguile their host with witty repartee and maybe soften the blow on Arty.

KP was reasonably impressed with the new arrival; Seamus was at his most charming, entertaining her with his cultural innocence.

"Are you staying long?" she enquired.

"Four weeks KP, but we'll see 'ow far me' money stretches, I may 'ave to rent me' self out."

She snorted a short laugh. "Arty's gonna be pissed with all three of you in his house you know," she said reluctantly. "You should have asked first."

"Can't you sweeten 'im up? It's only temporary, till we find somewhere else to live," appealed Pricey.

"I'll see what I can do, but I'm not promising anything."

Tom meanwhile, who was perched on the corner of a desk, had been persuaded by a mischievous Selena to have black eyeliner applied to his lids; he flicked them at KP.

"Did you like the recording we made the other night?"

The sight of him in make-up tickled her. "Excellent", she said. "We can do a lot with that."

Pricey's eyes narrowed with disdain, "Throw some shape inta ya' self," he chuckled gruffly.

Selena, whose face was inches away from Tom's as she applied the final touches, spoke in a sultry, breathy manner, "It's amazing; your eyes are exactly like Keira's."

It made Tom feel weird. "Alright," he snapped in mock anger, "I'm not ya' play thing, you can take it off now."

She laughed, applied some cleanser to a cotton wool pad and began wiping his eyes.

"Is ya' mum home?" he asked her.

"Sure is."

"I think we'll pay 'er a visit," said Pricey.

They left the Haze and headed for Jennifer's place and a spot of afternoon tea.

Jennifer lived in a trailer at the end of a small cul-de-sac off Speedway. It was a pocket Bohemian sovereignty of which Jennifer was the queen.

She kept a lovely little garden with flowering creepers, and pots and tubs full of pretty blooms; there was a patch of lawn and a patio set under a shady tree. Wind chimes tinkled in the minimal breeze and insects buzzed around the flowers.

Inside, the home was cluttered with clichéd couches, cushions and throws, tie-dye drapes, beaded curtains, crystals, Native American artefacts and jewellery, stacks of LPs, joss sticks and an exaggerated hubbly-bubbly pipe.

Jennifer appeared in a long flowing multicoloured gown, spliff in hand and 'tickety-boo' to be receiving new guests.

"Come in, come in," she said, ushering the boys into the sitting room.

"Toot anyone?" she asked in high tones, indicating to a dainty porcelain saucer on the coffee table containing a small mound of cocaine.

Fuckin' 'ell, thought Tom, it's offered like a bowl of peanuts round here.

"Very hospitable of you," said Pricey, "don't mind if I do."

He proceeded to scoop a little powder out of the dish with a debit card and cut it into a long line on the smoked glass table top; then he rolled a dollar bill from his pocket into a thin tube and snorted the whole line up a nostril, dabbing his finger over the excess granules before rubbing the residue on his gums.

Tom hadn't witnessed this ritual before, but realised that Pricey was a dab hand.

Seamus and Tom both declined Jennifer's generous offer.

"Earl Grey?" she enquired.

All took up her offer.

Tom asked if she didn't mind him putting a record on, Seamus got the full tour of the bedroom and the kitchen. He was in extreme flirt mode and Jennifer loved it; she had a penchant for younger men, well any handsome man really, and she was quite smitten with this one.

Tom found some Steel Pulse in the album stack. He'd been indoctrinated to them over the last couple of months. The melodic reggae music thumped out of the speakers and put everyone into an easy mood. When the kettle boiled the party spilled out into the garden.

The smell of Bergamot wafted beneath the parasol under which they gathered out of the searing sun. The chink of silver spoon on china cup made the afternoon feel very English. It was a lovely atmosphere.

The phone rang and Jennifer hurried inside to answer it. After five minutes she came back with a cautious look on her face. "That was KP," she said in her posh nasally accent. "Arty's hit the roof and wants you all out of the house."

The boys looked like they'd been on the receiving end of a stun grenade.

"She's trying to calm him down and will call back later."

"Drat and double drat," said Pricey.

Tom started to fear the worst.

Seamus started eyeing up Jennifer's bed.

Just then two heads appeared over the hedge.

"Mind if we join you?" asked the taller of the two.

"What's the password?" Jennifer quipped.

"Milk and one sugar," he replied.

Jennifer laughed. "Correct," she confirmed.

"Boys, this is Jack and Freddie, Jack is my neighbour and Freddie is his oldest friend."

The guys all shook hands, Pricey already knew Jack and Freddie; he sat back and rolled a communal joint.

The fellows were from New York State originally but had been here for many years. Jack was half Puerto Rican, had a mop of thick curly black hair, was at least 6ft tall, very muscular and had three days growth on his chops. Freddie in contrast was from Italian descent, short, olive skinned and balding, almost reminiscent of a young Paul Simon.

Jennifer considered Jack one of her closest friends; he was a gay man, but not in the least bit camp or effeminate to any degree. He was funny and knowledgeable and totally relaxed with his sexuality, he and his fiancé were planning a wedding in the not too distant future.

Tom and Seamus didn't have any homosexual friends in England, and neither of them had spent much time in the company of gay men, so for a couple of orthodox 'heteros', they were a little hesitant with the late arrival, but after a short while their apprehension had dispersed; Jack was just another bloke around the table.

Jack had an uplifting personality and easy liberal morals. He was also HIV positive.

Freddie hailed from New Jersey and was typically Italian; confident with a wry sense of humour, but not loud and flashy, he was kind-natured and immersed in marijuana, which rendered him with an endearing dozy expression.

"What are you guys up to today?" asked Jennifer.

"Oh drinking tea, getting stoned, you know, a usual day's work," replied Jack.

Pricey passed a spliff around, it went full circle; even Tom had a tug.

"Do you guys work at all?" he asked.

They both nearly pissed themselves.

"Oh, a little dealing here and there, nothing big time," said Jack.

"Gotta do what ya' gotta do," rapped Freddie smirking.

Another head appeared over the fence.

"Hey guys, smells like some good shit going down; can I join thee," the head said.

"Ross-I man," croaked Pricey, "come on down."

Ross-I lived behind Jennifer in another mobile home, his wild vacant stare, matted blonde dreadlocks and tie-dyed vest, illustrated that he was a complete stone head and had honed in on a free banquet over the hedge.

He enrolled with the party, taking his turn with the reefer. After some minutes he blurted out, "Are you guys from London?" as if suddenly registering that he was in foreign company.

"Watford, it's close to London," said Seamus.

"Wow, that's in England right?" he said with an upward inflection.

Everybody giggled.

"You shouldn't mock the I, and the I will not mock thee," he said in a measured manor staring at them with his dead, blue eyes. The jollity subsided, Ross-I may have been polished senseless by the dope, but one got the feeling that beneath the surface there poised a maniac anxious to escape.

The phone rang again.

It was KP. Arty had come to the realisation that the three lads could be useful after all. If they would work the door at the Purple Haze, they could stay at the house rent free, although he was still resentful that Tom and Pricey hadn't informed him that Seamus was coming over as well. The boys would have to tug their forelocks at him for quite some time.

Being driven back to Arty's house, stoned, with warm winds rustling his tainted brown hair, Seamus reflected on the fortunes of staying in rent free accommodation, cushioned by good natured, generous people, in a fascinating new country, with a thousand opportunities waiting to be exploited. The juncture seamed ideal, he was going to squeeze every last drop of juice out of this apple.

"Pinch ya' self, you're in America now son." echoed Pricey. "You must be dreaming."

After an eye popping meal at Fuddruckers, 'the world's greatest hamburger' joint, the excessively stuffed British individuals went home and changed into some evening apparel. Thinking that they had to look the part as doormen, they all dressed the same in dark Levi 501's, Airware boots and plain Polo shirts. A mistake that they were soon to regret, it being so breathtakingly hot still at 9:00 in the evening, meant they were steaming profusely out in the street. Tom and Seamus manned the front door while Pricey got the more relaxed job of monitoring the interior for trouble.

Playing this evening were two of Tucson's local buzz bands who had fair-sized followings. Fall from Grace, a gothic rock band fronted by skinny twin brothers, who styled themselves like grungy Marilyn Mansons. To Tom and Seamus' ears, they performed tuneless drivel, but a group of black clad, suicidal types jemmied some entertainment out of it.

Also appearing was the Host, a random horde of new age revellers fronted by a self styled demi-god named Odin. He had long flowing red hair, wore a cape and carried a small harp and a long sword shackled to his belt. He was audaciously charismatic; his disciples 'the Hosties' adored him, and he was unequivocally self-proclaimed to be the reincarnation of King Arthur. The Host were musically entertaining, with countless members, including Scorpion, on stage playing a variety of instruments, performing cheery if somewhat medieval ditties with a comical lyric. They had a great stage presence and good marketing skills with their merchandise, all of which went a long way in impressing the English lads.

Odin had a girlfriend called Gypsy, a very pretty girl, but alarmingly looked in need of a good wash; they had a son who inevitably, but somewhat unfortunately for the boy, had been named Thor. This three-years-old was often seen running amok, semi-naked and plastered in mud. His knotted long blonde hair obviously had never been acquainted with shampoo.

Tom was rather bewitched by the whole aura surrounding the Host, until he found out that Odin's real name was Chuck, which burst the delusional bubble in an instant.

Outside on the pavement, Tom was facing the road with his hands crossed behind his back, rueing his decision not to put on some shorts as sweat rivulets run down the inside of his legs from his soggy underpants. Feeling a slight disturbance on the front of his polo shirt, he presumed it was just another trickle of perspiration from his chest. He ignored it and carried on in conversation with some teenagers in the queue. Feeling a secondary tug at the material, he this time investigated, glancing down to see what was making a fuss. Staring back at him was a 6 in long black beast with open pincer jaws, long segmented antennae and armour-piercing spines on its neck, heading straight for his throat.

He exhaled a short, deep, guttural exclamation, before brushing the Kevlar-plated thing off, sending it clattering to the pavement like a black plastic alien toy. A girl shrieked and people scattered out of the way, before realising it was just a harmless Palo Verde beetle which had mistaken Tom for a tree, but never having seen an insect of those proportions before, Tom's heart was pounding as though he'd been under a zombie attack.

As the ejected beetle waddled up the avenue a crowd of reprobates took great delight in stamping on the helpless insect, squashing its yellow insides out onto the pavement.

Tom felt physically sick. He should have intervened and saved the poor critter's life, instead of witnessing the cruelty unfold in slow motion, glued to the entrance of the club still in shock. He finally came to his senses. "Oi!" he shouted, "What was the fuckin' point of that?"

One of the cheeky sods replied "It was only a fucking beetle, man; what the fuck?"

"Yeah, *was* a beetle, till you fuckin' splattered 'im. Pick on someone your own size, no better still, fuck off 'ome."

They were unfazed; they just shrugged. One of them had the guile to give Tom the bird.

He made as if to leave his position and run at them; they all took flight and legged it up the street. "Fuckin' numpties," he said to himself.

Minutes later the janitor, Sean Adams, came outside during the Host's performance; he was having an argument with one of the 'Fall from Grace' brothers, it was the most farcical thing to witness.

Sean stood at least a foot taller than the skinny goth and was at least six times as heavy, yet the lad was having a go. Tom hadn't a clue as to what they were arguing about because all they were saying to one another was "Fuck you." which rose in volume and pitch as each man ping-ponged it back to the other, practically head-butting their opponent with the force of the erupting words. After his tenth "Fuck you", a thunderous elongated roar worthy of a pissed-off Lycan, Sean Adams marched back into the Haze, wine-faced and incensed, leaving the scrawny youth kicking dust in the empty car lot next door.

"That was … insightful," said Tom bewildered.

The club emptied out around 2:00 a.m. leaving just the staff and a few band members clearing equipment away. The three Englishmen perched at the bar on lofty stools, each of them was pretty spent and rather parched. KP offered them all a pint of Jolt and then someone produced a bag of magic mushrooms.

Mexican magic mushrooms are monsters compared to their British cousins, with 2 inch diameter heads, so invariably you only need one to trip you the fuck out.

It's organic and it's food, reasoned Tom, what harm could it do?

Seamus and Pricey chewed their 'shrooms quickly, their faces distraught, as if they were eating cow pats, but Tom found his palatable, its taste was intense, sour, woody and earthy.

Within 15 minutes, blood was pumping around the boys' flushed faces like a Japanese bullet train, and they were giggling like nonsensical toddlers.

Everything was funny. Looking at each others' red faces, looking at other people in the room who weren't on 'shrooms, but who knew the score, thinking that what they were laughing at wasn't funny, and then laughing at that as well. It was hysterical and tears were running down their cheeks.

Seamus tapped Tom on the arm; he looked round to see Sean Adams sat on a bench against the opposite wall, arms crossed over his expansive belly, white beard flowing from his stony face, decked out in his blue dungarees, staring at them with a plastic cup adhered to his forehead at its base. The boys left their stools with uncontrolled hilarity.

Sean Adams just "ha-hummed," and slightly grinned, which made it even funnier.

Eventually the hallucinogenic effects paled and Pricey mustered up enough sensibility to drive them home as the sun was coming up.

Deadbeat and fading fast, Tom headed straight for the bedroom. He opened the door to an indelible sight. There passed out on top of his bed, wearing just a short grey t-shirt, was Rene, her vagina offering him a sideways smile, while her open mouth drooled onto his pillow. He stared at her momentarily, it was an astounding thing. He puffed air through his lips and wondered what to do. There it was right in front of him, a warm comfortable velvet purse, available and probably willing; he knew she had an inkling for him, but why was she on his bed?

Maybe they'd had a row or something, but this was too close to home to be comfortable and one doesn't shit on one's own doorstep.

He couldn't do it, couldn't take advantage of her or Arty. He covered her over with the sheet and went and lay on a bunk bed in the band room.

Pricey and Seamus ambled outside and smoked a large spliff before falling asleep on lounge chairs, where they stayed until around 11:00 a.m. when the whole household stirred.

The first thing Tom did when he awoke was to stealthily retrieve some swimming trunks from his room, stumble out to the patio and then dive into the pool. He felt like an overcooked turd, but the cool water miraculously revitalised his boiled body and brought him back into some kind of normality. The cure was contagious and soon Pricey and Seamus followed suit; in no time at all they were bombing and springing off the dive board like a trio of twelve-year-olds.

Natty turned up and wasted no time getting bare chested, although wild horses couldn't persuade him to take a plunge; he relaxed into a sun lounger.

Animal came round and revived Rene, who together, much to everyone's delight lay topless by the pool sporadically lubricating each other with sun tan lotion. This action sent

Natty scurrying around the patio not knowing where to sit next; he produced a camera from somewhere and eagerly took photographs of the prostrate ladies like it was an assignment.

After a bacon butty lunch rustled up by the Price, Seamus and Tom got out guitars and jammed in the full sun of the baking afternoon. Seamus had brought over with him his electric and an acoustic guitar. He plugged into Arty's little practice amp and they ran through a couple of Bob Marley hits, some Beatles classics, and then settled into creating some riffs and chord patterns.

Tom had already built up a base tan on his body, but Seamus had lily-white flabby skin, turning pinker by the minute under the midday grill.

A pair of Harris's hawks and three Turkey vultures circled above the house with the certain belief that it was just a matter of time before their next meal presented itself below.

"You oughta put some sun block on mate, ya' gonna frazzle out 'ere," Tom suggested.

"Na', I'll be alright," said Seamus ignoring good advice.

By sundown two huge bubble blisters had appeared on Seamus's shoulders, rising an inch from his skin. They were incredibly painful and needed to be burst with a pin, which Animal delighted in doing. Aloe Vera was then liberally applied to the wounds; its healing powers brought a modicum of relief.

They managed a few hours of sleep in the early evening then showered and got ready for work again. Natty prepared some Jamaican Jerk chicken with rice and peas; the boys were ravenous and devoured the meal with a passion.

Seamus spoke whilst chewing, "You're a great cook, Natty, where'd you learn it from?"

"Me' mamma teach me howda' cook ya' na', she was de' inspiration to me' gastronomicification, sim," Natty giggled at his own word-smithery.

"Fabulous," said Tom as best he could with a mouthful of chicken, "I appoint you 'ouse chef."

"'nuff respec' me' bredrin'," added Pricey.

The Purple Haze's star attraction tonight was bunch of upstarts from LA called S.N.A.F.U, a US military term used in the field meaning that things had gone awry. The LA kids were obnoxious, arrogant and rude, they had little respect for Tucson or its residents and every sentence that they spilled, was just a stream of profanity that diminished all power of the swear word. They dressed like skater dudes and were heavily inked.

The lead singer and drummer came out the front pre-gig, and were mouthing off.

"Dude this shithole ain't worth a fuckin' rat's dick, let's burn this fucker and kiss these assholes goodbye," suggested the singer.

"Watch ya' language mate, there's children present 'ere," said Seamus in a rare burst of authority.

Tom paid quick attention, he sensed trouble brewing, neither he nor Seamus were known scrappers, but Seamus had had some boxing training and had fought a few bouts. Pricey was nowhere to be seen, which was a shame because he had a reputation for breaking a few noses in the past.

"Dude …who the fuck are you?" the singer said with a rattled laugh. "I mean is that accent even for real … what the fuck?"

Seamus lost his temper; he was really taking this job seriously.

"I'll tell you who I am, *dude*, I'm the fuckin' security around 'ere and if I get any more shit from you I shall drag ya' back to your dressing room by ya' fuckin' 'air and you can stay there until ya' go on stage, got it?"

Venom was lashing from Seamus's tongue.

Tom stiffened and prepared for a fight.

The singer hacked up a greeny and spat it on the ground with contempt.

"You disgusting pig," said Seamus.

The singer smirked, Seamus lost it, lurching at him as he grabbed him by the throat and pushed him into the alcove. The line of teenagers waiting to enter the building all backed off in fear. Tom looked at the drummer and just shook his head, the drummer stayed put obviously out of his depth.

"Get back in that fuckin' dressing room before I push ya' fuckin' 'ead through this pane of glass ya' fuckin' little twat, cause I've 'ad just about enough of ya' disrespect, d'you 'ear?" Seamus shouted.

The singer's head was distorted against the glass of the door and his feet were leaving the ground. He couldn't utter a word, so he just gave a feeble nod, the terror apparent in his eyes.

Seamus let him down and backed off, giving him a death glare. The LA boys rounded and disappeared back into The Haze, shaken and disgraced.

Seamus winked at Tom and lit a cigarette.

"Well done mate," said Tom.

"Mouthy fucker … no manners."

Half-an-hour later KP came out to see what had transpired. "S.N.A.F.U.'s manager is going nuts in there, what did you do to the singer Seamus?"

"Embarrassed 'im I think. 'e was out 'ere swearing 'is 'ead off, gobbing and frightening the kids. I told 'im to go back inside, at which point 'e became really abusive and disrespectful to the club, to me and to England. So I gave 'im a mouthful, 'e shit 'imself and ran back indoors."

"You didn't hit him?"

"'it him? No, I just gave 'im a load of verbal, spoilt brat; 'e showed what a geezer 'e was."

Tom backed up the story.

"They causing trouble then, KP?"

"They're threatening to sue unless they get an apology, I'll have to go and sort things out," she said pensively. "Thanks for sticking up for the club Seamus, see you in a bit."

Katie Pirelli must have worked some magic on the S.N.A.F.U.'s manager that night, because there was no more aggression from the band, although they did trash the dressing room; but that's all run of the mill rock and roll stuff and the club just dealt with it.

After kicking out time, the staff were congregated around the bar, chilling and smoking a few J's, when all of a sudden a teenage girl who had been waiting outside for a lift home, burst through the doors, her face covered in blood.

She had been viciously punched to the ground in an unprovoked attack by a passing drunk, who then just nonchalantly meandered up the Avenue.

Everyone rushed outside. The boys, including some of the girl's friends, all gave chase to the assailant who had seen the posse, spooked, and was fleeing around the block.

The mob caught up easily and surrounded him in a dusty, barren, fenced-off car park. He reeled like a cornered cat pulling out a 4 in blade, and stabbing the air like he was in a sword fight with an invisible cavalier.

Halted by the sudden appearance of a weapon, the boys held off their arrest.

"Vuh … vuh … vuh." voiced the bum with his knife lunges. "Not so keen now are ya'?" he drawled.

Tom's heart was beating fast, he wanted to apprehend this nutter, but he didn't want to fulfil his father's prophecy as well.

The lads behind the drunk were inching closer, someone raised a boot and kicked the knife wielding hand, and then as quick as a flash a teenager jumped around his neck while someone else kicked his legs from under him.

He crumpled to the floor and a hail of feet and fists laid into him as he curled into a ball. Tom felt sorry for him now; he looked so pathetic cradled in the dirt.

"Alright, alright," said Pricey. "That's enough."

The kicking stopped and a volley of hands went in grabbing limbs, hair and bits of clothing, half-lifting, half-dragging the assailant through the dust back to The Haze.

The tramp was wriggling and screaming, and he stank like he had shat himself. By the time they got back to the club, a squad car had turned up and the attending officers arrested the rank individual. The English boys made themselves scarce and left all the glory to the teenagers, who must have imagined they were the dog's bollocks for capturing this arsehole.

Seamus had seen his fair share of aggro for the night and was longing for his bed; the boys slipped out the back door and headed home resolutely; drained.

***

A few days later Kelly decided that she needed her own space and moved into a small apartment closer to work. The vacant room was immediately commandeered by Natty who informed the boys that his wife was coming to visit him from Connecticut. The boys were stunned, as no mention of a wife had previously been articulated.

Natty asked the boys if they would build him a futon bed frame, giving the excuse he couldn't sleep on anything else. Some planks of wood and some nails were drafted in and a reasonable frame was cobbled together, topped off with a double futon mattress.

By the afternoon Natty had moved in, complete with wife, who turned out to be just a girl he'd met at a gig in Connecticut, and had happened to have stayed in touch.

She looked like a confused deer caught in the headlights, politely reeling against Natty's informal tactile attention. God knows what he had told her to convince her to come down to Tucson, but as for being his missus; she definitely was not.

That night an impromptu party was throne to celebrate Natty's arrival. His *spouse* Camille, frightened to death by the prospect of spending the night with the Rasta', turned to Pricey for protection. He took her under his wing and promised that he would get her on a plane as soon as possible, meanwhile she would have to stay here and ward Natty off with a big stick.

It appeared that everyone Tom had met so far in the States, had turned up for the party. A mountain of beer and champagne invaded the kitchen; MTV was pumping hard in the living room and shrieking semi-clad bodies were making good use of the swimming pool.

Seamus answered the doorbell and let in six valley-girls who just happened to be passing. They were all perfect teeth, long blonde hair, and severely out of their depth in this house of reprobates, like a small stack of neatly folded fresh laundry, on top of a heap of dirty clothes.

Pricey had scored some more magic mushrooms and he, Seamus and Tom gobbled up a large one each. The intense muddy flavour was quickly dispatched, then washed away with a large swig of beer.

Within half-an-hour the drug had taken effect and the boys were once again giggling buffoons and having a fantastic time. Pricey decided to leave with Camille and Jennifer on a cocaine hunt, which just left the two lads on 'shrooms in a room rammed with drunken people. Then they become separated, and were each bewildering individual groups of bemused revellers with nonsensical talk; the response to which was having a negative effect on Tom. What he was saying made perfect sense in his head, but emerged as total gibberish when it left his lips.

The sorority girls couldn't connect at all with the adults, especially Natty in hyper-drive, the proverbial bee around six honey pots. So they got up from the floor where they had been huddled in a circle and gingerly floated out the door, followed by Seamus who had latched onto one of them, a victim of the Montgomery charm.

The full horror of Tom's situation now hit him; he was alone in a room full of people he couldn't associate with, and they were treating him like an outcast. He was shrinking, getting smaller by the second; the room was darkening around him, fainter and dismal, till he was the only source of illumination, crouching on the floor trussed up tight in a corner. For the briefest moment he felt suicidal, understanding completely the reason why some people took their own lives; at that moment he too wanted to die.

"Are you okay Tom?"

A liberating voice broke through the cloudy resonance that smothered his head.

He turned to see Rene to the rescue.

"I'm 'shroomed out of me' 'ed and no one understands me," he babbled. "I feel so alone."

He must have looked pitiful.

She took his hand. "Come outside by the pool, it's quieter out there."

He followed her out and they sat on a lounger in a dimly lit corner of the garden.

She put an arm around his shoulders and cradled his head between her neck and chest, stroking his cheek with her other hand and rocking gently back and forth.

The warm night air was soothing, her hot body and rhythmic heartbeat relaxing and soon the demons evaporated and he became half-himself again.

Realising how this might look to anyone who may have glanced their way, he asked where Arty was.

"Oh he's gone to work," she said softly, "he'll be there all night."

Tom didn't intend on being a rat. He never ever wanted to hurt anyone; least of all Arty, who he liked and was extremely grateful to. But sometimes you are just carried away by the moment, and encouraged by the alcohol and intoxicated by the drugs; he succumbed to the carnal desires presented to him by a decent soul who had longed for him for weeks.

They lay back onto the forgiving sun-lounger and side by side kissed for the first time, the first kiss Tom had enjoyed in four months. Her subtle candy lips were moist and yielding and her delicate tongue penetrated his mouth, slowly probing for his own.

His free hand caressed the small of her back feeling the curve of her soft bottom pulling it into him so that their groins made contact. Her leg moved across his bringing him in even tighter feeling his rock hard passion pressing audaciously against her burning abdomen.

They writhed together for a while, their heartbeats increasing and their breathing laboured. She moaned a little as the juices began to flow, dampening her underwear and making her ache for penetration.

"Let's go in the band room," he whispered.

They got up in the shadows and silently melted into the empty darkness of the musty converted garage. Finding the nearest bunk bed, they wasted no time in stripping naked and laying back onto a stale fleecy blanket. Their hot bodies melded together perfectly, her small pert breasts felt like they were going to explode and her hard nipples pressed against his chest like two warm bullets on a cushion.

He pulled away from her, kissing her neck and chest with light butterfly touches making his way to those rigid little rosebuds, where he sucked and nibbled each one in turn, making them stiffen further from the attention.

She put a finger in her mouth and sucked on it, closing her eyes and surrendering to him completely.

He carried on a trail of tantalising kisses down over her flexing delicate tummy, stopping to poke her navel with his tongue, and then on past her fragrant soaking shield of pubic hair to her inner thighs, where he licked and teased her open legs right up to and around her dripping lips.

He paused for a second, tantalizing her a little more before burying his tongue straight into her sodden pussy.

She curved her back in ecstasy and groaned with pleasure, pulling at his hair and bringing his head closer with each lick of her clitoris till she neared a rising climax. Then, Tom withdrew his head and licked her all the way back up to her mouth and plunged his tongue between her lips, where she could taste herself upon him.

Finally with a thrust of his hips, he entered her throbbing wet channel, and with a gasp of delight she wrapped her legs around his waist, locking them in concert as they ground away like a pestle and mortar. They became a boiling, sticky, synchronised tangle of flesh which reached a crescendo in an unforgettable orgasm that nearly tore Tom's heart out and left deep impressions from Rene's nails in his back.

Rene's stifled screams left her weeping and incapable of movement, she just lay there quietly sobbing while he towered above her, arms outstretched like props upon the bed, his manhood pulsating inside her; breathing deeply like a sweltering big cat, his brain scrunched up like an ecstatic stress toy.

After some moments he laid back down on her resting on his elbows trying not to crush her.

"Oh my god, Tom," she said softly.

"It's just Tom when we're alone, dear," he japed, "no need to be formal. Come on, we'd better get back before someone notices we're missing."

He gave her a quick peck on the lips, they tidied themselves up and re-entered the party separately; it seemed no-one had noticed them gone and eventually both of them sloped off to bed in their respective rooms.

***

Some people waken to the sound of cockerels cawing, others to the sound of bastard alarm clocks; in this household it was the sound of snoring. The sun was high in the sky and the flimsy curtains diluted little of it. Tom's throat was drier than a talcum powder factory floor and the room smelled like the Devil's breath.

He turned his tired head on his pillow to face the double bed. Seamus's feet were protruding from under the duvet at the bottom and his arms were folded neatly across his chest, his mouth was open and cartoon Zs were coming out of it, expanding in size as they ascended toward the ceiling.

Suddenly an arm swung into view and flopped down across Seamus's face. A female arm, that caused Seamus to jolt and grunt. He stopped snoring briefly, but soon picked up the pace again and it got steadily louder.

Tom raised himself onto one fascinated elbow and focussed on their guest. It was one of the valley girls from the party. She had masses of bottle-blonde hair that had claimed Pricey's pillow, a cute face, but with a strong jutting jawline and an over large mouth.

She opened an eyelid and focussed on Tom with a sultry, sapphire-blue stare.

"Hi," she said with a gravelly, husky voice, "I'm Lara." She blew the hair off her face with a short puff from her bottom lip.

"Morning, I'm Tom."

"Boysie," croaked Seamus of the dead, "I'm just resting my eyes for a minute, mate," he yawned. "How the devil are ya'?"

"Knackered, mate, what time did you crawl in?" Tom sat up and leant his back against the wall.

"About two, mate, have you met Lara?"

Lara inched up, pulling the duvet under her arms to cover her bare chest. "We've just met Seamus, thank you for introducing us," she said sarcastically and loud.

"Mon pleasure," said the horizontal one, still with eyes shut.

Lara understandably seemed a bit ashamed to be naked in a stranger's bedroom with two men that she had only met the night before. She was 18, brazen, but not very worldly wise. Seamus had told her that he and Tom were like brothers; they lived together, ate together, worked together and slept in the same room, but not together. Lara was easily influenced and with the boys being English, it made everything that came out of their mouths seem quite correct and factual. This left her very open to a wind-up.

"Can I borrow ya' flip flops for a minute, mate? I'm desperate for a drink," asked Tom.

"Help ya' self dude … could you get me a glass from the fridge too?

"You guys really do share everything don't you?" squealed Lara.

"Yep," said Tom looking at her earnestly, "we always share everything, clothes, guitars, girlfriends—"

"Girlfriends?" she said, feigning shock.

"Yep, always 'ave."

Seamus was sniggering inside.

Tom pulled on some shorts and flapped off to the kitchen. He returned with two glasses of ice cold water only to find Seamus and Lara wrestling under the duvet.

"Don't mind me," said Tom, "I've seen it all before."

"Join in mate," came Seamus's muffled reply, followed by a thump and a yell.

"No," laughed Lara appearing from the sheets.

"We share *everything*," assured Tom looking at her straight faced. He could tell from her demeanour that she was definitely considering it.

"Get in, get in," whispered Seamus rather too keenly for his mate's liking.

Tom recoiled from the thought of sharing a spit-roast with his buddy. The sight of another man's erect penis near him would definitely extinguish the romance. Besides he didn't actually fancy Lara in the slightest.

He stood there, grinning, the scene far too comical for words, Lara was giggling and getting more excited by the prospect of a threesome. Seamus was teasing her with tickles and laughing maniacally; the covers were flailing in the air like loose sails in a storm and Tom was thinking that many a man would jump at this opportunity and that maybe it wouldn't come around again.

"Nah, not today, mate, you enjoy yourselves," he bequeathed.

Lara appeared a trifle disappointed as the duvet settled down around her ruffled form. Tom left them to it and meandered through the party devastation towards the bathroom to have a wee.

After a dip in the pool and some time drying off in the sun; where he replayed the events from last night in his mind, he left behind the blinding white sunshine and returned back into the dark cool living room to find Rene, Arty and Natty sitting around the breakfast bar munching on cornflakes amidst crumpled beer cans and empty champagne bottles.

"Morning, campers," he greeted cheerfully, "bloody 'ot out there."

"It's always hot out there," drawled Arty chuckling at Tom's naive remark.

Rene stared into her bowl, continuing to eat.

Natty spoke, "me' gonna 'ave a rehearsal today Tom, me' got a fren' comin' over from LA, him play d' trombone sim. An' Denny Kirk, an' Carl Strawberry an' Jamie Dinero from Mystic Lights, dem' come an' play rhydem' sim?"

"Nice," said Tom. "Where we gonna rehearse then?"

"Here in the living room," said Arty. "I'll rig up a PA, but ya'll have ta clean up the house while I'm gone okay?"

"No problem. I'll start now, the dustman's gonna love us."

Arty left the house to pick up a PA system from the club; Natty and Tom collected all the empties and put them in black bin bags, while Rene washed the glasses, cups and dishes. Once that was done Tom whizzed 'round with the vacuum cleaner while Natty cleaned the surfaces with a spray cleaner and paper towels.

Tom sidled up to Rene at the sink and asked her quietly if she was okay, she looked so terribly sad. He was feeling a bizarre mixture of guilt, conquest and pity.

She managed a little smile. "Oh I'm fine. Just a bit hungover that's all; I'll be alright later, don't worry," she lied.

"Okay then," he said rubbing her back. "You gonna be around for the rehearsal?"

"No, I think I'll go out with Animal, she'll be over soon."

Just then Seamus emerged from his pit closely shadowed by his prize.

"Mate, mate," he said, red eyed and bloated. "Ya' shoulda waited, I was gonna 'elp to clean up," he gestured.

Tom stared at his friend with his hands on his hips, wondering if Seamus knew that everyone knew that what he said was far, far from the truth.

"I've spent 'alf my life waiting for you, mate; it was a waste of time."

Natty was laughing while rolling a joint.

"We've got a rehearsal session this afternoon with Natty and a couple of lads from Mystic Lights, and Natty's mate from LA on trombone; should be blinding," said Tom.

"Oh, 'o, 'o," said Seamus, "sounds good Ras', looking forward to it, looking forward to it. Gotta' 'ave some breakfast first though, I'm starvingous."

Lara said her goodbyes and sheepishly scurried off, then Seamus fixed himself some bananas and honey on toast, and a cup of tea for Tom and Natty who spread out on the patio to bathe in the 90° furnace.

"Where's Pricey?" asked Seamus venturing to join them.

"Run off to get some Mary Jane with Jennifer and Camille, 'e 'asn't been seen since," informed Tom.

"Stolen me wife, an' run for som' ice," sang Natty, laughing.

"Probably still running," said Seamus joining in with the laughter.

A taxi brought Tyrell in from the airport to Arty's house; he was tall and stocky with close cropped hair, black and powerful like an American football player. He brought his trombone and a bag of clothes and was warmly greeted by Natty, who'd known him for some time.

He appeared a little confused to the reasons behind the rehearsal situation, but he was extremely amicable and keen to press on with the music.

Carl Strawberry and Jamie Dinero turned up next in Jamie's beat up estate car.

Jamie was of Mexican descent but considered himself a Rastafarian. He had dreads and a constant spliff in his mouth. He played bass with a really smooth style and knew all the tunes.

Carl was an enormous black dude of at least 500 lbs and 6-6 tall, and was easily the best drummer Tom and Seamus had ever played alongside. He was sharp, smart, driven and down on every beat with perfect timing. Yet, he played with such indifference, it was no more a struggle than breathing. He brought along an electronic kit that had the smallest kick drum in the world, basically a circle trigger the size of a golf ball for the beater to hit. The rest of the kit was small pads on a flimsy frame, with this giant sitting behind it. It looked ridiculous but made an incredible sound through the PA.

Sonny set up his keys and Denny Kirk rolled in wearing a dazzling white tracksuit and Tam, which was more akin to a test match than a band's rehearsal. His long dreads were tied in a ponytail that swayed across his back like a broken pendulum when he moved.

With Tom and Seamus, the band now comprised of an 8-piece with three guitarists, slight overkill on the skanking side of things that made Tom, the least accomplished player, feel surplus to requirements.

Natty had a tape of the songs he wanted to go through. The band listened to each song, picked out their respective parts and played along. Tyrell seemed to know all the songs and took the line of the brass section.

If a number didn't have the right vibe, Natty would stop it in mid-flow, shouting "rewind, rewind," or "reel and come again." at which point all the musicians would roll the music down like they were physically slowing a tape player with their fingers. This action was new and enthralling to the English pair.

After a couple of songs, Denny showed his frustration at there being too many guitarists all playing the same line. He took up the role of musical director and constructed different segments for Tom and Seamus to play; very simple skanks, counter skanks and riffs. This worked much better and he soon had his toothy smile back in place.

Carl Strawberry drove the band relentlessly and by early evening they had 12 of Natty's tunes licked. During a break Natty came up with a fresh idea; he mouthed some chord sounds to Denny and a bass line to Jamie, Carl picked up the beat, then every one joined in.

Natty started singing "Now this song dedicated to all me' bredrin' 'ere tonight, 'ere me now, Carl is a cornerstone for reggae, yes he is a cornerstone; Jamie is a cornerstone for reggae, yes he is a cornerstone …." He carried on for each person in the band, mixing it up with a reggae break down every other two lines and so it went on for 15 min, with everyone getting a big 'up' with various solos thrown in.

The session ended on a high; the band sounded excellent together and they all left happy, singing *Cornerstone* in their head.

Seamus is a cornerstone for reggae music, yes he is a cornerstone.

Tom is a cornerstone for reggae; yes he is a cornerstone ….

6
Wacky Places

"I've gotta car for ya' son," said Pricey, rubbing his hands together as he marched out to the poolside.

The announcement perplexed Tom, "Eh?"

"You've been after a motor for a while, so I've found ya' one. It's got tyres on it like that," Pricey held up two horizontal fat fingers, "an' it runs like a watch."

Tom squinted; his brother-in-law's back was against the low sun on the horizon, which diffused around him like a corona.

"What sort of car?"

"It's an estate, a big blue 'n; you could fit a double bed in the back."

"Could be 'andy … what they asking for it?"

"Nothing, Freddie's dumping it, so I've claimed it for ya', you can pick it up in the morning."

"What about tax and insurance?"

"It's got tags, don't worry about insurance, if you don't do anything stupid, ya' won't get pulled will ya'?" assured Pricey.

"A free car, eh?"

"On my life, all ya' gotta do is drive Fred to his new'n across town and the old'n's yours, straight up."

Tom pondered the deal for a second.

"Fair do's," he said stoically, "where've you been anyway?"

"We've been camped out at the Ramada Inn, all expenses paid for by Jennifer, I 'aven't been asleep for two days, courtesy of the old nose candy," he chuckled.

"Looks like it," said Tom eying up Pricey's crinkled appearance.

"Where's Camille?"

"She's in the front room with Natty, she's telling 'im that she made a big mistake coming 'ere; she's flying out in the morning, but she's gonna stay with Jennifer tonight."

"I don't think Natty's that bothered anyway, 'e's more excited about the band," revealed Tom.

Seamus and Lara tumbled out onto the patio, beers in hand.

"Mr Price," said Seamus, "where ya' been man, we've missed ya'?"

Pricey giggled a throaty laugh, "Keeping a low profile, son, who's this then, ya' new bird?"

"This is my friend Lara; we met the other night at the party."

"Very nice with chips," said Pricey laughing again.

Lara came over to greet the ginger one; she was wearing a light blue bikini and jean shorts that refused to be buttoned around her tanned puppy-fat midriff.

"Hi, very nice to meet you," she said shaking his hand.

"Nice to meet you two." He acknowledged her ample bosom.

Lara almost always carried with her an air of bewildered intrigue; she was both mystified and spellbound by the English sense of humour and as naive as a new born foal.

Tom spoke to Seamus. "Mr Price 'as found us a car; Freddie's giving us 'is old one, we can get it tomorrow."

"Sounds good, sounds good," said Seamus, "wos 'e want for it?"

"It's buckshee mate, non-spondulica."

Seamus tugged on his cigarette, raised his eyebrows and exhaled, blowing smoke up from his bottom lip past his face, "Sounds even better."

That evening after a glorious cold chicken salad dinner Seamus, Lara and Tom found themselves back in the pool. The night was smoulderingly hot and the tepid water provided the perfect complement. Pricey and Camille had sloped off again, Arty had gone to work and Rene and Natty were watching the telly in the living room.

A copious amount of Rollin' Rock beer was taking its effect and the boys were now naked and bombing the squealing teenager who had given up trying to preserve her make-up.

Tom clambered onto the diving board and proceeded to perform a series of bounces, first on one leg then the other, then mid-air splits. His tackle boogied freely like they were having the unrestricted time of their lives.

Seamus joined in, and they took it in turns to exhibit their dangly bits to the night sky and a rampant nubile air-head, before diving into the water with a series of comical styles.

Lara watched with wide-eyed intent, so excited that she almost came in the water.

Tom and Seamus thought this game had some longevity and carried it on until Seamus decided that he wanted to give Lara a seeing-to in the pool.

Tom left them canoodling under the diving board, he dried off, put on his shorts, then ambled into the living room where he found Rene alone and crying again. Without a word he picked her up like a child, carried her to his bedroom and closed the door.

***

The 1965 Ford Country Sedan station wagon could legally seat nine people, but seeing that Tom once crammed thirteen bodies and a guitar into his Hillman Avenger, meant that he could throw a party in the back of this beast and still have room for a disco in the front.

At 17ft long, it commanded the side walk outside Freddie's house. Its paintwork was a flat pale blue, which had long since seen a polishing rag, and it had a huge dent in the rear left hand panel where something heavy had ploughed into it, but these were its only blemishes. The plethora of chrome trim still shone like the day it was born.

Its blue leather bench seats were long enough to sleep on outstretched, and the dashboard instrumentation, column shift and steering wheel, deserved to be exhibited in a sci-fi museum.

Tom and Seamus were staring wide-eyed in through the side windows when Freddie bounced out of his front door with his strange elastic gait and came down the garden path to meet them.

"Hey," he said joyfully.

"Morning," said the boys.

"You guys ready to unleash the Thunderbird?"

"Sure thing," said Seamus, "where we off to?"

"Oh, the Southside, gotta friend who's selling me his hatchback, it's gonna be cheaper to run and bags of fun," rhymed Freddie.

"She eat a lot of fuel then, this old girl?" enquired Tom.

"Only if you tear it up," said Freddie "but if you just purr around town in her, she'll be gentle on the purse," he pitched.

The boys walked around the back of the Ford, it had Arkansas registered number plates.

"The Arkansas chuggerbug," announced Tom.

Seamus laughed, recalling the cartoon series Wacky Races.

They got in the passenger side and tentatively slid along the roasting bench seat. Freddie started her up with one twist of the key. She sounded really throaty, her ancient V8 engine combusting keenly into life.

Freddie looked very diminutive balanced on the edge of the patchy seat inside the expansive old can, and in Tom's mind Freddie was absolutely justified in opting for a tiny Japanese hatchback that would suit his stature perfectly.

"Cockpit check complete, we're clear for take off," Freddie said like a New Jersey pilot. "Fasten all seatbelts and extinguish all cigarettes, let's get this baby off the ground."

One side of his mouth turned up into a crooked grin, he yanked the column shift into drive, released the hand brake, brushed the accelerator and they peeled away from the curb like a sticky sweet leaving a cellophane wrapper.

In the Southern part of town Freddie parked outside an unkempt bungalow on a sandy featureless street and asked the boys if they wouldn't mind waiting in the car while he checked if Geraldo was up yet. He reached across them and opened the glove box, retrieving a parcel the size of a 2 lb bag of sugar wrapped in brown paper and done up with frantic packaging tape.

The lad's eyes followed the packet out of the door.

"I'll give you a signal from the porch if we're cool, then you can drive this honey away. Treat her sweet." He smiled that crooked smile again, the cigarette between his lips producing a smoke cloud that obscured his face. "Oh," he said exiting the car, "don't fill her up, there's a hole about half way in the fuel tank, you'll just lose it all." With that he bounced up the pathway to Geraldo's front door.

The boys searched each others faces, silent clogs engaging in their minds.

"We've just took part in a dope delivery," said Seamus agitated.

"Looks like it," said Tom, "best we fuck off sharpish."

A swarthy character appeared at the door looking like he'd just crawled out of a compost heap. Freddie spun around and gave the Brits the okay sign.

Tom wasted no time sliding over to the driver's position, grappling with the controls, and launching the old girl down the street without ringing too many alarm bells.

They were upset at being played like a couple of novices, but the free car more than made up for their disenchantment.

"Wos' she like to drive?" asked Seamus.

"Runs like a watch and 'as tires on 'er like *that*," said Tom mocking Pricey's gypsy spiel.

"But we need some petrol in an 'urry," he added, "got any money on ya'?"

"A couple o' bucks," said Seamus.

Tom looked at the petrol gauge; the needle was deep in the red.

In the past when he had bought petrol and also picked up something from the station shop, he had been questioned by the cashier as to whether he was paying for any gas or just for the drink that he was holding. Seeing as some people just used the shop as a convenience store, an idea appeared to him.

"'ow about this?" he said. "I'll put a quick twenty bucks of fuel in the tank, then pull off the pump and drive up to a parking bay, you go inside and buy a drink and say 'just this please', your accent's bound to bamboozle a local."

Seamus chewed his lip for a moment calculating the consequences.

"Alright," he said uneasily, "Let's 'ave a pop at that Circle K," indicating to a large forecourt up ahead.

The place was new and busy, perfect for a portion of petty theft. Tom whistled "I've been putting out fire with gasoline" from David Bowie's Cat People (*Putting Out Fire*), while he engaged the petrol nozzle into the Chuggerbug, and acting as apathetic as possible. Once the $20 was in, he casually rolled over to the parking area and waited, with the engine running, for Seamus to purchase a drink.

Inside the shop, the uniquely American smell of coffee, doughnuts and candy, embodied the convenience store culture; it was yet to explode onto British soil and was totally tantalizing. Seamus strode over to the self-service soda fountain and pulled off a gigantic takeaway cup from the stack. A Big Gulp holds 32 oz (roughly 1L) of fluid, an amount that he couldn't possibly manage to drink back home, but it being so fluid-sappingly hot over here, he could mop one up with ease.

"Just for the coke, sir?" asked the cashier.

"Mmm," replied Seamus sucking on the straw. He handed over $2 and got fifty cents change, with the obligatory, "Have a nice day."

Not bad for a tank of fuel, he thought and waltzed out of the shop a little light-headed.

He winked at Tom as he got in the car; they calmly reversed out of the parking bay and slowly drove away from the forecourt, holding their breaths, fully expecting someone to chase after them with a fist raised. Nothing happened.

When they got back to Kale Kuhn, they found Pricey in the kitchen whisking up some scrambled eggs.

"'ow's the motor?" he asked as they entered the kitchen. He was wrapped around the waist in a white bath towel, wearing nothing else, and making enough scramble to feed the entire neighbourhood.

"She's a relic, but pulls like a dragster," replied Tom. "You got enough eggs there?"

"Jen's coming over with 'er sister and a mate from London, thought I'd knock up some elevenses."

"It's 'alf-past-twelve," said Seamus.

"It's eleven o'clock somewhere," reasoned the Price.

"Could ya sling a few more eggs in that bowl mate? I'm starving," asked Seamus.

"Yeah me too," added Tom.

"No proplemo," Said Pricey, and cracked another four white shelled chicken embryos into the large basin.

"That Freddie stitched us right up this mornin'," said Tom. "We ran about two pound o' weed over to 'is mate's 'ouse 'idden in the glove box, without knowin' it. Probably what paid for his new car."

"The slippery toad," said Pricey, "I'll 'ave a word with 'im."

"Na, it's alright, we didn't get collared, 'e just should 'ave let us know that's all."

The front door cracked open and in bundled a felicitous fragrant chaos.

A trio of confident, sultry sirens, whose laughter, energised an erstwhile harmonious atmosphere.

"Morning everyone," said Jennifer. "This is my sister Fizz and my good friend Rose; they're down from New York and staying with me for a month."

Jennifer hugged each girl, her long dark hair swishing left and right like a pony's tail warding off flies.

Fizz was of mixed race, so Tom surmised she must be Jennifer's half-sister; she was a lot younger, around 21 he guessed, she had a round freckly face and a light coloured Jackson-five 'fro. She unveiled herself immediately as a vivacious coquette.

Rose was criminally pretty, raven haired, pale skinned, had captivating blue velvet eyes and a face not dissimilar to Vivien Leigh. Elfin and mischievous, she was a real live wire and highly spirited.

Tom fancied her instantly, but knew straight away that it would be hopeless to try. He lacked the dynamism that she demanded, and she possessed something that Tom did not; an air of certainty of getting laid.

"Scramble ladies?" said Pricey.

"You can put some bloody clothes on before you go anywhere near my breakfast," demanded Jennifer in her nasally upper class accent. "I don't want any of your chest hair languishing in my eggs."

Pricey giggled.

"Yeah, come on get the towel off," said Rose pulling at it impishly.

"Don't touch what ya' can't afford my dear," replied Pricey retreating from the kitchen.

Rose blew through her lips.

"Where y' from in London then Rose," asked Seamus.

"Kensington," she replied twirling round and jumping up to sit on to the work surface, her summer dress billowed all around her.

"Worth a few bob then?" probed Tom.

"I'm afraid not, Daddy's the one with all the 'dosh'; he owns an art gallery, but he's as tight as fuck, so I have to work for a living." Her face screwed up at the word 'work', like she had to clear up cat sick.

"What do ya' do then?" he inquired.

"Oh I'm a party planner for a corporate events company. Team-bonding weekends, award ceremonies, that sort of thing, boring, boring, boring."

"Lotsa' freebies though?" said Seamus.

"It has its perks, but one wouldn't abuse one's position," she said with abundant mirth.

"What about you Fizz?" asked Tom.

"I work in a funky boutique in Brooklyn … it pays the bills."

Her accent was just as posh as Jennifer's, only with a tinge of American.

"Nice," said Seamus.

Pricey came back to the kitchen, more suitably attired.

"Right then," he said rubbing his hands together, "let's 'ave some 'nosh'."

After breakfast Jennifer asked the boys if they wanted to go Tubing the next day.

Clueless, Tom asked, "What's *Tubing*?"

"Oh it's wonderful, four hours of drifting down the Salt River up in Phoenix, on inflated lorry inner tubes. We'll take a picnic and some champers; it'll be great fun, you coming?"

"I reckon we're up for that," he said.

"Umm," noised Seamus drawing on a cigarette, "take me to the river," he growled.

"We'll go up in the Arkansas Chuggerbug," said Tom, "it'll take six easy."

"The what?" said Jennifer.

"Our new mode of transport," he replied. "Freddie's old car."

"I saw it out front; it's a huge beast. We'll have to take mine as well because Jack, Mateo, Salina, KP and Glen are all coming too," she said.

"Sounds like a party," said Seamus.

"I love a good bash," said Rose seductively.

"So it's settled then?" Jennifer said. "Meet us at my place at ten o'clock and bring your swimming costumes, or whatever you guy's like to wear these days."

"Might not wear anything," said Seamus, "just dangle me little thing into the water."

Everybody laughed.

"Careful, there's fish in that river, they might think you are offering them lunch," said Jennifer. "Well maybe a starter anyway."

That evening at work outside The Haze, the boys were nurturing a rather limp crowd of gothic degenerates. The air was oppressive and the mood melancholy. Tom and Seamus had learnt their lesson on too much apparel, and nowadays wore as little as possible; the cut-down look highlighted their caramel limbs and helped to blend in with the populous. Their accents hadn't curved at all and this invaluable little weapon gave them a huge advantage over the locals; an asset that Seamus was employing ruthlessly on a petite little brunette in the doorway of the club.

Fixed to the front wall of adjoining properties next to Misinformed, was a public phone booth, a lonely battered silver and blue sentry, shackled to the concrete with a square canopy surround, providing scant protection from the elements or any eavesdroppers.

This communication device, a portal to another place, had seen no use at all in the time the boys had stood outside the club. Tom had been staring at it for a while now, wondering if it still possessed a pulse. He interrupted Seamus' play time.

"Do ya' think that phone works?"

Seamus stopped talking mid-sentence and studied the scruffy unobtrusive machine for a few seconds before opting to find out.

He flicked his fag butt into the road and walked over to the box. Picking up the receiver he held it to his ear.

"It 'as a dial tone," he said surprised.

Chancing his arm, he tapped in the international code for the UK, and then his home number expecting a voice to demand payment, but none came, instead he got straight through to his dad.

Seamus erupted with maniacal, throaty laughter, "I'm through!" he announced, astounded that he had a free hotline to the UK. He then proceeded to gush forth a torrent of information and questions as though he'd been absent for many years. He spoke to his mum and his sister respectively, each time explaining the gratuity of the magic phone box, interspersed with cackles and lines of amazement.

Seamus stayed on the phone, ludicrously, for a good 30min while Tom watched, fully expecting telephone engineers to turn up and kick Seamus off, or disconnect the phone, but nobody arrived; so when Seamus had finished, Tom, disbelieving that it would allow him to make a free call as well, took his turn and called his mum's house. Once again it worked, and an incredulous Tom spent a while chatting to his mum and step-dad.

There was obviously a fault with the AT&T machine, or maybe they just weren't expecting the man on the street to be phoning international numbers, who knew; but it worked and it would carry on working for months and months to come without repair, and Tom and Seamus milked it as often as they'd dare.

After his initial phone call, Seamus returned to his flirtatious activity with the brunette, who'd patiently stood in the doorway waiting for the suitor. Her name was Caryn Ventura; she was of Irish-Mexican heritage, smart, cute, around 5ft tall and quite hirsute, just the way Seamus liked them. He didn't realize it at the time, but this girl was poised to play a major role in his life.

***

The next day the boys woke at 9:00 a.m. Squeezed into their ill-fitting speedos, covered up with shorts, hurried a cereal breakfast and then rushed out into the sunshine of another Wedgewood blue sky day. The temperature was already in the high 80s, but prudence had taught them to lay towels across the bench seat of the Chuggerbug, so as not to torch their legs.

Tom started the engine, "Watch this," he said, "electric rear window."

He flicked a switch on the dashboard and the rear windscreen descended noisily into the tailgate and disappeared.

"Sweet," remarked Seamus contorting himself round to admire the 1960s gadgetry. "Does it sprout wings like Chitty Chitty Bang Bang?"

"Probably, 'aven't found that button yet."

They set off. With all the windows down it caused just enough rushed air to cool the interior of the car. The three lads were giggling and swapping stories from the night before when Billy Ocean came on the radio singing *Get outta my dreams, get into my car*, they simultaneously erupted with laughter.

"That's you the other night," said Tom to Pricey.

"She didn't wanna know," Pricey surrendered.

A few nights previous while walking towards Gracious Bob's with Natty to check out Mystic Lights, Pricey had tried to pull a 20-year-old blonde on the side walk. As Tom, Seamus and Natty walked on, Pricey could be heard saying "get into my car, come on get into my car." Wisely the girl rejected his offer and briskly walked off. The others shouted back words of encouragement, "Billy … Hey Billy … Get into my car."

Natty had nearly wet himself laughing.

"You can't blame 'er can ya? Some rampant sex pest trying to peel 'er off the street and bundle 'er into his Nissan," said Tom.

"I would 'ave been gentle with 'er," protested Pricey.

"You went at 'er like a loon, scared the life outta the poor thing."

Seamus hissed a wheezy laugh.

"'er loss," said Pricey.

"'er lucky escape," reasoned Tom.

On cue they joined in with the chorus, "Get outta my dreams, get into the back seat baby, get into my car …."

Outside Jennifer's home they were joined by Rose, Fizz, KP and Glen.

Rose insisted on sitting in the front, so squeezed herself between Tom and Seamus, much to Tom's delight. She wore a white bikini beneath a white see through cotton dress and a pair of sandals, and she smelt like a sweet shop.

Jack, Mateo and Salina piled into Jennifer's car, which took the lead. After filling up with fuel, this time paid for with a whip round, and stocking up on ice, beer and tortilla chips, packed neatly into two cool boxes, the party set off up Interstate10 towards Phoenix. Exiting near Mesa, they took the 202 east to Power Road and then on to the Salt River recreation ground. This area was in The Tonto National Forest, owned by the Apache people.

By now Rose had become extremely bored being in a hot sticky car for so long and decided to unleash her nefarious side on the boys.

"Let's see how fast this old banger can really do," she said thrusting her foot painfully on to Tom's flimsy deck shoe covering the accelerator. The lads found it funny at first as the old girl picked up speed forcing Tom to overtake Jennifer's car crammed with an audience of disbelieving faces.

The Chuggerbug reached 80mph and Tom supposed that Rose would take her foot off, but no, she forced all of her weight down on his and smiled wickedly, as though the devil had gotten hold of her.

Tom grimaced with pain, her wooden sole was grating on the bones across the bridge of his foot, and he was materializing concern for the integrity of the car. His passengers were making panicked suggestions that he should slow down, but instead the car carried on picking up speed. It reached 90 … 100, the mesquite trees and tumbleweed plants were flashing by at an alarming rate and dust was billowing behind them like the plume from a steam train.

"Slow down Tom," beseeched KP from the rear.

"I can't, she's welded me' to the floor."

Rose laughed insanely.

Still they picked up speed.

Acrid burning plastic smoke wafted into the front from under the dashboard, the Chuggerbug was about to ignite.

Frightened by their situation, Seamus uncharacteristically raised his voice at Rose telling her to get off.

Pricey joined in and gravely demanded she "Stop fuckin' about!"

A pin burst her bubble, reluctantly she obliged and lifted her foot; Tom applied the brakes and brought them back down to a more acceptable 50mph. Unfortunately that was that was the extent of intimacy between Tom and Rose; two sticky legs pressed together and a painful game of 'footsie'.

"Spoilsport," she said, feigning a sulk.

Tom looked in the rearview mirror and caught a glimpse of KP who was shaking her head angrily.

"You're a naughty girl," Tom said, like a father to a child.

"More than you'll ever know," replied the licentious girl.

"She can still shift," said Seamus trying to bring some humility to the table.

"Dangerously," said Pricey from the back.

The caustic pungent smoke eventually dissipated through the open windows and soon Jennifer caught up with them and resumed the lead. In a little over a mile they were in the car park of the recreation ground, where everybody piled out into branding hot sunshine like excitable, perspiring school kids on a coach trip.

The giant black rubber tubes cost $10 each to hire. They paid the guy at the kiosk, pitching in for an extra one to carry the cool boxes.

"We'll rope them all together to form a giant raft," Jennifer took on the matriarchal role. She'd been tubing before and knew all the tricks. It was an Arizonan tradition, a superb way to chill out under a blistering sky. The money raised from the Tubing went towards the upkeep of the Tonto National Forest, an almost pristine desert wilderness.

A yellow bus took them on a short journey down to the set-off point; the water was only a couple of feet deep and welcomingly cold.

A frenzy of de-bagging took place at the waters edge and while Jack and Pricey got on with lashing the tubes together with bungee cord, Tom and Seamus were introduced to Mateo whom they had not met before. He was a shy round faced petite man, alarmingly feminine, almost pretty in fact; he didn't have much to say apart from, "Hi."

Rose was the first one in; following a cartwheel she submerged herself under the fast flowing current and disappeared for a full minute.

KP was getting frantic, "Where's she gone?"

Jennifer scoured the water desperately, looking for a sign of her friend.

"Alligator's got 'er," said Tom dryly.

All of a sudden Rose burst through the surface like a mermaid released from a spell, making Fizz and Selena jump out of their skins, culminating in a water fight between the girls. This put everyone in high spirits and set the tone for rest of the day.

Tom parked his backside in an outer tube, facing forward he dangled his legs into the soothing cool river. Pricey handed him a cold, uncapped Michelob and the raft set sail like giant frogspawn gently meandering downstream, the tadpoles at the mercy of the current.

At times the river was as flat as a millpond allowing them to drift tenderly like petals in a pool, at others they were white-water rafting, rushing over short bumpy stretches of rapids that encouraged the flotsam to lift their butts out of the water or suffer a bruising.

They wound their way through sandy cliff canyons where nesting birds swept low over the water, catching insects for insatiable young. They passed scrubby desert, where wild horses came down to drink from the banks unperturbed by the human presence, and a family of Javelinas that fled as soon as they got wind of the approaching craft, the little rusty Reds grunting after the adults amid a billow of kicked-up dust.

A few large spliffs emerged.

Tom took a couple of hits laid back in his tube loving the contrast of hot and cold on his body, and felt content imagining how glorious it would be to spend the rest of his life right here; just like this.

After four hours of abandoned bliss they came up to the landing point. Jennifer shouted over that it would be easier to untie the bungee chords and paddle over to the bank individually. She warned everybody that the river became way faster and deeper just after the landing, so they should get over to the left hand side right now.

The girls didn't pay enough attention and were leaving it far too late to paddle across to shore. Fizz got caught in a current which took her farther out and she started to go to pieces, her flailing arms achieving nothing against the strong flow. Unbalanced she fell out of her tube, inhaling a lung full of mud enriched water. She resurfaced spluttering and coughing, but despite blurred vision, managed to grab hold of the slippery black tube. Clinging desperately to the wayward craft and kicking her legs wildly, she remained astonishingly stationary.

It had been hard enough for the men to pull their tubes to the shore, their arms ached with the effort, but Fizz was at her strength's end and the realisation of actually drowning was making her distraught, sapping vital energy from her bankrupt limbs.

A beautiful afternoon had suddenly turned sour; a disaster was rolling out before their eyes.

On instinct, Jennifer plunged right back in to save her sister, but the torrent was so strong, she too was now floundering.

Jack was yelling, "Form a chain … everyone form a chain!"

Linking arms, the party stretched out into the water, the smallest on the bank, Jack and Pricey up the front. Jennifer now assisted by Jack was able to stand up and take Fizz's hand.

Jack lunged for the inner tube just managing to claw on to the slimy rubber thing before it bobbed out of his grip, uncorking Fizz, who scrambled for Jack, latching onto his legs. This enabled Pricey to grab her waist; Seamus and Tom held on to him, Jennifer held on to Jack and between them all they hauled Fizz back into calmer waters where she clambered to shore and collapsed onto all fours.

Jack waded back to the bank looking like the thing from the black lagoon. "Fuck that shit," he said.

The girls surrounded Fizz and got her to sit down and relax; she was shivering uncontrollably and crying, obviously in a state of shock.

Rose and Jennifer cuddled her and calmed her down, the rest were pondering the situation and what might have been, in silence.

A bus driver who had witnessed the event came running over. "Everything okay here?" he asked.

"We're fine," said Jack, "just a little wet, nothing to worry about."

"'er tube's been lost though," said Tom pointing downstream.

The bus driver looked, "No problem, happens all the time, it'll get picked up some ways down the river, just as long as ya'll are okay."

"Yes, thank you," said Jennifer.

"Okay, the bus is waiting whenever you're ready, I'll take ya'll back to the lot."

"Cheers, mate," said Seamus.

The bus driver, his face a deeply furrowed nut brown, gave Seamus an inquisitive stare, then turned and left.

Within half an hour they were back in their respective cars, weary, brooding and hungry.

"Let's go back to mine and have a barbeque," suggested Jennifer, "I have some bubbly in the fridge and we can visit a supermarket on the way home and pick up more supplies, yeah?"

They all agreed; Seamus had left his acoustic guitar at Jennifer's house, so a singsong was on the cards.

Arriving back in the early evening, they found Odin camped out on the steps, quietly strumming his guitar.

"I sensed your presence heading towards me and felt obliged to await your return," he said poetically.

Rose, honed in on his magnetic personality instantaneously and sidled up beside him.

"Lady Guinevere I presume," he said gently, the magic settling all around them.

Rose's face lit up like a beacon, "At your mercy, Sire," she said, flattered by his charm.

He then proceeded to sing her a song about the lady in the lake he'd written ten minutes before.

Tom's heart groaned at the immediate loss, but it was inevitable; she wasn't ever going to be beguiled by him. He resigned himself to unloading groceries and helping to set up the barbeque.

"Bubbles everyone," Jennifer asked vibrantly.

"Rather," said Pricey taking control of the cooking.

"Why not," added Tom.

Seamus joined Odin and Rose by the patio doors and a series of Bob Dylan classics leaked out of their guitars, followed by Beatles and Rolling Stones hits, it seemed that there wasn't a tune Odin didn't know.

Every song called for, Odin smashed out with Seamus jamming along like a pupil following a grand master; and Seamus wasn't short of a few songs himself. Odin's dirty nicotine stained fingers were all over the neck of the guitar, mesmerising the assembly like the pied piper of Old Pueblo; everybody sang as darkness consumed a day that fought till the very end with another breathtaking sanguine sunset.

By 2:00 a.m. KP and Glen had gone home, Jack and Mateo had retired across the street, Selena and Fizz had disappeared and Pricey was crumpled in a corner seat, totally wasted and mumbling incoherently. Tom was so tired that he could barely focus, yet Seamus, Rose, Jennifer and Odin were still sparkling, propped up undeniably by the dandruff of the gods.

Tom decided to leave them all to it and as dangerous as it was, bid them goodnight and took the Arkansas back to Arty's house and the sanctuary of his bed. To his great relief, Rene wasn't waiting for him; he had the whole space to himself and so floundered onto the cool sheets and passed out in his clothes.

***

For some time now, Tom and Seamus had known a couple of girls who fancied the pants off them; the boys for their own reasons, wanted to keep it platonic. Tori, was the girlfriend of a sci-fi cartoonist and old horror movie enthusiast the boys had met at the club, by the name of Brandt Olofsson. He especially liked the works of Bela Lugosi, often quoting lines from the movie star's films. Although Tori loved Brandt dearly and would never cheat on him, she had this aching in her loins for Seamus. So her own, private little war was going on, which became blatantly evident every now and then. She was dark-haired, plump and lively; a genuinely lovely person.

The other girl was called Lena. Again, Tom had met her at the Haze; she had shoulder length curly blonde hair, brown eyes, was skinny, slightly hunched and had an odd blotchy complexion, somewhere between pink and beige, like some of her skin pigment couldn't make up its mind. She also had an ample amount of peach fuzz on her cheeks, which is never a good look.

Lena was slightly touched in the head, manic, and self acclaimed to be obsessively impassioned by natural life. Tom thought she was just a skanky cow and a bit lazy; she obviously wanted his knickers off, however, and possibly insanely for a virile young man, regarding this acquaintance he preferred to keep them on.

On this particular day, the boys decided they wanted to go to Old Tucson, the Western movie studio and film set. The girls determined to accompany them.

As a youngster Tom had a passion for cowboy movies and some of his favourites had been filmed there.

Old Tucson is situated west of town in the Tucson mountain range, just off Gates Pass. It took around an hour to travel there. It featured mock western streets, saloons and livery barns, and a working 19th century steam engine, complete with track, coaches and a station.

The church and Mexican town square, used in countless movies such as Three Amigos and Tombstone, is very recognisable, as is the ranch house used for the TV series The High Chaparral. When Tom saw this he was overawed and regressed with nostalgia. As a boy he used to watch this programme with his mum, curled up on the sofa on a Sunday afternoon with a box of Maltesers; the sight was humbling. Seamus and the girls were not so impressed and wandered off, but Tom stayed a while longer, leaning on the corral rails, imagining Manolito, Buck and Big John Cannon wrangling cattle or fending off Indians. He loved that show.

Little House on the Prairie, was also filmed there as was the original Gunfight at the OK Corral, with Burt and Kirk. All together some three hundred films, including four starring John Wayne. This place had an epic and distinct pedigree.

A staged gunfight erupted in the main street, complete with cheesy insults, blank cartridges and the predictable dead baddy, it was shockingly lame. After an expensive burger in the restaurant the guys reckoned they had seen enough. Lena suggested they go to her house for a swim. Of course, being the inquisitive type and indubitably sweaty, the boys eagerly agreed.

At the top of Gates Pass they pulled into a viewing point; a storm was passing through Tucson in the valley down below, it was a spectacle not to be ignored. On foot they climbed to an even higher vantage point. East and west, the panoramic vista from up here was massive; hazily stretching out for miles, an unprecedented advantage for watching a localised storm pass along a valley floor, and this one was intense.

Sitting down on rocks in brilliant sunshine while a slate grey cloud as big as a city slowly rolled over the desert nadir, engulfing Tucson ten miles ahead of them.

The cloud dragged behind it what looked like a heavy veil of silvered satin, stroking everything in its path, drenching the parched earth and soaking its citizens.

Multiple lightening forks, sometimes as many as ten at a time, crackled from within the cauldron and punched the earth with devastating electrical lashes, doing God knows what damage to the land beneath, whilst obscure mighty thunder groaned and rumbled again, echoing around the encasing mountain rim.

They watched mesmerized. The girls remained blasé, they'd seen it many times before, but were patient and informative. Half an hour passed, the storm moved south giving vent to a slab of glorious sunlight in its wake, evaporating the deluge in a matter of minutes. Before them, a distinct line denoted the border between dark and light, where the cloud was peeling away above a now dazzling mirror surface below, its shadow in full retreat like an ebbing black tide.

"Majestic," said Seamus at length.

"Uh ha," agreed Tom, his eyes still firmly fixed on the departing amorphous nimbostratus.

"Shall we head out now," asked Lena, "while we've still got a few more hours of daylight left?"

"Let's go," said Seamus, ever up for a new experience.

Lena lived on a small complex of single story rental apartments owned by her parents, in a remote location on the western fringes of Tucson. Her apartment was next to the communal swimming pool, and on first impressions Tom thought that the house would appreciate a lick of paint and a good clean.

She had cobwebs and spiders in every corner. Cockroaches and other bugs were very much in residence and a Black Widow had set up home under her double bed frame. Her empathy with wildlife was something to be commended, for sure; but there are limits. Obviously she wouldn't hurt a fly, but did she have to live amongst them?

"Doesn't it bother ya' living with all these insects?" he asked. "I mean isn't a Black Widow spider something to be avoided?"

"I leave them alone, and they leave me alone, it's a symbiotic co-habitation," she smiled.

Loony, he thought.

The pool was nice and clean though. The boys wasted no time emptying their pockets and stripping off their shirts, before enthralling themselves with water gymnastics.

In her absence, Lena had donned a slinky white bikini, whilst unabashed Tori had stripped down to her bra and knickers, the result of which was hardly the material for a glossy mag.

The air was thick and damp, but the water delightful. Dark clouds were forming up again, throwing the odd spit of rain to tap at their faces.

Long-legged, articulated, Golden Paper Wasps started to make a nuisance of them selves, by coming down to the surface of the pool for a drink. Seamus proceeded to get animated towards them; evidently he was terrified.

"What's the matter mate, they won't 'urt ya'?" said Tom.

"Bad experience when I was a nipper," he said between dodges from the fearless predators. "I was in the park with me' nan one day, when one of them fuckers crawled up me' shorts and stung me on me left bollock. It swelled up to twice its normal size, and she 'ad to dab calamine lotion all over me' 'nads', it was most embarrassing."

The girls were laughing, though they only understood half of what Seamus was saying.

"ow old were you?" Tom was curiously amused.

"Twenty-two," he said with a grin. "No, I was about five or six, but I've been scared of 'em ever since, and these bastards are massive."

"What's a bollock? asked Tori intrigued.

Seamus barked a short laugh, "me' soft fruits," he said, "me' wee testis."

"Bollocks … that's a cute name."

"You wouldn't say that if you saw 'em," said Tom.

Tori visualised Seamus' reproductive organs and turned rather chartreuse.

The wasps were becoming a proper menace and spoiling the afternoon's fun, so before long, all four of them got out of the pool and went into Lena's house to dry off.

Tom and Seamus had to work that night, so they bid Lena farewell and took Tori back to her house, thanking them both for an enlightening day.

***

At the Haze, Seamus got friendly with a nurse called Annie, who decided that she'd like to take his pulse, inside her preferably.

Unfortunately for the charmer, both Lara and Caryn had also turned up, eager to spend time with their man.

Seamus not wishing to dispense with any of his harem, spent the rest of the night hiding from all three, whilst still trying to put in a shift at work and managing to give excuses, to each girl in passing, as to why he couldn't spend any length of time with them.

Incredibly, he managed to outfox all three, and although suspicious of his actions, not one girl sussed what was going on.

Tom and Pricey were of course caught in the middle of it and were barraged by the girls for Seamus' whereabouts, to which they sent them off on wild goose chases throughout the club. It was like a comedy sketch; girls would ask where he was, they would get directions, and then Seamus would poke his head round a storeroom door, or toilet cubicle and say, "'as she gone yet?"

Pricey and Tom thought it funny for a while, but it soon manifested as laborious and eventually each girl got fed up and left the club on their own. Seamus was sweating profusely by the end of the night, like he'd run round the block a few times; he probably had in distance to be fair, with all the hiding. But now he was quite relieved to be able to walk freely around the place unhindered.

"Phew," he said to Tom, "I can't 'ave too many nights like this."

"Jack a couple of 'em in, then."

"Yeah, I ought to, I ought to," he said, knowing that he wouldn't.

7
Big Soup

Six a.m. isn't a great time to be shaken awake, especially when you didn't get in until 3:00. The sounds were barely registering in his grey mush, but Tom listened to them with a mixture of joy, relief and trepidation.

Pricey was leaving, going off on tour with a reggae band, to handle their merchandising, and he didn't know when he would be coming back.

His actions were hurried and determined, stuffing a suitcase with his few belongings. Tom raised himself from slumber to watch his brother-in-law pack.

"You can keep anything I've left behind," said Pricey. "Give my apologies to Katie Pirelli but this gig was too good to miss."

"Sure," said a bleary-eyed Tom. "What do I tell Keira?"

"I'll talk to her. Look after ya' self," he said, then squeezed passed the door jamb and was gone.

Seamus didn't stir.

Tom laid his fuzzy head back onto the pillow, not yet ready to deal with the information just handed to him, and drifted back off to 'the land of nod'.

At around 11:00, he awoke again and sat up on the edge of his single bed staring at his tan lines. Most of him was the colour of antique pine furniture, which in this light looked more like muddy water. Across his groin he had a lily white strip where his swimming trunks had kept him British. The contrast was ridiculous, like someone had striped him with white emulsion.

He cleared his throat and woke sleeping beauty in the double bed.

"Rasta'," said Seamus without opening his eyes.

"Pricey's left," said Tom solemnly.

"Eh?" said Seamus, slowly jackknifing to a sitting position.

"Gone off touring with some band 'e met last night, escaped as quick as 'e could early this morning."

"Fuckin' 'ell," said Seamus, "we'll 'ave to make our own dinner now."

Tom grunted a small laugh. He was glad that the nuisance had gone, but he felt more vulnerable, like a layer of protection had been ripped away from their bubble, annoying though Pricey was, they had lost an ally.

At the club that night, a widely advertised gig was ready to take place, an artist KP was terribly excited over and proud to promote.

The much elevated Andrew Tosh, son of the legendry ex Wailer, Peter Tosh.

Andrew was appearing with his band, a group that included a number of well-known reggae musicians, and the buzz around the Haze was feverish.

Tom and Seamus strolled into the office at around 8:00 p.m. to find Katie Pirelli distraught on the end of the telephone.

"Where the fuck is Natty?" She snapped. "He's supposed to be making a guest appearance and nobody knows where he fucking is," she continued to rage. Her eyes were wild and her chest blotchy with the stress.

"'aven't seen 'im all day," said Tom. "Thought 'e was out early."

"Pricey's gone off too, d'ya' think they've gone together KP?" asked Seamus.

"Gone off … what do you mean, gone off? He should be at work tonight, where's he gone off to?"

Tom gave her Pricey's story.

"Bloody nice of him to leave us in the lurch," she said.

"You've got us KP," said Seamus. "We're like Sure anti-perspirant, we won't let ya' down."

KP giggled a little desperately. "I'll have to call Glen in to replace Tom-one, he won't be happy," she continued. "Can you two man the front door while I try and locate Natty? He's been getting more and more paranoid lately, thinks everybody's being racist towards him or something!"

"Racist?" said Seamus. "Nobody's been racist."

The boy's gave one another a quizzical stare.

"Listen; can you guys come round for Sunday lunch tomorrow? I've been meaning to ask you for a while and just haven't got round to it."

"Sure," said Tom, "love to."

"Okay, we'll speak later, see you in a bit," she said picking up the phone again.

The boys walked out to the front and the great snaking line of people eager to get in off the street. The reggae vibe was intensifying throughout town, as was a sea of red, gold, black and green coloured clothing adorned by the masses outside, with a generous splattering of ganja leaf motif.

"Gonna take a few quid tonight," deduced Seamus.

"They'll be a relaxed mob at least," answered Tom.

Seamus' smoke-laugh almost whistled a tune as he exhaled through his pursed lips.

Arty had hauled in a bigger PA system and the stage had been enlarged to accommodate Andrew's ten-piece band. The club was filled to capacity and the air was thick with herbal essence. A couple of patrol cars parked across the street speculating for Pima county police funds, and Tom and Seamus had crept inside for a free show, expecting a rather salubrious experience.

Disappointingly, the set was tuneless and tedious, without a single recognisable song; all played with unremarkable musicianship. 15min in, the boys slipped back outside, bringing sweet relief to their ears. The Wailers, this band certainly was not.

Towards the end of the evening Caryn turned up and cast Seamus under her spell, the boys finished their shift and Tom left the couple to each other. He drove home alone, saying that he'd pick up Seamus the next day from Caryn's before driving to KP's house for dinner. Seamus was smitten and willing to walk off into the unknown without a stitch on or a dime in his pocket; his adventures tended to be greater that way.

Caryn shared a house with some students close to the University on N. Euclid Avenue; Tom rolled the Chuggerbug to a stop at the kerbside and honked his horn. Ten minutes later, Seamus appeared from the shadows, clambering through the screen door wearing a borrowed T-shirt and feminine sunglasses.

He received a quizzical squint.

"'ave a good night?" Tom enquired of his radiant friend.

"Corr', mate," he replied, "ya' wouldn't believe it."

While they drove, Seamus recounted the previous night's antics. Apparently they'd stopped on the way back at Mamma's for a slice of Margherita pizza, stayed up talking until 4:00 a.m. then had a bath together, drenching the bathroom floor and at one point slipping in the tub where Caryn hit her head on the bath taps. Then they'd carried on romping in her bedroom, and for good measure they'd had another wrestle Just under an hour ago.

"Phew," said Seamus, "she's a little wild thing I tell ya', covered in 'air, like a little monkey … and she's given my little thing a right seeing to, it ain't 'alf sore."

Tom winced into a bit of a frown, he didn't want to know about the state of his friend's penis, and hairy girls were not his bag.

Arriving at KP's on E. Fairmount Street, they pulled onto the dirt drive in front of the house.

It was a square bungalow with a small front yard and a veranda porch. Knocking at the front door induced laboured wheezy barking from a dog in its senior years. Glen answered with a wide welcoming smile and introduced the boys to Inkie, the couple's greying black Labrador cross. She had a red and black bandana around her neck just like Huckleberry and smelt rather ripe. She tried to jump up at the boys to say hello, but her poor old rheumatic legs wouldn't allow it. She settled instead for the wet nose in the crotch approach.

Inside, the cool dark rooms were laced heavily with pungent skunk weed, above which the feint smell of a roast dinner raised its head. The hum of a water-cooled air-conditioning unit spoilt an Eric Clapton tune that was wafting in from the dining room. A big old fashioned couch covered in a multicoloured woollen throw, governed the living room that it shared with a rocking chair, a heavy dark wooden chest and a couple of framed venue posters promoting legendary bygone rock gigs, with whom their host had been acquainted.

Katie Pirelli was sat at her desk in a bedroom that doubled as an office. Through the open door, Tom could make out an organised mess of cassette tapes, CD's, flyers and paper work littering the desktop and the adjoining shelves and tables.

"Hi," sang KP tunefully through a fog of marijuana smoke.

She peered at them over the top of her gold rimmed glasses resting on the end of her nose, the screen of her computer reflected in the lenses. "I'll be with you in a minute boys, go into the dining room and have a drink, I'm just finishing up here."

"Right 'o KP," said Seamus.

The lads followed Glen and sat around a moderately-sized, winged dining table that could easily seat six but which had been set for four, each place laid with an oval cotton doily and a set of silver cutlery. The scene appeared quintessentially English, apart from the smell of pot.

In a corner stood a tall oak dresser with leaded-glass, through which peeked a collection of fine china and cut glass tableware that must have made its way across the Atlantic some years previously; obviously one toe was still on British soil.

"Beer anyone?" asked Glen.

"Be rude not to," said Tom light-heartedly.

"Yes please mate," added Seamus, "any chance of a spliff?"

Glen laughed, "Sure, I'll roll a little appetizer in a moment, we've got some real good sensimella just come up from across the border this morning. I think you'll like it," he beamed.

"Lovely," said Seamus like a satisfied council official.

KP came into the room, red-eyed and starry.

"Did you enjoy Andrew last night?"

"Umm," they lied, not wishing to pour water on her campfire, "'e was good."

"I saw some strange dancing going on in the audience," Seamus added, "there were some very odd people in that crowd."

KP laughed heartily, "There're a lot of old hippies here in town, moved out from LA after the 60s, LSD leaves an indelible mark on some people."

Glen brought in two open bottles of Budweiser. "There you go," he said placing them on the table in front of the boys.

"Nice Welsh dresser you 'ave there," Tom nodded towards the corner of the room.

KP turned to the antique, "I keep my friend Tim's ashes in there," she said solemnly. "He was a drummer, he killed himself with a drug overdose five years ago. I miss him dearly, but he lets me know he's still around .…"

Tom and Seamus stared at her slightly open-mouthed, thinking that LSD had left a mark here too.

"He knocks on the glass every now and then .…" she laughed, appreciating that the boys didn't believe her.

Glen had quietly constructed a masterpiece of a three skinner, and proudly handed it over to Seamus who thanked him before wasting no time in sparking it up.

Taking a long draw on it, he held the smoke down till it tightened his chest to the point where he thought his lungs might rupture, then he exhaled through pursed lips like a steam train pulling away from a station.

"Was it heroin?" Tom asked KP.

"Yeah, he struggled with it for years." Tears were welling up in her thread-veined eyes. "We thought he was clean, when suddenly we had a hysterical call in the middle of the night from his girlfriend; he was dead before the paramedics got to him."

A dull silence swamped the room.

"I'll fix the dinner," said Glen, and wandered out to the kitchen.

Seamus changed tack. "So what's 'appening with Natty KP?"

"He's over at Sonny's doing far too much cocaine and as paranoid as fuck. Arty's been over there to try and straighten him out, but he thinks everyone is against him. We've got the Reggae Shakedown next Saturday in the back-lot at the Haze; it's totally advertised, tickets sold, PA hired, we don't want him to balls this up, it'll cost us a packet," she said.

"We're looking forward to that," said Tom apprehensively.

"He thinks that you and Seamus are only interested in working together and not with him," she added.

"We'll always write songs together KP, we've done it for years, but while we're 'ere we're up for writing with Natty, 'e just hasn't been around lately."

"Are you sure?" asked KP, like a doubtful parent.

"Absolutely," said the boys together.

"Okay then, I'll see that the rehearsal goes ahead next Friday at Denny's house. There's gonna be ten of you in the band."

"Cool," said Seamus. "It'll sound great."

"Who's the ten?" asked Tom.

"The eight that practised at Arty's plus a percussionist called Junior Roots and another keyboard player called Har-I, they're mates of Denny's," she said.

"Should sound pretty full, what time's the rehearsal?"

"Around midday I think, I'll let you know."

Glen brought in the dinner; it was a full-on Sunday roast beef, including Yorkshire pudding and gravy.

"Look at this … look at this," said Seamus. "It looks gorgeous."

"I did the Yorkshires, Glen did everything else," she said.

Tom winked at Glen; "You 'ave trained 'im well KP."

The food was perfect; the boys got stuck in and for the time being forgot they were abroad. More beers were brought to the table and the conversation about the band continued. A tour was in the planning stages, starting this June in the Midwest, down to Florida then up the Eastern seaboard to Chicago, New York and finally Canada. Eight weeks in total; the lads would be on $300 a week each, plus expenses. Natty was also considering taking them to Japan and recording an album in Jamaica.

Abruptly, a distinct double-tap sounded on the glass doors of the Welsh dresser. Tom and Seamus spun round and stared at the thing; no one was in arms reach of the cabinet; nobody in this realm could possibly have touched it.

The hairs stood up on the back of Tom's neck and he and Seamus looked at each other in disbelief.

"Tim," said KP gleefully nodding sideways.

Apart from that spooky voice on the ghost train in Disneyland, Tom hadn't had any spiritual experience in his life, and he still didn't wholeheartedly believe what they had just heard, but something definitely knocked on that glass.

KP chuckled. "Don't worry," she said, "he's just joining in with the conversation."

Tom might have ordinarily blamed the cannabis, but tonight he hadn't smoked any, so he just had to accept it was real; weird, but real.

The night ended, the lads thanked their hosts for their hospitality and kissed KP goodnight before heading for the car.

"She's good to us," said Tom as they pulled off the drive.

"Like a mum," said Seamus, "mum number two."

"What d' ya' think of 'ole Tim wrapping on the glass door?"

"I s'pose they could 'ave rigged up something to fall onto it," said Seamus.

"Bit elaborate though, don't ya' think?" said Tom, "just to put the willies up us."

"Umm," said Seamus, "I'm just thinking about going on tour, that money'll come in 'andy, 'cause mine's quickly evaporating.

"'ow much you got left then?"

"'bout three 'undred."

"Shit, that ain't gonna last long, let's 'ope it all comes off, otherwise we're gonna have to get jobs or something,"

"Bugger that, I'm on 'oliday," said Seamus, "If this don't work out with Natty, we'll get our own gigs, there's plenty of venues in town. Look at Mystic Lights, they're gigging nearly every night. Jah will find a way Rasta', nah take me home."

"Y' man," said Tom accelerating down Fairmount.

***

The day of the rehearsal came around; Natty had been considerably withdrawn all week, hanging out in his bedroom or by the pool on his own. The lads had tried to make conversation at mealtimes but he would only give short replies and then only relating to the music and the upcoming gig. It was hard work, so Tom and Seamus went out a lot, stealing petrol and photographs; they weren't even bothering to buy soft drinks at the gas station shops any more, they'd just pull up to the pumps, fill the tank and drive off. It was ludicrously easy, as long as they chose a different forecourt each time.

Denny's house was a whitewashed wooden shiplap affair with a low sloping grey shingle roof, not too far from Sonny's place. It had a baggy chainlink fence around a savannah of unkempt tall grass, in which three small children were playing. His wife Pepa was a singer herself and didn't mind in the slightest a large band setting up in her house.

In a vacant side room Arty had set up a PA system and half a dozen mikes on stands; the band members were arriving one by one and piling in their gear. Last on the scene were Natty and the boys.

After short introductions to the new fellows, Natty produced a set list of fifteen songs most of which the band knew. But Har-I, a short and pungent white rasta from Chicago with filthy blonde dreads down to his backside, dressed in a grubby pair of blue dungarees with a stained white t-shirt, and Junior Roots, a lanky nineteen-year-old Rastafarian wearing a long Bob Marley print string vest, red silk track suit bottoms and an oversized Jamaican Tam, were not very proficient musicians. The tunes kept breaking down, having to be re-started over and over again. It was going to be an extremely long afternoon and it was tremendously hot in there, made ten times worse by the extraordinary pursuit of every band member to roll a spliff at the completion of each song and smoke the whole thing to themselves. With the windows and doors shut it was like playing in the heart of a bonfire, so Tom escaped out into the clean air of the garden ahead of a rolling ball of smoke that could have alerted the fire department a mile away.

He was passively stoned and woolly-headed enough, so god knows how mellow the other guys were, but at least Natty was being more congenial, even happy for a change.

***

Saturday slipped into the early evening, pulling with it a thermal blanket over the town. It had been the hottest day of the year so far and the still air felt contained without a wisp of movement. The lads had swum, showered and dressed for the gig, only to feel like jumping back into the pool again; they were stifled and sticky like two sticks of sweating dynamite.

Eventually they left for The Haze with Natty who was as cool as a refrigerated coconut and smelt like one too. The car journey brought some relief from the heat, the rush of warm air over bare arms being better than no air at all. Natty was back to his usual smiley self again. This is what he lived for; this was his environment being driven to a gig, a great sounding band set up and waiting for him; PA, lights, outdoor stage, a large appreciative crowd and plenty ganja. Sublime. He closed his eyes and leaned his head back against the seat, his long dreadlocks dancing out the window like unfurled flags; he thanked Jah.

Arty had been busy all week setting up a temporary stage against the rear wall of the Purple Haze's backyard, and hired in a massive sound system that Scorpion was making ample use of. The reggae vibes were thumping out over the top of the building when the lads drove by. No parking spaces could be found, forcing them to abandon the car three blocks away and walk in.

Four hundred tickets had been sold and the queue to get into the club snaked a couple of hundred metres up 4th Avenue.

The boys went round the back and slipped in courtesy of Sean Adams on the gate.

"Tradesmen's entrance tonight," said Sean with a big rosy-cheeked smile.

"Good trade to be in though, Sean," said Seamus in cheeky response.

Tom just smiled, he was loving the occasion; this felt like the beginning of something big, something that he'd been building up to for his whole adult life. Years of practice, recording demos, unpaid gigs, writing songs, endless rehearsals, all honed in one direction; a career in the music business, fortune and fame, and this appeared to be the start of it. He felt heady and watery-eyed from the adrenalin, almost in a dream, like Pricey had suggested.

The whole gang were here, keen to see this project a success, none more so than KP who was a ball of stress and too flustered to give the boys a friendly greeting. Tom felt a little passed over, but realised that she had a lot on her plate tonight.

Tucson Kate introduced her children to the boys. "Hi," she said, "this is Holly and this is Josh."

The boys responded in kind. Josh was 16, a good looking lad with black hair and olive skin who exemplified his Mexican heritage; he was soft spoken and polite. Holly was 18, a shade heavier than she should have been; she had a round face and intelligent, deep brown eyes, wild bleached blonde hair that was bolstered by copious amounts of lacquer and an infectious giggle. She was into hard rock music so considered herself a bit misplaced at this gig, yet she was here to support the cause.

Seamus was already up on stage, chatting with Denny Kirk.

"Gotta go set up," said Tom, "I'll see you later."

Holly giggled.

The backline amps had been set in place for them; all they needed to do was plug in their guitars and play. Unfortunately Tom had been allocated a place next to Stinky Har-I, who was still in the same clothes as yesterday but had grown in fragrance.

"It's gonna sound bad, man," he said to Tom glassy eyed, in a trance-like state.

Not as bad as you smell, thought Tom in response. "I reckon you're right," he said.

Seamus looked over at Tom and screwed his face up in recognition of a stink; Tom nodded in agreement.

They went through a sound check to get the levels right. Everyone felt comfortable with their sound, and then they performed a number with only one 'rewind' to get the vocal levels higher in the stage monitors. The engineers were happy, the band was happy, Natty was happy.

"We're a happy family, sim," he said over the mike.

"Ire," responded the band.

At 9:00 p.m., the hordes were let in, soon filling The Haze to capacity. The band was in one of the rehearsal rooms chilling and having a smoke, Natty was meddling in a corner with some sniff. Carl Strawberry had brought along his girlfriend Poppy. The contrast between the two was astounding; he was a big, big black man of at least 35 st. and she was this tiny, slim Jewish girl of about 98 lbs. How they got it on in the bedroom was anyone's guess, but Tom supposed that she must have always ridden on top for fear of him squashing her like a fist on a grape. He pictured a matchstick straddling a Mars bar.

Caryn knocked on the rehearsal door and was let in; through the smog she found Seamus, who was surprised but pleased to see her. As luck would have it Lara couldn't make it tonight, so he could relax and enjoy the gig.

The band were called to the stage and snaked their way through the audience amidst cheers and clapping, Tom's heart was pounding fast, he wasn't nervous, just pumped.

Carl clicked out the time on his sticks and the band struck up with *True Love Never Dies*, they looped the chorus for 24 bars until Natty finally danced his way on stage to a rapturous noise from the bopping crowd.

Unusual gyrating was manifesting all over the yard, and Seamus and Tom couldn't help but focus on the more obscure amongst them. Grubby hippies and squalid new-age traveller types were gesticulating weirdly out of time to the music. They were obviously off of their faces, but nobody in the crowd was the least bit bothered, everybody was just doing their thing.

That tune finished to more applause and Natty introduced the next number, a new song. "Now this song called, *Life is Strange*," he said, in his thick Jamaican accent.

Carl clicked and rolled the number in. But it went horribly wrong, Har-I was playing a different song to the rest of the band and Junior Roots was all over the place. Natty glared round at the two new boys, put his hand up and reeled in the song. "Rewind, reel and come again!" he shouted. Denny was over and yelling the chords out to Har-I while Carl clicked in again. This time he got it right but a plastic key from his Yamaha broke off and sprang into the audience, who unknowingly trampled it into the dust. This ruined Har-I, his rhythm was now appalling, the sound on stage a complete mess. Tom couldn't distinguish his own chord playing from the other two, so just resorted to skanking on muted strings, Natty, frustrated with the vibe, forgot the lyrics, while Denny, getting more and more embarrassed with the whole affair, in desperation, tried to cover with an improvised guitar solo that sounded like he was wearing woollen mittens.

It was cringingly awful, but the crowd were unperturbed and carried on dancing. Seamus leaned over to Tom and shouted "they'll dance to anything this lot!"

Tom sniggered to himself knowing that his mate was spot on with his assessment.

Thankfully the tune was quickly wound up; Tom could hear Denny berating Junior and Har-I, "Bumberclart," he was saying, "me never been so embarrassed on stage, get it right ya

Rarsclart or ya'll never play with dis band again, sim." All of this, while Natty called up the next song.

"Now this song called … *Break down the Wall* … *of a Babylon* sim."

Denny's fury must have done the trick because the rest of the tunes ran through without a hitch and the stoned mob were, one nation under a leaf; contented.

The set ended and Scorpion struck up with a reggae disco. The band went backstage, congratulating each other, high-fiving and special handshaking. KP came in, over the moon, followed by Arty who was almost drooling with delight.

"Ya'll did great," he said, "that's the dress rehearsal out of the way—get ready for the tour."

"Yes I," they replied, "bring it on."

Tom was wondering where Rene might be tonight, why wasn't she here; he could do with someone to relate to. He casually asked KP in passing without appearing overly concerned.

"Oh, she's gone back home to Idaho, she's been missing her mum."

Tom knew better, his heart sank; he was hardly in love, but he had enjoyed the affection they'd shared, and he would miss that, so he was rocked by her leaving and more than a little sad.

"Oh dear," he said, "I bet Arty's upset."

"Not really, they weren't getting on anyway," she said, "it's for the best."

Tom suddenly felt like a fly on the wall, looking down on the party. Everyone was having a good time, Seamus was deep into Caryn and Natty was flying on nose candy. He found himself alone again. Grabbing a cold Rollin Rock he left the rehearsal room and meandered through the sweaty mass of boggling stone heads looking for a friendly face; he found one in the form of Tucson Kate, her jolly toothy smile beamed at him across the yard and he went over to where she was swaying in a big summer dress.

"Tom," she said, "I'd like you to meet Chad, he's staying with us for a while, he's a great drummer. I think you boys should hook up together and make some music."

Kate Norton was very intuitive; she carried this expression with her that made you think she knew something that you didn't. She was an empath, able to see emanating auras, and was satisfied she could tell your state of mind just by the colour you were radiating.

Chad was around 23-years-old, of the same stature as Tom, with short straight blonde hair and big smiley blue eyes. He was from Austin, Texas; an all-American boy, Tom liked him immediately. Chad was studying Sleep Deprivation at the U of A, had a part time job at a racquet club and was itching to join a band. Although touring with Natty Dread was high on the agenda right now, Tom said he could arrange a jam session with him and Seamus here at the club during the week; he just had to clear it with KP.

"Cool," said Chad "would you like another beer?"

"Sure," said Tom, "I'm drier than Death Valley."

***

The following Tuesday night, the lads had nothing to do. The sunset that evening had been formidable, the sky had turned blood red after the sun descended, replaced by a huge orange moon silhouetting the jagged charcoal mountains. Tom marvelled at the spectacle from a pool chair as the sky slowly shifted from purple into indigo, then the deepest black bejewelled curtain to decorate the heavens. He inhaled long and deep, it felt marvellous.

Seamus joined him on the patio.

"Look at all them stars," said Tom, his head fully tilted back.

"Majestic," said Seamus blowing smoke skyward and clouding the view. "There's a TV crew down at the Tap Room in Club Congress tonight, wanna go down and get on the telly?"

"What they doing?"

"Ah just Channel 34 doing a thing called Bar Talk, I think they set up a camera in the corner and film whoever turns up. I said we'd meet Jennifer there; it'll be a laugh."

"Sounds like a plan," said Tom, "let's go."

The Congress Hotel occupies the corner of E Congress Street in downtown Tucson. It was built in 1919 and is famous for being the respite of gang members associated with the notorious bank robber John Dillinger. The entire gang, including their boss, were captured in town in 1934, trying and failing miserably to keep a low profile.

Fashioned still in 1920's style, it was groaning with memorabilia, a step back in time, but had considered by some to be the best taproom in the country.

The bar was full to the gills, unusual for a Tuesday night. The TV crew consisted of a cameraman, a producer and a female presenter called Sophie.

The show was supposed to be a socio/documentary on the comings and goings of the patrons of a drinking hole, but the bartender, a skeletal balding jerk with a big nose by the name of Dan, thought that it was his one-man show.

Jennifer was perched inside a mahogany table booth with Carlos the producer, who she knew, nursing a swollen thumb that she was soaking in a glass of ice water.

The camera focussed on her, and Sophie asked her what had happened.

"I've come over here to avoid you lot," she said in her best Queen's English. "You were filming over there and I didn't want your camera in my face."

"But you have a story to tell," said Sophie, "and an enquiring mind wants to know."

"Thirty-five years of self-abuse, that's the story," replied Jennifer. "No, I shut my thumb in a car door earlier this evening and now I'm trying to get it drunk."

Sophie cackled and the camera panned round to the working side of the bar where Dan was making a martinI.

"You want olives and lemon?" he was saying to a female customer. "Oh, okay." Dan shook the cocktail and poured out the drink while the camera moved left and focussed on the centre of the bar where Sophie had honed in on Seamus and Tom.

Their fresh bronzed faces and colourful patterned shirts stood out a mile from the dowdy barflies and cowboys who sat on stools down the long bar, swigging from bottles of Bud and smoking Marlborough cigarettes.

"Can I borrow fifty cents?" Seamus asked Sophie unabashed.

"Sure," she said and reached in her jeans pocket to produce some loose change.

"'ere's a quick way to make fifty cents," he said winking at the camera. "'ow does a one-armed man count his change?"

"I don't know?" said Sophie intrigued.

"I'll show you," he said, and turned his back on her, slipping his arm down inside his jeans and undoing his fly.

Sophie turned to the camera with her mouth fully open as Seamus turned back protruding a finger through his zipper hole that sorted through the change cupped in his other hand.

Tom was cracking up between sips of beer while Sophie's shoulders bobbed up and down with laughter. Seamus kept the change.

"I've got one for ya'," said Tom.

Sophie turned the mike on him.

He told the joke about the paper cowboy being wanted for rustling, which had her in hysterics, hardly able to contain herself; it was a new joke back then.

Seamus followed up with, "What do ya' call an antelope with no eyes? No idea." At which point she became breathless.

The camera then panned back to a disgruntled Dan, who had lost the spotlight and his mike connection, and was pacing the length of the bar shouting, "Is this on … is this on?"

The conversation continued with the boys and Sophie who was captivated by the charismatic Englishmen, while Dan grappled with his cable connection.

"Where are you from?" Sophie asked through her tears.

"Where d' ya' think we're from?" challenged Seamus, with a cheeky grin.

"Australia?" she proffered.

Both boys barked out a laugh, amused at the idiocy of the common misconception.

Tom assumed an antipodean guise. "Yes, we are here on a boomerang throwing contest."

"I threw my boomerang and it never came back," added Seamus. "We're kangaroos, and we've hopped all the way from Australia."

"No, we're from Texas," said Tom confusing Sophie completely, she now didn't know what to believe.

"No, we're true Brits," said Seamus most sincerely. "'e's from a little place called Watford, sixteen miles north of London and so am I; we're a couple of corgis."

"Corgis, what's a corgi?" asked a girl at the bar.

"Are those corgis?" said Dan pointing at the boys beers and wanting to get in on the action.

Seamus took offence and shouted him down. "I'm just trying to explain where we're from and you've interrupted," he said.

Dan sulked off.

"Come on, are those accents for real?" said Sophie.

The girl at the bar decided to use a foolproof check to see if someone was faking an accent or not. Unbeknownst to Tom and Seamus some unscrupulous individuals would fabricate an English accent to get into the pants of impressionable young American girls.

Tom and Seamus were just being themselves.

The girl explained knowledgeably, "Someone is faking it if they make a two-syllable word out of a one-syllable word and a one-syllable word out of a two-syllable word."

"Like Bucking-ham palace?" said Seamus with a sarcastic mid-western accent.

The soundtrack faded back to Dan who had nothing to say, so the camera scanned the bar and focussed on a beautiful girl ordering a drink. She looked very much like a young Brooke Shields, only with almond-shaped eyes.

Tom had no idea at this moment that she would later become his girlfriend; her name was Gretchen, and he hadn't even noticed her.

The action shifted back to the boys who were now advertising for a bass player and a keyboard player by holding up a quickly penned telephone number on a sheet of paper.

Sophie said, "Look at these wholesome faces, how could you not want to play with these guys?"

Seamus and Tom were roaring with laughter.

"I love it 'ere," said Seamus to camera. "You can lie in bed until two o'clock in the afternoon, do nothing and then go back to bed again, it's great."

Sophie's shoulders jitterbugged again as the camera faded away.

Some time later, after the programme had gone off air, Jennifer introduced the boys to a couple of girls she had met in the lobby. They were 18, confident and not bad looking, but heavily plastered in make-up. Being underage for the licensing laws, the grown-ups had to get the drinks in. Even so, the girls coughed up their fair share for a round. After a few, Jennifer suddenly became quite tearful and was mumbling about being very old and unattractive. She wanted Seamus to take her home.

Doing the gentlemanly thing, he obliged, leaving the girls in the capable hands of a now atrociously drunk Tom.

They were from Phoenix, just down for a few nights and staying upstairs in the hotel. Their names were Carly and Tasha, and had been friends all of their short lives. They drank really fast, and Tom had trouble keeping up with them. He certainly had them entertained with his odd wit and his intoxicating accent and the drunker he got, the more attractive they became; even though he was of a different generation, it didn't seem to matter anymore.

Seamus arrived back after a short while, to find all three of them in raptures of laughter.

"'ow was she?" Tom enquired.

"She wanted me to stay the night, I 'ad to put 'er to bed, she was off 'er face. What are you lot on, I'll 'ave a pint of that?" said Seamus.

"Grab a beer mate, the girls 'ave kindly offered to show us around their room upstairs," slurred Tom unsteadily.

It was around midnight and the bar had almost emptied, save for a redneck who had a striking resemblance to Chewbacca, sucking on a bottle of Michelob at the end of the bar, his long curving moustache arced around his cheeks and became one with his bushy, rusty sideburns.

Dan the bartender served Seamus another Budweiser, glad to see the back of the supercilious Englishmen as they meandered out of the bar towards the hotel stairway.

A red patterned carpet fixed with highly polished Victorian stair rods cascaded down from the upper floors on a lavish lacquered wooden staircase. The party stumbled up it to the 2 nd floor where the thick carpet carried its theme right along the landing, contrasting the dark panelled walls and room doors.

Inside the girls' room, one could be forgiven for thinking that you'd stumbled into a silent movie; the décor was very much of that era. It had twin beds neatly dressed with thick red woollen bedspreads, flock wallpaper, heavy draped curtains and frilly lampshades on the stands. The net curtains were shifting softly with a light breeze and outside, red and yellow neon signs provided just enough illumination to see where you were going. An en-suite bathroom hid behind a door in the middle of the back wall.

Seamus noticed four cans of Heinz Big Soup on the bedside table and inquired as to why they were there.

"I love Big Soup," said Carly, "and it's cheaper than the restaurant."

"What … you eat it cold?" asked Tom.

"Uh ha," she chirped.

Tasha closed the drapes, plunging the room into darkness. All four of them sat on the beds, boys on one, girls on the other.

Tom's head swam, who's gonna make the first move? Carly was the prettier girl but Tasha looked the more likely out of the two of them to give up the goods so he plumped for her.

Moving over to her bed he found her hand and held it, draping his arm over her shoulder and finding her head he pulled it gently towards his. Their lips met and unexpectedly an inexperienced tongue pierced his mouth and wiggled around like a hot writhing snake.

He heard Seamus delve into action with Carly, who had been pulled over to the opposing bed. They crashed into the stack of soup tins on the bedside table sending them thumping to the floor, spilling the contents of a half consumed tin onto the carpet which Seamus then knelt in. "Shit," he said to her giggles.

Tom managed to calm the squirming serpent in his mouth, sensually plying the girl with seduction. His right hand delicately fondled her breasts on top of her shirt, before unfastening the buttons one by one, while her hand found its way to his bulging phallus and rubbed at it through his jeans, unfortunately, like she was scrubbing a stained carpet.

Gasps and whispers could be heard from the other bed mixed with a lot of muffled movement, until the bathroom door cracked open and Seamus and Carly slipped inside. Then Tom heard the sound of the shower running and cursed the choice that he had made, for Seamus it seemed had got the better deal, and with the prettier girl.

But to the job in hand, he unclipped Tasha's front loading bra and caressed her erect rosebud nipples one at a time, kissing her neck and making his way to her chest as she arched her back in anticipation. He sucked her nipples making her moan and bite her bottom lip while his hand worked on the crotch of her jeans. He undid the top button and released the zipper, then slid his hand into her cotton panties cupping the soft mound of pubic hair and the sodden hot lips that rose off the bed to meet him, the shielded malleable flesh, velvety and warm and demanding to be exploited.

He stopped kissing her and knelt upright, enabling him to grab a hold of the top of her jeans and pull them down. She helped him by twisting out of the tight fitting material and then took off her knickers herself, letting them fall to the floor.

Tom deftly took his own jeans and pants off and they lay side by side, half naked and almost blind in the darkness. He pulled her towards him feeling her supple little bottom in his hands which pressed his dick firmly into her belly. They rolled over so that she was on her back and she parted her legs so that Tom fell between them, then she wrapped her arms around him tight like a woman hanging on for dear life.

He entered her slowly feeling a modicum of resistance, he'd felt this opposition before and he couldn't believe his bad luck. She gave a muted cry of pain and contorted her body beneath him

"Oh, my god," she said.

"Are you a virgin?" Tom whispered.

"Ah ha," she replied, desperate for breath.

Tom felt himself deflate a little inside her. "Do you want me to stop?"

"No," she said, "carry on."

Tom felt reluctant for fear of hurting her. "Are you sure?"

"Ah ha, I want you to …."

A sudden rush of pride brought on by a girl that actually wanted him to pop her cherry sent his testosterone levels sky high, he swelled again and she felt it.

"Okay," he said, "I'll be gentle."

He moved his hips tentatively, every thrust a burning painful stretch of taught elastic flesh and she whimpered beneath him, her eyes screwed up tightly, her lips pursed shut, every muscle contracted, braced against the hurting.

It would soon be over, she kept telling herself, then she'd be a woman at last; it would soon be over. But it seemed to last an eternity, a heavy man squashing the air out of her lungs with a heat hotter than a furnace, sweat adhering them together and her friend in the bathroom doing god knows what. Then she felt it, a poker-hot explosion deep in her belly that made her catch a breath.

He exhaled a short sigh and stopped moving, his world dizzy for a few seconds, his heart pounding frantically, till he took a massive breath and held it briefly before slowly releasing the air like a punctured beach ball.

He kissed her on the forehead and retracted from within her, causing a sudden chill between her legs where he had once been. The withdrawal had stopped the rupture she felt inside, but an ache still remained, she hadn't enjoyed it at all, but she felt pleased, content that it was finally dealt with.

Tom lay still for a while, on his back, she nestled tightly beside him not daring to move an inch, the sound of the shower still splattering in the next room.

What have I just done? he thought. I came inside her, fucking idiot. "Are you on the pill?" he asked, as tenderly as he might.

"Uh ha," she said, "I take them to regulate my periods; have done since I was thirteen." She sat up and sniffed away a forming tear.

Tom rubbed her back, feeling her emotion. He sat up too and fumbled around the floor searching for his pants and jeans; he secured them, and awkwardly dressed himself

Tasha did likewise then sat back down again.

The shower stopped and the door peeled back, igniting the gloomy bedroom with piecing white light.

Seamus and Carly bundled in, wrapped in standard hotel gratuity towels, dripping wet and steaming. They bounced onto the bed laughing and giggling to themselves. They'd obviously had the better time of it.

"Phew," exclaimed Seamus, "that was majestic."

Carly giggled again.

"Come on mate, get dressed, we better be going and give these girls some sleep."

"Two minutes," said Seamus, "I'll be two minutes." He disappeared back into the bathroom.

As the boys clambered down the staircase, Seamus gabbled joyously of his acrobatic performance in the shower cubicle.

"She's a little devil," he said, "all over me like a rash, I didn't need to make any moves on 'er, she sucked me dick like 'er life depended on it, under the water, I don't know how she carried on breathing. I think it was the best shag I've ever 'ad. 'ow did you get on?"

Tom told him, they went quiet for a while.

They'd promised to see the girls tomorrow, though how they would feel in the light of a new day might be a different thing.

Returning to the Congress mid-morning, part intrigued, part concerned, the boys found the girls in the lobby phone booth, and were rocked by the difference in their appearance.

Gone were the made-up faces and big hair, the girls looked fresher and far more casual than the night before, more attractive in fact.

Tasha was acting elusive and Carly had simmered down somewhat.

Tom thought they were probably facing hangovers but the reality was quite something else.

The girls half expected to never see the boys again, and so were a little surprised when they'd showed up.

Carly finished her phone call; it was 11:00 a.m., scorching hot, and the boys had all day to do nothing.

"What d' ya' want to do," asked Seamus.

"Um, get something to eat? We're really hungry," Tasha was staring into the middle distance. "But we have no more money!"

Tom imagined that she was probably embarrassed to be in his company after what had transpired last night. She might also be feeling a little destitute and at the boys' mercy. He hoped that he could make the situation lighter with some buoyant conversation.

"Don't worry, we'll buy lunch," he said rather gallantly, seeing that he was spending Seamus' holiday money.

"Thank you," they said in monotone unison, lacking sincerity and chewing gum vacantly.

Tom drove them to a little favourite of theirs, a cool shady cafe on 4th Avenue called The Egg Garden; it had discrete booths and served up the best breakfasts in town. The house special came with home fries, an omelette of your choice and a toasted English muffin. They also managed to brew up a decent cup of tea.

Over breakfast, the girls spilled the beans on why they were here in Tucson.

Tom nearly dropped his Lipton's.

The girls weren't 18, they were 16 and they had run away from home.

Seamus paused from eating for a moment to digest what he had just heard. Both boys were reeling inside, no longer wishing to be involved with these two, but also feeling an alien responsibility for their wellbeing; almost like adults in fact.

An enjoyable breakfast turned sour with the invading taint of paedophilia. Uncertain of the legal age of consent here in Arizona, they pondered if these two were jailbait? Last night abruptly appeared like a huge mistake. A rewind button would come in very handy right now.

"Why 'ave ya' run away?" enquired Tom hoping to untangle the ball of knots manifesting in his mind.

Carly spoke. "I don't get along with my stepdad too well, he's forever grounding me and I hate school and I hate Scottsdale, and I hate my stepbrother, and I just had to get away. Tasha came with me because her boyfriend is really abusive."

Tasha looked visibly guilty, like she had been the one who had instigated the whole deal.

"Does anybody know you're 'ere?" he asked.

"Only my friend, Bernice," said Carly. "I spoke to her this morning."

"Did you mention us?" asked Seamus.

"No," she sang, looking down at her food. Seamus knew that she'd lied. These two were professionals at it, and he couldn't believe another word they said.

"We're gonna go to the bathroom," said Tasha scanning the restaurant for the Ladies. "Be back in a minute."

They obviously were going for a confab, which gave the boys perfect opportunity to discuss exactly what they were going to do with them.

"Fuckin' 'ell, we're facin' nick 'ere if they run to the 'Old Bill'," said Tom crapping his pants.

Seamus lit a cigarette and chewed his bottom lip.

"We've gotta get rid of 'em as soon as," continued Tom.

By the time the girls came back it had been settled. Seamus was going to pay for them to stay another night in a motel, somewhere far away from where the boys lived. They would promise to call them later in the evening, but that was the end of the line. This is where they washed their hands of them. As long as the girls didn't squeal to the cops the boys would be off the map. A little heartless perhaps, but they really couldn't afford to get any more involved with this messy situation.

They chose a bleak, no frills motel on Miracle Mile, paid the unconcerned receptionist upfront for one night in a twin-bed room, and took the girls and their bags into the inglorious shell.

"That's the most expensive shag I've ever 'ad to pay for," said Seamus on the drive home.

"Could've been a lot dearer mate," concluded Tom.

8
Altered States

"Natty's moved out," announced Arty as the boys arrived home.

"What?" said Tom astounded.

"Gone back to Connecticut, quit, thrown in the towel, finished."

Arty's dark eyes had lost their lustre, he was thoroughly pissed off.

"Why?" asked Seamus wondering if it had anything to do with them.

Arty sucked in some drool that had gathered in his lower jaw with a short rasping sound. "Ya'll ain't to blame," he said, "He just never settled in, and the Mary Jane was fucking with his mind. So he's broke the contract. Now we've gotta try and sue his ass, get some of our investment back!"

A look of bewilderment smudged across the bon vivant boys' faces. What the hell were they going to do now, with only a hundred bucks between them, no job and no prospect of a tour? Their stay in the US of A looked to be stunted at best, and worst of all they had lost another friend.

Tom suddenly felt utterly vulnerable. "Can we carry on living 'ere?"

"For the time being, as long as ya'll keep working at The Haze, but I'm considering giving up the lease, it's costing too much to run it on my own," Arty confessed.

The reality check was a nasty pill to swallow, but at least the boys weren't in immediate danger of being thrown out onto the street; they had some grace in order to find work and a place to stay, but where to start?

"Thanks Art," said Seamus, "we appreciate it mate. Oh by the way," he said, randomly changing direction. "What's the legal age of consent 'ere in the States?"

Arty gave him a probing quizzical stare, "Why, what ya'll been up to?" he asked proffering his toothy grin.

"Just covering all bases," replied Seamus playfully.

"It's eighteen here in Arizona, you stay above that ya' hear, otherwise ya'll be prison pussy."

Seamus barked a small laugh. "I'll remember that," he said faking innocence.

***

Two days later the lads were in Workshop Music & Sound, a music store on Speedway. Seamus was buying strings for his Stratocaster and Tom was fiddling with various guitars on the racks.

The assistant in charge, was a diminutive Hispanic man, all of four-foot tall; not a dwarf, just a miniature person in proportion to his own size.

His name tag labelled him Ben Lucero; he was astride an amp and playing some intricate bass lines. Serving customers with his Ibanez slung across his knee slapping out ultra fast riffs and smiling at his own ability, he was a confident little gnome who took an instant interest in the Brit invasion of his shop.

Tom and Seamus were blown away by Ben's competence and asked him if he would like to jam with them one evening after work.

They settled on the following Monday evening, because the lads had to work at the club over the weekend and Ben didn't do Sundays; he was a devout Christian.

Tom pondered over his and Seamus' heathen life style for five minutes and wondered how Ben would fit in, but if anyone wanted to live a chaste, honest, virtuous, pious existence, then that was their problem; for now, they'd let him play bass with them.

Ben arrived at Arty's house bang on 6:30 p.m. and brought along with him a miniscule practice bass amp. They set up in the band room and jammed three or four tunes the boys had written. Ben liked the funky-pop vibe and laid down some driving grooves to compliment the chord structures. Seamus loved the wee guy's style and all three of them agreed to take it a step further and book some proper rehearsal time.

"I know a drummer," exclaimed Tom out of the blue. "I'd forgotten all about 'im. Maybe 'e'll come along to a rehearsal."

It surprised Seamus. "'ow do ya' know 'im then?"

"I met 'im last week after the gig, 'is name's Chad, lives with Tucson Kate."

"Brilliant," said Seamus, "give 'im a shout, what's 'e into?"

"He mentioned some names, but I've never 'eard of 'em. 'e seems alright, I'll give 'im a bell later."

Ben was enthralled by Brit speak, his ample lips drew back revealing a perfect broad white toothed smile. "You guys are off the scale," he said.

"Off 'ome if we don't find jobs," replied Seamus necking a cold beer.

The boys told Ben of their desperate money situation. The look of concern aged Ben's face for a moment, before he had an idea. He knew a man who might be able to help; he would get back to them.

The doorbell rang, it was Lara. She bounced in with her usual effervescence, all teeth, hair and suffocating perfume.

Ben made his exit and Tom went off to phone Chad, leaving Seamus to his feast of flesh.

Chad was pleased to hear from the Englishman and keen to rehearse. Arty said they could use the backroom of The Haze on Saturday afternoon, which was fine with Ben because he only worked at the store in the morning.

***

A Heavy Rock Friday night at the club featuring local band The Sidewinders, was taking its toll on the boys as they pushed their trolley around Fry's supermarket on Saturday morning. They'd had limited sleep and were yawning through the aisles spending the last of Seamus' cash on a week's supply of groceries.

The usual trick worked at the till with two wallets of developed film and on the way home they drove off without paying for another tank of petrol from a Circle K filling station.

They sat in sweltering silence, the open windows making little difference to the temperature within the car. Tom drove on autopilot, his mind attempting to focus on their future instead of concentrating on the road ahead. A blank canvas unfurled in front of him with not a single glimpse of what lay in store, just an endless white monoscape where the immediate surroundings petered out and nothing began. His head felt like it was being mummified; he tried to breathe but couldn't inhale. His lungs were refusing to function, panic gripping his throat, the muscles constricting between his eyes and forehead.

"Red light Tom … Tom!" shouted Seamus piercing the muffled pressure in his friend's ears.

Tom reacted instinctively and brought the car to an abrupt halt.

The fright snapped him back to the present where he was he able to gulp some air and clear his mind.

"Didn't ya see it, Rasta'?" asked Seamus.

"No, I was daydreaming. How much cash you got left, mate?" he said, changing the subject. He wanted to clarify their situation.

"A dollar," said Seamus resignedly.

"One dollar—you've got one dollar left?"

"Yep," said his mate.

The lights turned green and Tom accelerated away.

Both of them looked at each other and started to laugh, the absurdity of their circumstance suddenly seemed ridiculous.

"What the fuck are we gonna do?" asked Tom making a rueful surrender.

"'ave you seen Midnight Cowboy?" asked Seamus.

"I ain't suckin' anyone's cock! I'd rather swim home."

Seamus laughed mischievously through his cigarette smoke. "Don't worry Ras' some ting will turn up," he said imitating Natty. "Trus' the I."

The backroom of The Haze was treated like a junk/storage room. It had a large window on the rear wall that overlooked the yard, purple unkempt carpet on the floor, stacks of cardboard boxes and discarded equipment piled against two of the whitewashed walls.

Sean Adams, who seemed to be living amongst this disarray, let the boys in.

"Hey guys, good to see ya," he said in his deep croaky resonating voice. "Ya' buddy's already out back, come on through."

Chad had got there early, had set up his kit up by the partition wall and was adjusting the cymbal stands as the boys walked in.

"Hey, guys," he said through a nervous smile, "How's it hanging?" He came around from his kit to greet them with an outstretched hand.

Tom introduced his best mate, who bonded instantly with the drummer, in a way that is ostensibly unique to Seamus.

"Pleased to meet you," said Chad, his blue-eyed smiley face wrinkled with glee. "How's it going?"

"Not too, too bad," Seamus said from his weary chops.

"Great playing the other night by the way, I had a blast! You wanna wait for the bass player to arrive, go through some stuff now, or have a drink, d', d', d', der, da, da, da, dar?" asked Chad singing the last phrases like the missing lyrics to a song.

Seamus yawned. "I didn't know what I was doing really; just bluffing my way through it, but the crowd seemed to love it. Erm, I think we'll set up the gear first and then maybe grab a pint of Jolt," he said wheeling his amp in opposite Chad's drums. "That's a nice kit you 'ave there, mate. Are those electronic pads?"

"Yeah, it's a Roland Octopad; it has more than a hundred studio samples stored in it. I can use it to trigger another sound source, or sample my own sounds, d', d', d' der, da, da, da, dar."

"Nice." Seamus sparked up a single skinner.

"What we gonna sing through?" asked Tom scanning the walls for equipment.

Sean Adams intervened. "There's a small PA in the office," he said, hands tucked inside the bib of his trademark blue denim dungarees. "I'll help you bring it through."

"Won't Arty mind?" asked Tom.

"What the eyes don't see, the heart won't grieve over," reasoned Sean.

As Tom and Sean hauled in the speakers and the mixer head, Ben rattled the glass on the front of the club with his car keys. Sean opened the door and helped Ben drag in a Peavey stack system bigger than the bass player himself. Between the two of them they looked like a circus double act rolling a prop into the ring.

Everyone shook hands; Tom felt a surge of adrenalin but canned his excitement with an air of typical English reserve. He had set up in hundreds of practice sessions before and acted like it was no big deal, but deep down he was experiencing an old nervousness, an apprehension for sharing his own material with a stranger, baring his soul. It was like appearing nude in front of an audience, he was as anxious as a kitten in a bag.

"Who wants a drink then?" he asked, offering his services as bartender.

Everyone took a pint of Jolt into the back room and after another brief introduction of Chad to Ben, they were soon into the first number; a Montgomery/Reynolds composition entitled *Halfway Woman*, the lyrics of which were written about Lela's indecision.

After twenty minutes of jamming over the song, they wound it down.

"Sounds good, sounds good," encouraged Seamus.

Chad stopped the little tape recorder he had brought along for prosperity. He played tight, kept excellent time and wasn't too flashy. As a unit they gelled perfectly.

Sean Adams who sat in a corner clapped his big hands together in appreciation, "That was great guys," he told them sincerely, "and you, Tom, sing like a bird."

Tom could feel his cheeks warming up. "Yeah, a roast chicken," he joked self- deprecatingly.

They all laughed.

"You got some more songs?" enquired Sean.

"Loads," said Tom, "let's see now … try this."

He ran through a chord sequence that Seamus knew all to well, a funky bit of pop called *Sacrifice*. Ben followed the chords and Chad picked up the rhythm, the song had never sounded as good.

Seamus hit a blinding guitar solo midway through the song that so surprised him he nearly fell over, and when the song finished he was laughing himself silly. "Phew," he said with a big rasping puff of air, "I nearly spontaneously combusted!"

Ben smiled his big smile, he found these two Brits fascinating to listen to. "You guy's are really off the scale," he said.

"That's a good name for the band," said Tom.

"What, *off the scale*?" asked Chad with mirth in his voice?

"Why not, if that's what we are?"

"Off me nut," said Seamus, "with all that Jolt, I'm buzzing man, buzzing."

Sean Adams was chuckling in his seat, "Off The Scale," he confirmed.

They ran through another six songs over the next four hours until KP and Scorpion turned up with Sasha and Selena to get the club ready for the night.

The sun was below the skyline now and purple light flooded the room.

KP liked what she heard. "You guys play well together," she said, "are you going to keep it up?"

The boys all looked at each other nodding.

"I think so," said Tom.

"Well you can rehearse here as much as you like. Feel free."

"Thanks KP," said Seamus. "You're way too kind."

They broke down their equipment and arranged to meet again on Wednesday night; all four of them seemed excited about the prospect. Possibly providence had brought them together for good reason.

***

Before the practice session began on Wednesday, Ben told the boys he had secured them a job with a builder he knew from church. If they wanted, they could start on Monday.

A few days ago their future stay in America looked decidedly bleak, but suddenly the borders of their world seemed more clearly defined. They had a band, a cash-in-hand job and a place to stay, for now anyway.

It was the beginning of June and hotter than either of them had ever experienced in their life. Temperatures were creeping into the high 90s, an energy sapping heat that contradicted the ethos of manual labour, especially for two blokes who came from a cold climate and hadn't exerted themselves physically for months.

They met up with Dale McKenzie the owner of a construction firm who was building houses in the foothills of the Catalina Mountains, a couple of which were completed, but the site needed to be cleaned up and the waste materials put into a dumpster.

Dale instructed them on what to clear away and what to leave in neat piles, and gave them shovels, brooms, wheelbarrows and cleaning products. He drove off in his four-wheel drive pickup, leaving the boys in a choking cloud of wheel-spun dust. The pay would be a measly $2 an hour each and he wanted them to work for 8hrs per day; 'wetback' money.

Tom was keen to get stuck in straight away and do as much as they could today, leaving less to do on the morrow. Seamus wanted to finish his roll-up first.

He stared down the length of the desiccated earth road, enjoying long pulls of tobacco smoke filling his lungs with acrid poison, numbing the craving effects of his addiction, when something caught his eye. A bird the size of a small skinny pheasant but with long thin legs and mottled brown and beige feathers, sprinted out of the brush and stood motionless in one of the baked ochre tyre ruts.

It had a long pointed beak, big eyes and a crest of brown and beige that swept back over the top of his head like a boring punk Mohican. Its tail stuck up at a ninety degree angle from its body and contained a few dark blue iridescent feathers in its span.

"'ere, Tom, look at this," he said gently, nodding in the direction of the bird.

Tom put down his shovel and slowly crept over to Seamus trying not to spook the critter.

It cocked its head to one side, giving the lads the once over, took a couple of quick steps forward then stood statuesque again.

"'ave a word," said Tom, "it's a Roadrunner."

"Meet, meet," said Seamus, inevitably.

The bird allowed the boys to creep within 10ft of it before it fled down the track, sprinting like a goose-stepping North Korean soldier without arms, very comical, but at nowhere near the expected speed portrayed by Wile E Coyote's arch rival, which was disappointing.

They took up their shovels and went to work.

"Let's start upstairs," said Tom. "We can position the wheelbarrows underneath the windows and throw the shit out. Then we can clean the glass and move on downstairs."

"Sounds good Ras'." Seamus was leaning on his broom and making another roll-up.

Two hours into the job they were sweating bucket loads. Most of the water rations they'd brought had disappeared, they had no money to buy more and the mains water had yet to be hooked up to the house.

The cement dust they were kicking up from sweeping the bare concrete floors filled the rooms with a sharp fine particle cloud that the motionless air wasn't clearing at all, even with all the windows open.

Tom couldn't believe how parched he was, his gullet stuck together every time he swallowed and he felt suffocated by the density of the dust, but had to ration his water because he only had a couple of swallows left to last the rest of the day.

They went outside for a breather and sat down in the slim shadow of the house. It was quiet out here on the outskirts of town and in this infernal heat hardly a creature stirred, save for the ever present Turkey Vultures that were circling above waiting for something to fail.

"Fuck me, I'm dying of thirst," said Seamus flopping his head back against the stucco wall.

"Shh, don't let them vultures 'ear you say that," managed Tom from arid lips. "Doubt if I can make it through the whole day without a proper drink."

They were a long way from any neighbouring properties, otherwise Seamus would be over there like a shot, 'poncing' a tall drink and something to eat without question.

The boys found American hospitality to be supreme and the locals couldn't resist inviting two such charming lads into their houses, and right now the boys had to capitalise on any handouts they could get.

They refrained from taking another drink from their cherished lukewarm liquid supply and went back indoors.

A pile of dust and debris had been brushed up to the wall under the window in a front bedroom, the window was open, held ajar by a long brass stay, and Tom was gingerly shovelling cascading amounts through the gap between the opener and the frame. Sweat was running off his forehead, getting into his eyes, making them sting and blurring his vision. Irritated, he brought his shoulder up to wipe his eye while holding a shovel full and inadvertently lifted the window stay with the pan, at the exact moment the only gust of wind of the day happened to blow.

The resulting crash sent splintered shards of glass across the front yard and almost certainly woke the dead. The two grubby workmen stood agog in a cloud of filth stunned by the fluke accident.

"For fucks sake," said Seamus.

"There go the wages," resigned Tom.

Seamus ran through the possibilities, "We'll just say the wind blew it shut, it's near enough what happened anyway."

"Today. What wind? And besides the glass is out there."

"No problem, we'll tidy up in 'ere, clean the windows and bring all the glass back inside and scatter it on the floor."

Tom calculated that apart from putting his hands up to the deed and taking a hit on his meagre wages that Seamus' idea was worth a punt.

"Brilliant," he said, "let's do that."

The boys spent another 4hrs on site, stacking unused materials and cleaning the downstairs rooms. Finally they could stand the heat exhaustion no more; they were close to collapse and almost rabid from lack of fluid.

When reaching home they each consumed a pint of ice water from the fridge then ran fully clothed into the pool. This felt marvellous and there they stayed for an hour, cooling their inner core and ranting about the job. Neither of them wanted to go back the next day, but they were so broke they really had no choice.

Lara came round and Seamus got out of the water straight away leaving Tom resting his chin on his crossed arms on the margins of the pool, staring at Huckleberry laid flat out on the patio, his slobbery jowls resting on his crossed front paws and droopy bloodshot eyes staring back at Tom.

"Ain't we a pair," Tom told the dog.

The next day was the same arduous torture, only this time, with foresight; they had brought along plenty of water and some bananas to see them through. They managed an uneventful 8hr day, but the rate of achievement was very poor, even for a slacker.

In the evening Ben called round unexpectedly with a resigned smile upon his face.

"Hey Ben, what's up?" enquired Tom at the front door.

"Bad news, guys," he said entering the house. "Dale can't employ you any more."

"What … why's that?" asked Seamus coming barefoot into the hall.

"You don't have green cards and he's not prepared to break the law. He gave me this to give to you." Ben handed the boys $50.

Tom counted it and said, "We earned sixty-four; we put in fourteen hours each."

"Yeah but he took off some money for the broken window," replied Ben awkwardly.

"But that wasn't our fault," protested Seamus, "the wind blew it shut and broke it."

"Happened on your watch I guess," shrugged Ben, "anyway I'm sorry guys, but that's all he gave me."

Tom felt the leaden weight of despair back in his stomach and his eyes glazed over as his mind drifted from the present to the probable.

"It's not your fault, mate," he said to Ben, accepting his bass player's remorse. "You still alright for tomorrow's session?"

"Of course, I'll see you guys over there at six-thirty, right?"

"Look forward to it," said Seamus, "see ya then."

Tom closed the door and turned to Seamus. "That's fucked that then."

"We've got food money for a week Ras', maybe something else will turn up. Don't worry, come on we've got a party to go to," said Seamus jubilantly.

"Is Lara coming?"

"I think so, why?"

"Maybe she knows someone who needs some odd jobs done."

"Maybe. I'll ask her."

Jennifer was throwing a midweek birthday party for herself featuring her good friend Rainer Ptacek on guitar. He was extraordinary, a definitive 'musician's musician', born in East Berlin in 1951 to a Czech-German family. Rainer and his folks fled from oppression to the States when he was five-years-old, first to Chicago then Tucson in the early 70s, where he took up his musical career. He had just released an album entitled *'Barefoot Rock'*, with his band Das Combo and it was being aired on the stereo as the lads arrived.

He would give a rendition of his own tunes later, thrown in with a variety of traditional blues songs, none of which the boys had heard.

Tom had never taken to the blues despite being exposed to plenty of it in his early years as a budding songwriter, when the boys used to frequent and perform at a Sunday afternoon blues venue in Watford called The Pump House. Here they were introduced to all manner of styles from good, and not so good artists, from the local community and a scattering of 'nearly made its' who were decent musicians and singers, but who for various reasons, didn't quite fit the criteria of the day.

Seamus on the other hand, could get off on any music and found Rainer to be spiritually inspirational.

Jennifer had festooned her garden with lanterns and fairy lights, and had laid on a big spread of delicious homemade finger food. Several large cool boxes were loaded with ice and champagne bottles and all the usual suspects were in attendance, plus a few bodies the boys had not yet met.

"Boys, boys, have some champagne," offered Jennifer who was three parts pissed already. "Toot?" she enquired.

Ross-I, who was sitting down in a garden chair, leant his head backwards allowing him to look at the boys upside down, it was a disconcerting sight.

"Try the weasel-dust man, it's a killer," he said.

His pupils were as big as Smarties and his dirty dreads hung from his skeletal face like a damp mop.

Not if it does that to ya' face, thought Tom. "Just a drink for now," he said.

Seamus looked over at the food table. He hadn't eaten anything apart a couple of bananas all day and was ravenous, salivating at the sight of a pile of roasted chicken legs.

"Is it all right to 'ave a bite to eat Jen'?" he asked.

"Of course, darling, that's what it's there for, help yourself. Come on, there's some people I want you to meet." She took Tom by the arm and led them towards the food table.

On the way the boys said good evening to Selena, KP, Glen, Tucson Kate, Jack, Freddie and Mateo who were grouped together round the champagne coolers, in extremely high spirits, laughing, smoking and fooling around.

It was a lovely atmosphere; the air was tinged with orange blossom and laced with Zydeco music, a perfect gathering to celebrate Jennifer's birthday.

A couple of people who the boys hadn't met before were filling their plates with salsa, curried rice and tortilla chips. They stopped midway through piling on big spoonfuls of potato salad when Jennifer spoke their names.

"Pete, Maisy, I'd like you to met Tom and Seamus, and Seamus' lovely girlfriend Lara." Lara flushed at the thought of being Mrs Seamus.

"They're from Hertfordshire, but have decided that the people on this side of the pond are much more entertaining," she embellished.

Pete was of slight build, had thick, curly black hair and wore John Lennon style glasses. He was from London and reminded Tom facially of Robin Williams.

Maisy was from the Isle of Skye, Eilean a' Cheò, in her mid-30s, had long black hair highlighted with fine wisps of grey, a smiley Celtic face and an apparent penchant for long hippy dresses.

Maisy taught the Gaelic language in various schools in town and gave private lessons in homes to supplement her income. Pete was an English teacher.

"Pleased to meet you," said Pete juggling his plate and glass to offer a hand.

"How do you do?" said Maisy. Her voice was soft and rich with a hint of devilment to it.

"'ow's the chicken?" enquired Seamus placing food high on his list of priorities.

"Haven't had a chance to sample it yet, but it looks great," replied Pete eyeing up the mountain of poultry on the table.

"I'm starving," said Seamus.

"I'm Pete," said Pete grinning widely.

Seamus barked a false laugh.

"So what are you two guys doing with yourselves in Tucson town?" asked Maisy.

"We've just formed a band actually," said Tom, "although we're also looking for work if you know of anyone who needs a couple of slaves."

"A band, eh, that's very interesting, I have need of a band, what type of music do you play," said Maisy, flickering interest like a youthful courtesan.

The spark of possible earnings ignited Tom's suppressed business instinct and he flared into action.

"We play our own songs and a few well-known soul covers like *Baby Now That I've Found You*, *This Old Heart of Mine*, *What Becomes of the Broken Hearted?*; you know, old Motown and Staxx numbers, but we can adapt to anything. What do you 'ave in mind?"

Seamus was heaping his plate with food like he was testing the ceramic's capabilities, stacking it high with a little bit of everything.

Lara scrutinized him with an unhealthy scowl.

"A colleague of mine is organising a charity gig for Gay Pride. Would you be interested in performing?" asked Maisy.

The word charity poured a pail of pool water into Tom's cocktail; it rendered the drink unpalatable.

"No pay then?" he said with diluted enthusiasm.

"No, but we can provide you with food and ample quantities of alcoholic beverage," she said with an optimistic smile.

"When is it and where do we play?" He felt obliged to accept, even though the prospect of actually being Stateside for much longer was looking evermore doubtful.

"It's two weeks from now, at the El Casino ballroom on 26th Street. Can you do it?"

Tom turned to Seamus who had cheeks like a hamster, a greasy mouth and a chicken drumstick in his hand.

"Do ya' think we'll be ready for that in two weeks?"

"Mmm," mumbled the rodent with his mouth full, "no problem."

***

At the rehearsal session the next night, the boys broke the news of their first gig to Ben and Chad. The drummer was all smiles, "two weeks, huh," he said contemplating the timeline. "Are we the only act?"

"Uh ha," said Tom.

"Well we better pick up the pace, learn some more songs, we'll need at least an hour and a half to fill or we'll have to wing it with some long guitar solos."

Ben looked really troubled.

"I, I don't think I can do that gig fellas … it goes against my religious beliefs to promote homosexuality." He was clearly distressed.

Seamus was innocently perplexed, Ben was obviously intelligent, how could he let his indoctrinated beliefs get in the way of a chance to perform in public?

"It's only a gig, mate," he proffered, "can't ya' just turn up and play, then bugger off?"

"Booger what?"

"Bugger off, go home."

Ben gave a half smile.

"I'll have to consult my minister about this," he said rather solemnly, "I dunno guys," he shook his head.

Tom felt it all falling to bits again, so tried to pluck a compromise out of the stale air.

"Do ya' 'ave to tell ya' minister? I mean can't ya' just keep the gig quiet?" he asked.

"Not really Tom, that would be deceiving God," he said earnestly. "We'll carry on the rehearsal for tonight and I'll let you know my decision tomorrow."

Tom and Seamus had little choice but to press on with showing the guys some of their material, knowing that for one of them it was probably a waste of time. Even so, the music sounded great and it would be a devastating shame to destroy the timbre they had so far developed. At the end of the session they packed away their equipment in a somewhat sombre mood.

On Thursday, the boys got the inevitable news they had been dreading. Ben had quit the band for moral issues. He offered his apologies but that wasn't going to play the bass notes in two weeks' time.

They went to see Jennifer, to ask her to let Maisy know that they probably couldn't do her gig. Jennifer was sitting in her front room with her legs up on a pouffe, glued to the TV watching tennis at Wimbledon.

"I don't do anything for two weeks while Wimbledon is on," she announced imperiously. She had a tall glass of Pimms in one hand and a spliff in the other. "Help yourself to a drink boys, there's a big punch bowl in the kitchen."

The lads dutifully complied with the request and then rejoined Jennifer in the living room.

Several portable electric fans were encouraging a reasonable breeze through the mobile home, their gentle hum together with the subdued commentary from the BBC created a serene ambience, enticing Tom to melt into an armchair and focus on the game in progress, a quarter final between Boris Becker and Pat Cash.

Becker had the upper hand, having won the first set 6-4, and now he was up 3 games to 0.

"What did you want to ask me boys?" said Jennifer while the tennis players took a short break between games.

They told Jennifer of Ben's departure.

"I know a bass player who'll help you out," she declared. "His name's Stu' but we call him Hot Pot."

"Hot Pot," said Seamus with a snigger.

Jennifer smiled, "Yeah, he plays with Raucous Raccoon; they're quite busy but I'm sure he'll find the time to lend a hand, shall I call him for you?"

"If ya' could Jen," said Tom, "can ya' see if 'e can make a rehearsal this Saturday afternoon?"

"I'll try, but can't promise anything," said Jennifer, her eyes wandering back to the TV as Becker and Cash resumed play on Court 2.

That evening Jennifer called the boys to let them know Hot Pot would be pleased to help out, and his band were playing tonight at The Chicago Bar on Speedway if they wanted to go meet him before hand.

"Good idea," said Tom, his fire reignited, "We'll get over there for nine, cheers Jen." He put the phone down and rubbed his hands together. "We're off again," he said to his buddy.

The Chicago Bar was a live music venue, offering local bands 7 nights a week. It stood alone on a grey tarmac parking lot at the junction of N. Sonoita Avenue, a rectangular building sporting the Chicago Bears football team's blue and orange colours, fronted with black glass panels and a Las Vegas style white, illuminated box sign at the roadside, displaying this week's artists.

Inside it was dark with a noticeably low hung ceiling, masses of dark wood panelling, picture mirrors, beer advertising merchandise and sports memorabilia adorning the walls. A fully occupied pool table filled one corner and dangerously low ceiling fans cut through the cigarette smoke like airplane propellers in fog. The Chicago Bears colours were omnipresent throughout the bar.

Raucous Raccoon were in full swing on stage, dutifully churning out a cover of the Beatles, *Get Back*.

"That's apt," shouted Tom above the music.

The stage wasn't set far above the floor; it was in an alcove 20ft wide, proudly exhibiting a wall of used and broken cymbals on its left hand side, trophies from bands gone by, and a wood carving depicting the Chicago skyline across the back drop.

The English boys, decked out in shorts, sandals and vest tops stood out like tourists amongst the local hands, whose preference for head gear seemed to be reversed baseball caps and Stetsons.

They sashayed over to a long sticky wooden bar that ran the length of the club down to the stage where they perched themselves on stools.

Seamus ordered a pitcher of draft Michelob, then they swung round to watch the band.

Raucous were a four-piece consisting of two guitarists, a drummer and Stu.

He was a tall slim rockabilly with jet black hair styled in an exaggerated Elvis bouffant and long pointed sideburns that traversed his jaw line like the go-faster flashes on a Gran Torino. He wore a red and white check shirt that had the sleeves hacked off at the shoulders, skinny jeans and pointy cowboy boots. For comedy effect he had an elasticised guitar strap that he kept elongating, bringing his bass down to his knees. He did this so many times that it ceased to be funny.

The audience tonight was on the thin side, just 4 people dancing, making the worn out orange linoleum floor look like the loneliest place on earth, and anyone attempting to cross it to feel like a penguin on the Bonneville salt flats.

Forty-five minutes later, after a repertoire of middle-of-the-road covers and mild rock numbers received with lukewarm applause, the band took a break.

Tom and Seamus walked over to the stage and introduced themselves to Hot Pot who was placing his guitar on a stand.

"I saw you guys come in," he said. "You're lucky you haven't been lynched wearing clothes like that. This is Redneck country, not a poolside bar," he quipped with an iniquitous smile.

"We got some funny looks on the way in," said Seamus. "I thought those guys on the pool table fancied me."

"They'd fuck you up alright," said Hot Pot.

Tom didn't know if Stu was joking, the bassist's gaze was expectant and probing, waiting for a response.

"Can we buy you a beer?" Tom asked.

"Sure, I'll have a bottle of Bud," he said still grinning like El Diablo.

"Hey guys," he said to the rest of his band, "this is Tom and Seamus, they're a couple of Brits new in town and they're gonna buy us a beer."

The Americans looked over curiously and smiled. One of them came over to shake hands. The lead guitarist and main vocalist, a short round-faced bloke named Kris; he was a decent musician, and along with Stu was obviously the force behind the band. But the other two members let the side down, especially the drummer Brin, who dropped the beat occasionally and was sloppy at the best of times. He was more intent on sucking the face off his girlfriend, who was now straddling his lap whilst he slouched on his drum stool.

Tom went to the bar. Stu couldn't resist scrutinising Seamus' leg. It had a wide 6 in. woolly brown mole on its shin, a birthmark Seamus had always had a complex about, and until only recently kept it hidden from the world. His new fondness for wearing shorts had exposed the beast and recently he felt less embarrassed over it, almost liberated in fact.

"Hey Seamus, you've got shit on ya leg," said Hot Pot with a dry grin.

Obviously Hot Pot had a sardonic nature, but Seamus was like a sponge, he could soak up loads of punishment and still remain buoyant.

He laughed a breathy whistle, blowing smoke through his pursed lips. "Yeah I've tried t' wipe that off many times, but it won't budge" he replied. Staring at the stage, Seamus eyed up Hot Pot's gear. He had a Peavey stack and a Fender Bass. "Nice guitar ya' got there Stu," he said encouragingly.

"What … the Fender P, yeah I've had it a while, it does a fine job," replied Hot Pot suspiciously protective of his axe.

"Everybody round 'ere seems to prefer Peavey amps, d' they sound better?"

"It's a copy, I got it in Korea, those slanty-eyed bastards can make anything, it's just like the real thing, I tell ya' man, you go into a workshop over there on a Monday and tell em what you need, they'll have it fixed up by Friday for a quarter of the fucking price. I checked it in with my luggage didn't cost a fucking thing to bring back."

"Fuckin' 'ell," said Seamus raising his eyebrows.

"Fuckin' A," said Hot Pot raising his.

Tom came back with another pitcher of beer and four bottles of Bud for the band on a tray, and duly handed them out. "So you're up for filling in on this gig we got at the El Casino Ballroom then Stu?" Tom topped up his and Seamus' glass with fresh Michelob.

"Yeah, Jen said something about that, what's the deal? We gotta keep our backs to the wall or what's going on there eh?" said Hot Pot sarcastically half joking.

Tom smiled, "I think there'll be a few 'friends of Dorothy' on the dance floor." Seamus punched out a laugh, as Hot Pot performed his mistrustful leer again.

"Yeah I'm down with that," he said, "when's the rehearsal?"

"This Saturday afternoon at The Purple Haze, d' ya' know it?" replied Seamus.

"Sure I know it; my wife's gotta clothing store on 4th Avenue right across the street, d'ya wanna meet up around two o'clock?"

"Yep, that'll be great," said Tom "I'm looking forward to it."

The boys went on to explain how they ended up in Tucson and the predicament they were in financially. Hot Pot was semi-sympathetic to their plight but he was a jingoistic homeboy who was cruel-witted and very guarded, almost wary of these two Englishmen. On the plus side he was a good bass player, knew loads of tunes, could sing back-up and was enthusiastic about 'depping' for them. Once more they had a band to gig with.

Raucous Raccoon returned to the stage for their second set and Tom and Seamus went back to their bar stools. The dance floor didn't get any busier, but the drummer's girlfriend Marta put in such a performance that it kept the boys entertained for most of the set, twirling and pirouetting like a lone cowgirl Prima ballerina.

Before the final song Tom and Seamus sloped off, waving to Raucous who were sweating under the hot stage lights, grinding out a tired version of *Route 66*.

***

The Saturday afternoon practice session went well; Hot Pot, the senior man at 34-years-old, gelled well with Chad who was the youngest, and he knew all the cover songs that Seamus and Tom threw at him. The originals however, being on the funky side were slightly awkward for him. He was more of a straight rock and roll sort of guy, but he persevered with the rhythms and found some middle ground, which changed the dynamics of the songs, lending them a rockier feel. The boys didn't mind, it was experimental anyway and potentially only for one gig.

After the rehearsal Hot Pot asked the boys if they wanted to go back to his house for dinner. Chad couldn't make it, he had to go home and study, the boys were keener but they didn't have much gas left in the Chuggerbug.

"That's no big deal, we can go in my truck and I'll bring you back here tonight, you have to work right?" said Hot Pot.

"'ave to start at nine, "said Seamus, "If ya' don't mind, that'll be beautiful."

"Beautiful, eh, okay, let's get going," said Hot Pot amused.

They broke the equipment down in double time and left The Haze in the capable hands of Sean Adams.

Hot Pot's truck was a large, square Ford pickup, wide enough to get four people and a couple of dogs on the bench seat and still have room for two shot guns on a rack behind the head rests.

He lived on the north-side, a good 10mls away, giving them plenty of time to talk.

On a 4 lane one-way street coming out of town they were approached by an elderly lady in a small silver Toyota that had obviously taken a wrong turn. Hot Pot veered towards her like he was hoping for a head on collision. At first the boys thought he was mucking around, but when he forced the old lady into the curb, bump up onto the grass verge and grind to a stop, they realised he was disturbingly serious. The octogenarian was clearly terrified, but Hot Pot wasn't content with that.

He pulled close along side her, wound down his window and shouted at her, "You're driving the wrong fuckin' way!" at the top of his voice. Incomprehensibly, he was totally infuriated with her and his eyes were bulging out of his face with pupils as big as chocolate buttons. "Fuckin' idiot," he said winding up the window. "People like that shouldn't be on the fuckin' road."

Tom and Seamus sat there stunned, they couldn't believe just how upset he had become at the old dear's simple mistake, an error that could have been rectified without any aggression at all. They stayed contemplatively quiet, being at the mercy of a slightly disturbed individual. It put a strange mark upon their new friend.

Stu's house was a good-sized redwood timber bungalow situated in an acre of ground within a spacious neighbourhood. It had a well-groomed garden and a fair-sized swimming pool. Inside, the rooms were cool, shaded and modern and featured many Native American pieces of art. Evidently the couple were making a reasonable living doing what they did.

"Very nice," said Seamus as they drove through the gateway and parked on the limestone chip drive.

Hot Pot's wife was in the kitchen preparing the evening meal when the boys ambled through the front door, the smell of grilled swordfish steaks seasoned with black pepper and drizzled with lime juice was elevating. Tom breathed it in like it was essential. "Cor, that smells good, Stu," he said in the hallway.

Hot Pot led them to the open-plan kitchen which over looked the back yard.

"This is my wife, Fenella," he said, as she turned from the sink to great them.

She shook her hands free from water and wiped them on a tea towel before coming over to meet the boys.

She had masses of long dark curly hair, a pretty face, large framed spectacles, a full figure and sizeable breasts, perfectly round and firm, almost like two small balloons had been pushed up her jumper.

Tom guessed her to be around 30-years-old; she had an impeccable smile and lovely soft brown eyes.

"Hi," she said with a mellow melodic voice, "very nice to meet you both." She held out her hand and shook both of theirs.

"We've got swordfish and a tossed salad for dinner, I hope that's okay?"

"Beautiful," said Seamus finding Fenella's charms intoxicating.

"It smells delicious," added Tom, "I 'ope we 'aven't put you out?"

"Not at all," she replied, "we have people over all the time."

"Yep, it's party central here," said Hot Pot, "now let's eat. Beer anyone?"

"When in Rome," said Tom.

Over the course of dinner the boys discovered that Fenella's shop sold second hand retro and ex-army issue clothing, and was doing reasonably well. Together with Stu's gig money they were able to live quite comfortably. She was intelligent, flirtatious, well-schooled and showed tiny signs of being interested in Seamus when her husband wasn't on guard. Seamus was his usual whimsical self, being disingenuous was just one of his fatal charms.

The time passed quickly and too soon they were back at The Haze, working the door, with full bellies and reasonably satisfied with the way things were going.

"I think Fenella fancies you," said Tom to his smoking buddy.

"Uh hum," Seamus sang, "very nice with salsa."

***

As morning broke, Tom slipped into consciousness to the sound of a distant jackhammer gunning at the road, "Why are they doing road works on a Sunday?" he whispered, until he realised it was in fact Seamus snoring in the next bed. Unable to move his paralysed limbs, he drifted back to oblivion and dreamt he was participating on an Army assault course with the menace of muffled machine gun fire sporadically erupting in the woods beside him.

At around midday the bedroom door swung open and in bounded Lara like a cross between Pooh Bear and Barbie; she leapt on Seamus, jolting him from slumber with the speed of a sprung mousetrap.

"What the … what the fuck ya' doin' woman?" he said uncharacteristically enraged.

Lara laughed to cover her embarrassment. "I wanted to surprise you," she said like a hurt child.

"Ya' frightened me to death," he said, his anger subsiding.

"It'd be more of a surprise if ya' didn't come 'round on a Sunday morning," said Tom without opening his eyes.

The sarcasm went unnoticed as she poured into her preamble. "Guys, I've got some great news. Tom I've found you a job."

Tom who was lying on his stomach, head half-buried in the pillow, opened an eye and stared at her like a semi-attentive Cyclops. "Doing what?" he asked after a moment.

"Some friends of mine need the wall painted around their house and they are willing to pay two-hundred dollars for a week's work."

Tom rallied himself and swung around so that he sat against the wall with his legs over the side of the bed, the sheet barely covering his modesty. "Wait a minute," he said, "why 'ave I got the job and not Seamus?"

"Well," she hesitated. "I thought you would be more qualified for the work," she lied.

Tom knew she just wanted to spend more time with Seamus and splitting the boys up would be an ideal opportunity for her to get more claws into him. But he didn't mind taking the workload for a week; they desperately needed the money, he'd been spending Seamus' cash and it didn't matter which way it came in.

"Great," he said, "where do they live and when do they want me?"

"Well, their names are Saul and Caitlyn Berns, they live on Orange Grove Road and they want you to start tomorrow, isn't that good?" she flourished.

Tom nodded silently, pouting his bottom lip as he contemplated the job in hand. Painting was easy, something Seamus' dad once said to him echoed in his mind. "If you can piss, you can paint." True enough, he thought.

"Okay, tell 'em I'll be there at eight, paintbrush in 'and," he said.

"Rasta far I," bellowed Seamus, finger snapping his right hand like a smacked arse.

"Cool," said Lara who then tunnelled under the sheets to cuddle up to Seamus who was still prostrate in the X position with his eyes shut.

Tom raised one cheek and shook his head, got up, and left them alone.

9
Orange Groove

Orange Grove Rd intersected North Oracle at a junction highlighted by the Del Oro Plaza on one side and a 76 filling station on the other. The massive orange 76 ball on a pole landmarked the turning from a good 400yd distance.

The road here comprised of 3 lane traffic, in each direction, separated by a high-curbed gravel meridian and hedged by formidable brown telegraph poles, the lines of which glinted in the morning sun, cutting through the arid azure sky like the taut silver wires of an endless six-string egg slicer.

Tom entered the left hand lane and waited for the filter light to give him the all clear. At 7:50 a.m., he was already sticking to the seats of the Arkansas Chuggerbug, and desperately parched after missing the essential breakfast cup of tea.

Once on Orange Grove, 3 lanes became 2; he passed a 4 bay do-it-yourself carwash on the right, refreshingly painted in aquamarine and white, it stood out amongst the usual desert browns and sandstone coloured buildings. A cloud of high pressure spray obscured an early morning enthusiast.

Palo Verde and towering Eucalyptus trees lined the pavements, scattered with tall palms here and there, like shaggy haired giants nodding at the shining metal boxes passing by. The entrance to an apartment block was bordered with orange trees; a possible remnant of a once larger plantation perhaps, Tom wondered why their trunks were painted white, an ostentatious waste of materials he thought.

The road narrowed once more down to a single lane, Tom slowed to read the house numbers on his right; this was it, the 2 nd house along, number 550. The property was fenced by a 5ft painted block wall the colour of dried mud, and a single panel wooden electronic gate, which had been rolled back for his privilege and now lingered besides a brown and gold pickup at the foot of the drive.

Tom turned in and onto the red-printed concrete cobble stone surface which rumbled up to the front door along a short avenue of date palms and neatly trimmed Box hedge, contained in raised brick planters.

The turn-around outside the house could park 4 cars easily, only one posed there, baking its metallic candy apple red paint, an open-top Jeep with massive chrome plated wheels and over-sized knobbly tyres.

Tom was unsure where to put his antique, it looked too abandoned to dump by the front door. So he swung it around and drove back to the bottom of the drive and shoehorned it in next to the pick up.

A heady aroma of orange blossom pleasantly caught his nostrils as he exited his leviathan. The outlying flanks of the front garden were indeed a citrus grove, heavily laden with this year's crop, mostly oranges, but also some grapefruit, tangerine and a single lemon tree, their limbs arced almost to the ground with the burden of nurturing so much fruit.

Around each tree, a circular brick wall had been constructed like a wellhead, to retain water from the irrigation system running throughout the garden. Tom pondered again over the trees whitewashed trunks, which gave them an artificial expression; a folly or a fashion statement surely, he imagined.

Before he got to the dark oak double front door, shaded by a porch covered in purple Bougainvillea, a man and a woman appeared in the shadows of the open garage space to the right of the house, which sheltered a burgundy Lincoln Mk IV, a wood panelled Wagoneer and a dark blue Lincoln Continental.

He was tall, square framed and looked to be at least in his late-60s. Dressed in a navy blazer and light coloured slacks, with an open necked blue and white striped shirt, he had slick, thin, dyed-black hair and tortoiseshell rimmed glasses that pinched the end of his nose. The lady was in her 40s and was wearing a white two-piece suit with a red lacy top beneath. She had straight bottle-blonde hair that curled inward as it reached her shoulders, inquisitive bulbous blue eyes and a round, cheerful face.

The man was chewing on a cinnamon stick, the brown juice of which had dribbled down the front of his shirt.

"You Tom?" he enquired with a gravelly Bronx accent and a suspicious glare.

"Yes." Tom replied extending his hand.

"Saul Berns, this is my wife Caitlyn."

Tom caught just the fingers of Saul's well-manicured liver-spotted hand. He thought the shake to be very limp, and that his hands were disproportionately small for the size of the man.

Caitlyn said good morning and stood beside her husband grinning like she was waiting for a birthday present, while Saul scrutinised the scruffy young Brit.

The wife had nicely shaped lips that were over-highlighted by bright glossy red lipstick.

"Where did ya' put ya' car?" Saul asked.

"Down by the pickup."

"Good, you can leave it there." Saul cleared his throat. "I'll show ya' whatcha' gotta' do, follow me."

Tom span on the balls of his trainer-clad feet and shadowed his new employer to the garden tool shed that sat snug beside the garden gate to the left of the house, against a short wall dividing the front and back yards.

In amongst the various spades, rakes and pruning shears were several gallon pots of cream coloured masonry paint and a couple of 6 in brushes.

Saul stood with one leg in and one outside the shed, taking stock of its contents. "I wantcha' t' take this shit and paint it on the fuckin' walls around the grove, can you do that?" he patronised.

"Yup," Tom replied enthusiastically. "Both sides?"

Saul looked at him like he'd just asked a stupid question. His wise brown eyes appeared over the top of his glasses. "All the inside and just the outside at the front," He explained. "The fuckin' neighbours can paint their own fuckin' sides."

"Right-o," said Tom venturing into the relative cool of the shed.

"I'm going a' work now," drawled the boss, "The fuckin' gardener is around some place, the dopey shit. He'll help ya' if ya' need to move anything; I'll be back around five."

With that Saul disappeared back into the house momentarily before coming out again, getting into the big blue Lincoln and growling off down the drive.

Tom opened the lid on one of the pots with a screwdriver, found an old bamboo plant support, and stirred the thick paint slowly for a couple of minutes.

He liked this shed, it would be a little sanctuary away from the intense heat that was building up outside. When the paint was stirred he stepped back out into the brilliant sunshine; he was wearing only a pair of running shorts and a vest, but was perspiring heavily already and he hadn't done a stroke yet. Today was going to be difficult, without any refreshments and very little money in his pocket; he was relying on Caitlyn making him something to drink later on.

He began painting beside the shed, reaching as far back between the wall and the building as he could stretch, but it was slow going; the honeycomb surface of the wall made it near-on impossible to penetrate all the little cavities. It was more of a splodge and dab action, than a brushstroke, and it was going to take an age.

The side gate clicked open and through it came a Hispanic man in his mid-50s with tough leathery chestnut skin and a thick Magnum PI moustache. He wore a blue cheque shirt, jeans and a wide brimmed straw sombrero.

Tom stopped what he was doing and turned to smile at the gardener who returned the gesture with an upward nod of the head.

"Tom," said the speckled painter holding out his hand.

"Ruben," replied the Mexican, and then something in Spanish Tom couldn't translate.

The gardener removed some tools from the shed, took off his hat and fanned his face with it. His black hair was wet and flattened against his forehead. "*Mucho calor*," he stated.

Tom deduced that he meant it was very hot. "*Si*," he replied.

Ruben replaced his hat and sauntered off again to the rear garden.

Chatty, thought Tom.

By 1:00 p.m. he had only managed to complete a 20ft section of wall; he was desperately thirsty and decidedly hungry, and curiously, he hadn't seen hide nor hair of Caitlyn all morning.

He checked the change in his pocket, just a $5 bill and a few coins was all he possessed. Popping the lid back on the paint pot, he took the brush to the shed and found a plastic bag to wrap it in to keep it supple. Then he set off down the road on foot towards the filling station on the corner. There he bought a cheap, pre made egg mayonnaise sandwich and a bottle of summer fruits Gatorade, and took it outside to settle on the grass beside the road, in the shade of a robust Eucalyptus tree.

This purchase left him with just $3.20. A loan till the end of the week was deemed a necessity.

After a short respite he trudged back to the house to resume painting, all the while thinking about what a cushy deal Seamus had got, he was probably still in bed, humping that sticky pink thing that had procured Tom this job.

In the opposite corner to where he had been working, secluded under an orange tree, was the prostrate snoozing figure of Ruben lying on flattened cardboard, sombrero over his face and snoring like a warthog.

Siesta time supposed Tom, and went back to his commission.

The buzzing noise started around 2:00, first with one beast then another, and another, until there were hundreds of them going at it high in the trees, sounding like a Rampant Rabbit test site. Tom tried to locate the source of the annoyance, but for the life of him couldn't pinpoint any creatures in the branches at all. He zoned them out and pretty soon they became just background noise amidst the passing traffic and occasional fly past of aircraft from Davis Monthan.

Now and then he caught glimpses of a fat-faced woman with glasses and a mop of bushy black hair in the subdued light behind the kitchen window. It turned out to be Ruben's wife Gracie, who did the housework for the Berns'. She smiled at Tom every time their eyes met. Tom raised a hand in reply.

At 5:00 p.m. Saul rolled back up the drive and came over to inspect what the Limey had achieved, roughly 30 ft, by the end of the day.

"Is that all you've done?" he snapped.

"It's pretty 'ard to cover," said Tom. "Ya' can't just brush it on; you 'ave to stab it to get inside all the little 'oles."

"Hah," Saul barked whist chewing gum. "You'll have t' do better than that, or you'll be here for fuckin' months, it ain't the fuckin' Sistine Chapel, just get it on the wall."

Tom looked despondent.

"Pack ya' things up and I'll see ya' t' morra', use the well tap t' wash up." Saul ordered before walking away.

Not a good time to ask for a couple of quid then? thought Tom. He drove home in a forlorn mood; he was dehydrated and feeling the effects of sun stroke, the skin on his bent arm and leg joints fused together with sweat, unfolding like cheap Sellotape from a roll as he moved. There was little fuel left in the tank and even less in his belly; he hoped Seamus had prepared some dinner for his return.

Gloriously, Lara had come to their aid with a family bucket of Kentucky fried chicken, fries, coleslaw, biscuits (like scones without the currants) and gravy. Colonel Saunders needed to be knighted.

Tuesday was almost a carbon copy of Monday, Saul greeted Tom in the drive, told him how much wall he wanted him to paint, then drove off to work. Caitlyn never showed her face and Ruben fell asleep under the orange tree.

The only difference today, Tom had brought along his Sony Walkman cassette player and a bunch of tapes, which blotted out the monotony of dabbing on dazzling cream paint onto the Great Wall of Orange Grove.

During the morning he took a breather for 10min, stole an orange from a branch and sat on the wall of the tree in the shade to enjoy it.

The fruit was amazing, like nothing else he had ever tasted in his life; the flavour was exactly the same as orange blossom, sweet, fragrant, incredibly juicy and so more-ish he just had to have another. He enjoyed fruit, but had never had the inclination to eat one orange after another, yet these were phenomenal and he couldn't resist. He contemplated a third, but thought better of it, he would hate to be caught nicking from his boss after just 2 days, and besides he had to speed up operations or he would be getting the old heave-ho anyway.

Revitalised, he went to the well tap, washed his sticky hands, arms and face, binned the orange peel evidence, then went back to splodging on exterior emulsion to the sounds of U2 and Everything but the Girl.

Saul came back at 5:00 and marched over to inspect today's achievements. Tom had reached halfway down one side of the garden, still only roughly another 35ft.

The boss stood there in a short sleeved shirt, chewing gum in one side of his mouth, his ebony eyes creased from the glare of the afternoon furnace.

Tom waited for a bollocking, like an urban artist expecting the law's critique.

"Could ya' paint faster if ya' had ya' buddy here?" Saul said at length.

"Sure," replied Tom with surprised relief.

"Okay, okay, bring him along t' morra'; let's get this fuckin' job done."

"Okay, thanks Saul, we'll be 'ere bright-eyed and bushy-tailed in the morning."

"What?" Saul snapped. Tom's accent made English hard to decipher, and Saul had little patience to want to try.

"We'll be 'ere in the morning," Tom revised.

***

Seamus blagged $20 out of Arty that night and the boys went out to Geronimo's for a Guinness and a slice of pizza to celebrate their joint employment.

The bar was on campus and the only place in town where they served the black Irish stout. The décor was typically Southwestern, a mixture of rustic and modern subdued interior with a long polished wooden bar running the length of one wall and high stools and tables throughout. The pizzas were immense and as cheap as chips.

"What's the old man like to work for?" Seamus enquired with a mouthful of Veggie Volcano.

Tom washed his slice down with a long swig of the ice cold bitterness. "Er, a miserable fucker. It's like 'e's on the verge of being angry all the time, and it's an effort for 'im t' speak t' ya'."

"A bit like your old man." Seamus laughed, knowing Tom's dad all too well.

"I don't think 'e's violent… But then again, I've only known 'im for two days—he might be?"

"I'll give 'im some of the old Montgomery charm, that'll chill 'im out."

Tom scoffed, "You'd need a walk-in freezer."

Seamus clenched his teeth and laughed like Muttley. "Ya' man. Ha, ha, ha. What about 'is missus, what's she like?"

Tom continued to eat, the pizza was superb and he was famished. "I never see 'er. She's always in the 'ouse so must work from 'ome or something."

"Is she worthy of the old pork sword?"

Tom creased his forehead, vexed by the question; it hadn't crossed his mind at all. "Leave it out, she must be at least forty-five; I bet she's seen more action than Chuck Norris."

Seamus did his Muttley impression again, and then said in a Leslie Phillips voice, "Umm, a mature lady." Before raising his eyebrows whilst drawing on his cigarette.

"Yeah, tenderised like a battered steak," joked Tom.

"Ooh," grimaced Seamus. "Hammer me tenderloin."

The next morning, the lads walked up the cobbled drive with fuzzy heads and sleep deprived eyes. They had crossed the street last night to Gracious Bob's and joined a group of jocks who were celebrating a birthday. The frat' boys welcomed the Brits into their fold and wouldn't let them spend a cent on beer, which was a shame. The party ended when the bar closed its doors at 2:00 a.m. spilling incoherent legless specimens out into the street. The drinkers became a massive swaying entity, clinging lovingly to each other, singing at the tops of their lungs and being sick in the gutter.

Seamus drove the pair of them home, though he couldn't remember doing so.

Saul and Caitlyn were there to meet them outside the open garage.

The lack of slumber must have been apparent in the boys' appearance. Caitlyn studied them with her hands behind her back, sucking in her lips to suppress her amusement.

Her husband looked bitterly disappointed.

"Morning Saul, morning Caitlyn." Tom felt like his tongue had been carpeted. Unbelievably the words came out in the right order.

Seamus said morning as well and offered the boss his hand. "I'm Seamus," he said with fetid breath.

"What?" snarled Saul. He held a cinnamon stick between his fingers like he was gripping a cigarette.

"Seamus … I'm Seamus."

"You're fuckin' hungover," chided Saul. "Can ya' hold a fuckin' paint brush?"

"Absolutely," said the red-eyed lush.

"Then follow me, I want ya' t' use it t' put some paint on a fuckin' wall, if ya' got the gumption."

Saul strode towards the boundary wall with Seamus close to his side. Caitlyn smiled and gave Tom a slow wink, letting him know that everything was just fine. Tom turned and followed the other two, slightly more enlightened to his governor's temperament.

"So whaddya' do t' earn a buck then Saul?" Seamus asked as they traversed the grove.

"Real estate," intoned the boss.

"Right, right. Selling 'ouses and stuff? Bet ya' make a packet. I know an estate agent, 'e's only twenty-four, 'e drives a Porsche, lives in a four bedroom 'ouse, 'e's—"

"You talk too much," interrupted Saul. "Just paint the fuckin' wall."

"Right, right, gotcha, gotcha," answered a gagged Seamus.

Saul sighed through his nose and looked over the rim of his glasses at the sorry sack in front of him. They had come to the front wall were the blocks met the gate post.

"With the two of ya' here, you'll come to this point by the end of the day. If ya' need more paint, ask Caitlyn t' go buy some from Home Depot, I'll be back this afternoon."

"Okay Saul, 'ave a good day," Tom said.

"Okay," drawled the boss. He went to turn away, but hesitated then turned back. "That stupid blonde introduced you t' us didn't she?"

Seamus looked up. "Lara, yeah, she said 'er parents knew ya'."

"That fuckin' dumb shit, she's a pain in the ass," Saul sneered. "Did ya' get the juices?"

Seamus gave a short laugh at Saul's terminology. "Ah ha," he replied.

Saul presented a lopsided vicious smile. "What about the mother-daughter act, did ya' get the mother daughter act?"

"No Saul, not yet," humoured Seamus, "but it would be nice."

"Ha," barked Saul in agreement before finally sauntering back up the drive.

"What's the mother like?" asked Tom envisaging the scene.

"Not too bad," said Seamus.

"The juices," mimicked Tom in Saul's voice.

The sun beat down on the two workmen. They stripped off their shirts and carried out their task bare chested, sweat evaporating off their backs before it had the chance to run. They dabbed the wall with a sloppy monotony, talking endlessly about the night before, Seamus getting more paint on himself than on the objective. They were losing fluids fast without realisation, and were awfully parched. Still Caitlyn hadn't made an appearance with an offer of refreshment, so Seamus took it upon himself to go up to the front door and ask for a drink.

Gracie answered, her chubby face a picture of joy, squinty eyes and curly hair. Behind her appeared four nosey dogs that she was struggling to hold back with her legs.

Seamus bent down and stroked the two golden retrievers, one of which stood up on her hind legs and placed her front paws on his bare chest.

Gracie berated the dog, "Down, Fonda."

The other two hounds stayed further back in the house, cocking their heads to one side inquisitively. Although Gracie didn't speak much English, eventually she got the drift that the two boys desperately needed a drink, so she trotted off to ask Caitlyn if that would be alright.

The lady of the house came to the door looking flushed, as though she'd been exercising or something. "Oh sure," she said, "but you can't come in. Saul wouldn't like that. I'll get Gracie to fix you guys up with an ice cold orange juice, we have plenty of it."

"Nice dogs you got there, Caitlyn," said Seamus ruffling Fonda's ears.

She smiled and exposed her dimpled cheeks for the first time. "That's Fonda and Reina, my two dogs, and those two back there are Saul's; Myko, he's a three-year-old male, and the little black one is a two-year-old bitch called Jolie, Tres Jolie. She's always happy, but Myko can be a little grumpy, just like Saul." She laughed.

"What breed are they then Caitlyn?"

"Oh, they're Japanese Akitas, they were bred for hunting bears, don't they just have bear faces?"

Seamus looked at the two fluffy beasts and thought they just looked like dogs to him. "Yeah, I can see that, Caitlyn."

She smiled sweetly again then slipped off into the shadows of the inner sanctum leaving Seamus on the doorstep wrestling fur.

Gracie brought the drinks out in tall, pint-sized glasses topped with bobbing ice cubes. The juice was divine, not just because the boys were near death with thirst, but because it was the sweetest, most fragrant orange juice on the whole planet and was polished off in no time.

"God that's gorgeous," said Seamus sucking out the remnants of his glass through the ice.

"It's the same with the oranges mate, you just can't get enough," said Tom licking his sticky lips.

"Shall I ask for another one?" said Seamus.

"No, don't take the piss. This is the first drink she's given us, don't strong it."

"I'm gonna," said Seamus, and strode over to the house again.

Tom cringed inside, he would have liked another glass too but he wouldn't take liberties, unlike his friend. He got back to painting, waiting for Seamus to return empty handed, but sure enough, back he came with two more filled to the brim glasses of wonder stuff.

"Yambozee," he said and laughed like Sid James.

Tom always tried to do what was expected of him, even though he was easily led astray. Seamus on the other hand always entertained Seamus first, with everything else taking second place. He'd take as many fag breaks as he could, engage people in time killing conversation and generally just do enough work to show that he had at least been there.

Today he was writing 'go fuck yourself' on the wall in big letters and giggling while Tom was chastising him and trying to paint over it before anyone could see. His arms were now decorated right up to his elbows and splodges and flecks adorned his laughing sun-kissed face.

Unexpectedly, Saul came home at 2:00, just as the surreptitious insects struck up their matinee performance.

He scrutinised his labour force as he purred slowly up the drive, then again when he got out of his car before entering the house.

The boys kept working, Seamus kept talking.

They reached the end of the first wall by a wide compost heap made up mostly of palm fronds and fermenting date fruit.

Saul came over simmering with dissatisfied fervour. "This is all ya' done? I could have pissed farther."

The boys turned to Saul, steaming hot in the frazzling heat, paint splattered, semi naked, glistening with sweat and tanned to a ruddy mahogany brown.

"It's pretty 'ard going Saul, the wall just soaks up the paint like no-ones business," protested Seamus.

"Blow it out ya' ass. You'd do a lot more work if ya stopped fuckin' talking, ya' dumb shit." Saul singled Tom out. "Tomorra' you come in, an' ya' buddy can stop at home, goodbye." He sauntered back up the drive leaving the boys bereft of words.

Tom was more disenchanted than Seamus seemed to be. For Seamus it meant longer in bed and no more toil, but for Tom, he had to slog all this way for the next week and a half and bake his brains out under a relentless sun without a soul to talk to. But as tedious as it was, it meant money, so he resigned himself to put up with it.

"I can talk and work, work and talk, I still get the job done; what's 'is problem?" said Seamus petitioning his innocence on the way to the tool shed.

"Obviously Saul doesn't see it that way mate, 'e's well-old school, perhaps we're supposed to go to 'im cap in 'and or something," said Tom, trying to find a compromise in the situation. Internally he was feeling let down by his mate.

The journey home was a sombre affair, made the more aggravating by an irritating squeak that the Arkansas had developed in a rear wheel.

"Never mind Ras'," said Seamus, "we've got the gig at the weekend to look forward to, n' that'll be a laugh."

"Mmm," said Tom feeling like the fall guy.

They rehearsed for the first time that night at The Haze, in a newly converted mobile site office, which had been craned into the backlot. It was sound proofed and snug, contained a PA system, but without air-conditioning, so in no time at all it turned into a sauna that emitted visible steam when the door was opened, which was often.

They had roughly an hour's worth of material in the bag, it would have to suffice for the charity gig. If the band were well received, they could drag out the tunes with elongated guitar solos.

Tom had completed the week of grilled drudgery and managed to reach the opposite corner of the front garden wall. His reward was $200 in cash, plus $40 for Seamus' day's toil. He felt suddenly whole again, money in his pocket seemed like a safety net beneath him, at last they could get in some decent food.

***

The El Casino Ballroom first opened it doors in 1947. Since then it had hosted many a family milestone plus a multitude of touring musical acts; even illustrious names such as James Brown and Fats Domino had graced its cavernous arena. It boasts one of the largest spring-mounted wooden floors in Arizona which is kept exquisitely glass like, for gliding across effortlessly one would presume.

The high vaulted ceiling and white painted walls give it a cold, exposed, sports hall type of feel, and acoustically it was unsympathetic. Positioned inadequately on the deep wide stage, the boys' tiny amount of equipment looked rather pathetic, reminding them of their first attempts at putting a band together, practising in the All Saints church hall in Horseshoe Lane, Garston. A musty smelling bit of Victoriana, with creaking floor boards and orange drape stage curtains that wouldn't close properly.

A capacity audience at the El Casino would number around 1200; alas all it could boast tonight were 100 souls to rattle around the disinfectant-smelling hall.

Jennifer, the two Kate's, Selena, Pete and Maisy, Holly, Freddie, Jack and Mateo were all milling around, clinging to the food tables and circulating the void. A number of overtly lesbian women chatted in the alcoves, one such crew cut lady in a lightweight trouser suit came up to the stage and introduced herself as Cath Pearce; she was the event organiser and mighty pleased that the boys could accommodate the evening.

"No problem," said Seamus, "we're only too, too pleased to perform for you."

Cath appeared a trifle bemused by the English accent, and stepping back from the testosterone on stage she said, "Help yourselves to the food table." Then reversed towards a group of similarly inclined ladies.

"That's very kind of 'er," said Tom, "we could do with a table back 'ome."

Hot Pot leaned in, his bass languid around his neck. "Bearded clams are on the menu tonight girls," he murmured.

After a short welcoming speech and the proclamation of Jack and Mateo's imminent wedding, Cath introduced tonight's entertainment.

"Ladies and lesbians, I give you, Off the Scale!"

A feeble applause clattered from the sides of the hall as Chad clicked in the first number, The Foundations hit, *Baby Now That I've Found You.*

As if being controlled by underfloor magnets on sticks, a several couples were drawn onto the dance floor and obeyed the beat in a very formal fashion, but unlike any other gig that Tom had sung at, the couples were of the same gender, which was far too surreal for his naïve eyes. The closest he'd ever been to a host of gay folk before was watching The Village People perform *YMCA* on 'Top of the Pops' and to see two really butch ladies smooching right in front of him while he was trying to concentrate on the song was rather disconcerting. They were kissing passionately, two women snogging like it was an everyday thing and nobody batted an eyelid. They certainly didn't look like the kind of lesbians that he'd been exposed to in grainy videos and it was redefining some of his adolescent fantasies.

The band played The Isley Brothers, *This Old Heart of Mine* and Bell and Clay's, *Private Number*, then threw in a few of their own songs, which drastically cleared the dance floor, only a couple of langered gay men doing the Bump and Jennifer and Kate Norton, remained steadfast on the parquet.

Seamus took the initiative and struck up the opening line of *Johnny B. Goode*. This got everybody back on their feet, so the band followed it up with *Jailhouse Rock* and then *Great Balls of Fire*. The party was really swinging so they put in Bob Marley's *One Love* and UB40's *Red, Red Wine*, then slowed it down with the delectable *Waiting in Vain*.

This drew everyone together; especially Hot Pot, who came between Tom and Seamus and nodded out towards a pair of moustachioed men eating each other's faces on the fringe; one guy clenching the other by the buttocks pulling him in until their crutches were writhing together.

Stu sneered his one-sided smile which made Tom laugh and trip up on the lyric. Blotting out the scene he re-focused, imagining that this was just an ordinary crowd. But for a small town boy like Tom, this was a crash course in alternative lifestyles.

Eventually the band finished with two Blues Brothers classics, *Sweet Home Chicago* and *Everybody Needs Somebody to Love*, squeezing in far too many guitar solos for comfort; but it received a tremendous response from the now well-oiled crowd.

Jack came over sweating like a Turkish masseur and took Tom's hand. "Thank you for doing that for the boys," he said. "It's been a great success."

"They enjoyed it, didn't they?" replied the elevated Brit.

"We sure did." Jack smiled at Tom with bloodshot, brown-rimmed eyes, seemingly overdosed on the weed.

Pete and Maisy trotted up to the stage.

The Scottish woman was smiling like a wild cat. She unveiled a small gap between her front teeth and her rosy apple cheeks shone like polished Cox's Orange Pippins. "Well done, well done," she enthused. "I didn't expect you to be that good, very entertaining."

Tom jumped down from the high stage, and sent a sharp pain up through his bad ankle, a remnant from a vehicle accident back in '85. "We aim to please," he said modestly.

Pete was grinning from ear to ear. "I'm impressed. I didn't realise I was in the company of such talent."

Seamus jumped down next to his buddy. "You're too, too kind," he said, "we were only jamming really."

"Well it sounded polished to me," said Maisy, "and I think that Cath is over the moon." She gave Tom a youthful beam.

"Well that's the main man pleased then," Tom said with his tongue in his cheek.

Pete laughed, "That's fighting talk 'round these parts," he whispered, "and we're outnumbered, remember."

Tom made a face that said oops.

"We've got a proposition for you boys if you're up for it," Maisy said.

"We're up for anything," said Seamus chomping at the bit.

"What are you doing for the next two weeks?" asked Pete.

Tom wondered if a mini tour was in the offering. "Well I'm painting a garden wall for a week and then nothing," he said.

"I'm also doing nothing," pitched in Seamus, "for the whole two weeks."

Maisy kept on smiling. "How would you like to housesit at our place while we go on holiday?"

The lads weren't expecting that.

"Err, sure," Tom said flummoxed, "where d' ya' live?"

"On East Mabel Street, it's off of Euclid Avenue … off Speedway."

"Oh, I know," replied Tom, vaguely imagining the area. "When ya' going away?"

"On Monday," said Pete. "Sorry it's short notice. We did have someone lined up for it, but they've let us down and you two seem like well-balanced individuals, a couple of trustworthy chaps, fellow Brits and all that—"

Maisy cut him short. "Do you like cats?"

"We're quite found of pussy," said Seamus, who then immediately blushed. "Sorry, I don't know what came over me then."

Maisy and Pete were laughing, talk like that didn't bother Maisy at all, she had grown up with four brothers and was quite used to the way men talked about the opposite sex.

"Why don't you come 'round tomorrow and take a look," suggested Pete, "you can make your minds up after you see the place."

They set a rendezvous point of midday, giving them plenty of time to sleep off any activity that might befall them this evening.

Hot Pot packed his gear away and wished the lads a fond goodnight. Chad stowed his drums in the back of his VW camper van, then asked Tom and Seamus if they wanted to have a drink at the racquet club where he worked. Always up for somewhere new, the boys eagerly accepted. So, leaving the party in the hands of a man wife with a couple of turntables, they bid their friends adios and followed Chad over to Country Club Road for a snifter at the new drinking hole.

The club was at the dead-end of the street, a floodlit leisure complex that boasted scores of outdoor tennis courts, indoor volley, racquet and basketball courts, a couple of swimming pools, a gym and sauna facilities, housed in a large white building that clung to the south bank of the Rillito river.

Chad worked in the bar, and therefore could invite guests to use the facilities if he accompanied them. The only facility the boys were interested in tonight was the beer taps and as a bonus, Chad also received a discount on any purchases.

Working the bar tonight was his good friend and colleague, Julie.

Standing just 5-2, she looked diminutive behind the long pine expanse and was equally dwarfed by the tall beer spigots. She was pulling a pitcher of lager as the trio entered the room.

"Hey Chad, can't keep away, huh?" Her eyes flicked over his two companions before resting solely on the liquid being poured.

"Jules, I'd like you to meet my two buddies here, this is Tom and this is Seamus, they're from England and we've just performed our first gig together."

"Really, wow where was that?" She finished pouring the beer, and then placed the pitcher on a round wooden tray along with four tall beer glasses.

"At the El Casino Ballroom," he said screwing his face up like it was the most obscure place in the world to perform. "Our audience was err … interesting."

She leaned into the bar with both hands. "Oh, how come?"

Chad curled his top lip revealing his perfect teeth. "It was a benefit for our local gay community—a freebie."

"Oh, dad would be so proud of you," she announced as she sashayed off toward a table of sportsmen.

"Why would 'er dad be proud of us?" questioned Tom.

"Long story. Her dad came out of the closet a few years after Julie was born. Apparently he'd been fighting it for some time."

"Fuck … is she cool with that?" asked Seamus following the girl to the table with his eyes.

"Ah, yeah, they get along just fine. I think it helps that he's a millionaire. Never bite the hand that feeds right," Chad joked.

Julie had a cute little figure, thick dark medium length straight hair, eyes like coals, but unfortunately no neck. Seamus fancied her immediately.

A couple of beers later Seamus and Tom had Julie charmed enough to want to spend the rest of the night with them. She had been invited to a party by one of the staff in an apartment block across the road. Julie in turn invited all three boys.

She was an intriguing character, coy, certainly intelligent and demurely sophisticated. Tom found her appealing and great company, but not sexy enough for a shag. Seamus on the other hand considered her delectable.

When they arrived, an ethereal eerie silence shrouded the apartment block where the party was supposed to be, like the building was encased in a mysterious invisible vacuum. The night air was warm and still, every light in the house was on, the doors were all open, but not a soul was to be found inside.

They climbed the exterior steps to the 1st floor of the white building and went in. A massive seawater tropical fish tank centred the open-plan living space, combining the kitchen, dining room and lounge. The boys peered in at the formidable marine eco system and marvelled at the beautiful fish therein, mesmerized by its crystal clarity and the fantastic colours of the coral.

It was all too intangible. Where were the owners? If this was a party, where were the guests? Where was the drink? Were they in the right house?

The boys followed Julie down to the basement. The apartment was built on a hill and the back had three floors, as opposed to the two at the front.

Down the steps they found the booze, a large barrel of beer already tapped and some plastic cups. Instinctively they helped themselves.

All of a sudden, people were pouring in from every direction like the deluge of some long distance conga line, music started up and hey presto, the party was in full swing.

Tom and Seamus just looked at each other and shrugged. Fortune favours the brave, thought Tom and poured himself another beer.

By 2:00 a.m. they had drunk enough to be considered appropriately soused. The quartet meandered out to the pool area which was typically fenced and gated off to the public with black-painted iron railings. But it held no barrier to the lads who quickly scaled the fence and opened the gate for madame.

Stripping bollock-naked the three boys hopped into the hot tub, which was bubbling away like a lonely cauldron in need of human ingredients.

Julie whose excitement couldn't be screened, peeled down to her off-white bra and knickers and plunged in, her nipples projected like two brown bullets through the sodden cotton and her thick black bush could clearly be seen beneath the water.

The situation felt glorious, a statically charged harmonious air engulfed them as they frolicked in the spume, talking gibberish and telling anecdotes of times gone by. Seamus was in devious form, and it seemed to be having the desired effect on Julie.

After a while they were fully cooked, so extracted themselves from the froth and ran to the pool with a commotion that would rouse the ancients. The temperature change was shocking and momentarily took their breaths away.

"Wow," shouted Seamus, "fuckin' 'ell … fuckin' 'ell."

"Jesus," said Tom. "I'm getting back into the jacuzzi."

All four of them ejected from the pool like the family from Atlantis, slipping back into the hot water and leaving a drenched trail between the two ponds.

"Me' old fella's never been so small," remarked Tom blaming the cold water for his acorn sized 'willy'.

"Mine's disappeared altogether," joked Seamus.

"You guys," said Chad.

"You can't blame the water for your inadequacies boys, but hey, size doesn't matter, right?" teased Julie.

Apartment lights were flicking on in the surrounding building and raised voices could be heard above the drone of the party music. Abruptly two gun shots cracked the raven sky with an ear splitting suddenness that startled the rampant quartet into frozen hysteria.

"Get outta my pool!" shouted the anonymous secreted gunslinger in a western drawl.

The occupants needed no other instruction. They scrambled out of the hot tub, hurriedly snatched up their respective piles and speedily exited through the gate like exposed water nymphs, their bare arses disappearing into the night.

They ran and hobbled as best they could on a dirt road, back to the car park of the club, never once looking back until they reached the relative safety of the Arkansas Chuggerbug, where at last they could catch their breaths and put their dampened 'togs' back on.

Their breathing was laboured, and once his shorts were on, Tom leaned back against the car. "Bit unnecessary wasn't it?" he gasped. "All 'e 'ad to do was ask us to leave."

Seamus was panting, "Fuckin' 'ell, good job we got outta that jacuzzi, I pissed me' self."

"I guess we pissed *him* off good and proper," said Chad, who had turned extremely ghostly in the moonlight.

Julie put her uniform back on in silence and said, "We should report that guy for firing a weapon in public like that— that's totally against the law, even in Arizona." She was obviously scared out of her wits, shaking not just from the cold.

Chad put an arm around her and squeezed her tight. "Hey, we're okay, hun, nobody got hurt," he said comfortingly. "I'll drop you off home and sleep on the couch if you're scared."

Julie nodded, she felt very assailable just now.

Seamus wished he had gotten in there first.

The friends said goodnight and departed the car park in their respective vehicles. On the way back to Arty's, the boys couldn't help but laugh at the near scrape.

"Did you really piss in the water?" asked Tom.

"I nearly turned the fuckin' water brown," replied his buddy before cackling at his own admission.

Tom giggled back before saying, "Would 'ave been the perfect parting gift."

***

Sunday morning came way too soon. Tom was so tired that even yawning was an effort. His eyes ached like they'd been stubbed by a finger during the night and his limbs behaved like sandbags dangling from his unresponsive torso.

He focussed on his watch; 11:30 a.m. A ripple of angst pulsed through his brain. They were supposed to be at Pete and Maisy's house in half-an-hour, they'd never make it in time. Then the cringe hit him, a wave of fear gushed from his head to his toes, and laid hot and heavy in the pit of his stomach. They could have so easily been killed last night. God knows where the bullets went. He rolled onto his side and surveyed sleeping beauty in the next bed, a snoring behemoth in complete abeyance. Tom wondered where his dreams were taking him.

"Seamus," Tom pushed a foot onto his buddy's exposed leg. "Seamus, come on, we're gonna be late."

"Just resting my eyes Rasta'; two minutes."

Tom sat up with great effort, exhaled, then giddily stomped off to the bathroom.

Pete and Maisy's place was a bungalow on a corner plot, in a classic Tucson suburban street. Fenced off with low chain link, the unkempt front yard sported rocks, dust, tufts of long grass and scrubby Mesquite trees. The boys meandered up through the mini desert and climbed the steps of the veranda, opened the fly screen and rapped on the front door. A selection of wind chimes tinkled lightly with the disturbance of the still heavy air. It was 1:00 p.m. and the clandestine army of chirping insects had started up early, further fuelling Tom's inquisition.

Pete answered the door, gushing with a smile, certainly pleased to see them both.

"Come on in, lads," he offered, "we'd nearly given up on you."

"Sorry we're late, mate," said Seamus quasi-apologetically. "'ad a bit of a late one and couldn't peel myself from the sheets," he yawned.

"Ah the squalls of youth, I remember them too well, do come in," beckoned Pete.

The dim coolness of the room was in complete contrast to the ultraviolet intensity outside. The lads removed their sunglasses in order to avoid furniture.

Shutters and curtains drawn against the exterior radiance meant the occupants lived by lamplight, which gave everything a subdued atmoshere. The living room was of a similar fashion to their circle of friends; New Age hippy, with sprinklings of the mystic, Celtic and the psychedelic and, of course, the telltale signs of a couple of pot heads.

Maisy sauntered in from the bedroom wearing an orange and red tightly-wrapped Sari, her rosy apple cheeks supremely exaggerated by her smile. "Have we intruded on your hangover boys," she said with her soft Scottish accent.

"*Somnus rumpus*," added Pete, "sleep interrupted."

Seamus yawned again. "I could manage another 'alf an 'our Pete, if you've got a spare bed."

"Sleep all you want when we are away old boy, you have a choice of four beds."

A girl of maybe 12-years-old appeared from the kitchen, she was also in a Sari, freckle-faced, the double of her mother.

"This is Seashell," said Maisy, "Jorge is somewhere in the house, possibly digging up the vegetables in the back yard."

"Oh, you grow your own grub?" said Tom.

Pete replied, "Just a few squash and some tomatoes … something that you'll have to water I'm afraid, if you decide to stay here. Can I get you a drink; tea maybe?"

The boys accepted some Earl Grey and took a tour of the house. There were three extremely lived-in bedrooms, furnished with futons of various sizes and a sofa bed in the large living room. Tom surmised that they must enjoy having guests sleep over.

The kitchen was untidy, but not dirty, had a back door with a cat flap in it and three food bowls on the floor containing various stages of consumption.

"We have three cats," interjected Maisy, "another reason for having house sitters while we're on our 'jollys'."

"Cool," said Seamus. "D' ya' mind if I 'ave a fag in the 'ouse?"

"No, but can we show you the garden?" Maisy opened the back door and held it for the lads to follow her.

Stepping out of the water-cooled air-conditioned bungalow was like taking the meat from the fridge to the oven, seriously searing the flesh on the boys' bare shoulders.

"Christ it's 'ot today," said Tom wearily.

Pete proudly presented his rows of desperately withered ground vines. Tom who had knowledge of gardening perused the lines of veg with a mind of conjecture. Some of these plants were just gourds, they certainly were not edible.

"You don't eat these, do you Pete?"

Pete chuckled, "Only the Butternut Squash, the rest are for the school, they make great shakers for the music room."

"Right," said Tom, thinking that you can never have enough shakers.

"Well what do you think?" asked Pete when they returned to the house.

Seamus gave Tom the nod of approval; they could have some fun in here, treat it like their own pad.

"We'll take it, sir," confirmed Tom, "what time are you off tomorrow?"

Pete was chuffed, he explained that they were going mid-morning and would be back in 15 days. He would give them a key today and they could come back at their leisure, help themselves to the food stocks and party if they wanted to, just as long as they kept the cats and the plants alive, and didn't wreck the place.

"You can count on us," declared Seamus believing that he meant what he was saying.

"Excellent," said Pete, "just make sure that you dispose of your condoms away from the house."

"We only use the edible ones," proclaimed Tom.

Pete baulked at the thought and chugged. He opened the front door to let the boys out.

"Don't worry, your home is in safe 'ands," said Tom to the couple who were going on vacation "Where are you off too anyway?"

"The Baja, Mexico, might do a spot of whale-stroking in the bay."

"Ah," said Tom none the wiser. "'ave a good trip."

"Indeed we will," replied Pete, "see you in two weeks."

The boys got back into their roasting tin and headed for the Egg Garden, for a spot of much needed all-day breakfast.

***

By the end of Tuesday Tom had finished painting the Great Wall and Saul had given him another task, to paint the trunks of the citrus trees with a coat of white wash. The young Brit finally had an answer to the nagging question which had bothered him for a while. The paint reflected damaging ultraviolet light away from the delicate bark of the trees, but because it was emulsion it still allowed the skin to breathe.

There were more than 50 trees, some of which had distinctly low, dense and thorn covered branches, so it was going to take some effort. A bit of an arduous task in Tom's mind, but it secured more money.

The mid-July heat was intense and temperatures were hitting all time highs. He laboured away in just his flimsy Le Coq Sportif running shorts, permanently soaked around the waist band. Sweat vanished from his mahogany back before it had a chance to form rivulets. He was venting his body fluids at a dangerous rate, blissfully unaware of his grave circumstance, ensconced inside a bubble of music provided by his Walkman.

Softly singing to himself and making long lazy strokes with a paint encrusted brush on a particularly bare branched specimen up near the house, he felt a cold tap on his baking shoulder.

Startled he turned around to find Caitlyn standing behind him dressed like a cast member of Dallas, manicured, fresh, that just out of the salon look, and wafting of heady Poison perfume.

"You'd better come in, it's a hundred and ten degrees out here. You'll die if you continue to work in this."

Tom removed his headphones, it was definitely scorching hot, but not oppressive, an arid heat unlike anything he was used to. "Oh, okay," he said, welcome to have a break and interested to see inside the forbidden palace.

After putting his brush in the shed, Caitlyn led the way to the house, her fragrance pulling him along like loosely attached reins.

The temperature drop inside was considerable, at least 50° and the rooms were intensely darker than his eyes were attuned to. He shuddered with the shock.

"Would you like a cold drink, Tom?"

"Lovely, some squash would be great."

"Come into the kitchen, but don't let Saul know okay, he'll be mad at me," she said in low tones.

The two Golden Retrievers and the black Akita bitch came trotting up, instantly inquisitive of the new house guest. Fonda reared up on her hind legs and placed her fore paws on his chest, her tongue like a piece of pulsating ham lolled out of one side of her mouth.

"Get down Fonda," chastised Caitlyn.

Tom didn't mind, he made a great fuss of all three of them. He loved animals and these three seemed to enjoy him. The male Akita, Myko, who was lying on the living room floor, barely managed to raise his head in acknowledgement of someone new entering the building.

The living room was vast, sunk down a step from the hallway and entered through a white-walled arch with a bare brick trim. Its dominant features were dark wood panelling that covered the entire left hand wall consisting of cupboards, drawers and shelving, a massive white L-shaped couch that could seat a whole football team and the rear and right hand walls that were made up entirely of bronze framed double glazed patio doors that stretched from floor to ceiling. There was too much bling to take in, a room adorned with a multitude of fine art and sculptures, was like Alcázar to a poor fella from the suburbs.

Caitlyn swayed to the right through another arch into a circular dining room with a round table that could seat eight comfortably. This room was glazed with a quarter round bay window, had large paintings hung on the walls, and grand tropical plants residing in Japanese style urns.

Through yet another arch was the kitchen area, the rear part of which had more patio doors, in front of these stood the biggest TV that Tom had ever seen, accompanied by two huge rattan chairs with oversized, extremely comfortable looking white cushions. Obviously this is where the couple spent most of their time in the evening. A snug at the end of the kitchen, where his lordship could recline in front of the box while his lady presented him with tidbits from her larder.

In the kitchen proper, a spacious rectangle tightly-fitted with walnut cabinets and all the latest appliances, stood Gracie at one end of the central island attending to a pile of ironing. She smiled at Tom through the steam while pressing another one of Saul's shirts and said sweetly, "*Hola.*"

Caitlyn approached an enormous double-fronted fridge with a pint glass in her hand.

"Ice?" she asked the wide-eyed Brit.

"Oh yes, please," replied Tom expecting her to open the freezer and pull out an ice tray. Instead she placed the glass into an alcove in the fridge door, depressing a lever that allowed ice cubes to free fall into the vessel. A magic fridge.

"Fresh OJ?"

"That would be splendid, Caitlyn."

"Go sit yourself down in front of the TV. You can relax inside for a while and let your body temperature return to normal—here." She handed him the remote control, "Wander through the stations, there may be a movie on HBO, if you can stand the commercials."

Tom smiled; he felt a little spoiled, a bit guilty and a tad exposed sitting in the governor's chair, oozing testosterone in front of a middle-aged housewife that he barely knew, and getting paid for it.

Raising Arizona was playing on the movie channel; a comedy starring Nicolas Cage, Tom found it gloriously funny and soon lost himself in the big chair.

Caitlyn disappeared into the labyrinth and Gracie continued silently ironing. By the time the film finished it was 3:00 p.m. and high time Tom was back decorating the fruit trees. He thanked Gracie for the orange juice, which was just as amazing as before and exited the house via the side door that opened into the garage.

Greeted by a brazier of an afternoon Tom strolled to the tool shed to retrieve his paint pot and finish up on today's mission.

On the way back to Mabel Street, the noise coming from the back of the Chuggerbug was steadily increasingly, to the point where it was grating on Tom's nerves and attracting concerned looks from fellow motorists. His embarrassment mounted, and with the fear of something hideous becoming imminent, he drove on tenterhooks, every muscle tense for the inevitable breakdown, praying for the old girl to limp home. Obviously with no breakdown cover and no funds to pay for it, it would be a rather painful walk home, and the prospect of losing his job for want of transport was depressing.

Midway on the journey, the smell of burning alerted him to a trail of grey smoke billowing from the rear, poisoning his tracks, "Fuck it," he said. He was on fire.

Pulling into the nearest strip mall, he rolled up outside a Chinese launderette, rapidly turned off the engine and shot out of the car. The rear wheel had seized up and had been burning rubber for a good quarter of a mile. The hub of the wheel was glowing hot and the smoke was making quite a screen.

Tom ran into the laundry and frantically asked the attendant for some water.

"Your car is on fire, sir," exclaimed the dim-witted girl.

He couldn't believe his ears, "Yes I know. That's why I want the water, love, 'urry up."

The girl, knocked back by his curtness, dashed off into the rear of the building.

The prospects of a petrol fire explosion were playing havoc with Tom's neural system and the thought of a plate glass shower wasn't something he relished.

A dull thud, like the sound of someone saying boo through a tube, preceded orange flames flickering round the tyre under the wheel arch.

Stunned for a second, Tom thought it best to leg it. He burst through to the back room where the girl was filling a bucket from the sink tap. Grabbing her by the hand as he passed, he dragged her out through an open rear door into a dusty yard.

"Wait here!" he yelled. "It's gonna blow up."

Her face was the picture of confused terror as Tom left her and ran up the street. Five seconds later a fireball erupted in front of the shop, sending a plume of black poisonous smoke high into the air above the building like a mini atom bomb mushroom.

"Fuck!" he hissed vehemently and stopped in his tracks. It occurred to him that somebody might have been caught by the blast. Overcome by guilt; he turned and raced back to the parking lot in front of the launderette. A few cars had stopped and the occupants were out beside open doors gaping at the scene, but thankfully no-one had been close enough to be injured. The windows on the car had all caved in and the interior was a raging inferno.

It upset Tom, who attempted to appear just like an onlooker. The laundry window was miraculously still intact and the girl was nowhere to be seen, so he slipped away and took to a slow jog on the sidewalk, his attire of running shorts and a vest top being his guise. Hopefully he wouldn't raise suspicion, leaving the Arkansas Chuggerbug unattended at its own cremation.

He could think of nothing he'd left inside to incriminate him or Seamus; the car didn't have any legal ties to them whatsoever, but now he was bollocksed, both for getting home and for getting back to work.

10
Super Sport

Freddie dropped Tom off outside Pete and Maisy's in the early evening. He had begrudgingly responded to a frantic phone call and felt responsible enough to leave his bong and go pick up the stranded Englishman from a call box on North 1st Avenue. Deeply concerned by the burning hulk of his ex-car, he told Tom that if the police came calling he'd say that he sold it some months ago to a random guy he'd met at a swap-meet, and hadn't seen either it or him since, and hope that the story held water. Jennifer would give him an alibi for his whereabouts this afternoon.

"You're 'ome late," Seamus said as his buddy rattled in through the back door.

"She's gone mate," replied Tom looking thoroughly despondent.

"What, what, what … who's gone, wos' 'appened?"

Tom gave his buddy the low down on the demise of their transport and how he'd narrowly escaped death once again inside a fireball. Seamus was agog, he sparked up a cigarette.

Tom sat down on a kitchen chair and rested his elbows on the table; his hands cradled his worried face.

One of the cats, a skinny tabby female rubbed incessantly at his bare legs, marking him with the scent from her cheek glands. Like Tom, she wanted feeding, but there was no sign of dinner on the horizon.

The silence was oppressive, the irritation of the cat and the smell of the cigarette smoke nauseated Tom; he needed to be outside again.

"'ave you watered the plants yet?" he probed Seamus, who spluttered a feeble excuse.

"No, I was just waiting for the sun to go down a bit before I went out there."

Tom got up. "I'll do it," he said striding for the back door. Although he was tired, sticky and famished, a spell alone with the hosepipe would give him time to contemplate their situation. "You can put the dinner on," he said letting the screen door spring back and clatter against its frame.

Sometime later the smell of chips came wafting out through the air-conditioning unit and prompted Tom to leave the irrigation alone for the night.

"Mushroom omelette and 'ome fries," announced Seamus as Tom came in.

Tom looked at the plate on the work top. "Aren't omelettes supposed to be yellow?" he said sardonically.

"These are a little suntanned Ras', I got a bit distracted feeding the cats while Rome burned."

"They're Nero 'nough chargrilled mate."

"Nero 'nough, ha," barked Seamus.

"Listen, I'm gonna 'ave to call up Saul and tell 'im I can't make it in tomorra', till we sort ourselves out with another car, but fuck knows 'ow we're gonna do that unless somebody else gives us one, and I can't imagine that—"

"You can always get the bus," interrupted Seamus.

"Yeah I suppose I could," yielded Tom. "I ain't been on a bus for years, where's the fuckin' bus stop?" he shrugged, "I bet I'll 'ave to change somewhere, it'll take forever to get there. Bollocks."

Seamus placed tonight's culinary effort in front of his mate. "'ere eat ya' dinner, 'ave a shower and then phone Saul, 'e might 'ave an idea, ya' never know."

"Perhaps 'e'll lend me the burgundy Lincoln, it never leaves the garage," declared Tom.

"Umm," said Seamus with a mouthful of food, "pimp my ride."

Later on, Tom telephoned his boss and nervously explained his predicament.

"What?" snapped Saul, "Your car caught fire? Did ya' get hurt?"

"No, no, but the car's a 'write-off'."

"What?"

"The car's destroyed, so I don't know 'ow I'm gonna be able to get to work tomorra'."

The line went silent for a moment, and then Saul spoke in softer tones. "How about ya' buy my pickup from me for fifteen hundred dollars?"

"I don't 'ave that sort of money, Saul."

"Ya' can pay it off, a hundred dollars a week, there's enough work here to keep ya' busy for a while, whaddya' think?"

"That's a generous offer Saul, but I don't think that Seamus and I can survive on just a hundred dollars a week."

Again the phone line went silent. The pause was broken by, "What if both you and your buddy work here and I take a hundred and fifty dollars a week from ya'?"

This was a much more agreeable idea, but Tom thought it best to talk it over with Seamus first.

"Can I call ya' back in five minutes please, Saul, I've just gotta run it by Seamus?"

"Yup, don't be too long, it's getting late," growled the boss.

And so it was agreed, although Seamus would be giving up his precious time and half his sleep, the slick little El Camino would become theirs as of tomorrow. They still had to get over to Orange Grove in the morning, so a pleading call was made to Jennifer who was all too willing to send Salina over first thing. Salina was not so keen.

***

A fine mantle of dust dulled her metallic bronze paintwork; she had a flat rear tyre, no tags and had sat there sulking ever since Caitlyn's brother Charles had sold her to Saul many months before when he was desperate for money.

The little Chevrolet had chrome five spoke wheels, a 5.7 litre V8 engine; the words *Super Sport* emblazoned in gold along the lower body side, framed by stripes, and even though she was an automatic, she flew like shit off a shovel. Her only fault was a broken speedometer, so the boys never got to appreciate just how fast she really was, but she purred and throbbed like a dragster.

They stood admiring her at the foot of the drive, her beige interior was in decent shape for a ten-year-old car and there wasn't a scratch on her body, but for all her good looks she was still considered by her manufacturer to be just a utility vehicle. The boys deemed her to be something else; transport to the stars.

Saul ambled down to meet them, his brilliant white shirt unbuttoned to his chest, spoilt by a dribble of cinnamon juice.

"You can stare at it all ya' fuckin' like when you get it home. Right now ya' gotta work the fuckin' payments off," he bellowed.

Half-heartedly the boys rounded and greeted their boss, then strolled with him in silence as he delivered today's instructions.

He wanted them to finish painting the trees, paint the electronic gate with brown wood stain and then make a start on painting the driveway's cobble stones with red floor paint.

Mid-morning, Caitlyn appeared in the garage offering two cold cans of Coke; the boys readily accepted them and stood in the relative cool of the open garage to down them and take a breather. Caitlyn herself had a can of diet, caffeine-free Coke and stayed with the lads for a chit-chat. She was most interested to hear about Tom and Seamus' backgrounds and very keen to learn more about England. Talking of course, was Seamus' forte and a ten-minute break turned into a half-hour history lesson, at which point Tom was bored and kicking his heels, itching to get back to work.

"Is the Jeep yours as well then Caitlyn?" asked Seamus.

"It's my son Jamie's. He's away at college in Alaska right now studying engineering, but he'll be home soon after the summer," she replied, her face displaying unconvincing pride.

"It's a beautiful car Caitlyn, I bet it's fun to drive," continued Seamus.

"It can be a little bumpy, but it attracts a lot of attention, which is what Jamie wants of course; the young girls love it."

"Sure, sure," confirmed Seamus imagining himself at the wheel.

Tom severed Seamus' indulgence. "We'd better get back to work Caitlyn; Saul's given us a lot t' do today. He said that you'd give us a lift down to a gas station later, to put some air into that flat tyre on the El Camino."

"Oh sure, later this afternoon, I have to go out now and buy you guys some more floor paint from Home Depot, I'll be back in a couple of hours," she replied. She turned and wafted back inside, leaving her sweet aroma languishing in the car port.

Seamus puckered up his lips and drew in of the perfume. "I would," he said in all earnestness.

Tom grimaced. "Mother-fucker," he mocked.

They went back to the trees.

At lunchtime they bought a gallon container of apple juice each and drank it all within an hour. The plastic containers then became ideal water containers that were replenished from the well tap and kept in the tool shed fridge. They were drinking so much fluid, but because the liquid was venting through their pores and evaporating fast, they never once had to urinate during the day.

The bugs in the trees were the loudest they had ever been now, maybe the infernal heat was getting to them too.

When Caitlyn came back from shopping and asked the boys to unload her trunk full of goodies, Tom asked her if she knew the source of the frustrating racket.

"They're Cicadas," she said, "big ugly flying bugs that sit in the trees, they feed on sap and lay their eggs in curled up leaves. I think that the noise is a kinda mating call, irritating though it is."

"They've been driving me nuts for weeks, I can't see 'em, it's like they're invisible or something."

"They have big transparent wings, and their bodies are the colour of the branches that they sit on, so they're very hard to see," she informed them.

"Are they here all year, Caitlyn?" enquired Seamus.

"Oh no," she hastened to say, "They go somewhere else when it gets cooler."

"Thank God for that," said Tom. "Noisy critters."

Two gallon cans of red floor paint were lifted out and added to the original pair in the tool shed. This next operation was going to take careful planning so as not to paint one's self into a corner.

First the boys tried sweeping the drive to remove the dirt and vegetation from between the lines of printed concrete, but this proved painstakingly infuriating. So they shifted to jet-washing it down the drive with the garden hose and a Hoselock spray attachment. This worked, and turned out to be quite a meditative and thankfully cooling task which both lads wanted, while the other one swept. Of course Seamus turned it into a game when he was in control of the hose and thoroughly drenched Tom with childish aplomb.

The damp concrete dried rapidly, giving them a couple of hours to lay down some red.

Furnishing two new 4 in brushes and starting around by the garden gate area, they left a little triangle for Ruben to step out on before launching himself on to the dirt of the grove; they'd come back to that later. They made their way round the front of the house, managing to reach the section where the drive met the turn around. They ceased activity when Saul pulled up and cast his critical eye on the project.

"Looking good, Saul," enthused Seamus, hoping for a commendable reply.

"Looks like Kate's fuckin' lipstick," he drawled.

It was a bright postbox red and in marked contrast to the old darker claret shade, a dye that was almost certainly mixed in with the concrete.

"Should tone down a little when it's dry Saul," said Tom trying to placate the New Yorker.

Saul chewed gum noisily in one side of his mouth. "Fuckin' wants to, it'll be like driving over a fuckin' whore's mouth every mornin'. Did ya' get ya' tyre fixed?"

"Yes, Saul, it just needed some air," replied Seamus.

"That's good, you can drive the fucker home, an' I'll see ya' t'morra."

They put the equipment away and headed for their new toy. Being the eldest, Tom elected himself as the first driver. He couldn't wait. Inside he noticed for the first time she had an eight-track cassette player, a true relic from the 70s.

"'ow we gonna play our demos on that?" he jested.

They drove to the gas station and proudly put $20 in the tank. It had been a while since they had actually paid for some gas, so it felt weird, but this car was a keeper and with the pair of them at work now, Tom felt confident that they could afford some legitimate fuel.

The El Camino was a dream to drive, light, yet so powerful, you could steer her with one finger and she glided effortlessly while cruising the urban sprawl back to Mabel, but could roar like a chained dragon if you needed to put your foot down.

Nearing home, along Speedway, they were neck and neck with a blue sedan, Tom had his window down and his sun-kissed arm angled out on the door frame to catch the breeze. A flirtatious brunette in her late teens rolled down her window alongside him, and with a devil of a beam asked, "Are you a super sport?"

Tom smiled, thinking that the Arkansas never got him this sort of attention; he said, "That depends on what game you are playing."

The girl laughed wickedly as her driver girlfriend sped off causing her long semi-permed curls to flap around her pretty eclipsed face.

"Very nice," said Seamus realising the car's potential.

"A fanny magnet," Tom responded.

That night, at Pete and Maisy's, Seamus got a call from Caryn. She had gone to stay with her dad in San Antonio, Texas, and wondered if he would like to come and visit for the weekend. A flight would only cost $90, but he'd have to ride the Greyhound bus up to Phoenix to catch it, another $20, which would leave Seamus 'skint' again. But Caryn assured him he would not have to spend another dime, so he jumped at the chance; he would go on Friday night.

After Saul left for work on Thursday morning the lads continued to paint the drive; it hadn't toned down at all, much to Saul's discomfort. But they had started now so were reluctantly urged to carry on. They asked Saul to park in the bottom lot when he came home this afternoon, then they could stay on and paint behind his car so that it would be dry in the morning. They didn't get that far.

At around 2:00 p.m. that day the rains decided they should begin, and begin in earnest.

From a faultless clear blue sky in the morning, over the mountains came a black cloud so dense it looked like a trillion tons of coal dust unfolding from the heavens, undulating down the Catalinas and devouring the foothills. Day turned to night, lightning bolts frazzled the pressurised oxygen all around them and thunder shook the very foundations they stood on. Water cascaded from on high like they were at the foot of an eternal waterfall; not droplets, but sheer sheets of warm rain causing the boys to run and take shelter under the porch from fear of being hurt.

Caitlyn joined them out front to witness the spectacle, the lads were sodden and mildly in shock, especially Seamus who hadn't been subjected to anything like this in his life.

They watched, as not only the fresh paint they had applied this morning, but also yesterday's coat as well, was ripped apart and washed away down the drive into storm drains along the road.

"Oh dear," said Caitlyn, "Saul's not going to be pleased with this."

Seamus brushed a water droplet from his nose with the back of his hand. "Bit of a waste o' money Caitlyn."

Tom tried diplomacy. "D' ya' think we bought the wrong product?" His dark wet skin appeared a deeper mahogany in the subdued light under the porch.

"Well I did get floor paint," said Caitlyn in her defence, "perhaps it's only meant for interior use; we better check the label on the can."

Sure enough when the small print was scrutinised, the instructions were for inside use only. It was never going to last on the drive.

"I'd better call Saul and tell him what's happened, see what he says," she said and slipped back into the house, leaving the two Brits to stare at the deluge.

"At least it's shut the cicadas up," reasoned Tom.

Amazingly, apart from a few fallen oranges, none of the trees had sustained any damage; they just looked very forlorn, drooping with the added weight of the water on their branches. Caitlyn came back within a couple of minutes smiling like she'd achieved something.

"Saul says that one of you can come with me to the store, while the other one waits here and cleans up the mess that the storm has made. Who wants to come?"

Seamus was fastest to react, sensing another adventure. "I'll come Caitlyn; I've never been in a Lincoln before."

Tom rolled his eyes; he was quite used to Seamus' time-wasting exercises. He was a patient man, his time would come.

Caitlyn became quite girly and excited, "We'll go when the rain stops. You guys come inside and watch TV. I'll fix you a drink; coffee?"

"That'll be splendid, you're too, too kind Caitlyn," flattered Seamus.

A couple of hours later, it was like there had never been a storm at all. Not a trace of a cloud could be seen anywhere; it was freaky. The sun blazed down and rapidly dried up all the surface water The only evidence left was the flowing washes that had erupted all over town.

While they flew off to Home Depot, Tom got to work with a broom. Slivers of paint had gathered in the lines of the concrete pattern, they adhered frustratingly to the grooves and were going to take an eternity to shift.

He stopped after a bit and retrieved a fallen orange. Sitting on a tree well to peel and eat it, an enterprising idea occurred to him. Surely the Berns' had more than enough fruit here than they could ever use. They wouldn't miss a few sacks of oranges if they happened to be whisked away before they were accounted for.

Tom could easily sneak a few into the car, behind the seat, each day, and when they had enough, they could sell them at a local swap meet and earn a nice little packet on the side. It seemed like an opportunity staring him in the face. He made his way to a part of the grove that couldn't be seen from the house and gathered up a shirt full of fruit, then casually meandered to the El Camino and deposited the booty behind the driver's seat. Clicking the door shut he smiled inwardly, thinking of how clever he was.

The Lincoln returned a short while later, but alas the only floor paint available was the type they had already used, so Seamus had come up with an enlightened solution to the dilemma, and they had purchased several gallons of clear varnish, a translucent sealant that may well armour the paint enough to keep it on the drive.

It was too late in the afternoon to start painting now so the boys packed up and went home a little early. Tom told Seamus of his get rich quick scheme with the oranges, Seamus thought it a brilliant idea; they would gather more fruit tomorrow.

That night they swapped bedrooms, just to mash it up a bit; the hard unforgiving futons took a little getting used to, but once he did, Tom had the best night's sleep that he could remember and woke revitalised.

A different approach was needed for the epic driveway paint job. If this rain was going to appear every afternoon and spoil their efforts, they would have to manage by swiftly painting small sections in the morning, and then cover it up with a tarpaulin to give it a fighting chance. When it was dry, apply the sealant then cover that up. Or they could just wait a month till the rainy season had passed, but Saul wanted it done now, so manage it they did.

Sure enough at midday an impeccable sky turned pitch-black and ominous, drenching the plain with such a deluge that houses were in fear of being swept away.

The boys sheltered in the garage, Ruben in the tool shed. Caitlyn, who had a female friend visiting, invited the boys into the kitchen to meet her.

Macy Moore was a large lady dripping in gold, who was abrasively abrupt and ostensibly dogmatic. She was a divorcee, had two teenage kids, bred Akitas and had been left twenty-three million dollars by her late father.

Macy was in her mid-40s with cropped curly grey hair, and was somewhat robust; masculine even and yet showed a feminine side in a way that was both coy and amorous. She wore loose fitting cream pants and a frilly yellow cotton shirt, open to the cleavage that revealed many chains adorning her ruddy chest.

Her eyes were too small for a face that was round and small featured, and she wore no makeup whatsoever.

The two young steaming, bronzed, semi-naked Englishmen, standing dripping in front of her, ignited a flame within her depths that hadn't been fuelled in many a year. Something green awakened. These two belonged to Caitlyn but she wanted one.

They were certainly charming, but she'd have to work cautiously, pull one in slowly, like an angler with a fish on a line, reeling towards her keep net a degree at a time.

"So you're going off for the weekend Seamus to see your girlfriend. What are you doing Tom?" Macy enquired. She spoke rapidly and to the point.

"I plan to indulge in some erstwhile activities like drinking beer, playing the guitar and enjoying some fine home dining Macy, how about you?"

"Oh I've got a dog show to go to, up in Scottsdale, but if you're not too busy you could help with a problem that I have."

"Oh what's that?" enquired Tom hoping that it didn't involve dusting out some old cobwebs from a disused tunnel.

Caitlyn was instinctively suspicious.

"I'm having the daughter of a friend of mine come and stay for a week or two; she has just finished a long-term relationship and is very down in the dumps. You can take her out for dinner on Sunday night. I'll pay, any restaurant that you like, and you can borrow my Cadillac; you can cheer her up, show her a good time. I don't want her moping around the house for a fortnight, good Lord."

Talk about being handed it on a gold plate, Tom couldn't believe what he was hearing, of course he would do it; he felt a little farmed out, but why not, the cherry was ripe for the picking.

They set a time of 8:00 p.m. for Tom's arrival at Macy's house off Sunrise Drive in the Catalina foothills, a very swanky piece of real estate.

The rain stopped and the boys went back to work. Macy paraded out to her car, a brand new white Elegance. She told Caitlyn she would call her, waved and sped off feeling rather smug that she'd cast a line and got a nibble straight away.

Caitlyn was agitated. Macy was a close friend and confidante, but when it came to stealing her boys, the gloves would have to come off.

***

Sunday's sunset was magnificent, made the more spectacular by a bluff of lingering clouds hugging the horizon. A conglomerate of orange sorbet ice cream, rosé wine and blueberry bubblegum faded into the slow approaching grey-black of the evening.

Tom spent the day doing very little; he showered and put on his best cream trousers and a long sleeved leaf-green Ralph Lauren shirt. The clothes were far too heavy for this weather and he regretted the need to dress up; his legs were sweating already. He had an hour to go before picking up Annabel, so he was taking his time getting ready and enjoying a peach iced tea and the view from the front porch as the day retired.

Just then the house phone rang, it was Seamus. He'd got back into town on the Greyhound bus and was at the terminus next to the Congress hotel. He wanted collecting because he had no money left for a cab.

It was a twenty minute round trip, so it would be cutting it fine, but if he hurried, Tom would still be able to pick up Seamus and get over to Macy's for his date. He left immediately, agitated, it was added stress he didn't need.

When he arrived at the bus station Seamus was nowhere to be seen. Tom got out of the El Camino, went into the shelter and looked around, nothing. He cursed Seamus' name, got back into the car, and drove around the block once to see if his mate was just wandering around, but still nothing. With time running short, he decided to go back to Pete and Maisy's to check the answer machine for messages.

He ran into the house, spotted the dreaded red light blinking, pressed the play button, and sure enough; two unwelcome pieces of communication that fractured his corona.

Mate, don't bother picking me up, I'm gonna go into the Tap Room in the hotel and see if I can ponce a drink.

Mate, sorry, can you come and get me after all there's no-one in here, I'm in the Tap Room.

"Fuckin' bloke," shouted Tom at the answer machine, "I'll be fuckin' *well* late now. Bollocks."

He stomped out of the house again, ran to the car and sped off towards town again completely on edge, and hotter than a steam iron.

When Tom found Seamus he was perched on a bar stool, relaxed and in mid-conquest of a drunk student who was languishing on the bar. Seamus was laughing like a lunatic and untroubled by Tom's angst.

Tom scooped up Seamus' case. "Come on," he demanded, "You've made me well-fuckin' late."

"Alright, alright Rasta', let me finish me flipping beer," said Seamus necking his Coors Light. "This is Cheyenne, by the way."

"Nice to meet you," Tom said disapprovingly.

The girl limply raised a hand off the bar in salute.

Tom turned and left reluctantly followed by his buddy.

They sped back home all the way with Tom venting his spleen at Seamus' indifference. The two rarely argued, but this time Tom felt enraged at his friend's audacity.

Tom dumped Seamus' case on the pavement and got back into the car. It was 8:30; he was already half-an-hour late. He was just about to hit the accelerator when Seamus put his head through the window.

"Mate, can I borra' twenty bucks me' old mucker, I wanna go back out?"

Tom couldn't believe the liberty. "For fuck's sake!" he shouted. He got out of the car, reached in his soggy pocket and pulled out a note, screwed it up and threw it at his friend before jumping back in and wheel-spinning off.

Seamus tugged on his roll up, bent down and picked up the bill and said, "Mm, ha, ha, hee, hee," before entering the house unruffled.

Annabel, Annabel. Tom rolled her name over in his mind as he journeyed into the foothills and conjured up an image of British tennis beauty Annabel Croft. Quintessentially fine, English totty, in a white cotton summer frock and a crown of daisies on her long flowing chestnut locks, meandering slowly through a sun-drenched summer meadow, running her hands atop the tall grass and flowers, awash with hazy orange light. The ogress that presented herself however was in stark contrast.

This Annabel had a mop of hacked, wiry ginger hair, wore a shirt and trousers not too dissimilar to Tom's apparel, and had all the mannerisms of a bloke.

The disappointment must have been evident in Tom's face, even though he tried to disguise it with jovial charm.

Macy kissed him on the cheek with thin stiff lips and welcomed him inside.

"Sorry I'm not on time ladies; Seamus was late coming in to the Greyhound station and asked me to pick 'im up."

"Better late than never," observed Macy. "It's good to see you in something more presentable than just your running shorts." She smiled revealing a missing tooth on the right side of her upper jaw as her beady eyes almost disappeared in the folds of her flesh.

Annabel was introduced, she shook hands with Tom and in the light of the hallway he could see that she had an abundance of freckles, a mutation that rarely appealed to him.

No wonder she's single, he thought. Mind you, so am I.

She was also depressingly sullen, definitely in need of a good time.

Tom would try his best. But all he could think of right now was food; he was extremely hungry but had the sense to have booked a table for 9:00.

Macy's house was low-level, long, with white painted walls and a Spanish pan-tiled roof. It had manicured gardens and kennels in the right-hand wing. At this point Tom had only entered the hallway; it had sealed dark terracotta tiles on the floor and white walls adorned with expensive paintings and Native American art.

"Run along now," commanded Macy in her high-pitched cartoon voice. "You'll miss your table—where did you book?"

"Le Rendezvous."

Macy gave a vague response. "Ha."

"It's a French restaurant on West River Road. Tres cher, but according to Caitlyn, une cuisine d'excellence," he quoted.

"I know that," snapped Macy comically, her catchphrase was an insecure response to disguise her lack of data. She gave Tom the keys to her Cadillac and $200 in $20 bills. "Bring it back in one piece," she insisted.

"Annabel or the car?" Tom joked. He smiled tentatively; he hadn't had much luck with automobiles lately.

"Both," Macy barked.

"I'll 'andle 'er with kid gloves," he replied.

"The car as well I hope," retorted Macy, darting a wry glance at Annabel.

No fear there, he thought, not even with a pair of welder's mitts on.

Le Rendezvous was typically Tucson on the exterior, a square box of white stucco walls, with iron grills at the windows that were canopied by plastic moldings in the style of the French tricolour. But inside Tom felt like he'd been transported back to a Britain in the mid-70s.

The restaurant was carpeted with a heavy patterned woollen weave of scrolled fern leaves in hues of red and gold. White net curtains hung at the windows followed by hefty red velour drapes. A strong accent of dark wooden furniture, partitioning and wall-panelling complemented the semi-papered walls of gold patterned flock.

White embroidered cloths shrouded the tables that were adorned with far too many knives and forks, and little table lamps with multicoloured fabric tasselled shades that were better suited to a country cottage.

The expectations of having a lively conversation and a few laughs soon dissipated. Annabel was not only miserable; she was also obnoxious and spiteful. Tom tried a few attempts at humour, but received only curious looks in return.

It was no surprise her bloke had pissed off.

They had a fistful of cash to spend, so Tom picked the dearest thing on the menu, Dover sole, $40 a pop, which was flambéed in brandy and butter at the table by the waiter. It remains to this day the best fish he ever tasted, falling off the bone and melting in his mouth. It was accompanied by boiled baby new potatoes and some blanched green vegetables, washed down with a cold bottle of Bergerac Blanc.

Despite the moody bitch sat opposite him, Tom was in heaven, ordering a perfect twin chocolate mousse with fresh cream for dessert, followed by an Irish coffee; he couldn't have felt more sated.

Annabel pushed a filet mignon around the plate, but hardly ate a thing.

Tom deemed it such a waste of food and disrespectful to the chef. This drew even more contempt for her, although being her escort for the night, he would barely show it. The evening was topped off by a little gem of providence when Annabel inadvertently knocked a full goblet of red wine over herself. It seeped and spread like a crimson flood on blotting paper and despite the waiter's best attempts at mopping her up, she left the building rather more tie-dyed than she came in.

This gave great joy to the Brit who smiled inside at the time and laughed aloud after he had dropped her back at Macy's.

When he finally arrived at Pete and Maisy's house, Seamus still hadn't returned, so he just retired for the evening very content. The lad stumbled in at around 2:00 a.m. and woke Tom up by falling onto his bed and insisting upon subjecting him to a lengthy slurred recital of how the young student girl had plied him with Corona all night, and then paid for a cab to bring him home.

Seamus then promptly fell asleep and snored like a basking elephant seal, forcing Tom to change bedrooms, opting this time for Seashell's single futon.

***

On the Tuesday night the boys got wind of a party going on not too far away on E. Florita Street. Chad's friend Dave had been invited, so that meant they had all been invited. It was at a house rented by a couple of Uni girls, a tiny little two bedroom bungalow, one of three that bordered a small lawn that lay behind a low brick wall, a few paces off the main road. They reminded Tom of the chalets from a Butlins holiday he'd been on with his parents in the 60s.

Giving up on finding the place, they were turning the El Camino round to head off back home when Seamus spotted Dave's blue Mustang in the street. They had stumbled upon the place by chance.

The party was in full swing as they strode up the garden path to the sound of loud cheery voices over the top of Salt n Pepa's *Push It* thumping out on the stereo.

Nobody in the sardine packed room was above the age of 22, people were dancing on the furniture, swilling beer out of plastic pint glasses, draped over each other singing abundantly, somebody was pissing out of an open window, a plastic keg was half full on the kitchen table and it was wall-to-wall pretty girls.

Seamus looked at Tom. "My kinda place," he said raising both eyebrows and dragging on a cigarette.

Tom spotted the beautiful Sasha sat on an arm of a worn-out living room chair, he caught her eye and wondered over to say hello. Scorpion wasn't here and she was in a rare chatty mood. Tom thought he might be in with half a chance despite her rumoured disease, maybe if he didn't kiss her, the herpes wouldn't jump across.

He then beheld something else, something far more appealing; Venus personified, the girl from the Tap Room on the night that they got involved with the runaways.

She moved with breathtaking confidence, detached from the crowd within a sphere of demure supremacy, the rest of the world just background noise.

Her looks were Eastern European, a delectable cross between the actress Brooke Shields and the model Paulina Porizkova. She had olive skin, long silky straight chocolate hair with an undertone of gold in certain lights that fell in front of her beautiful face, causing her to push it back behind her petite ears now and again. She had cocoa dark eyes and heavy black brows, not a hint of make-up on and the most kissable lips possible, he was captivated immediately.

The boys languished there for a few hours, mostly in the kitchen next to the keg, pacing themselves, getting leisurely inebriated and extracting as much fun as could be from the natives. As the party thinned, it became clear that the house belonged to the one arresting Tom's heart.

Gretchen shared the little rented bungalow with her classmate, Sian.

Only a few bodies remained in the living room, it was around midnight and the atmosphere was trance like. Some mellow acid jazz was wafting out of the stereo speakers as Tom wandered in and found a seat on the back of a small couch that rested beneath a large paper map of the world, blue-tacked to the wall.

He had always been intrigued by maps, he loved the topography and the staggering amount of exotic place names; places he longed to visit, sights that he had planned to see, the geography and the location of familiar countries. Fascinatingly this map was scribed in Russian.

Whilst he studied the details, she came and sat next to him, attracted by this foreigner studying one of her prized possessions, undeniably sharing her interest for the world.

"You read Russian?" She asked alluringly. Her voice was golden, soft and sultry; her intelligence almost smothered him.

"*Het*," replied Tom attempting to be clever.

"*Akh ty, govoryat na russkom*?"

"Ya' got me there, I know about two words I'm afraid, yes and no."

"Oh I bet you know more than you think you do, what about Cosmonaut?"

"Yep."

"Soyuz?"

"Yeah."

"Sputnik, comrade, vodka, what about Kremlin?"

"Yes, all of those."

"See you're halfway there and you didn't even know it."

Tom raised his plastic cup. "Nostrovia," he attempted.

"*Na Zdorovie*", she corrected.

"It sounds so much better coming from you."

"Oh I'm not very good; we're only in our second year of study."

"We?"

"Sian and I, we've both taken the same class." Gretchen nodded towards her friend, a plain looking girl of medium build with a round potato face accentuated by a dark bob hairstyle and a pear-shaped figure, who was presently being entertained by Seamus in an armchair.

"Hi, I'm Gretchen, Gretchen Olsztyn Von Leysen," she held out her hand.

Tom took it and gripped it lightly; her hand was more delicate than brand new chamois leather and a thousand times more beguiling. He could feel her pulse and looking into her eyes he feared he would melt into a pool of wax at her feet if he held her any longer. He let go.

"That's Prussian isn't it," he said stabbing in the dark. He was spot on.

"Yeah, long ago my great, great something was a Count of somewhere way back, but I'm as American as Idaho potatoes, although I'd like to be a foreign diplomat someday," she gushed.

"A Prussian princess," he announced captivated. "'ow about that?"

She smiled. "Where's that?" she snapped, placing her finger on the map.

It landed in the Middle East, on a country next to the Mediterranean Sea.

Tom had to wrack his brain for this one, just below Turkey, he thought. "Syria," he announced proudly.

She was really impressed now; most Americans couldn't point out their own country on a globe. "And that?" she asked gesticulating to another part of the world, it was in Central Asia below Russia and although the letters on it were all back to front, he knew it instinctively.

"Mongolia," he declared with gusto. "And where's this?" he said trying to play her at her own game, forgetting that she could read the map.

"Hmm," she said feigning perplexity, "let me see ... the moon?"

Tom realised his mistake, but relished in her clever humour. At last he'd found someone he could relate to; she was stunningly beautiful and seemed to have an interest in him.

They continued to talk beside the map as time disappeared; apart from Russian she was also studying politics and was very interested in world affairs.

Tom had limited knowledge of these subjects but from somewhere managed to dredge up enough information to keep Gretchen enthusiastic.

The party fizzled out, Chad and Dave had long since gone home. Two college lads were asleep on the chairs in the front room and Seamus had disappeared into the secrets of Sian's room.

"Oops," said Tom surveying the carnage left behind. "All the bed spaces 'ave been taken."

"Not quite," she said delicately looping her arms around his neck. "You can stay in my room." Her doe eyelashes fluttered and Tom fell into her ebony pools.

Their faces came together and for the first time her sweet alcoholic breath caressed his lips before they touched hers in a slow butterfly soft kiss that melded them together. A warm watermelon Bacardi Breezer, melting caramel, passion fruit and strawberry firm embrace, that span the room around them like they were the centre of the universe.

Her bedroom was at the back of the house, entered by a door through the little kitchen. It connected to the bathroom in the centre of the building, which in turn led to Sian's room at the front.

She held his hand and pulled him into the cedar-scented moonlit half-light. He closed the door behind him and embraced her once more. They were roughly the same height and locked together like two pieces of a puzzle.

Static electric blue sparks crackled and danced away to nothing as they undressed each other, dropping garments in a heap where they stood. They were soon naked, both of them tanned, hot and lithe, but it was not frantic and fumbled, only serenely calm and graceful.

Her breasts were perfectly formed, uplifted, with brown perky nipples, fully aroused. Her pubic hair was full and dark and neatly trimmed; she was moist, Tom could feel it on his leg as it glided in-between hers.

His erection pressed into her belly like a stick of fused gelignite; she pulled him in tightly as they kissed, their tongues exploring fresh fields. He kissed her neck, her cheek, her earlobes; he breathed faintly into her ears making her shudder with pleasure. She gripped him even tighter as he reached down and slid his penis between her legs, not inside her, but just between her legs at the velour entrance to her wet cave, teasing her, throbbing as the blood pulsed through his veins, he caressed her bum cheeks with both hands.

Letting go of him she got down on her knees and took his explosive device in both hands. She tossed her head back, flicking her damp hair from her face, which glinted in the moonlight, and slowly brought her mouth onto his glistening purple helmet, taking him all the way down to the back of her throat as far as he could go.

Tom sighed as the warmth of her mouth surrounded his aching tool, mixing saliva with seminal fluid, providing the perfect lubrication for her to slide up and down his shaft. She licked and sucked for a delirious ten minutes until he thought he was being too selfish and that she deserved her share of oral pleasure.

He withdrew and lay her down on the bed, basically a mattress on the floor with a sheet cover and a light duvet. He kissed her again, kissed her mouth, her nose, her eyelids, her chin, the hollow of her throat, her chest, her nipples, where he spent some time sucking in her erect firm buttons, slurping on each of them, the cool of his saliva making them stiffen further. He licked down a line to her belly button, over her flat stomach and around the patch of female fur to her inner thighs that were now soaked with excitement. She parted her legs and pulled at his hair, she desperately wanted the feel of his probing tongue on her twitching clitoris. After a tormenting minute of licking around the periphery he finally yielded to her desire, tasting her salty sweet tanginess for the first time. She moaned with delight, catching her breath and biting hard on her soft bottom lip.

He lapped away for what seemed like an eternity, inserting a couple of fingers into her, thrusting them deep, hard and slow, bringing her close to orgasm. Her juices trickling down his chin and soaking the bed until his aching jaw could take it no more. He pulled away on the brink of her climax, her body arcing, the tummy muscles taught, her mind lost on some misty horizon.

Bringing himself down upon her laboured softness, he supported his weight with his elbows and tucked his arms around her hot back, clamping his hands around her shoulders, giving himself full leverage to penetrate her hard.

Kissing her again, so she could taste her own love juice upon his lips, he positioned his cock with ease and it slid in with scant resistance, right up to the hilt until their pubic bones ground together in a rhythmic pumping rotation.

It didn't take long before Tom could feel the boiling flood of no return erupt from the depths of his balls through his shaft and shoot into the warm tight folds of her femininity, causing his eyes to screw up tight, a soft sigh to escape and his fingernails to almost pierce through the flesh on her shoulders.

The French are so apt in calling it La petite mort, for a split second he was definitely not of this earth. He relaxed; the tension had almost brought him to tears. He lay there inside her flexing his manhood, squeezing out the last few drops of life and Gretchen responded, tightening her muscles around his cock like a gripping fist.

"Did ya' like that?" he whispered.

"It was wonderful," she replied, "but I can never cum from penetration, I never have."

"Oh," said Tom, feeling a mix of selfishness and inadequacy.

"It's alright though; I enjoyed the oral, maybe we can work on that."

In this light Tom couldn't work out if she was being despondent or kind; he withdrew from her gently and rolled onto his side, then pulled the duvet over them both to hamper a slight chill. It was boiling outside but the small air-conditioning unit was busily whirring away keeping the house cool.

"Do ya' think we might see each other again then?" he asked provisionally.

"How could I resist an intelligent, handsome man like you, of course, I want to see you again." She was on her side as well now facing him and twirling his hair around a finger making little ringlets out of his short locks.

"You think I'm intelligent?"

"Sure, you're the cleverest boy in the room," she joked.

Tom gave a short husky cackle. "And you're the most beautiful girl that I've ever held." He meant it with all his heart, although it came out a little too contrived.

"Oh I'm really quite plain," she replied disparagingly. "You should see my mom; she really is beautiful."

This encouraged Tom no end, thinking there might be a long-term relationship here. "I'd love to."

They gazed at each other for a long while, not saying another word until sleep finally beset them both and they drifted off to slumberland.

Morning came too soon in the form of an old-fashioned alarm clock, a round faced little fellow with three legs and two small bells on his head that were being hammered enthusiastically by what seemed like Thor himself.

Gretchen leaned across Tom and switched the thing off.

Sunlight beamed in through a crack in the curtains, brightening the small box room strewn with rumpled clothes and piles of school work.

The two connecting doors to the bathroom were open; evidently Gretchen had been to the loo during the night. Tom lay there for a moment staring at Sian's naked, pear shaped arse that was exposed from receding sheets in the other bedroom and smiling at him. It was rather pale, he thought to himself.

"Morning sweetness," he said to the gorgeous girl lying naked beside him.

She rolled over and put her head on his chest. "How come you look so good in the morning?" she said enviously.

"I've 'ad a lot of practice," he joked, not believing her for one second, although he *was* a morning person and never had any trouble jumping out of bed like a spring lamb.

Gretchen's words tantalised his skin. "Would you like some tea?"

"That would be lovely, what's the time, I'm afraid we 'ave to get to work?"

"Seven-thirty, I've only got strawberry tea, is that okay?"

He had never had anything but regular before, but liked the sound of a cup of strawberry tea.

"Smashing, I better wake Seamus."

She got up and put on a long blue shirt that became a mini dress.

Tom sat up and admired her exquisite form; for him there was something terribly horny about a girl getting dressed, but he had no time for that, they needed to walk back to Mabel and get their car, that was if he could rouse his mate.

He shouted at him from the loo while taking a leak, the prostrate monster finally responded with, "Me up Rasta'," although Tom knew that Seamus' eyes would still be shut.

Tom washed his bits, cleaned his teeth using his finger as a toothbrush and then got dressed. The tea was a delight, they sipped it together out on the porch, shaded from the rising sun. The air was warming rapidly; the sprinkler system on the communal lawn had been to work during the night and the smell of damp grass fragranced the still morning.

Gretchen stared out into the neighbourhood.

Tom stared at her profile, her perfect face, her flawless skin, those kissable lips, a light breeze flicking her rich chocolate hair. He couldn't believe his luck, he felt so at ease and inexplicably content. Today was going to be a glorious day.

After exchanging phone numbers, the boys were on their way, the sun was shining, love was in the air and their feet barely touched the tarmac.

"'ow did ya' get on with Sian?" asked Tom.

"Well, I was so knackered, I sloped off and found a bed and put me 'ed down. Next thing, a girl got in beside me," replied Seamus, "a great little fuck, 'n even 'ad a shaven haven."

"Smooth. Did she teach you any Russian?"

"She taught me a new position, reverse cowgirl, I just 'ad to lie there and think of breakfast, ha, ha, ha." Seamus took a last draw from his cigarette then flicked it into the curb. "'ow was the lovely Gretchen?"

"She's nobility mate, of Prussian descent, one of her relatives was a fuckin' Count."

"Careful how you say that," said Seamus. "Did she give up the strudel?"

"With a great dollop o' cream," replied Tom.

***

On the Thursday morning Tom awoke in the living room on the sofa bed to the beeping of his little white alarm clock. This was the third different bed he had slept on in Pete and Maisy's house and by far the most comfortable. He stretched under the single sheet causing the linen to ride up over his feet and gather round his middle. He yawned and sat upright, considered what day it was and then reluctantly swung his legs over the side of the bed.

Seamus came down the corridor from the master bedroom in his Y-fronts performing a comical animated sideways walk. He stopped short of the living room and then proceeded to reverse course in the same oblique motion. Then he came back, doing it again.

Tom screwed up his face, questioning his friend's sanity. "What are ya' doin'?" he asked.

Seamus continued his ridiculous routine and said "'ave you 'ad any itching boysie."

"Itching?"

"Yeah, itching down below."

Tom was perplexed before it dawned on him. "Crabs … you've got crabs!"

"I think so, little black fuckers under me' skin, 'ave you got 'em?"

"I don't think so, I 'aven't been scratching, I better go and check. Fuck, where did ya' get them from?"

"Must 'ave been from a dirty toilet seat or something, I couldn't 'ave got 'em from Caryn."

"What if you've given 'em to 'er, and Sian? Fuck … ya' might 'ave infested the whole fuckin' 'ouse. Shit, they'll be 'ome in a few days; we better wash all the fuckin' sheets and 'ope the bastards don't get into the mattresses."

The shock of Seamus' predicament had turned him pale. "I better get something to kill the fuckers from the chemists," he said.

"We'll go to Wal-Mart on the way to work. Come on, get dressed or we'll be late again."

Tom waited in the car outside the store; it was 8:40, they were sure to get another bollocking from Saul.

Inside Seamus was perusing the aisles stacked floor to ceiling with medicinal treatments, hoping that a cure for crabs would jump out and nip him on the nose. It was hopeless, he didn't know the technical term for the little blighters, the clock was ticking and he was itching like crazy. There was nothing for it; he would have to consult the pharmacist.

Only one old lady was in line for the man in the white coat, who was eyes down behind the counter filling a container with a measure of pills.

A queue started to form behind Seamus and was now three deep and the anxiety of asking for crab-killer was growing inside him. Seamus had plenty of front, but this was going to be humiliating.

"Can I help you son?" asked the cheery-faced pharmacist.

"Yes err, good morning." Seamus cleared his throat. "I've got some err, visitors, err, you know, in the downstairs department, and I wonder if you err, have something to cure, the err, problem?" He coughed again.

A snigger came from behind him.

The pharmacist looked curiously at Seamus, who had now turned scarlet. "Oh you mean pubic lice! Sure, we've got all sorts to cure that," he said jubilantly, "What would like to try, shampoo, cream, a louse comb, powder?"

A woman behind interjected. "Try the shampoo, it worked for me."

"And the comb," said a burly trucker type. "You'll need a comb."

Now the whole store was privy to his dilemma, it didn't seem such a humiliation and obviously quite a common condition in these parts. He opted for the shampoo and the comb, thanked everybody for their help and made a rapid exit.

"Pubic lice," he announced when he got back into the car. "That was very fuckin' embarrassing, every fuckin' customer in there knows what I've got now." He ranted as Tom sped off to work. "I've got the gear to eradicate the bastards tonight; ya' better dose yourself in it too just to be sure." Seamus surmised.

Tom agreed, although he was horrified at the prospect of actually finding any of the tiny spiders burrowing into his flesh.

After a sweltering, infuriatingly maddening day Seamus was relieved to get home and straight into the shower. He thoroughly doused his nether regions with insecticidal shampoo, then liberally anointed his whole body with the stuff just to be on the safe side. Then whilst still under the lukewarm water, he got to work with the louse comb.

Managing to remove a few creatures, the task proved near on impossible because the lice had decisively taken up residence under his skin. He could see them burrowing away just beneath a thin translucent layer of flesh, which made him feel violated and unclean. It was going to take quite a number of washes to rid this particular infestation.

He handed the shampoo to Tom when he came out of the shower. "'ere give ya' self a go with this, just in case you've picked them up," he said.

Tom had been busy stripping all the beds; they had slept on all of them over the two-week period and would be absolutely ashamed of themselves if they passed on a dose of crabs to the returning family.

"Alright, I'll just put this first lot of washing on. Wha' d' the crabs look like?"

"Not like the ones ya' get at the fishmongers mate, ha, ha, ha. These are tiny black dots with legs that are tunnelling under me pubes; d' ya' wanna 'ave a look?"

"Nah, I'll give that a swerve mate, I ain't got nothing like that, but I'll use the shampoo any way, then we better go tell Sian the 'appy news, she'll be ecstatic."

"Humm," said Seamus despondently.

Sian worked part-time in a record store on the U of A campus mall. Tom waited in the car while his buddy sheepishly slid in past the glass door.

The shop's windows were heavily dressed with music posters of newly released albums and singles, and promotions for local gigs, but Tom could just see into the murky interior and make out Sian behind the counter. She seemed to be taking the revelation in a casual manner.

Seamus strode out of the store like a man leaving a prostate examination, glad it was all over and feeling quite brave.

"Wha' d' ya' tell her?" asked Tom.

"I 'anded 'er the shampoo and said that she may 'ave to wash 'erself in this as a precaution, because Caryn may 'ave caught the cooties and may 'ave passed them on to me."

"You didn't actually tell 'er that you've got 'em then?"

"Fuck off, she's an 'andy little shag I might 'ave to revisit at some point."

Tom laughed. "Not when she starts scratching 'er minge ya' won't be."

"All's fine Rasta', drive on." Seamus smirked.

Tom reversed out of the bay and headed to 'The French Quarter' on East Grant Road, it was open mike night and they were hoping to get a spot and maybe meet some talent.

Inside the packed Cajun themed bar, it was impossible to get a seat, so the boys put their names down on a list at the door, then went and grappled for a beer at the bar.

On stage was a dude wearing a sleeveless denim jacket and a blue bandana wrapped around his head. He was wringing the blues out of a Fender Telecaster like it was his erogenous appendage, his facial expressions depicting every note.

"Johnny Thunder," applauded the clubs host after a couple of numbers that brought the house down. The lads clapped their appreciation for the charismatic guitarist; maybe they could get a word with him later, he seemed an affable sort of bloke.

An hour or so in, their names were called; Seamus had bought his Strat along and the pair of them took to the stage.

Tom asked the house drummer, bass and keyboard player to stay up there with them and after a short tuning check, Seamus showed the band a brief chord progression to one of the boys' own songs, a west coast groove in the key of E.

Muffled voices and the odd clinking of beer glasses filtered in from a wall of smoke and stage lights.

Tom approached the mike and said, "Good evening ladies and gentlemen, we're from a little place called Watford in the UK and we'd like to perform one of our songs for ya'," The room faded to silence. "This is *Believe it All*."

Seamus started up the rhythm, the drummer picked up the beat and the other two joined in. It sounded nothing like their original recorded version, it was organic and it grew into something of an infectious Latin beat that snaked its way over 15min and several solos from Seamus and the keyboard player. Tom sung the melody to a fashion and then ad-libbed a version of Boz Scaggs' *Lowdown* over the looped chords, which fitted in perfectly, before ending with a multiple chorus.

Surprisingly the audience responded handsomely with applause and whistles. Tom and Seamus were chuffed to bits; they would have to do more of this.

The white-walled club was on 3 levels. The stage dropped down to an audience pit that covered maybe 20 tables, then a stairway climbed to the bar area opposite the stage which potentially held another 10. Johnny Thunder controlled one of those tables looking uncannily like a version of Mickey Rourke in biker gear.

As Seamus and Tom passed by he congratulated them.

"Hey, nice job guys, where did you say you were from?"

"'e's from a little place called Watford and so am I," said Seamus.

"In England, right?" questioned Johnny.

"Just north of London," said Tom, "within the M25."

"Right, right," said Johnny none the wiser.

"Listen, I've just come out of doing a two-stretch in the Pen, for a little misdemeanour, and I'm just high on life right now, and even though I ain't used to your style of music, it sure sounds great to me. Next time maybe we can rock out together, how's that sound?"

Seamus raised his eyebrows. "That'll be brilliant mate, you down 'ere every week?"

"If there's a jam session in town, Johnny will be found brother." He sat there with a cheeky smile, legs and arms wide apart resting a Budweiser on his thigh, his dirty blonde hair poking out the top of his bandana.

"I'll 'old ya' to it," said Seamus.

Johnny winked at him.

The boys retired to the bar and got liberally lubricated before driving home.

***

On the Friday night whilst working at The Haze they received a terrible blow; Arty was moving out of the house this weekend and they would have to find an alternative place to live. This also meant the job at the club would come to an end, with all its perks and status. Tom could sense a black hole appearing under them again; anxiously he went to seek out KP in her office.

She brought sweet relief, Tucson Kate would gladly take them in at her house; she had a spare room, and with Chad living there too, they could practice as much as they liked at home. It was a fair way out of town, on the southwest side, but beggars could not be choosers, so they were fully grateful. Also, they could carry on rehearsing at The Haze indefinitely. On top of this KP had preliminarily pencilled in some dates for Off the Scale to play at the club; they had two weeks to get their act together.

11
Slick

West Canada Street situated in Drexel Heights seemed remote, far away from the Tucson the boys had become acquainted with.

Tom and Seamus had put Pete and Maisy's house back in order on the Sunday. They'd washed all of the linen; remade all the beds and fed the cats for the last time, watered the plants then left the key under a plant pot in the back yard, as instructed.

Then they had driven over to Calle Kuehn, packed their bags and tidied their room in Arty's house. The tall fella was there loading up a U-haul truck with all of his furniture, helped by his wingman Scorpion. He was moving to a much smaller house closer to the club.

Tom was a little melancholy to be leaving this place, they'd had some great times here; it had the essence of Rene and she was a sweetheart.

The boys, already hot and sweaty, helped Arty with the heavy and bulky things for an hour, a small redemption for his massive generosity. This wasn't goodbye at all, they would still see him at The Haze, just not as much as previously.

They dumped their dusty suitcases into the back of the El Camino and headed for 4th Avenue where they were due to meet Tucson Kate.

She had been dropped off earlier by her daughter Holly, spent a few hours chatting with KP and was planning to navigate the boys back to her house, squashed between them like a fragrant marshmallow sandwich.

The drive took them first downtown, then south on 6th Avenue until it met West Ajo Way, then they drove west for a couple of miles till they hit South Mission Road where they turned left and headed south again.

Small talk and jokes extinguished, the conversation took on a more sober refrain.

"So where are you guys working now?" Kate enquired.

"Oh we've got a cushy little number up on Orange Grove Road, doing some gardening and maintenance work for a wealthy couple," said Tom.

Kate chortled, "a cushy number?" she almost gargled when she laughed, the boys spoke an exotic language that she found rather amusing.

"Sometimes 'e's a miserable old git but 'e's giving us plenty of money and letting us buy this car with weekly payments," said Seamus, who was squashed up against the passenger door almost half out of the window.

"What does he do for a living?" asked Kate in her soft toned manner.

"'e deals in real estate," Tom replied.

Kate was growing more and more suspicious, her eyes narrowed. "What's his name, this real estate broker?"

"Saul Berns," said Seamus

Kate caught her breath. "You work for Saul Berns … You work for Saul Berns?" She was almost choking with disbelief. "Oh my, you work for Saul Berns?" She laughed with incredulity.

A question arose in Tom's mind; what was wrong with the fella?

"Do ya' know 'im then?" he asked.

"Do I know him?" Kate laughed again. "He's the biggest crook in town; oh my, Saul Berns." She changed her tune and spoke softly again. "I used to work for him as a secretary around ten years ago, until I realised he was part of the mob. He tried to involve me in a crooked land deal, till I hightailed it out of there. You guys had better watch your backs, he's a mean son of a bitch."

"'e's been alright to us," Seamus said innocently.

"For now," chuckled Kate, "Oh my, Saul Berns … just be careful."

Before Mission Road turned into a single carriageway, Kate indicated that they should turn right into West Canada Street. This was going to be their home for almost a year.

On the exterior, the house resembled more of a secure federal building than a home. It was a drab featureless red brick rectangle with black iron bars at the windows and a decorative wrought iron gate over a heavy dark wooden front door.

There was no front garden to speak of, just an area of dirt between the house and a brick boundary wall. The silver mailbox lent backwards at an unhealthy angle, the product of an unwanted shunt from a careless driver parking on the curb. It looked somewhat unappreciated.

Tom pulled onto the drive and all three of them rolled out of the car like belly fat let loose from a pair of trousers two sizes too small. They entered via the front door where it was cooler by several degrees; the ancient water cooled air-conditioning unit on the roof straining to keep up with the demand, reluctantly providing some respite.

The house had a 'Tardis' effect, seeming much, much larger on the interior and containing a labyrinth of rooms.

Entering a large office/reception room, the boys' new bedroom was through a doorway to the left. It contained two single beds, bare white walls and cream and brown patterned lino on the floor. Through an arched doorway was another room containing Chad's spare drum kit, a small room but plenty big enough for the three of them to rehearse in.

This room led via yet another door to a corridor that would take you to Kate's room on the left, a large bedroom with an en suite bathroom at the back of the house; or if you turned right would take you down a couple of steps into an L-shaped open plan living room/dining room.

The kitchen was off to the left of this, separated by a breakfast bar, a plethora of antique pine cupboards and doors and a massive fridge.

Towards the front of the house, off the lounge, up a step and in through an alcove was another door. This led to Holly's bedroom, a dark mysterious gothic sanctuary, which was apparently out of bounds.

Chad's room was on the right hand side of the house at the back, entered via a door in the dining area. It was long, light and airy, and just wide enough to accommodate a double bed.

Tom and Seamus' room had recently become available due to Kate's vacating son Josh, who had gone to live with his dad in New Mexico.

The backyard was accessible through double glazed patio doors; it was a fenced off square of unkempt grass that was supporting a tattered, raised, round swimming pool, 3ft deep and 30ft in diameter.

The family kept two dogs, a large white shaggy coated congenial fellow called Arnie, who somewhere along the line must have had Old English Sheepdog in his genealogy, and a little grey Shih-tzu complete with a customary blue bow in his hair, called Fonzi or sometimes Misha shoe, a mispronunciation of the French title of *Monsieur Chou*.

Also inhabiting the abode was a mischievous and often entertaining character that went by the name of Buster, an African green parrot, multi-skilled in impersonation and regularly pulling pranks on his house mates.

Buster spent much of his time on an open perch and although he had his wings clipped, would often attempt to cruise around the living room upsetting all and sundry in his path with disastrous aplomb.

Kate and the boys settled on a lodging fee of $50 per week, a price that included all food and laundry, and another surrogate mother.

The house wasn't the most lavish that the boys had ever stepped into, the family were clearly on the breadline; Kate and Holly didn't have jobs, so Chad's and their money seemed to be the only income for the household, but getting by they clearly were, which suited their carefree attitude.

A five minute walk away was a handy Circle K gas station/convenience store and a small strip mall, which included a bar frequented by Mexicans and Indians; in front of this a powder dry car park held a swap meet once a week. Tom thought it a perfect place to offload the stolen oranges that were piling up behind the back seat of the El Comino. They would give it a couple more weeks though, so they could build up plenty of stock.

Tonight's menu was set to be fried chicken, curly fries and corn on the cob, washed down with dozens of bottles of cold Rollin' Rock beer.

Also invited for dinner were Holly's friend Rosita, a short chubby Mexican lesbian and Cynthia, the niece of the chief of the Pascua Yaqui tribe, a full-blooded Native American princess; coffee skinned and slender, with long, straight, silky, black hair she could easily sit on.

Rosita was always cheerful, the epitome of a fun-bundle; she had a wicked glint in her eye and was undoubtedly in love with Holly.

Cynthia was 23-years-old and as sweet as raw honey, but let herself down with some airhead moments and smelling of mothballs.

Kate was seeing Cynthia's uncle, a great man, a legend in Pascua Yaqui history. He was not only their chief, he was also their medicine man, a dual position rarely attained and although the chief 21 children, not one of them was eligible to acquire both titles.

The Chief had fought in World War II as a patriotic American and in 1964 he had played a major part in persuading the White House to set aside 202 acres of desert land where the tribe's identity and sovereignty could be asserted and maintained.

In 1978 the Pascua Yaqui tribe of Arizona became federally recognized and the reservation became part of American soil after being scattered in pueblo's across their native Mexico and other parts of South America following wars with the Spanish, the Mexicans and later the American cavalry that endured for nearly four-hundred years.

The Chief was the Chairman of the Pascua Yaqui Association, the Vice-Chairman of the Tribal Council and an

Elder of the tribe. He was a teacher, a tribal historian, and the political and spiritual leader of the Yaqui peoples. Kate was his latest flame.

While the boys made themselves at home, Kate and Cynthia went out for some late provisions. Kate asked Tom to keep an eye on her waterbed that was being filled via a hose from the garden. Tom agreed then duly sat down on the sofa to watch an American football game. Not understanding the rules, he and Seamus became fully engrossed in the match, even though Buster was doing his damnedest to distract them by stealthily edging along the back of the couch and biting their ears with his razor-edged beak.

Partially through the 3rd quarter, the girls came back laden with Safeway carrier bags. They went straight into the kitchen to unload. Cynthia peeled off into Kate's room to use the toilet, slowly returning a few minutes later with a quizzical expression.

"Kate, I think there's something wrong with your bed," she dozily informed the suddenly panicked matriarch.

Instantly slapped back to his prior responsibility, Tom leapt from his seat and ran into the bedroom to behold a mind-boggling sight.

The waterbed had expanded to three times its intended size, almost round in shape, like a cartoon puffer fish on helium; it had literally lifted off of the bed.

It was a miracle that the thing hadn't burst its seams and engulfed the entire house with a mini tsunami, a testament surely to the manufacturer's quality.

Without hesitation Tom rushed out through the patio doors and turned off the tap, unscrewed it from the spigot and let it fall to the ground, actuating a flow reversal.

All Kate could do was to hold her hand to her mouth, eventually laughing at the ridiculousness of the incident. A fiasco was diverted, but only just. Cynthia remained puzzled.

Tom wrote some letters home during the week, advising his mum and Lela of his new address. He'd been on the phone to Gretchen a number of times, had taken her to dinner at a quaint little Bohemian café on Congress Street, then stayed over again at her place, while Seamus stayed at Caryn's. She was now back in town and just happened to live on the same street as Gretchen, so it was easy for Seamus to take the car and pick up Tom, fresh and smiling radiantly like the sun was emitting from his core. Life was wonderful all of a sudden and the pair of them were jubilant, even when it came to work.

Sean Adams was playing at The Purple Haze on the Saturday night with his three-piece band, an outfit that the boys hadn't seen yet, but if Sean's wonderfully melodic voice was anything to go by, this band were going to be a real treat.

Tom dropped Seamus off at Caryn's; they would meet them at the club later and he then drove on to pick up Gretchen. The couple parked up on 4th Avenue and walked along the street for a few blocks. The night was immensely hot and still humid from the earlier rain. They held hands and strolled on the sidewalk, Tom saying hello to at least a dozen people he knew as they approached his former workplace.

Gretchen was pleasantly impressed, "Gee, you know more people in town than I do."

It hadn't occurred to Tom until then, but he had made quite a number of acquaintances along this street. He smiled at her hoping this was a plus point.

They queued with a small number of goths to get into the club, ahead of a disturbing yet comical sight. A young couple dressed in matching black wet-look PVC jumpsuits, attached to each other via an 18in long stainless steel rod, manacled to black leather studded dog collars around their necks. They wore identical makeup; white face powder, black lipstick and eyeliner. He had highly lacquered Robert Smith style ink black hair, while she had dolloped a handful of something greasy onto her locks and combed it back so it stuck to her head like a filthy mold. But the most hilarious thing was when they tried to enter the building. They couldn't fit through the door side-by-side, so had to contort themselves at an awkward angle, the girl first, and being shorter than he, she nearly throttled him.

"True love," jibbed Tom.

Gretchen chuckled.

They paid nothing to enter; Salina was on the door and waved them through raising an incredulous brow at Tom's gorgeous girlfriend.

The floor space was crammed, mostly with young music fans and a few older metal heads. Sean Adams was popular in town too, and many had come to pay homage.

Seamus and Caryn arrived a short time later and the foursome chatted enthusiastically, with high hopes for the evening's entertainment.

Scorpion faded the house music down to nothing, the lights dimmed on the crowd and dry ice was pumped in from stage left as eerie ultraviolet light illuminated a backdrop of a crucified dollar sign, complete with a crown of blood soaked thorns.

Three hefty silhouetted figures stomped through the fog, backlit and silent, dressed for all intents and purposes like the cast from the Texas Chainsaw Massacre, only with Sean Adams in a white hockey mask like Jason's from Friday the 13th.

The drummer clicked in at an incredible rate and the loudest ear piecing speed metal exploded from the stage like a bomb blast, before Sean began screaming like an adrenalin-fuelled demented Harpy. It was a wonder the plate glass front didn't shatter. The boys were used to loud music but this was insane. The girls clamped their hands to their ears for fear of losing one of their senses, while all around them wild-haired head bangers were going mental and testing their neck vertebrae to the limits.

The quartet could not stand it for more than one song, which barely lasted 90 seconds before another one struck up immediately. They headed for the street before their ears started to bleed.

"Sorry about that," said Tom to the girls as they headed for the cars, "I 'ad no idea it would be anything like that, Sean normally sings country."

"Nearly rattled all the teeth out of me' 'ead," said Seamus, "for fuck's sake."

"What shall we do now?" wondered Gretchen.

"'ow about Gracious Bob's? I think Mystic Lights are on tonight and it's close to your 'ouse," suggested Tom.

So it was agreed and the four of them spent the evening in much more temperate company.

***

Ruben stood in the kitchen doorway, the epitome of subservience, ringing his Sombrero with his hands, he looked like the forlorn friend of Speedy Gonzales; he was getting fired. It had come to Saul's attention that he'd been having a siesta under an orange tree every afternoon for 2 hrs at a time; it really had nothing to do with the boys and yet the pendulum of blame was swinging their way, although they hadn't intentionally grassed up the gardener, it may have accidentally slipped out.

They were all in the kitchen when Ruben was told that his services would no longer be needed, and of course he felt that the lads had pushed him out of a job. He pointed at them both individually, slowly, and then ran his thumb across his throat. The boys laughed nervously wondering whether the action was in jest or in fact; not. Surely he wasn't going to execute them Cartel style, was he?

Gracie kept smiling her chubby little face off. Better to be cheerful, and grateful she still had a position with the Berns'.

Now it meant that the boys had the gardening work to do as well, and from then on, each morning Saul would take them on a tour of duty, barking out his orders, only half of which would ever get done because Caitlyn was getting progressively friendlier and regularly inviting them into the house to liven up her day and keep her entertained.

Also, Pricey came back this week from touring with the reggae band, evidently loaded with cash. He temporarily went and stayed with his mother until he could find a place of his own to rent.

Off the Scale's first gig at The Haze was coming up this Saturday; Tom had been busy making small A4 posters and putting them up all over 4th Avenue to advertise the show, and Macy had, as part of her game plan, bought Tom a new Fender Stratocaster with a sky blue body, and a new Fender Princeton amp. But Seamus was still lacking a decent guitar amp, so Pricey offered to lend him the money; he could pay it back when he could afford it. Tom knew this usually meant Pricey wanted in on the act, but strangely enough he wasn't showing any signs of infiltration at the moment.

The Chicago music store opened its doors on East Congress Street in 1967. A massive red, glass-fronted building, that takes up a quarter of a block. Inside, its three levels offer a wet dream of instruments to make any ardent musician drool. Dealing mostly in guitars, amps and drums, it is rammed packed with vintage, rare, new and used delights more akin to a collection than a salesroom, each piece lovingly racked and presented. One could spend hours in here perusing the aisles and trying out the gear. The family-owned business had a unique flavour, a quirky relaxed attitude that even encouraged haggling for a price, and all the staff seemed to have adopted a dry sense of humour. Out the back in the basement they had a workshop that fastidiously restored all manner of instruments and employed a full team of enthusiastic craftsmen.

Seamus spent some considerable time early on Thursday evening testing several amps with vintage guitars, but couldn't decide on which was the right combo for his needs. He had to meet Pricey that night in the Chicago bar where Mystic Lights were playing, to collect his cash advance. Whilst there, he couldn't see why a swift half would do any harm.

Two hours later, after playing pool and guzzling lager with Pricey he had got the flavour and fancied a spell in Café Sweetwater on the corner of 4th Avenue and 1st Street, where Javier Marquez was playing with his jazz band. At 1:00 a.m. after 3 pitchers of beer and several shots of Crown Royal, he thought it best to drive home while he could still see.

The El Camino was parked on the curb outside the café. Staggering to it he noticed an attractive black woman passing by.

"Where's the party sweetheart?" he slurred.

The woman, in her mid-20s, was wearing a miniscule tight fitting red shiny skirt and an electric blue boob-tube, had long glimmering legs terminating in a pair of chunky yellow stilettos with a four inch heel, and her buoyant afro was pinched by a lime green scarf that was tied neatly into a bow.

"You wanna party, I'll show you a party," she responded.

She was like a one woman discothèque and the doors were wide open with a VIP entry pass waved in Seamus' face.

"Where we gonna party?" he asked openly.

"Anywhere you want sugar."

"Jump in," he said feeling unbelievably gifted.

She got in and giggled her head off, her brilliant perfect smile lighting up the passenger space.

They didn't drive far, just around the block to a Circle K with a small vacant lot. It was dark and relatively quiet.

A lazy dog gave a reluctant bark in a garden close by, fighting an instinct to warn off marauding wolves.

Seamus left her in the car and went and bought a six pack of Budweiser.

Getting back into the driving seat he cracked a can and handed it to his guest, cracking another one for himself.

"What do people call ya' then?" he drawled, commencing with verbal foreplay.

"Oh you can call me Sunshine," she said with her enormous smile, and with that she reached across and started rubbing his stick shift through his shorts.

Before he knew it, she was gliding her soft full lips over the length of his manhood while he leaned back into the seat, a beer in one hand and a 'fag' in the other.

This is the life, he thought, I'm in America now son.

Five minutes later they were in an impossible position, she was bent over double, her head down in the footwell, her feet touching the roof lining and Seamus had lifted her skirt to reveal that she wasn't wearing any knickers, and although she was brown on the outside, she was very much pink on the inside.

Gripping onto the waistband of her skirt like he was clinging to a lifebuoy in rough seas, he pumped her like a steam locomotive piston, till the life shot out of him in a climax of lightning proportions.

Sunshine let out a muffled groan, like the final bellow of a slaughtered beast, Seamus wasn't sure if she was enjoying the rump or just being concertinaed to death, but frankly he didn't much care, she had served her purpose as a receptacle, the sole purpose of their coupling.

He dropped her off in an alley behind a house not too many blocks away, in a neighbourhood with houses that appeared prefabricated. Then rolled home slowly, fully satisfied with the evenings dividends.

Tom opened his eyes to the sounds of frantic rummaging in his bedroom, the sounds of a person at the end of their tether, desperately trying to locate something that wasn't where it was supposed to be.

He peered through the gloom and blearily focussed on the stooped hulk of Seamus turning the room upside down.

"What ya' lost Ras'?" he said wearily.

"That fuckin' bitch, she's 'ad it," Seamus replied lifting his discarded shorts upside down and spilling loose change all over the lino. It rolled and span and settled in far corners while Tom tried to make sense of what Seamus was talking about.

"Who … what bitch 'ad what?"

"That cunt from last night, it's not 'ere."

Seamus left the room and went out of the front door, streaming arc-welding bright light into the house that sliced across the office floor with razor shape precision.

Two minutes later he was back inside the room like a headless chicken zombie, turning his bedding and looking in places that he knew it couldn't be.

Tom swung his feet onto the floor and scratched his head. "What 'ave ya' lost?"

"Pricey's money … the two-hundred fuckin' dollars 'e gave me to buy a new amp … she must 'ave rifled me' pockets while she was sucking me' knob. Pricey's gonna be fuckin' livid, I can't ask 'im for any more."

Tom was suppressing the humour that was evolving in his head. "Who was sucking ya' knob, where?"

Seamus relayed last night's tale, as Tom did his best to control his laughter. "Go check the car again; you've probably dropped it behind the seat."

"I've looked, I've looked!"

"Go look again."

Seamus did, and was back again in one minute, still fuming.

"It's not there. I'll 'ave t' go round 'er 'ouse and front 'er, the fuckin' 'slag'. What a fuckin' thief."

Caitlyn Berns had lent Tom the Wagoneer to get home with, because Seamus had gone off early to look at amps. Saul was away for a few days, so he didn't know.

"Why don't ya' take the Wagoneer, it might give ya' more leverage," said Tom.

"Good idea," said Seamus.

He went to the bathroom while Tom lay back down on his bed. It was only 7:00, Friday morning, far too early to face the world yet.

"I've got a purple ring around me' cock," said Seamus as he came back into the bedroom.

"Eh?" Tom didn't think he'd heard him right.

"Fuckin' lipstick; good of 'er to autograph 'er 'andiwork, the fuckin' whore."

This time, Tom did let out a cackle. "Sorry mate, but that is fuckin' funny. You gonna be alright?"

Seamus was tying up his boots whilst sitting on his ransacked bed. "I'll just demand that she gives it me back. Or I'll call the Old Bill."

"Yeah but don't go steaming in 'er 'ouse, she might 'ave a gun and use 'er right to defend 'erself."

"Fear not Ras', me' no intention of getting shot today. I'll see ya' later."

With that he was off, closing the front door behind him and plunging the house back into forgiving darkness.

A menacing block of a man opened the door at Sunshine's house. He was wearing red sweat pants and a dazzling white vest, which allowed him to exhibit an impressive muscular upper body with huge biceps.

Another brother craned his neck around a corner to see who had come calling so early in the morning. This one was around 6-4, built like a brick shithouse and frowning.

The guy who answered the door said nothing, just gave an upwards nod as if to say what do you want.

Seamus put on his best breezy repose. "Morning mate, is Sunshine home?"

The guy stared at Seamus intensely through the fly screen, his dark eyes boring into the Englishman's face.

"Who wants to know?" he said irately.

The other guy strode closer to the door inquisitive as to why a white dude with a funny accent was calling in this neighbourhood.

Seamus was thinking on his feet, there was no way that he was going to intimidate these two with his stature, he would have to come up with a cunning ruse to frighten them into redemption.

"Seamus Montgomery, New Scotland Yard."

The black guys just stared at him unfazed.

"I'm a British police officer on exchange with the Tucson Police department and I—"

"I ain't stole nothing!" came an unseen voice from somewhere within the house.

The first guy looked back into the house and then at Seamus. His face screwed up angrily. "She ain't stole nothing, Homes," he said folding his big arms across his chest in a show of defiance.

Seamus, sensing he was on a hiding for nothing, tried one more time to remonstrate with girl. He hadn't mentioned any crime yet, so it was obvious she had stolen it.

"Two hundred dollars Sunshine, I had it with me last night and this morning it's gone," he said loudly projecting past the doormen, "Just hand it back and I'll say no more of it."

"You got the wrong girl, sugar!" she sounded from down the hall.

"You heard her white boy, now why don't you run along back to Scotland or wherever y'all from and tell it to ya' mama."

Seamus was furious at the audacity of the girl, but he clearly wasn't going to get past these two bruisers.

The bigger guy was coming his way like an Iberian fighting bull, nostrils flaring and steam coming out of his ears.

"Right," Seamus said backing away, "you'll be hearing from the police this morning, I'm going straight there now."

It was a pathetic threat that rebounded off the two homeboys with the force of a falling leaf, but at least in his mind he had tried something and perhaps he had worried her a little.

The dudes weren't in the least bit daunted; they shut the door and went back to cutting cocaine in the kitchen.

Seamus spent the morning looking for Pricey to tell him the unfortunate news. He discovered that the Price had left town again, so now he was amp-less for tonight's gig, if only he had bought one yesterday instead of being indecisive and leaving it until the last minute.

Tom, had got up refreshed, had a cup of tea and then opened a letter from Lela, just a short note, the content was getting smaller as time went on. In it she told him that she had been visiting his mum in Harefield with Kit and they were getting along fine. She enclosed a couple of photos of Kit on his first birthday which made Tom really melancholy. The torch he carried for Lela still burned brightly, but he was no longer under her spell; Gretchen had cast a new one, which was overpowering the previous hex. She would be coming to the gig tomorrow and he couldn't wait to show off his band to his Prussian girlfriend.

He unpacked his lightweight, grey chequered suit and hung it out to decrease, this would make an excellent stage outfit, but staring at it, it looked like he had been sleeping in it for the past six months, as foreign a task as it was to him, he would have to give it an iron.

On the Saturday, the band met up at The Haze in the afternoon to great excitement; a 5-News team were there, doing an exposé on the club. Off the Scale would be filmed during a sound check and the footage would go out during the early evening news as a 'Look around town' bulletin.

This brilliant chance for American TV exposure was not to be sniffed at and the boys leapt at the opportunity.

Tom called Kate Norton and asked her to video tape the news—they were gonna be on the telly!

Tom let Seamus use his new amp, while he borrowed Chad's old Peavey practice amp. Once the stage mix was to their liking, the lads burst into a rendition of one of their original songs, *Suspicion*, a jaunty pop tune, another one in part written about Lela.

Hot Pot wore a white dress shirt and black bolo tie, Chad and Seamus wore charcoal-coloured suits with white open-necked shirts, and Tom, his baggy grey chequered suit. The news crew used three cameras, shooting from different angles during the performance, the footage and the sound quality were great, and the channel aired around 30 seconds of the song, along with a brief that told of two English lads playing live tonight at The Purple Haze. The clip finished with the three news anchors jigging robotically in their seats, and the female saying "So that's what's hot in town tonight." The boys later included the footage in their home movie *And for Desert*.

The gig itself got a mediocre reception, the mixed audience of Gothic Punks and Midwestern Rock fans weren't accustomed to Britpop and didn't quite know what to make of it, so mostly they just politely clapped at the end of each song.

A few people danced and some, like Chad's friend Dave were quite enthusiastic. Gretchen remained regally reserved, if somewhat conservative in her praise. Tom got the feeling his music wasn't her cup of tea, and yet she would support him wholeheartedly.

Hot Pot had a second helping that night, because Raucous Raccoon were also on the bill, with their mix of authentic Americana covers; they connected better with the older crowd, who suddenly came to life from the shadows, to revel in the familiar tunes. The boys were unperturbed, their game was a lot harder to play and they would have to start on the bottom rung and heave themselves up the grizzly ladder one step at a time.

Later, after a rather strenuous bout of bedroom Olympics, Tom was beguiled by the interest Gretchen was showing in his tackle.

"Is there something wrong with it?" he asked, worried that he might be a disappointment.

"Oh no, I think it's very cute," she replied toying with the flaccid thing.

"Cute?"

"Compact, it's all there, all very tidy."

Tom smiled, but hoped that she wasn't saying it was small.

"I had a boyfriend once who only had one ball," she said, "I used to say to him, are you hiding your Easter Egg in there, at which point he'd get very upset, I'd joke about it all the time."

Tom was tickled, he was totally falling for this girl; she was perfect.

***

After a fortnight living on West Canada, the boys had enough oranges to fill half the bed of their pickup, and a swap meet was in progress on the space to the rear of the Circle K. Enthusiastically the lads created a cardboard sign that read Oranges, 6 for $1, and then loaded the truck with their ill-gotten goods, in large boxes they had picked up from the supermarket.

It was a desiccated day, not a hint of a breeze, the hot metal of the El Camino was barely touchable so thankfully they didn't have far to take the vehicle.

Parking up on the end of a well-established line of stalls, they opened the tailgate, placed their amateur written sign on top of the fruit and waited, cheerfully, for their fledgling fruit empire to take its initial steps.

Hours passed without a single bit of interest from the locals. They had exhausted their banter to each other from last night's activities and about forthcoming events, and even the conundrum as to why the goods weren't selling, maybe they were too expensive.

Then an elderly Hispanic man with a gnarled walnut face stopped by.

"Oranges, sir," said Seamus, "the best you'll ever taste."

"You won't sell any oranges around here," he informed them.

The boys were floored.

"Everybody has a tree in their back yard," he chuckled.

Seeing that the lads were suddenly dejected by this revelation, he took pity on them. "I tell ya what, I'll take a half dozen, they better be as sweet as you claim, or I'll be back." The man handed over his dollar, picked out six of the biggest ones, then dropped them into a tatty old hessian shopping bag.

"Well that's that fucked then," said Tom cancelling the fiesta, "might as well fuck off 'ome."

"Why don't we go into town and try flogging it off down there?" suggested Seamus.

"Could go down to 4th Avenue and 'ave a go, they might be a bit more vitamin C receptive."

"Let's do it."

Parking the car on East 7th Street, they found themselves quite by accident to be next to a couple of wild orange trees, no other props were needed.

This pitch proved a little more successful, an offshoot of the busy shopping parade that was home to The Purple Haze. They got some footfall and yet were still tucked away from any officials that might try to move them on.

An hour later, they had managed to offload half a box of oranges, but that was it and they were restless, hot and disillusioned.

"What we gonna do with all this fruit?" enquired Seamus.

Tom pondered it for no more than a second.

"We'll just leave it 'ere, let the people 'elp themselves, we ain't ever gonna eat all this lot, what a waste a' time, we could a' been sacked for a few fuckin' dollars."

Seamus remained buoyant. "Never mind Ras', there's a party tonight at Stu's friend Randy's 'ouse. 'e's a great guitar player, should be a hoot."

"Yeah but we ain't invited," replied Tom gloomily.

"We'll invite ourselves—no fuckin' problem."

Randy Peters was a big cuddly bear of a man, with a bushy beard and a gentle nature. He played guitar in an easy listening country band and sometimes jammed with Hot Pot and Raucous Raccoon. He lived out in the foothills of the Tucson Mountains off Ironwood Hill Drive. It took the boys ages to find the house and when they did, the sun had dipped below the horizon and the party was in full swing.

All the guests at this shindig were adults; everyone a stranger to Tom and Seamus, apart from Stu and Randy, who was celebrating his 33rd birthday.

They walked around the long modern bungalow, a canal tiled building that was timber clad in shades of black and grey. Flip-flops crunched on large grade aggregate as they gingerly trod through the neat low maintenance cactus garden to the expansive paved patio area, surrounding a kidney shaped pool.

Guests were in abundance and politely nodded to the two visitors as they weaved their way through to the house, passing music equipment that was set up at one end of the pool, in readiness for a jam session. On a guitar stand gleaming like a priceless religious icon was Randy's brand new Gibson 335, a golden maple hollow bodied semi-acoustic electric number with double f-holes, a beautiful precious possession.

Hot Pot was surprised to see the lads suddenly turn up, his eyes shifted between his bandmates and the host who came over and greeted them both like they were fully expected, strengthening Tom's observation of just how welcoming Americans can be.

Maybe, he thought, it stems from the days of the early settlers, creeping west across inhospitable lands, setting up homes in remote outposts where any visitors apart from pissed off tribal people, must have been a welcome sight, and to those travellers, hot and fatigued on the apprentice trails, a far flung homestead would beckon like a much appreciated sanctuary.

Food and drink were always offered when guests arrived, and tonight was no exception; the boys were pointed in the direction of the kitchen, through a quadruple set of patio doors, whilst a light rumour began to ripple amongst the jamboree that the new Beatles had arrived.

Within the spacious open-plan, well illuminated kitchen, stood a number of guys protectively hovering beside a work surface littered with bottles of booze, a 40-pint barrel of beer and a couple of glass demi-johns containing a clear liquid.

This was the place to be, so advancing towards the stash, Tom and Seamus bewitched the keepers of the hooch, who as usual were predictably mightily interested with the English way of doing things, and likewise keen to counter the British charm with a show of American machismo.

The boys were poured a pint each from the keg, a lager with an alcohol content of just four percent, something that Americans seemed to get drunk on but the Brits could drink all night with little effect.

"What's in the glass jars?" asked the ever curious Seamus to a heavily moustachioed guest.

"Homebrew, mescal tequila," he announced proudly. "Made from the peyote cactus, mighty fine too,"

Seamus' eyes lit up.

"Is it strong then?" asked Tom.

"Contains mescaline, a hallucinogenic used by the Natives for centuries to get off their tits, they normally chew dried segments of the plant, which can make you vomit before you'll get high. But I make mine into tequila, which is much more civilised." He laughed and his friends giggled, having been off their tits many times previously.

"D'ya' mind if I have a wee dram?" asked Seamus, keen to represent Great Britain in the liver punishing event.

Not wishing to be disregarded in this discipline, Tom volunteered to have a shot as well.

It burnt like a creeping flame that rolled down the gullet and ignited the stomach; they may as well have swallowed petrol and thrown in a lit match for good measure, the shot caused the boys to exhale with gusto in order to extinguish the fire.

"Phoar," said Seamus turning a deep scarlet colour, "woo, that tickled me' tonsils."

The veterans, who had looked on with expectant anticipation were now jubilant in welcoming another two initiates into their clique.

"Fuck that," said Tom. "I'm not having another one of those; I'll stick to me' beer."

"I'll 'ave another go," said Seamus bent on self-flagellation.

"Yay," said the wide-eyed one with the moustache, pouring out another shot from the demi-john, expertly using two fingers in the glass eye holes and a fancy backhanded manoeuvre.

Seamus sunk that shot in one go, looked like he was going to have a coronary, burped a huge gaseous belch and glowed again like a Chinese lantern.

Tom shook his head at his partner's glut for punishment.

Seamus ordered up another one.

Randy, Hot Pot and a couple of other guys had struck up a jam outside; the mood in the house was joyous with the lads entertaining the party people in their inimitable style. Tom was merry but completely in control, Seamus on the other hand was showing signs of incoherence, something the boy never did; he could normally drink all night and not seem in the least bit inebriated so evidently the peyote was taking another prisoner.

A short while later, a call was put out over the microphone. "And now ladies and gents, we give you Tom and Seamus, the new Beatles."

Whoops and cheers erupted from the poolside and the sound of many hands being put together in keen anticipation.

Dubiously, unprepared and pissed, the lads ambled out onto the patio to meet their audience.

"What we gonna do?" whispered Tom over Seamus' shoulder.

"Jus' follow me," slurred the intoxicated one, and then, with one wildly misplaced forward leg, launched Randy's birthday present off its stand and sent it clattering to the concrete slabs. A sickening, clanging of wood, metal and feedback silenced the crowd and stopped the Beatles in their tracks.

Randy rushed over to rescue his beautiful gift, amidst tangible consternation from the speechless onlookers; it thankfully had only sustained a couple of small chips to the lacquer. He told the boys not to worry and in his gentlemanly manner asked them to resume their appearance.

Sheepishly they walked the mile to the equipment, where Seamus pulled on an acoustic guitar and sat on a stool. Tom tried to vanish behind a mike stand while Seamus struck up the opening chords to *You've Got To Hide Your Love Away*. They managed one verse and a chorus before Seamus fell off the stool and collapsed into an embarrassing heap on the floor, incoherent and unable to use his limbs, at which point the new Beatles, with some assistance, quickly vacated the building.

***

One languid night in early August, Kate Norton enticed the lads to go outside with her to watch the Perseids meteor shower. It was a cloudless sky, the air temperature hung around the mid-80s with not a whisper of wind on bare arms and legs. They wandered into the front yard each clutching the neck of a cold Rollin' Rock and felt the darkness.

Even with the subdued nominal street lighting on West Canada, the heavens were a spangled spectacle a thousand times clearer than the firmament back home.

The more Tom stared at it, the more it appeared to be a reachable ceiling, a palpable inky blanket littered with tiny searchlights. He felt like it was cradling the Earth, nestling it, keeping it warm.

They were promised a performance tonight with meteors dropping in twos and threes at a time, more than 90 fireballs per minute.

Tom lay on top of the perimeter wall, looking straight up; Seamus was on the ground, while Kate leant against the wall and craned her neck skyward.

Sure enough, the silent white fireworks streaked and faded into view at fantastic speed, bright arcs that appeared out of nowhere and disappeared without warning, in pairs, singular, triple and even quadruple; an ethereal onslaught to the upper atmosphere from the direction of the constellation Perseus.

Watching in wonderment, hypnotised by cosmic magic, the boys listened to a fantastic tale unfurled by their adoptive mother.

The subject matter had turned extra-terrestrial; Seamus had asked Kate if she believed that aliens existed.

She laughed, her gappy front teeth flashing in the moonlight. "Oh, they do," she laughed again, "man, they do."

Kate went silent for a bit, reflecting, and then she began. "I've met some. My friend Dana and I were introduced to a group of people who lived at the end of 1st Avenue, way out high in the Catalina's, Magee Road. Man, they were a tall race of people, around seven feet I'd say, and all blonde. They looked very peculiar, kinda all the same, with milky white skin and big blue eyes, very long fingers and limbs, they wore white coats, kinda like scientists I guess."

She paused again and looked pained, like she was reliving the experience. "They wanted to do some experiments on us, wanted to take some fluid samples, some blood, saliva and you know … some vaginal fluid, God I even think they wanted to take some eggs from our ovaries … Dana agreed but I was having none of it, I freaked out a little, so we left."

"She agreed?" said Tom astonished.

"Well, they were so damn attractive, mesmerising in fact, I felt almost compelled to do what they wanted, it was like I had no control over my own decisions. Dana went back another time and I think she had these things done to her, she was quite willing to cooperate with them."

"Blimey, she was brainwashed," said Seamus from his position on the ground.

"Charmed more like, they were such beautiful people."

"Did ya' know that they were aliens at this point?" enquired Tom still captivated by the shooting star extravagance above.

"They certainly weren't from Tucson, man," she cackled.

"Did ya' see a ship or anything?"

"No, but they did have a Chevy minibus," she said, then curled her tongue up over her front teeth.

Tom was thinking that either his new mum was completely mad or that she had seen something few people would find credible, Kate certainly seemed to believe in it, he sat up wanting to know more. "Did ya' see 'em again?"

"No they split town suddenly and I never saw them again, but it's left me in no doubt, they were real alright, man and they're living among us right now."

Her affirmation was utterly sincere; it made Tom's skin crawl.

The lads deliberated over it for days afterwards, Tom even mentioned it to Holly who verified the account saying, "Yeah, that shit freaks me out man, big time, my mom's goofy about shit like that."

Fact or fantasy, Tom believed that Kate believed it to be true.

***

"I've got you a gig at the U of A," said Gretchen over the phone.

"Really, that's great," replied Tom. "How d'ya' manage that?"

"Oh it's not a major gig, it's just a lunchtime deal in The Cellar Bar, but it'll be packed with students, so it'll be great exposure. My friend Carlos runs the bar so it was easy to swing it. You get the door money, it won't be a lot, it's only a dollar to get in, but you can drink as much beer as you want."

"Fantastic, when is it?"

"Next Thursday, if you like I can put up some flyers in the bar."

"Brilliant, we'll take the day off work; I'll make some flyers and bring 'em round tonight."

"Okay, I'm working at Gracious Bob's tonight, but you're welcome to come back to mine afterwards."

"Oh, are you behind the bar?"

"No I'm waitressing; it's minimum wage, one dollar and one cent an hour. But I get to keep all the tips, seventeen per cent of the bill is the customary tip, the same as the tax, it's exploitation, but apparently I can earn around fifty bucks a night and I really need that money right now."

"That's more than I earn a day."

"You can always try waitressing."

"The uniform might not suit me."

"Oh I don't know," she teased.

The Cellar was just that, down in the basement, brightly lit with a contemporary design. There were rails and partitions of stainless steel and glass, a walnut bar with matching satellite tables, stage decking also of solid walnut, with a backdrop of plain dusty pink bricks. The band had somehow expanded to a five-piece, due to the sudden appearance of a Mexican conga player who just set up by his own accord and asked if he could join in. He said his name was Jesus; he was short, stocky and sported a long handlebar moustache.

Chad knew his way round the campus, of course, being a student there; he said hello to many people coming and going through the halls. The boys wore their suits again, the air-con making their stage gear bearable.

Gretchen wafted in and made herself comfortable at a table in the middle of the room, she was clutching an armful of books and folders and preceded to study while the band set up, hardly acknowledging Tom at all, who just assumed that she was preoccupied with her workload.

With the sound levels set, Tom walked up to the microphone in order to introduce the band. Touching his lips to the mike connected him via a fault in the house wiring system, through his guitar to the mains electricity supply. The force zapped him in the face with a static punch, knocking his head back like he was on the receiving end of a jab from Sugar Ray Leonard. It felt like a wasp sting, he turned to Seamus.

"Did ya see that, I just got a shock from this mike!"

Seamus looked curious, but not alarmed. "Don't touch it, mate, stand off it," he said.

Easier said than done, thought Tom, it was going to be like trying to sing into the end of a cattle prod.

He approached the mike again this time gingerly keeping a distance. "Hello, we're from London," a few heads in the crowd looked up. "We're called Off the Scale and this is a song of ours called *Tell all the People*."

Seamus struck up with the intro and they were off.

The percussionist blended in well, the band sounded fluid, the reception was warm, and Tom kept getting smacked on the lips like a moth in a fly zapper. After the tenth time of this painful disorienting treatment, he'd had enough, so took off his guitar terminating the circuit, and allowing him to continue with the gig unhindered.

Gretchen disappeared halfway through the set, obviously she had classes to go to, but a little salutation would have been nice, thought Tom.

Carlos paid the boys $98, all the money from the door receipts, and re-booked them for a fortnight's time. The boys welcomed the gig, they were after higher paying jobs, but this was like a paid rehearsal. Chad and Stu got $25 a piece while Tom and Seamus split the rest. The conga player left his phone number and took off, never to be seen again.

***

The bullshit list of jobs which Saul had given them on Friday never got done, in particular the trimming of the large Cypress trees in the back 40. Saul had gone away for the weekend up to New York to visit his cousin Oren who according to Caitlyn Berns, was in the adult entertainment business. The boys decided that because they had taken the Thursday off, they should go in on Saturday and finish the list, to bump up their money.

The tall columned evergreen Cypresses seemed neat enough already, but Saul had a penchant for uniformity, for plants to be trim and regular, unnaturally impeccable. Tom preferred the random beauty of natural selection and considered topiary as something sacrilegious, but that's what he was being paid to do, so reluctantly curbed his morals and got on with someone else's ideal.

Seamus just wanted to get the job done as quickly as possible and get out of there, albeit with as much jollity as he could muster.

The trees were around 20ft high, so the lads used a set of fruit ladders, some steps and long handled pruning shears to get to the furthest reaches. Shorter shears catered for the lower branches.

The first tree they operated on, looked like it had suffered at the hands of an apprentice hairdresser on his first day in a salon, without the guidance of an experienced stylist. Chunks of growth had been hacked away on one side like someone had taken a bite out of it. They hoped Saul wouldn't notice.

They were roasting, balanced on the ladders, presented to the sun like marshmallows to a campfire, slightly hungover and rather bored. To entertain themselves, they started to talk in a simulated German language, complete nonsense, but it sounded plausible and tickled them no end.

"Ik bin ilanden staffenbinken stoff."

"Ya boshen nafen devere von bikcht."

A termite man arrived in the backyard, complete with grey overalls, boots, yellow hard hat, a mask, chemical tanks strapped to his back and a spray gun in his hand, making a fair impression of one of the GhostBusters.

The boys nodded to him and then carried on with their tedium, continuing to speak *German*.

"Didi staps unfearon der vosterstien."

"Ida kyla dash dishver von botton."

The bug man sprayed the entire ground area with termite death, not saying a word to the two foreigners up a tree, until he had finished, when Seamus and Tom said goodbye.

"Hey, you guys speak pretty good German," he said in his naivety.

"Thank you very much," Seamus replied, highly amused.

"I learn it from a book," said Tom mimicking Manuel from Fawlty Towers.

"Oh, okay," said the Terminator.

Tom instantly understood that this guy would believe anything you told him, but to lead him on would be cruel.

"Where are you guys from?" asked bug man.

"Australia," said Seamus clipping away at a mid-section.

"Really?" said the poor man.

"Yes, we're over 'ere for the Wombat competition," mocked Tom.

"Wombat?" said Seamus.

"No I'll bowl," replied Tom.

"Oh," said the absent witted individual, "cool."

He left feeling rather underachieving and insignificant.

They finished the pruning around 1:00 p.m. that afternoon, cleared away the debris and dumped it on the compost heap, raked the dirt, brushed the paving and put away the tools. They made a fuss of the dogs for 10min then headed off to Putney's sports bar on Oracle for some lunch, a beer and a game of pool.

Monday morning came around far too soon; they strolled up the drive with the same excitement one gets going to the dentist. Saul was still eating his breakfast in the kitchen, so Caitlyn came out through the side door to give them their orders. She was wearing massive rimmed brown sunglasses, indoors, the purpose for which eluded the boys, and a blue polo neck holy jumper, which was far too warm for the kiln-like temperature outside.

"Good morning," she smiled joyfully at their approach.

"Morning Caitlyn, 'ow the devil are ya'?" asked Seamus.

"Très bon mon ami, et vous?" she said laying on the French far too early in the day. The boss's wife not only tried too hard to impress the lads, she was also playing schoolmistress and imparting the romance language onto them in bites.

"Je suis très heureuse de faire votre connaissance," replied a glassy eyed Seamus stumbling over the pronunciation.

"Très fatiguè," admitted Tom, "aren't you 'ot in that jumper?"

Caitlyn blushed, she definitely was. "Saul wants you both to wash the cars first thing this morning before he goes to work and then he'll tell you what else needs doing okay? You can use the hose, there are buckets and sponges and shampoo here in the garage; oh and vacuum the insides as well." She smiled sweetly again and trotted back into the cool relief of the house.

Seamus tugged the peak of his red baseball cap in mock servitude, then the boys got to work on the Lincolns that were both out on the turnaround at the top of the drive.

After hovering and dusting the thermal interiors of the baking cars, the cold water from the hosepipes made this first hour of the week, an almost ecstatic, pleasurable, one. Tom lost himself in a daydream laced with Gretchen, who, like the water, had been chilly this weekend.

Seamus woke Tom from his thoughts with a deliberate broadside burst in the face, refreshing though it was; the bugger had to have some back, so Tom flicked him with a quick spurt right in the nuts, drenching his shorts. Seamus then escaped to the relative safety of the opposite side of the Lincoln, where he launched a heavily sudded sponge at his buddy's face. Tom ducked and it went rolling in the dirt, gathering a scintilla of dead plant material.

Not wishing it to escalate into a full blown water fight in front of their mafia Don, Tom let it lie and just laughed. "Missed," he said.

Seamus replied with a "Ha," then went and retrieved his sponge.

It hit Tom in the back of the head with a dull squelch. "Bastard," said Tom and gave Seamus another flick with the jet spray; it got him straight in the ear.

"When you two have finished fuckin' around, I'd like to get to work!" bellowed Saul from the garage.

"Sorry Saul, we'll just be two minutes," Seamus said earnestly.

"Humph," said Saul and went back to his breakfast.

When the cars were leathered off, they dried instantly, leaving just a faint powdery covering that was easy to buff up with clean rags.

Saul came out to inspect the motors, his critical eye on maximum. He was smacking his fat lips as he chewed a stick of gum; he ran a manicured hand over the paintwork of his big blue Lincoln.

"Not bad," he said quietly, "let's take a walk." He sighed.

Apprehensively the lads fell in behind their boss as he sauntered into the backyard, up the steps and along to the back 40. He stopped by the first Cypress tree.

"Ya' didn't cut these trees on Friday," he said scornfully.

"They've been cut, Saul," informed Seamus cheerfully.

"They haven't been cut," insisted Saul raising his voice a little.

"They 'ave been cut," reiterated Tom.

"You didn't cut the fuckin' trees on Friday, so who cut the fuckin' trees? Did God cut the fuckin' trees?"

Seamus and Tom glanced at each other.

"We came in on Saturday, Saul," admitted Tom.

"What!" Saul gave them both the death stare.

"Ya' not supposed to be fuckin' here when I'm not, who let you in, Caitlyn?" Saul stared at them over the rim of his glasses, they knew that they had committed a mortal sin and now they were going to drop his wife in it too.

"Ah ha," regretted Seamus.

The boss walked further along the line of Cypress trees, looking up at every one of them.

"Ya' done a pretty good job," he said at length, "follow me."

Relieved at not getting concrete boots for Christmas and amazed that Saul thought the trees looked okay; the boys shadowed their beneficiary once again to the tool shed.

On the floor were several new ten-litre pots of exterior white emulsion, a couple of new paint rollers, paint trays and two extension poles. They were to paint the asphalt on the flat roof of the house, which was basically the whole roof, in order to repel the sun.

Saul shot off to work and the boys got the double extension ladder out from the garage. Having roofing experience Tom went up first while Seamus went inside the house for a skive.

Apart from the air-conditioning unit, which looked like an aluminium chicken coup on stilts, there were just a scattering of stench pipes coming up through the roof and a parapet wall that encompassed the house.

"Easy," said Tom to himself.

Five minutes in however, he was back down the ladder to retrieve his buddy and a pair of sunglasses. The mirror glare coming off the paint was so intense he had a white-out and almost lost his bearings.

Seamus reluctantly left the cool of the office where he had been playing virtual pool on Caitlyn's Apple computer, and joined his mate at the end of a paint roller.

The pair of them resembled inmates on a chain-gang work detail, only in running shorts and Ray Bans.

This was the hottest day to date by far, and it was assaulting them on two fronts; the 'currant bun' above, and the solar reflection bounced back by the paint they were applying. It felt like they were literally being fried in an enormous white skillet and had to take several breaks in the shade, just to regain some cohesion.

"This sort of thing oughta be done at night, it's ridiculous," complained Seamus.

"That'll look good," said Tom sarcastically, "a novel concept, painting by moonlight."

"Perhaps we could wear those glasses that let ya' see at night, like a couple of owls," suggested Seamus leaning on his pole.

"T-wit," responded Tom.

Sweat made purchase on the poles challenging, each dip of roller into paint tray a laboured trial they could do without. Dollops of white gunk splattered the roof surface like the spoils of a punctured icing bag, before being smeared across the surface in a haphazard frenzied pattern inching its way in reverse across the asphalt.

Saltwater dripped off the end of their noses and ran into their eyes, stinging and blurring their vision, and their shorts and socks were soaking from the toil.

The sun blazed down drying the white paint almost as quickly as they applied it, and the two hombres to the core, ensuring that when they finally reached the end of the paint job, the part where they stepped off the roof and onto the ladder, there would be nothing left of them but two dry crispy husks in boots, welded to a couple of paint poles.

It was a ridiculous affair, but it had to be done, so they allowed themselves a 5min break, before re-ascending to apply more viscous emulsion.

Tom poured more gloop into his tray from a heavy 10gal tin spilling a large splatter with the motion of moving the thing.

Seamus had desecrated *the* golden rule of floor painting and boxed himself into a corner against the air-con housing and was now contemplating his options. He could wait up here till the paint dried, which wouldn't be long in this frying pan, but he was failing fast. Alternatively, he could tramp over the wet slippery glue leaving a trail of footprints, while decorating his trainers at the same time. Option B it was, carrying his roller pole, paint tray and re-fill tin like a juggler on ice, he traversed the surface.

Tom watched his partner with dismay and wondered how he had got this far in life.

"Hold it, hold it," he said when Seamus had almost reached him. "Ya' can't leave footprints like that in the paint; Saul'll go mad if he see's that."

"D'ya' think 'e'll come up 'ere?" Seamus said irritably.

"'e might … 'ere, 'and me the tin and the tray, you'll 'ave to go back an' roll over the paint while it's still wet."

"For fuck's sake. I'm roasting up 'ere."

"So am I. Do it sharpish, then we can go down for another break."

Reluctantly Seamus retraced his steps and smoothed out his signature, but now his soles were plastered in white mush.

"You'll 'ave to take them off before ya' go down the ladder, ya' gonna get it everywhere," advised Tom.

"Fuckin' 'ell, that ladder's gonna burn me fuckin' feet."

"Yup."

Seamus scrambled down the aluminium rungs like it was a state-of-the-art bathroom radiator, shoes in one hand, and bisected the drive to the garage like he was walking on hot ashes.

"Ooch, ouch, ooch, ouch, ooch, ouch." He said with each step—it was the funniest thing.

When the exercise was finally over the boys were bushed. Tom was so relieved to finally climb down the ladder, he felt like a firefighter who'd been on the front line of an inferno for the past two hours. Thankfully they were invited into the kitchen to normalise their systems.

Caitlyn recommended they take a dip in the pool to cool down, it would be their first venture into the inviting oasis and they needed scant persuasion.

Quickly discarding their footwear, they hurtled in enthusiastically, like pre-pubescent boys into a lake. The lukewarm fluid was almost orgasmic, like being wrapped in soft cool velvet drapes that swathed around their boiling bodies, warming up the water a few degrees just millimetres from their skin before dissipating into the blue sparkling rapture of the pool.

Caitlyn bought them out a tall glass of Tequila Sunrise each, brimming with ice and sat there in the shade of the palo verde tree, indulging in her boys and fuelling her fantasies. They did little else for the rest of that day.

***

Bryce Breville leant against the bar in the Tucson Racquet Club like a lonesome ranch hand looking for work. He'd been for a swim and was now nurturing a cold bottle of Coors Lite, fastidiously peeling the label off with his thumbnail and eavesdropping on the boys' conversation.

Another gig at the Purple Haze was looming in a week-and-a-half's time, followed by another stint in The Cellar. The lads wanted to add some more original tunes to their set. They had written some new stuff whilst jamming at the hacienda and also wanted to bring in a couple of old favourites from the past. Chad was keen for them to play the Spinners' song *I'll Be Around*, but the boys had never heard of it.

Bryce started singing the chorus; it was now suddenly familiar to them and suited the other songs they had been covering.

"You a musician, mate?" Seamus asked craning his neck to see who had joined in with their discussion.

"I'm a music teacher over at the U of A; I play saxophone, clarinet, flute—"

Chad interrupted, "I thought I'd seen you somewhere around, seen you in the halls."

"You a student?" Bryce asked indifferently.

"Yeah, majoring in sleep deprivation, something to fall back on if this music thing doesn't take off."

Bryce didn't know if he was joking or not, "Do you have some gigs coming up?"

"Not as many as we'd like," said Tom, "but we're getting there."

"Fancy a jam some time?" asked Seamus optimistically.

Bryce came over and sat in a vacant chair; he was a big character, around 6-3 and weighing roughly 250 lbs. He had a large round face, thick rubbery lips, a mop of golden brown curls that cascaded onto his forehead from a side parting and a foot long ponytail down his back. His beep blue eyes were rimmed by dark circles and heavy lids which gave him the appearance of being half asleep. Dressed in a black vest and tight sky blue slacks he looked anything but a teacher, but this wasn't a school day, and this *was* Tucson.

"I'd prefer to rehearse a little beforehand, would you guys consider coming back to my place to go over a few songs? It's just down the street."

It didn't cross their wholesome little minds one ounce that this guy might be a homicidal, cannibal maniac, luring them into a hatchet strewn, blood-soaked torture chamber. Instinctively they all thought it would be groovy.

"Trouble is, mate, I don't 'ave me guitar with me," Seamus then said.

"I have a guitar, an acoustic." Declared Bryce, "can you work with that?"

"Well let's go then," said Seamus energised.

Tom and Chad were more reserved, but keen to know if this guy was genuine.

Midway down a narrow dirt alley, the back entrance to Allen Road, off Country Club, stood a tiny ramshackle home, forgotten and dilapidated, probably an obstinate resister to some developer's plan.

Chad squeezed his camper van up to a fence amongst some overgrown plants and unforgiving tyre ruts, allowing just enough space for another vehicle to pass.

Bryce led the way through a barely functioning fly screen and an unlocked front door, into a pitch black hovel that smelt of stale food and mouldy clothes.

The sax player rummaged around in the gloom and found a lamp switch, lighting up a cramped living room strewn with brass instruments and musty furniture. Thankfully there were no rancid cadaver's, but it *was* the kind of place where you had to wipe your feet on the way out.

Bryce cleared some room on the couch and rearranged a couple of chairs so that everybody could be seated and face one another.

Tom noticed a polystyrene bust perched on a dirty sideboard and wondered why Bryce should have such a strange ornament amongst his empty takeaway boxes and instrument cases; perhaps it was a fraternity remnant.

The guitar was nice, an Ovation with a walnut body and a mahogany fret board; it played beautifully.

Chad picked up a set of dusty bongos and slapped them into shape while Bryce set a reed into a silver Alto's mouthpiece.

It took a minute or two of tuning before Bryce was playing some warm-up scales and trills; his tone was excellent, he was a marvellous player, surely he should be a professional musician so why was he living in such squalor?

Before too long Seamus had shown Bryce some licks from one or two of the boys' original songs, the sax man had not only picked up on the essence straight away, he had taken control of the tunes and improved the melodies and figured out harmonies to the lines. The song *Rosa* came alive, and a new song called *Be Mine* suddenly morphed into something utterly commercial. The boys were excited; they jammed for a good couple of hours, losing all sense of time.

"Fuckin' 'ell it's midnight," said Seamus glancing at his watch, "the time's flown by."

Chad was yawning, "We'd better be getting home gents, I'm deadbeat."

"Yeah, work tomorrow," added Tom.

The boys explained to Bryce where they worked, then asked him if he'd like to join them in rehearsal tomorrow night at The Haze. In a sedate measured manner he said he would be happy to.

Three buoyant lads talked joyously all the way back to Drexel Heights; they couldn't believe how well it sounded for an acoustic jam.

When they arrived home, Chad retired straight away, being the studious type, he took school hyper seriously.

Holly was up; smoking a fat doobie on the couch and watching Metallica bang out a tune on MTV. Tom concluded the thrash metal band had little melody that he could pick up on; he liked rock music but to him this was just noise. Holly however idolised this bunch of straggle-haired, leather-clad, guttural banshees and plastered her bedroom walls with their glossy posters.

The boys nestled either side of her and partook in the herbal offering. Holly rolled them fat and strong, a couple of tugs was all Tom needed to 'mong-out' and become cotton-mouthed, then he would listen to anything, adhered to the settee on a half-second delay.

He liked Holly; she had a wicked sense of humour, a tungsten shell, an untroubled attitude and although no centrefold, she oozed sex appeal. For an 18-year-old she was carrying a few unnecessary pounds, but her dark smouldering eyes could pull a man in like a tractor beam.

Fifteen minutes of brain dead metal endurance was all the lads could stand, so in slow motion, they took their leave, to their very agreeable beds.

***

Wednesday nights rehearsal was a revelation, Bryce knew all the cover versions the boys raised and added a truckload of sparkle to their original tunes, they really thought they had something special now, until at the end of the session when Hot Pot announced that they'd better be looking for a permanent bass player soon because he was getting far too busy with Raucous Raccoon and his work commitments, to fill-in any more. He kindly offered to stay though, until they found a replacement, which was handy because the gigs were starting to roll in.

After Stu had packed up and gone, Chad said he thought he knew a bass player at school who was available; he would ask him to come to The Cellar gig tomorrow.

His name was Jules, he sounded like an accountant and looked like an IT engineer. He was chubby, round faced, had sensible black hair and round rimmed black spectacles that he kept nervously pushing back up over the bridge of his nose with his middle finger.

Chad introduced him to the Englishmen, who greeted him warmly. Jules seemed to find everything they said funny and though obviously intelligent, chuckled away jollily after every other sentence like an awestruck teenager.

"Yeah it's a bit of a kick in the bollocks that our bass player's leaving us Jules, we're sounding really good right now, but 'ave a listen 'n see what ya' think," said Seamus to the short, pursed lipped academic.

"Kick in the bool-lacks, what's bool-lacks?" chortled Jules.

"In the bollocks ... bollocks ... in the nuts," explained a titillated Seamus.

"Oh, oh, a kick in the nuts. Bool-lacks is that what you guys call them?"

Tom laughed, still tickled as to how the mother tongue had been so sanitized here across the pond.

"Plant ya' 'Aris' on a stool, take the weight off ya' 'plates' and keep ya' ear out for a conga player, 'e lurks about in the dark, ready to elbow 'is way in on the act." Tom said deliberately trying to confuse the poor soul.

Jules chuckled again.

"I've no idea what you just said," he replied.

"Let us know what you think in the break," Tom said slowly, and then walked to the stage, thinking, what the fuck have we got here?

Gretchen didn't even show up for this gig. It bothered Tom throughout the performance; he knew she had a lot of revision to do and nagging her to come would have only stretched the thin membrane of a relationship that he now feared they had.

He'd hardly seen her in the last two weeks and he could tell in her phone voice she wasn't as keen as she had once been. He felt an inevitable break-up was on the cards, it was a bitter taste that he didn't want to swallow. He thought perhaps he loved her but he had never told her so.

Today's performance was better received than the last, with a certain amount of whooping coming from a rotating audience.

Bryce, a familiar figure to the music fraternity, made the band an instant hit with his students, many of whom had taken their break in The Cellar today.

Jules too was impressed and let the boys know it; he forwarded his services wholeheartedly and even though Tom and Seamus hadn't heard him thumb a note yet, they welcomed him along to the next rehearsal at The Haze on Saturday. This brought a modicum of relief to Hot Pot, whose wife had been giving him a hard time of late for never being home. He would do his last gig for Off the Scale on Saturday night and then he would hand the job over to Jules, who happened to be a talented musician, if somewhat overzealous.

Yet again the band had notched up a gear and was sounding as tight as a pair of yoga pants on a hot chick.

Early Saturday evening, the boys moved their equipment out of the rehearsal room and onto the stage at The Purple Haze. A thunderous storm was shaking the foundations of the building and sheet lightning was flaring the early darkness like a faulty fluorescent tube beneath the steel grey clouds.

The massive drops of rain were like cups of water precision-launched from on high, thoroughly soaking the lads on the short journey between the two buildings. They were glad to be inside at last and literally steaming in the accumulated heat inside the club.

Hot Pot arrived sodden, looking like he had just stepped out of the shower in his clothes. He asked for assistance getting his amp in from the truck. Seamus found a sheet of polythene and together they made a makeshift tarpaulin to bring it in reasonably dry.

The sound check was going well; Scorpion knew Off the Scale's requirements well by now and settled them in quickly. KP and Arty were busying themselves and Selena had turned up to manage the door. The club was coming to life.

Also on the bill tonight were Harriet and the Underground Railroad, and another band Taste of Eden, two local rock groups who would never be mentioned again in the scrolls of history. Their members and hangers-on were milling around listening to Off the Scale and itching to get their own sound checks underway.

Midway through a song, the tall imposing figure of Bryce Breville, who'd been home to change clothes, paced along the sidewalk past the plate-glass of the club and burst in through the front door like a raven-clad gypsy cowboy, drenched from the deluge.

The boys stopped playing as he stomped across the black sticky floorboards, sax case in hand like a hit man with his weapon of choice.

It was like Bryce, only different. His long greased ponytail swung down his back as usual, but gone was his mop of baby soft curls and in its place was a wet shiny bald scalp perfectly circumnavigating his dome from forehead to the back of the parietal bone.

The lads on stage were suddenly dumbstruck; the use of the polystyrene bust in Bryce's lair had now become apparent, a stand for a 'syrup-of-fig'.

Bryce was as cool as a Nordic gherkin, acting like nothing was amiss, yet this must have been a very revealing moment for him, almost akin to coming out of the closet; yet he remained totally unfazed and stoical, his courage apparent.

Seamus broke the silence with the best of intentions. "Very slick Bryce," he ribbed.

12
Blue Funk

"I can't see you anymore."

"Why?"

"It's complicated. My ex has come back into town, I thought I was over him, but I'm obviously not. You've been really kind; I've had a good time, but … I still love him …."

Tom replayed the conversation constantly in his head, desperately seeking a fleck of gold embedded in the dense ebony magma entombing him.

She said he was kind, which surely must be endearing; she'd had a good time, not a great time, he wasn't great enough for her. She loved another, not him, never him; her ex, some superhuman fucking Lancelot Tom hadn't even laid eyes on. Did he exist or was she just saying that as an excuse to dump him because he didn't tick all the right boxes? Either way she didn't love him like he loved her. Why didn't he ever tell her, would it have made any difference? It might have but he doubted it.

He felt really low; the recurrence of a familiar desolation for him, yet another failed relationship. It must be him, he thought, or it wouldn't keep happening. He felt heavy limbed and lethargic.

Seamus said, "It's only a bird, mate. Let's go out and 'ave a beer, pull a couple a 'sorts', a 'bunk-up' will soon sort ya' out."

But he didn't want to; he couldn't see how any other girl could possibly compare to Gretchen. He just wanted to lie on his bed and let the weight of the world crush the life out of him.

Seamus went out on his own; he was furnished with a tougher exterior than Tom, and had never, ever shown any sign of losing his heart to anyone as long as the two boys had known each other. Apart from a 'pull yourself out of it' line of advice, he was short on any other form of counsel, he just wanted to venture out and have some fun.

Tom stayed there in the quiet warm stillness of their room, his eyes wet and heavy from a monsoon of tears, until finally the distant tinkering of his foster family and the echoing words of his former girlfriend faded away, as he shifted into sleep and a dream about flying above an indoor swimming pool, performing trapeze style acrobatics around the steal A-frames beneath the opaque wired-glass roof windows.

His little white alarm clock woke him, a single sonic note repeated four times, then a pause, followed by four more, over and over till the thing was smacked on the head by a groping listless arm. The sound usually just meant 'get up you lazy bastard', but today it sounded like fear itself, the call to rise above the trenches and walk slowly towards the enemy machine guns armed with nothing more than an orange and a paint brush. The fear a condemned man must feel waking up on his last day on Earth in a cell next to the gallows; dread, abasement, resignation. Realisation, knowing that this was reality and the bliss you had just departed from was only a figment of your imagination, even though it was your preferred state of being.

Seamus rattled his usual aria in the next bed, immune to love and unaware that it was time to get up.

Tom didn't want to go to work today; in fact he wanted to go home, back to England, he felt isolated and remote, misplaced and unwanted.

Somehow his sense of duty prevailed, he was expected at the Berns', so that's where he would go; he woke Seamus.

"What time is it Ras'?" The big fella yawned.

"Seven," replied Tom wearily.

"Fuck me, you missed a good night last night."

Tom didn't reply.

"Me and Caryn went to the Cushion Street Wine Bar to listen to The Larry Redhouse Quartet and ended up in this frat 'ouse on the campus, pissed out of our 'eads and smoking the biggest bong that I've ever seen, the fuckin' tube must have been a meter long, I nearly fuckin' passed out with me first draw, it was fuckin' ridiculous."

Far from feeling jubilant for his friend's joyous evening, Tom just felt even more excluded. He wasn't just depressed; he was also depriving himself of a remedy.

"Do ya' want tea?" he found the energy to say.

"Two sugars please, mucker," said Seamus straining to become upright.

"'ere, you 'ad a fuckin' enormous black spider on ya' chest when I came in last night, I 'ad t' brush it off, it looked like it was eying ya' up for dinner. It was so big it ran out of the room and slammed the door shut behind it!"

"Should 'ave left it there, it might 'ave done me a favour," said Tom sullenly heading for the kitchen.

On the journey to work Seamus had to put up with Tom's laborious over repeated break up monologue with Gretchen, and his dissection of her explanation and the faint possibilities of reconciliation.

Seamus knew otherwise, Tom should forget it, the woman didn't want to know, and having never been down that dark bleak cul-de-sac himself, he only had scant words of comfort to offer his friend.

"You gotta change the fuckin' record mate, snap out of it and move on."

"Yeah but—"

"Yeah but nothing, it's 'er loss, fuck 'er."

Tom knew he was right; it was just going to take time to peel his heart off the floor and place it back in his chest.

Caitlyn Berns called them into the kitchen as they neared the house; Saul wanted to have a conversation with them while he ate his breakfast.

The smell of sweet coffee percolating in a pot and English muffins with eggs Benedict, almost drove the boys into ordering a couple for themselves, all they'd had was a cup of tea and a couple of Oreo biscuits each.

The dogs came sniffing round; especially the Retrievers who were keen to get their noses right into the boys crotches and nuzzle like it was the acceptable thing to do.

Miko just sneezed, took a few laps from the giant water bowl, and then went back into the living room to lie on the cool stone floor. Jolie sat and stared at the lads, her black sweet head cocked to one side and her little pink tongue panting in and out of her soft mouth.

"Caitlyn and me are going away to Florida for the weekend, and we want you guys to watch the house, so that it don't get fuckin' broken into." said Saul whilst chewing a mouthful of food.

"That is if you're not doing anything of course," added Caitlyn.

Saul's dark eyes peeked over the top of his horn rimmed glasses, expecting a response.

"Yeah, no problem," Seamus said enthusiastically, "Only be too glad to."

Tom felt a mixture of apprehension and excitement, the responsibility burdening the latter. He nodded in agreement with Seamus.

Saul put down his fork and wiped his mouth with a napkin, throwing it to the table, he sighed and got up. He never gave too much information away at any given time and was always scheming, building a platform from which to work things in his favour; these two Brits were going to come in very handy, if he played them right.

In Saul's mind, the boys hadn't been on a tour of the house yet; Caitlyn's manipulation of her playthings was kept in a parallel universe of which he had no knowledge. So he took it upon himself to show them around. Tom and Seamus feigned enlightenment as they went from room to room.

"One of ya' can sleep in here," he said of the rear office/bedroom, "and one in Jamie's old room. It's got a fuckin' water bed in there, I hate the fuckin' thing."

When they came to the master bedroom he said, "I don't want any fucker in here period, unless there's a fuckin' thief coming into the house." He reached under the bed and pulled out a 12-bore shotgun and a big black handgun.

"If any fucker tries to get in the house, I want ya' to shoot the bastards with these …."

Tom's eye's widened and he stiffened at the thought of using a gun on somebody. He had fired a 410 shotgun before, only at a metal dustbin on some waste ground, but the sound of that was near deafening. And he had used air rifles as a kid, but shoot a human being at point blank range? Surely this was only the stuff of movies and cop shows, wasn't it?

"… but make sure they are in the fuckin' house, not in the garden, otherwise you'll be charged with fuckin' murder, half in the house is fine, just not outside." Saul put the guns back under the bed and continued the tour quite pleased with his directorship so far.

I ain't touchin' 'em, thought Tom, they can rob the fuckin' house if they like, I ain't shooting anyone.

They went back to the kitchen; Saul stopped by the TV and picked up the remote control.

"This is for the TV," he then pointed to the mute button, "and this is for the fuckin' commercials."

He showed them the kitchen appliances, mentioning the microwave he said "This is where you cook ya' food," pre-supposing that the boys knew little about the ways of culinary preparation, when in fact they were now both dab hands at knocking up a meal.

"We're going Friday afternoon; Caitlyn'll draw you up a list of things that want doing while we're away, I don't want any of ya' fuckin' friends in the house, and if one of my dogs gets hurt, you'll get hurt." Saul glared at the boys with the cold-hearted look of an assassin. They knew that he meant it.

"One other thing," their boss said before they went walkabout in the garden, "The professor has written a song that he wants put to music."

Caitlyn handed them a purple coloured A4 sheet of paper containing the words to 'The ballad of Rincon Valley'. It was a poem written by Dr Kevin Launcher concerning his coalition's fight against Ron Ruby and his cohorts plans to metropolize the desert. Saul's name was mentioned within the song, decisively on the *Green's* side, but of course his part in this uprising of the masses against capitalism, and thwarting the developer's plans, was just a way of shitting on Ron Ruby.

"Take that home and put it to music," Saul said smiling viciously the only way Saul could. "There's a press meeting on Thursday night at some bar in town, where the coalition are putting their case forward to the news teams, get ya' self in front of the cameras and make it sound good," he snarled.

At a cursory glance, the lyrics meant little to the boys, but the double line couplets lent themselves to a blues format, so they would work something simple out when they got home.

***

Stomping into their own living room at the hacienda after work, they were greeted by a wonderful smell. The boys as usual were sticky and dusty and wanted nothing more than an ice cold beer from the fridge, but tonight Kate Norton was cooking a red snapper curry and the aroma swathed them in ribbons of enticement.

A giant commercial-kitchen sized pot rested on the stove, lidless and softly bubbling away with a *ploth-plar* noise one usually gets when boiling up some porridge oats.

Beside this pot resided another one of equal proportions gently simmering some aromatic pilau rice.

They went over to test the dish with a teaspoon.

"Umm, needs a little more curry powder I think," said Tom.

"Oh you think?" said Kate reaching for the cupboard door above the cooker where she kept the herbs and spices.

A scurrying sound, like light raindrops on rice paper petered out as unwanted house guests ran for cover. Unfortunately one of them lost its spiny footing and fell out of the cupboard, landing unceremoniously upside down into the yellow molten liquid beneath.

The cockroach, which was an inch long, coloured a shiny reddish-brown and sporting some impressive antennae, kicked his little legs furiously trying to escape the indignity of being boiled alive along with a dead fish.

"Whoops," said Kate hastily ladling it out and battering it in the sink.

"Tough little critters they are," she said retrieving the curry powder. "They can survive a nuclear attack."

The boys flicked a look of concern at each other before reasoning with themselves that the food remained unsullied.

Hearing that his band mates had come home, Chad came out of his hidey hole extremely excited. Some guys on a music engineering course at the Uni, had offered the band a day's recording session in the 24 track studio, valued at around $500, absolutely free.

"Fantastic Chad," Seamus said after swigging a long draw from his bottle, "let's celebrate."

"Already with ya' buddy," replied the drummer, who was very fond of a beer himself.

"When can we go in Chad?" asked Tom mustering up a little enthusiasm.

"Oh I told them that I'd run it past you guys first, see what you think, d', d', d', der, da, da, da, dar, and then get back to them. They're pretty flexible, but its part of their course work so they'd like us in there fairly soon. So shall I tell them next week and we'll wing it from there?"

"Brill," said Seamus, "If ya' can tell 'em next Monday, we'll 'ave the day off work cause our bosses are away."

"Cool," said Chad.

With that, Buster, whose wings had been clipped recently and shouldn't have had the ability to fly at all, launched himself from his Choya cactus perch towards the stove and landed flapping and squawking right in the curry pot, emulating the previous squatter.

Four people rushed to his rescue and pulled the soggy parrot out of the goo. These extra ingredients surprisingly didn't spoil the flavour one bit.

Rosetta and Holly came out giggling from Holly's bedroom arm in arm, then lay on the couch hugging one another, Rosetta stroking Holly's hair like she was a favoured pet. The boys perused them in wonderment.

"I think Rosetta's rather fond of Holly," remarked Tom.

Kate just shrugged as if to say 'so what'. Tom got the distinct feeling that love was love in this house, no matter who it was between. He shrank away from that scrutiny slightly perplexed.

Kate wanted a word with the boys; she lowered her tone and gathered them close to her.

"Some friends and I are going to do a deal that involves storing a quantity of grass in the house for a week or so, before moving it on. I thought I'd let you guys know what was going on before the goods arrived, to see if you'd object."

"What d' ya' plan to make out of it," enquired Seamus soberly.

"Oh a hundred and twenty-five grand split five ways," replied Kate casually.

The penny dropped as to how the family survived without any obvious income.

"Wow, that's a lot of dope," said Tom assuming that Pricey must be involved somewhere along the line.

Kate laughed her gappy tooth chuckle. "Yup," she said.

Tom thought it over for a moment. They were involved with enough illegal shit already, how could they possibly mind? It was one more thing to worry about, but if they weren't directly involved, how could they be accountable?

"Alright with me," he said at length.

"No worries," said Seamus.

"It's your ass," concluded Chad.

More giggles imparted from the sofa; Rosetta was now lying on top of Holly with her head on Holly's chest.

"When's the shipment coming in?" asked Tom.

"Oh within a week or so, we just need to gather our funds to pay for the shit, which is proving a little tricky just now," she replied.

"Things a little tight Kate?" said Seamus.

Their surrogate mother laughed a chesty gurgle, "Yeah you could say that, man, but we'll get by, we usually do." She wafted off towards her bedroom in a loose fitting turquoise cotton dress, like she was floating on air, assisted surely by some kind of substance.

Rosetta suddenly sat upright on the sofa straddling her hostage like she was sat across a horse. She was short enough to be a jockey, had jet-black cropped hair that was tonight moosed into a Mohican style and dressed entirely in black; jeans, shirt, waistcoat and cowboy boots sans spurs.

"Hey you guys wanna go to a party?" she hollered to the boys.

"Oh, not for me," Chad gracefully declined, "I've got to study with a six-pack."

"I'll come," said Seamus, "where's it at?"

"A friend's house in town, you wanna party with two gorgeous eighteen-year-old girls Tom?" she said suggestively.

Tom didn't feel much like partying, but he didn't want to stay in either, so he took the bait.

They went in Rosetta's little blue Toyota, parking on a suburban street on the South side. The girls were in wild spirits, they smelt of the alluring combination of cheap perfume and bubblegum, that tantalising cocktail of provocative innocence.

Approaching a white, timber clad, two storey house which was spewing music and people onto the street, Seamus asked Rosetta what was the occasion.

"It's just a party, man … a man party," she giggled.

"What, so it's just blokes?" asked Tom.

The girls laughed.

"What, is it gay party?" he said with some concern.

"Everyone 'ere is gay? said Seamus wanting affirmation.

"Apart from you two," she laughed again.

"And me," insisted Holly much to Rosetta's thinly disguised disappointment.

This revelation of Holly's gladdened Tom although he still wasn't absolutely convinced.

Inside, the building was like a humongous sweaty version of sardines, wall to wall men with barely enough room to filter through air, let alone more bodies.

The high energy music was ear-splitting and it was hotter than a Blacksmith's armpit. The quartet jemmied their way through the crowd, led by Rosetta, forcing disgruntled guests to make way as she parted the pink sea. Tom made himself as thin as possible, scared to death that he might touch, or get touched by somebody indiscreetly.

In the kitchen at least, there was some room to manoeuvre and the keg stood unmanned, an opportunity not to be missed. They filled up four plastic pint cups then filtered out into the front yard, where a table and four chairs presented themselves as reasonable sanctuary.

After an hour or so of people watching and 'piss taking', Seamus felt the urge to relieve himself. He got up and walked towards the house, stopping to ask a bleach blonde Billy Idol look-alike the way to the toilet.

"Ooh, call me Spike," said the delicate individual.

"Is this your house Spike?"

"Oh no," replied the punk excitedly, "but if it was I'd lead you straight to the bedroom," he gushed.

Seamus went to say something, but cut his sentence short after the first syllable.

Spike laughed outrageously, cupping a hand limply over his mouth. He then explained to Seamus the route to the bathroom, up the stairs, first door on the left.

As Seamus ambled off he could hear one of Spike's friends say in an outrageously camp voice "Who was that guy?" The catchphrase would stay with the boys for a very long time.

"I've just been chatted up by a bloke," said Seamus on his return to the table.

"You sure he was chatting you up?" asked Tom.

"'e was as camp as a row of tents," responded Seamus, and went on to tell them what Spike had said.

"You d'narf attract 'em," said Tom, "Remember Ronnie from the Crown in Garston? Come back love!" Tom mocked and went on to tell the girls how as a 15-year-old, Seamus had been plied with drink in the local pub by the flamboyant manager and enticed to stay after all the other customers had gone home, then lured up to Ronnie's room on the pretence of having some more alcohol. Seamus being green and greedy readily accepted and followed the pervert up the stairs. Only when Ronnie lent over and tried to kiss him did Seamus realise what his true intentions were and reacted by punching the poof on the nose, and making a hasty escape to the sound of the fading and now infamous line "Come back love!"

Tom was nearly crying with laughter recounting the tale, but the girls could only manage a smile, glinting at Seamus with a suspicious gaze.

***

Thursday arrived; the boys were introduced to Dr Kevin Launcher in the lounge at Orange Grove. He was the ultimate lecturer, long, lean, Greek bearded, wearing an olive green corduroy jacket with leather elbow patches and donning 60s style black-rimmed glasses with a really strong lens.

He wanted to hear the boy's rendition of his protest song in advance of them performing it tonight in front of the TV crews. Saul was surprisingly intrigued, he wore a lopsided wry smile, almost certain that the lads would churn out a load of old drivel, not that he cared much; he just wanted another stab at his arch enemy.

The Berns' sat down on one part of the expansive white sofa whilst Dr Kevin remained on his feet. Seamus got out his guitar and ran a quick tuning check. Miko cocked his large bear like head to one side, having never heard a stringed instrument before and Jolie just sat there inquisitively, her pale red tongue heaving back and forth, like a baby dragon; brightly contrasting against her jet black face.

Tom felt more nervous than he'd ever done; as if they were on trial for some misdemeanour. He gripped the A4 sheet of lyrics like he was holding on to a life preserver, causing it to crush and indent with his fingers' clasp. Seamus struck up the tune and they were off.

The blues had never been murdered in such a fashion before, the ill-fitting rhymes and un-poetic content made it a tongue twister that Tom struggled to keep within the bounds of a twelve-bar, and had to squash or stretch some words in order to complete the sentences.

When it came to an end, their audience gave a mixed reaction. Caitlyn was almost bursting with hormonal eruption, the good Dr was grinning like an Athenian cat and Saul just carried on chewing gum and staring at the boys with a sort of smug 'I knew it would be crap' look on his face, mixed with, 'so they can play and sing, so what?', demeanour. The dogs both huffed and laid down on the cool stone floor unimpressed.

"You guys really did a good job," Kevin said, breaking the nauseating silence.

"You ain't no Tony Bennett," wisecracked Saul airing his critical prowess.

"More like Gordon Bennett," added Seamus.

"What?" snapped Saul.

"Just a bit of English humour."

"Blow it out ya' ass," said Saul, "just sing that fuckin' song in front of the news people tonight. We'll watch it on the TV."

"Saul, I think these boys can go really far, what do you think, honey?"

"I think they should go back to work, there's a mile of dog shit to pick out there.

"Right you are Saul," said Seamus putting away his guitar.

Tom said nothing, he knew the song was a pile of pants, but the chance to get on national TV again was worth a little cringe. He got up, and the boys stepped out into the incinerator heat of the day, removing their vest tops immediately and heading for the tool shed.

Dr Launcher thanked the Berns' for their hospitality and left to go back to the university filled with pride and confidence that the song would provide some popular culture and some amalgamation amongst his fraternity.

Saul Berns chuckled; he was looking forward to throwing more sand in Ron Ruby's eyes.

The whole thing flew past it seems, quicker than the time it takes to recall it. Seamus took forever to get ready and they were running late as usual, driving at speed to the East side, to a restaurant bar called Rojo Gila, where the TV crews and the media hounds had gathered in force to report on the latest publicity stunt organised by the eminent professor and his green buddies.

Impatiently waiting at a set of traffic lights on a major three lane junction, the boys were discussing their tactics for performing the song and then retiring to a secluded table in order to eat something enormous from the menu, because they hadn't had the time to grab any food at home.

Gradually they became aware of the approach of screeching tyres, the inescapable sound of a car desperately trying to stop, but failing.

They instinctively looked both right and left on the carriageway that crossed their path, whilst still carrying on their conversation, then scrutinised the road ahead to see if the noise was coming from that direction; nothing looked amiss, yet the squeal was getting louder.

"Where the fuck is that coming from?" pondered Tom.

The answer came in the form of repugnant black, burning rubber smoke, which billowed past, over and around them in a rapid dissipating cloud. Apparently the out of control vehicle had been on an imminent collision course with them from behind.

A white Pontiac Trans-Am with a blue firebird emblem on the bonnet was now stationary at an awkward angle, just inches from their bumper. The driver and his pals, ashen faced and white knuckled from bracing themselves for impact, their fingernails embedded into vinyl and leather upholstery, sat with their hearts in overdrive and their lungs arrested.

Seamus glanced at them in his rear-view mirror, then at Tom, barely registering the incident before relaxing back into his seat. The lights changed, he casually slipped the El Camino into drive and they slipped away from the scene as if nothing had happened.

"They'll be needing some new tyres then," satirised Tom.

As they finally pulled into the car park of the bar it became apparent that both factions of the argument had turned up *en masse*. There were protesters with placards and slogan strewn t-shirts, both in and outside the restaurant. News network vans bristling with huge satellite dishes took up all the parking bays, forcing the boys back out onto the street to find somewhere to disembark. A grassy corner spot on the next block provided a harbour, so Seamus mounted the curb and put her down there.

Grabbing his guitar from the flatbed, the pair raced to the bar, where it was a struggle to convince the burly overwhelmed doormen that they were in fact the duo performing the live protest song for the cameras tonight, and not just a couple of glory hunters trying to get their mugs on TV.

They met with Kevin Launcher inside the tightly packed and chaotic dining area, who introduced them to a couple of his peers and to a KGUN9 reporter who was feigning empathy for their cause.

"This is Carla, she's featuring you two guys tonight; it's going out on the nine o'clock slot, are you all set?"

"No worries, Kev', we are fully rehearsed and primed to go," bullshitted Seamus.

Tom just smiled. This is gonna be hideous, he thought.

Carla directed the boys towards a couple of tall stools that were set up at the bar in front of the media circus. Tom sat uncomfortably on the edge of one whilst Seamus retrieved his guitar. A technician handed Tom a mike and set up another one on a stand level with Seamus' sound hole.

The noise in the room subsided as expectant do-gooders waited in a high state of anticipation.

"Roll VTR, and action!" shouted Carla.

Seamus launched into the chord progression with gusto, playing the round twice before Tom found the pitch and piled in with the lyrics. They managed two verses and a chorus before the surging started. A tide of people shuffling sideways against their will and bundling right into the performers, knocking the boys off their stools and sending squealing equipment to the ground, that was engulfed by the horde.

Seamus cradled his guitar like a harnessed baby and found himself unceremoniously herded towards the Professor who was making a stance with outstretched arms in a feeble attempt to stem the flow of bodies.

This was unmistakably Ron Ruby's henchmen's instigation, to upset the protest and turn it into a fiasco. They had succeeded to a degree, but the film crews were there to capture the events, which highlighted the green faction and also showed up Ruby's team to be the bully-boys in the fracas.

Saul watched the debacle unfold on a special live news bulletin, barking out a loud laugh when the mini riot erupted. It upset Caitlyn; she was quite looking forward to hearing her boys performing on the TV and was recording the programme on videotape for them to watch the next day.

"That fuckin' stupid whore's son," growled Saul, "He's just shot himself up the ass, ha, ha, ha."

Tom managed to somehow stay upright, pinned against the bar by a sea of anxious people ebbing across the restaurant in an attempt to flee the building. He spotted the back of Seamus disappearing into the throng and decided the best thing to do would be to go with the flow and try and catch up with him. After a lot of pushing and squeezing and far too polite apologies, he found his buddy outside near the entrance laughing his head off at the ridiculousness of the situation.

By now punches, placards and beer were being thrown across the void in the bar and the police were wading in while frantic conservationists were spilling from the building like ants from a flooded colony.

"Time to go," said Tom to his mate.

"I was enjoying that," laughed Seamus, seriously entertained.

***

On North 4th Avenue, very inconspicuously sited between a bookstore and a rock shop, was the lads new found dining experience, Rosa's Cantina. A Mexican restaurant capable of seating no more than twenty people, although each time they visited they had the place to themselves; tonight was no different.

Seated on the left of the long orange walled dining room, at a rustic wooden table, they received a complimentary bowl of nacho chips and house salsa.

"'ow does this place ever make any money?" wondered Tom.

Seamus was stuffing the delicious home made chips into his mouth like he had entered an eating contest, and had managed to decorate his chin liberally with the tangy red dip.

"Mmm," he said, "I'm starvingous," as he carried on munching.

Brightly coloured ornate paintings hung from the walls, interspersed with antique advertising signs and a golden framed Bandera de México. Tom's scrutiny was interrupted when two bottles of Corona arrived stuffed with fat wedges of lime and plonked in front of them.

"Are you ready to order Senor?" enquired the rotund waitress.

They had no need to peruse the menu, they knew exactly what they wanted, one 14in-long refried bean Chimichangas on a mountain of salad, topped with large dollops of sour cream, guacamole, jalapeño peppers and salsa, and a spare plate. The dish was massively oversized for one person and quite adequate for two; being priced at just $4, the owner couldn't have made a dime out of the English boys, yet they were always welcomed with a smile.

"Looking forward to resting me' 'ed on that double bed tomorrow night Ras', 'ow about you?" said Seamus between forkfuls.

"Gonna seem weird not 'aving them two around, I 'spose they must trust us now or they wouldn't let us stay."

"Mmm, this Chimichangas is beautiful, beautiful!" resounded Seamus, "I 'ope Caitlyn stocks up the larder before she goes, cause if we're on lock down an' there ain't no food in the 'ouse I'm gonna waste away."

"I think you've got plenty in reserve ole boy," Tom mocked, nodding towards Seamus' spare tyres.

"I'm eating for two," replied Seamus happily.

"Well you are a Gemini."

The food was divine and after another cerveza they settled the bill, then headed up the street to Café Sweetwater wherein they were approached by a vivacious tequila cowgirl in a black leather mini skirt, waistcoat, boots, Stetson and a loaded shot-glass sash, offering body shots at $1 a go.

"What's a body shot?" enquired Tom innocently.

"Oh, you can lick the salt off any part of my body!" said the bubbly blonde earnestly.

"Anywhere?" said Tom.

"Uh ha!"

This could get messy, he thought.

He gave her a dollar and requested the inside of her wrist, a moderate place to start. He gave it a lick, she smelt of a soap that reminded him of Avon products his mum used to buy in the 70s. The cowgirl rubbed in a pinch of salt she took from a small pouch on her belt, poured out a shot of Cuervo gold and handed it to Tom with a wedge of lime.

"Bottoms up," she announced.

That might be next, thought Tom.

He took the glass and the lime, licked the salt off her arm, downed the drink in one and then bit into the lime.

The rush from the giddy mix of all three flavours stopped him short and made him wince.

Seamus watched in keen anticipation, intending on a more daring platform.

"Whooow!" blew Tom, "that arrested time and space, 'ave a go, Monty."

"I choose the chest," Seamus proclaimed.

"Sure," said the girl thrusting forth her ample assets.

Seamus nuzzled into her cleavage and took a long lick of her left bosom breathing in her scent and tasting her skin.

Again the ritual three step manoeuvres were adhered to, she giggled when Seamus lapped up the salt and he took to the drink with gusto, appearing to have just received an electric shock whilst holding his breath.

"Wowzer!" he said at length, "grapple me grapenuts, that cleared out the cobwebs."

The bar was fairly relaxed so the lad's commotion was causing a little interest with the other customers.

"Where are you guys from?" asked the cowgirl.

"Across the pond," said Seamus, "from old Blighty."

She didn't comprehend.

Next, Tom had a lick of her right inner thigh where he discerned that she was wearing black lacy panties and not afraid to flaunt them.

Seamus went for the killer stroke and asked for a lick of her butt cheek, for which she duly obliged, bending over revealing her thong to the rest of the patrons who were now taking a determined fascination. He chose the right buttock and she unashamedly plastered it in salt, before performing a contortionist's move in order to pour the tequila and hand out the lime.

A few cheers erupted from the onlookers as the bitter cocktail went down in one acidic action.

The thought of going for the 'fanny' crossed Tom's mind, and even though he was fired up enough, he thought it too base to ask. Instead he opted for her lips which surprisingly, she was all too willing to offer.

She licked her own lips and dabbed on the salt, she was an attractive girl and the booze that had now cleared away all of Tom's inhibitions had turned her into a goddess. He leaned in and kissed her like she was the love of his life; she tasted like a spearmint mermaid and he stayed there longer than required before pulling away and necking the shot to a rowdy cheer from the bar.

"Arreebar!" someone shouted, and at least two people whistled.

The cowgirl was enjoying the attention and laughing along with the excited customers.

Tom's head was now swimming with intoxication and he knew he'd had enough. But Seamus was still intent on his third go.

"I'll take the belly button!" he shouted.

Tequila girl obliged, his tongue could feel the faint hairs that ran the course of her abdomen from her pubic area to her pierced navel, and the licking aroused her for the briefest of moments. Seamus swallowed his final shot and slammed the glass onto the bar top as if in triumph to some Olympic feat.

"Do you want more?" asked the saleswoman.

The bigger of the two Englishmen was game, but the more restrained of the pair decided they had work to do tomorrow and should be off, even though he hated to leave this deity behind, knowing he'd probably never see her again in this lifetime.

The girl moved on to a new set of customers gratified that she was doing her job well and that two men had been thoroughly titillated.

"'ow many blokes d' ya' think 'ave licked that tonight?" asked Seamus reflecting on what had just occurred.

Tom suddenly felt rather unclean.

"'adn't thought of that," he said distastefully.

They walked back to the El Camino unsteady on their feet, a little dazed.

Back at the hacienda Seamus went to bed while Tom went to see if Holly was still awake. Of course she was; she never fell asleep until the wee hours. He knocked lightly on the closed bedroom door.

"Yellow," her words sliced through the smoke haze.

Tom entered; he felt a tinge of excitement in the pit of his stomach as he crossed the boundary of the girl's mysterious inner sanctum. She was laying on her back on the bed, fully clothed, her legs bent up at the knees, her head resting on several pillows that were arranged up the wall to give her a comfortable viewing position to watch her TV, an ancient set placed within a crammed wooden wall cabinet at the opposite end of her room. MTV was on as usual and blurting out mild heavy metal tunes featuring big haired spandex covered dudes that Tom had never heard of.

Holly was smoking a regulatory fat doobie, surrounded by an assortment of faded cushions and a snuggled up Fonzi, although through Tom's drunken eyes he envisaged her to be an elfin princess reclining on a mattress of moss and feathers in the moonlit mists of a forest glen.

"Still up then?" he slurred.

She giggled, "It's too darn early to be going to sleep, where have you guys been?" Tom went and sat on the end of the bed and relayed the night's activities to her, she thought it all so very funny and laughed throughout most of the tale until it came to shot drinking, then she seemed a bit perturbed.

He asked if he could have a toke on her joint, she passed it his way; he took a large pull on it and held it in, making him feel so lightheaded he thought he might pass out. He gave her it back and stared at her thinking that with her deep black eyes and her cascading blonde locks, she really looked quite captivating tonight.

"Can I lie beside you?" he asked, imagining that it would be quite alright.

"No you can't old man;" she snapped, "go back to your own room!"

"I'm not old," he protested, "I'm only twenty-seven."

"That's ancient, man, I'm only eighteen!"

She had a point, although there was only nine years between them, she was still a teenager, with a teenager's mind; getting cosy with a grown up must have seemed quite heinous.

She threw a cushion at him that hit him square in the face. The dope had taken effect and he was feeling particularly out of phase.

"Your loss," he said, getting off the bed and searching for his balance. He went to walk out with the cushion but turned and threw it back at her, it missed and fell to the floor, she giggled. Fonzi didn't stir an inch; he just lay there curled up like a ball of angora knitting wool.

Holly went back to staring at the maniacs on the telly and wishing that Tom had been more persistent.

***

Feeding schedule for the Berns' Dogs

In the morning, all four dogs get a little ham (Reina gets very little, but Miko gets a lot.)

Reina: She is fed only once a day; that is, first thing in the morning. She gets her "diet" doggy food, which is in the laundry room. Mix about three medium handfuls with warm water and close her in the laundry room. At night, she may have one or two doggy biscuits.

Fonda: She receives a medium meal (about half a small dish) of mixed kibble in the morning; in the evening, she may have about a quarter of a bowl of mixed kibble. Naturally, she receives about two biscuits in the evening.

Tres Jolie: She's ravenous in the morning, and if you don't feed her right away, she'll forage for whatever she can find in the yard. So, about 7-ish, give her any leftover food from the night before, but make sure Reina and Fonda are out of her way. Then about 8 or 9 a.m. give her a medium bowl of mixed kibble. Between 6 and 7 p.m. she gets a small bowl of mixed kibble – <u>outside with Miko</u>. She gets two or three biscuits in the evening.

<u>Miko:</u> He's not crazy about eating first thing in the morning, but if there's anything left over from the night before, try to feed him that about 8:00. Otherwise, he'll just eat his ham and wait for a <u>big</u> meal in the evening.

In the evening, give him the larger sized bowl of kibble, and as many biscuits as he wants.

<u>Kibble Recipe:</u>

Mix dry dog food with warm water, add canned liver dog food (or substitute pastrami or chopped ham); and a stick of butter. Add a little Mazola and add one tablespoon of brewer's yeast (in fridge) and mix well.

Remember, feed Jolie and Miko outside by themselves! Miko will growl and try to steel Jolie's food, but tell him a stern "No!"

<u>Things to do:</u>

Move the Wagoneer and let her run 10 minutes every day.
Lock side gate every afternoon after 4:00.p.m.
Buy flowers for planting (Bedding plants).
Pick mixed fruit for Gracie to make fruit compote.
Clean brass pots inside.
Replenish potting soil for plants inside house and two large jade plants outside.
Move cactus (Agave) to empty pots and place under porch.

Take dogs for tick dip 10:30 a.m. Saturday.

Saturday, Dixon Exterminators will be here between 10:30 and 1:30; ask them to bomb garage; and please enquire about what we should do with vacuum cleaner (spray it?).

Change Saturday's appt with Andie to Tuesday or Wednesday (325-4663).
Put answering machine on whenever you are both outside.
Work with Jolie about an hour each day (split time up) for show ring

Where we can be reached in Florida: Bob Horn, St Petersburg, 1-813-347-8423; Al Schwartzkov, Orlando, 1-407-679-0159

"Fuck me, 'ave ya' seen this? The fuckin' dogs eat better than we do," said Seamus after scanning through the list that Caitlyn had left magnetised to the fridge door.

Tom read it through. "Talk about anal, 'aven't we got enough things to do?" he said after reading the bullet marks out loud. "We'll 'ave no time to enjoy ourselves; it'll be like being at work."

Seamus laughed, "She can't be serious, surely she's just doing this for Saul to see ain't she?"

"Dunno, but we better do it all, otherwise he'll know, now it's all itemised," reasoned Tom.

Very little else happened over the weekend, the boys stayed at their post, they took care of the dogs, they cooked, they ate, they worked, they watched TV, they found Saul's porn collection and watched a couple of those movies.

The highlight for Tom was the waterbed in Jamie's old room that he commandeered; it was a different type to those he had come across before, in the fact it had 12 long interconnected tubes running the length of the bed making up the mattress, but instead of giving you the 'all at sea' effect every time you moved, they behaved independently and were thus so much more comfortable. The water was heated, of course, and the bed was expansive giving him the best night's sleep he thought he'd ever had.

Also there was a large screen television in the room with cable TV and he was able to watch almost newly released movies on HBO, the funniest by far being 'Midnight Run' staring Robert De Niro and Charles Grodin.

The dog training had been a recent introduction. Caitlyn thought that Jolie would make an exquisite example of Akita breeding; she was a pretty dog, and the boys should be the ones to show her off in the ring. Several dog shows were on the horizon and Jolie needed to be put through her paces so she knew how to behave when in competition. The trouble being, she was a dog who held little regard for instruction and seemed intent on following her instincts, which, sweet as she was, would be a recipe for last place.

The 'training' happened on the stone deck area out by the pool. The other dogs had to be kept indoors otherwise the exercise just turned into a farce. Tom kept Jolie on a short lead to his right and trotted around in a circle of 20 yds diameter, at a pace of around 5 mph. Each time a circuit was complete they would stop and Tom would position the dog upright with her front legs together and straight, her rear legs angled backwards and slightly apart. Her tail, which was curled in a tight swirl, had to be upright and not flopping to one side.

Each time after the positioning, Jolie would immediately sit down, panting in the arid heat, her tongue forever lolling back and forth.

It was hopeless, yet Tom persevered and at least succeeded in getting her to trot by his side.

For some reason Seamus was exempt from training the dog, yet felt it necessary to give instruction on the methods used from the luxury of a rattan pool chair in the shade of the big palo verde tree, his bare feet up on another chair and a cold glass of fresh orange juice in his hand.

"D'*you* wanna do it?" snapped Tom in frustration.

"No tanks, me' quite comfortable 'ere," replied a very chilled Seamus with a dubious West Indian accent.

"Fuck it," said Tom, "this'll do for today, it's too much like 'ard work."

He let Jolie off of her lead and she ran for cover under the shadow of the patio veranda, Tom followed her and let the other dogs out into the yard, he needed a drink too.

The first dog show was in a couple of weeks' time in Sierra Vista, they wouldn't stand a chance, but were all too willing to go and visit the town, and get paid for the privilege.

***

The footage filmed on Caitlyn's camcorder, rounded the pillar on the corner of the rear office and shakily entered through the open door into the shrine where Seamus had spent the night. Tom's poor attempt at a David Attenborough impersonation took up the narrative.

"We find ourselves making our way through this labyrinth of a cave system, searching for one of the world's rarest creatures, *Horizontalis Championi,* and here he is surrounded by his two hounds of hell, Fonda and Reina." The dogs stirred at the mention of their names and Seamus' exposed feet twitched as if brushed with an invisible feather, the white rippled sheets were draped across his naked tanned body resembling a Roman Emperor flaked out on his back from an orgy the previous night, still swaddled in his toga.

He yawned and raised his head a little off of the pillows.

"Dude," he croaked.

David continued. "To the surprise of us all, we find that the great Goliath actually possesses a crude form of language, as yet undecipherable to the human ear." Tom pressed the stop button and lowered the camera. "Time to get up mush, we're due in the studio in an 'our."

"I'll be two minutes," countered Seamus.

Tom knew better.

An hour and a half later they met Bryce, Chad and Jules at the main entrance to the studios at the university.

"Glad you could make it guys," said Chad sarcastically.

"Sorry, sorry guys," pleaded Seamus, "the traffic was terrible," he lied.

Tom shook his head, "Where we going Chad?"

"Right this way gents," said the drummer who led them to a spacious two-room studio in which his drum kit had already been set up.

The décor was dark brown wood with acoustic foam tiles on the walls. A state of the art mixing console hogged a large portion of the control room; racks of gear lined one wall including effects machines, samplers and sound modules. Jules' bass amp was in here too, he scurried to his axe and annoyingly started to show off, slapping away at the un-amplified strings whilst Tom and Seamus marvelled at the array of studio equipment.

Seamus wheeled in his amp and set to tuning his guitar while the engineers, a friendly and extremely patient couple of geeks called Clem and Darryl, got a sound on Chad's kit.

The idea was to record three songs, *'Be Mine'*, *'Rosa'* and *'Murder on the 4th June'*, with Chad and Seamus playing live, then to record the bass and the Sax, redo the guitar parts, then add the vocals; and if they had time left, to overdub some backing vocals.

He didn't know if the bloke was nervous or just naive, but Tom was infuriated by Jules' constant barrage of bass slapping in the control room. Everyone knew the lad could play, but he didn't have to remind the world relentlessly.

When it came to the bass player's turn, he overplayed everything and Seamus found himself directing the fellow with kid gloves to get him to simplify his lines. Thankfully Seamus had the tact to carry this off without too much pride being spilt and the recording went like a dream, considering the time allotted, and they managed to produce three decent sounding tracks which would easily suffice as a demo recording of the band, good enough to play on the radio.

"Good job guys," said Chad high-fiving Clem and Darryl after the finished product was given its final airing.

Tom and Seamus felt very pleased with the day's work and couldn't wait to air it to their friends. The demo was mastered onto chrome cassette tape and copies were made on a multi cassette dubbing machine for all of the band members.

Now it was time to bandy the product around and try to get some paid work from it.

***

As time progressed, the teasing and flirting between Tom and Holly intensified; Kate pretended not to notice, but it was all too obvious what was occurring here. Tom tried to stifle his feelings, but Holly's antics were making her a right little minx.

Midweek, the boys attended a birthday party for Pete and Maisy's daughter. She had just turned 13 and the lads were asked to sing a few songs for an audience of cheeky children. They sang a rendition of the Beatles *'Michelle'*, but substituted the main lyric for *Seashell*. The girl was made up, believing that the boys had written the song especially for her, they didn't burst her bubble, and let her carry on thinking that that she was that special.

On Thursday, Off the Scale played another gig at The Haze, supporting local bands 'Marshmallow Overcoat' and 'The Cattle'. It was the first of three this month and they were gaining momentum and seeing some regular faces in the crowd.

This was Jules' first gig with the boys and his anxiety surfaced with frantic thumb slapping on the neck of his guitar, alas, also his habit of laughing at everything the lads said backstage. But the performance was great and they received a warm response from the cosmopolitan midweek audience.

"Friday night, next week, mate," said Seamus as they exited the stage.

"Woo hoo, big time," said a now relaxed Jules, "can't wait."

"Moving up another step on the ladder old boy," reassured Tom.

***

Another weekend, another party. Hot Pot was hosting an all night jam session at his house. Raucous Raccoon set up in the living room and a whole host of muso friends were invited to do their 'thang'; this time the English boys were on the guest list and it turned out to be a blast. Seamus and Kris from Raucous were hardly off their guitars in a sweaty dual of whose fingers knew the most chords, as song after song reverberated through the night.

Fenella laid on a lovely spread of Mex-American cuisine and alcohol flowed in copious amounts. In the small hours Tom found himself in the mild waters of the swimming pool, under the stars, treading water and talking to a lounging river Naiad stretched out along the coping stones in a white gossamer dress that in the moonlight shone like it was made of silver filament. Part of the dress draped lackadaisically into the pool and it mattered not; she was barefooted, laid on her side with her head rested on the upturned hand of an arm bent at the elbow and angled towards her face, her golden hair cascaded towards the water like a miniature falls and her big blue eyes glinted like molten pools of mercury.

Lena had followed Tom out into the night; she still had a damp patch for him and although she looked the loveliest he'd ever seen her, like a shimmering featherlight fairy, she still didn't turn him on.

Rescue came in the form of Seamus having finally given his blistering fingers a break and wandering out to the poolside to join his friends.

"You got swimming trunks on Ras'?" he asked.

"Those, I 'ave not," concluded Tom, "I am bare arsed." He smiled.

Seamus started to peel off his moist clothing and said "I'm coming in."

With that he did his famous one bent leg belly flop dive into the pool, causing a mini tidal wave that drenched the giggling Tinker Bell so much that she thought it best to just fall in and have a muck about with her clothes on.

The shenanigans went on for a while until Tom, bored with it; extricated himself from the water and got dressed, leaving the other two social butterflies to discover each other; she'd get her oats and Seamus another notch on his bedpost. Tom just wanted his bed; he thanked his hosts and slipped off in the El Camino drunker than a designated driver should be.

The phone rang on Sunday morning; Seamus called and asked to be picked up from Lena's house. It was no biggy for Tom to drive over and get him and it just so happened to tie in with Kate Norton's request for the lads to be out of the house today when the 'shipment' arrived.

"'ow did ya' get on?" asked Tom when the unkempt one fell onto the boiling passenger seat of their car.

"She fed the fuckin' pigs by 'and—she's a fuckin' nutter," responded the bedraggled lad.

"I could 'ave told ya' that mate; what pigs?"

"The fuckin' Javelinas, wild ones that come to 'er fuckin' door, she feeds them bits of old carrot and cabbage by 'and … big stinking 'airy fuckers with 'uge yellow tusks. I stood well back, thought she was going to lose 'er fuckin' fingers, she's mental."

"What … a whole bunch of 'em?"

"About six of 'em; a whole fuckin' family."

"Christ I've 'eard that they can be right vicious, she's lucky she's still got arms."

"Yeah, what with that fuckin' black widow living under her bed an' all, I was frightened to death to fall asleep in case it fancied a nibble of me in the night."

Tom barked a hearty laugh. "What she got a black widow living under 'er bed for?"

"She thinks it likes 'er."

"Fuckin' cranky cow, she's not gonna be with us for long is she?"

"Good fuck though, I just 'ad to lie back and listen to the bed springs."

"Sounds about right," wound up Tom. "Anyway, we've gotta be out of the 'ouse for a while; the package is arriving and they don't want us around, fewer witnesses I s'pose. So we'll go for brunch somewhere, what d'ya' fancy?"

"Fuckin' 'ell me armpits stink mucker—"

"An' ya' knob!"

"An' that wee fella as well, I was looking forward to a shower when we got back."

"It'll 'ave to wait mate, the Egg Garden?"

"Ooh," said Seamus, his taste buds igniting, "'ome fries and an omelette, take me there, Daddy."

Following a superb meal at their favourite breakfast haunt, in a cool dark booth with few other customers around, the twosome paid a visit to KP to play her the new demo and kill a couple of hours. The English lady seemed very enthusiastic for the recording and promised to get them several interviews on KXCI community radio.

She shared a killer joint with the boys and although she never mentioned the deal that was going down, Tom and Seamus presumed she just might be involved.

Late in the afternoon they crunched to a halt on West Canada, the temperature was in the upper 90s, warm enough to roast chestnuts on the dashboard.

Seamus felt like he was one of those chestnuts. A cat's paw breeze stroked his face as he got out of the car, laced with the undeniable whiff of skunk weed. The stuff was so strong that the sniffer dogs at Tucson International must have been running round in circles, and the airport was five miles away.

Everything was as per normal in the hacienda, no one seemed perturbed by the fact that you could actually get stoned just by breathing normally, and Kate Norton was floating around as usual, multitasking between preparing dinner and collating the archives for the Yaqui tribal museum.

"You took delivery then, Kate," said Tom stating the obvious.

She gurgled a laugh. "You could say that, man," she laughed again, "let me show you." Provocatively, she led the boys to the spare room.

In it stacked to chest height were 250 parcels individually wrapped in black bin polythene and secured tightly with packing tape, each roughly the size of a shoe box, weighing 1 lb and valued at $1,000.

"Gonna need a few 'Rizzlas' to get through this lot Kate," said Tom astounded at the amount of room this consignment took up.

"What are Rizzlas?"

"Cigarette papers Kate," enlightened Seamus.

"Oh, yeah man," she giggled, "but these babies aren't staying here for long, they'll be gone in a few days, then if all goes to plan we'll be able to pay the back rent and buy a few Christmas presents too."

"Ah ha," said Seamus. He yawned and said he was going to jump in the shower.

Tom went to see what Holly was doing; he'd been thinking of her all day.

For weeks after the shipment had left the building on a dark night, when a Chevy van had reversed down beside the house and a mystery man had taken the medicinal herbage away; the boys were sweeping up handfuls of spillage from the packages. It was very welcome plunder, and a wickedly strong strain.

13
North

Just inside the perimeter wall of the front yard at Orange Grove, ahead of where they parked the El Camino each morning, resided the compost heap. A mound of rotting palm fronds, Agave stems, Dates and mouldy citrus fruits, swollen to a height of a yard and a half and a diameter of around five.

It wasn't just a fragrant eyesore, but an ecosystem, an insect metropolis without planning consent. And Saul wanted it vacated and demolished with immediate effect.

To tackle this Caitlyn had hired a three ton U-Haul box wagon, not the most ideal transport solution; a tipper truck would have served the purpose better, but adequate enough to take the debris away.

Armed with pitchforks, leaf rakes and shovels, the boys set to the task with loathing and despondency, their orders were to make the yard spotless, exterminate the inhabitants of the compost ghetto and dump the detritus on a specified piece of land belonging to the enemy.

"The fuckin' roaches can go live with the King fuckin' roach himself," Saul had decreed.

Manoeuvring the truck inside the walls was tricky, there was barely enough room to turn the Lincoln Continental around, yet alone a removal lorry; but after several frustrating point turns Tom managed to back the thing up to the decomposing pile and with a hiss of the air brakes, brought it to a stop, switched off the engine and disembarked.

"Nice one, Tom," said Seamus leaning on his pitchfork like a yokel.

The cab master warranted no praise, he used to drive lorries around London for a double-glazing company, and if he could squeeze seven tones of metal through the narrow alleys and width restricted roads of his capital city then parking one in an Arizona garden was simplicity itself.

Forking in the fronds was easy at first; the fresher ones behaved themselves and stayed on the tines until they were launched towards the back of the truck. But the smaller pieces and rotted stuff, was far more argumentative, and the fruit impossible. Seamus tried spearing the oranges, which was fun, but then he couldn't get them off the ends of the forks, so abandoned that sport, they'd have to be dealt with by shovel.

An hour went by; the lads were a couple of pounds lighter from venting steam, so they took a water break. The well water from the fridge in the tool shed had a slight burnt hair smell to it, but was a mighty relief under the intense August heat. They polished off a gallon each and set back to work. Even though the truck was quickly filling up, it seemed like they hadn't made much of a dent in the compost heaps demise and the strangest thing was, they'd hardly seen a critter amongst it at all.

By lunchtime the pile had gone, the ground raked and every last leaf loaded onto the truck. The boys threw the tools in the back and plodded up the drive, answering a call from the lady of the house, "Seamus-Tom … lunch!"

Entering the kitchen they must have smelled like a welder's jock strap from the amount of effort they had put in to loading that truck but Caitlyn didn't seem to notice.

"*Assoyez-vous*," she requested, starting today's French lesson.

"*Merci Madame*," countered Tom.

Seamus thought for a few seconds, and then worked out what to say. "*Ce qui pour le déjeuner aujourd'hui ?*" (What's for lunch today?)

"*Ah, puits fait mon ami, nous prenons le ragout de palourde*," she said showing off.

"What … what … what?" augmented Seamus befuddled.

Caitlyn found herself amused and returned to English for the sake of her poorly educated guests.

"Clam chowder, the best soup you'll ever taste, mind you this is out of a can and nowhere near as good as the real thing served down on Fisherman's Wharf in the San Francisco Bay. Oh my god, that chowder down there is to die for. You guys really should go there while you are over here; it is my favourite place in the whole world. I used to live there before I met Saul; that's where Jamie was born."

She started singing 'I left my heart in San Francisco,' badly.

"Mmm, this is lovely," slurped Seamus behind his silver spoon.

Tom thought it just tasted like mildly fishy potatoes.

"Have some soda bread, I bought it especially for the soup," Caitlyn said enthusiastically, and went back to French, *"La phrase d'aujourd'hui est, Je suis très fatigué et je veux aller au lit,"*

"What does that mean?" enquired Tom.

"I'm very tired and I want to go to bed."

"I'm not stopping you," he joked.

Caitlyn smiled wickedly imagining that she'd just been asked to bed, but that was far from Tom's mind.

She got the boys to say it several times before she was happy with their pronunciation. "Learn a phrase each day and you'll be speaking French in no time," she insisted.

Fat lot of help that was going to be at a monster truck fest in Tucson, considered Tom, but then again, there was always La Rendezvous!

The lady of the house disappeared and left the boys to finish their lunch; it was alright, nothing special, but they were grateful, once again they didn't have to break into their softly earned cash to buy a meal.

After their break, Tom drove way out East and headed down Old Spanish Trail, a familiar route that once took him to his Sister's house near Colossal Cave.

On the left they found the dirt track road they were after and pulled in. A metal sign advertising land for sale was hanging limply from one nail on the corner of a wooden board, it flapped as they passed it, dusting Mesquite bushes with trail powder from the furrows.

The land on which they were about to trespass had been bought some time ago and was part of Ron Ruby's big expansion idea for a massive housing development and resort.

Creeping at a snail's pace along the unmade surface for half a mile, scraping the paintwork on overhanging branches and rocking the cab in the large pot holes, Tom eventually halted at a chain-link gate padlocked shut with a hefty chain. A metal plate wired to the gate read 'Private—Keep Out'.

"Balls," he said, "'ow we 'sposed to get in there then?"

Seamus took a long draw on his cigarette and said, "Why don't we dump it 'ere Ras'?"

Tom studied his buddy, he had one foot rested up on the dashboard and his arm out of the window.

"'ow am I gonna turn it around down this narrow lane?" he said.

There was barely enough room for them to traverse the road, let alone perform a three-point-turn.

"What if you break the lock with the lorry?"

"What … like a battering ram?"

"No, just drive up to it slowly and push it, it's bound to break!" said Seamus confidently.

"You reckon?"

"If it don't we'll 'ave to take this fuckin' lot back to Saul's an' he ain't gonna be 'appy with that."

"Let's give it a go," said Tom.

Tenderly he nudged the truck up to the gate until they were touching; not wishing to damage the paintwork on the front of the cab too much, he pushed the accelerator to some degree and inched his way foreword a little until the tensile strength of the gates and the chain became compromised, resisting the weight that was bearing down on them.

They held fast.

Conscious of the fact that they were only a short distance from the road and not too far from nearby homesteads, Tom didn't want to draw unnecessary attention to their activity, but he had to break this padlock, so he gave it more throttle, causing the rear wheels to spin in the dust and more noise than was comfortable.

"Go on Ras'," urged Seamus from the passenger seat.

Tom gave it more on the floor, revving loudly at 3000 rpm. Unexpectedly with a shattering ping; the whole gate broke at its hinges and was slammed to the ground by the force of three tons plus, converging on it.

The hire truck flew through the opening into barely traversed scrubland, and then scrunched to an abrupt stop, shifting Seamus out of his seat and almost through the windscreen.

"Ha, ha," he chortled, "That did the trick."

Worried that they must have been heard, Tom manoeuvred the truck in a circle so as to face in the opposite direction, bumping over rocks and crushing small bushes and disturbing gods knows what desert dwellers in his haste.

Once back on the uneven road with the rear end level with the broken gates he stopped the truck once again and switched off the engine.

"Right 'ere'll do," he said indicating to Seamus that they should get out and empty the contents as quick as possible.

The lads hurried to the back and elevated the roller shutter, climbed in the box and began forking and raking the pile out of the lorry like their lives depended on it, all the time expecting a visit from some nosey neighbours or the cops, or even worse Ron Ruby's men, having been tipped off.

Frantically extracting the detritus and dripping in sweat they neared the bottom of the pile, where it became chillingly apparent to where all the residents from the compost heap had taken refuge. The bed of the truck was a shimmering russet crunchy carpet, as cockroaches, scorpions and spiders of all sizes clambered over each other in an attempt to find cover. Black widows, funnel-web and wolf spiders climbed the walls and cascaded off of the end of the flat bed into the hot sun like an insect waterfall and scarpered.

The clandestine chore of frenzied labour had just turned into a scene from a Hitchcock movie and the lads were rendered immobile as invertebrates and exoskeletons clambered over the boys' boots and started to ascend the hairy vertical slopes that led to the moist dark sanctuary of the lads' nether regions.

"Okay, nobody move," said Tom mimicking Michael Caine's line from 'The Italian Job'.

"We're gonna get fuckin' bitten to death 'ere Ras'," muttered Seamus.

"I'm sure they're more scared of us than we are of them," Tom tried to reassure his buddy to little avail.

Seamus held up his broom like he was wielding an axe, defending his square of aluminium like it was his pledge.

Kicking off the unwanted attention and brushing off the advanced individuals, then doing some kind of informal truck-bed tap dance, the boys devised a conclusive and courageous plan. They would use the two large headed brooms and sweep from the back of the box in one hefty stroke, ridding the beasts and the last of the debris from the van onto the desert floor in a oncer.

This gargantuan swoop succeeded bar a couple of big buggers that had climbed up the inside walls. They were soon dispatched with a flick of bristle and the boys were shutter down, back in the cab, and creeping quietly away from the scene.

At the road junction, Tom tentatively nosed his way out on to the main road, half expecting an armed road block to be waiting for the lawless desperadoes they'd become, but nothing was occurring, just a heat haze warping the tarmac in the distance and a lone pickup truck some way off travelling in the opposite direction.

They were safe and out of there as long as police forensics weren't going to get involved, making a plaster cast of their tire tracks and tracing it back to Saul, but that was highly unlikely seeing that no one had been killed, apart from a few cockroaches, but that was hardly to be considered homicide, maybe insecticide, or was that something else? They were on the road, job done, *comme ça*.

"Arac-no-phobia," quipped Tom at the wheel.

"The only roach I wanna see again," said Seamus, "is in the end of a spliff."

But all the way back they were spooked by phantom spiders triggering hairs on their legs and up their shorts. They wouldn't be free of that feeling until they had both had a scrub down in the shower tonight.

***

On Friday night, Off the Scale played another gig at The Haze, supporting local rockers Gila Bend, and Train of Thought.

They went down reasonably well; it was a good rehearsal for the next gig midweek at the Rialto Theatre on Congress Street.

The humidity that night was insane, like wandering through invisible kettle steam and for the first time in the States, Tom's lungs were tight, an asthma attack seemed imminent, which would have been disastrous because he hadn't brought an inhaler with him.

Seamus wanted to be dropped off at Caryn's house, so Tom obliged, then headed back to the hacienda alone and went looking for Holly.

As usual for this time of night she was holed up in her sweat lodge, tugging on a fat one.

"What ya' up to?" Tom asked cutting through the smoke like a rescuing fire-fighter.

"Oh nothing, just kicking back," replied the teenager disingenuously, hoping that he'd come around.

"D' ya' mind if I 'ave some?" Tom indicated towards the joint.

She offered it to him feigning reluctance. "You boys; why dontcha get your own shit?"

"I don't smoke."

Holly laughed, she had a very distinctive gurgle, her dimpled apple cheeks took over her face and she lit up like a golden lantern. "You smoke all of mine," she giggled.

Tom lay on the bed next to her and got cotton mouthed within minutes. Surprisingly the smoke helped relieve the itchiness in his lungs.

"How was the gig?" she enquired indifferently.

"Reasonable," he said but complained that Seamus was still using his amp and that he should get his own.

"Get your rich girlfriend to buy you a new one," she replied with a hint of animosity in her voice.

"Is that a spot of jealousy I hear my dear?"

"No," she giggled.

Tom turned over and rose on all fours, then straddled her and began tickling her sides, to which she squirmed and giggled and half-heartedly tried to push him off. He held her wrists down on the bed and sat firmly on her tummy; she smelt divine, their eyes locked and a surge of adrenalin boiled in his belly, rising up to his chest.

It felt like the most natural response in the world, he descended on her slowly, locking onto her full soft lips with his and they kissed like they'd never been kissed before. They bit and nibbled and sucked and explored with tongues like bubblegum tentacles. He cradled her face in his hands and their bodies entwined like coiling snakes on hot sand. She gripped him tightly with her legs, never wanting him to escape as their groins ground together, dry humping like a millstone and quern pummelling sacks of corn.

He was so hard he felt like he would rupture, but try as he might, she would not yield to his attempts to undress her. She was having none of it; her flesh it appeared was definitely off the menu.

After an age of getting nowhere more than a Jack Russell on a stuffed toy, he decided that he was better off in his own bed before he got blue bollocks. He bid her goodnight, convincing himself she wasn't a lost cause; she just needed a little more persuasion.

Frustrating though it was, she let him go, her presupposition being that the Englishman was no more than a libertine skirt chaser, and she was partially correct. But this young lady wasn't going to be just another mark on the stock of his rifle, though she really could have done with a notch herself tonight.

***

"What's the difference between whiskey and bourbon then?" Tom asked the bartender.

The lads were killing time on high stools, sat alongside three members of Raucous Raccoon, amounting to the sole patrons this evening, and aligning the ancient polished mahogany bar top of the Tap Room in the Hotel Congress. The barman, Jed, a handsome fellow in his 30s with a shed load of integrity and a very welcoming demeanour, was taking great delight imparting his hard earned knowledge of the history and variety of all things liquor.

Five fresh shot glasses were placed in front of the musicians on the bar and a measure of Jack Daniels slopped in each.

"Now ya' Jack here is Tennessee sour mash whiskey, made from corn, a little bit of rye and barley malt, but the real secret ingredient they say, is the iron free spring water drawn from a place they call The Hollow."

The guys all took a swig.

"Course it's then filtered through ten feet of charcoal and left to distil in oak barrels that are made on the premises. You getting a honey type of overtone?"

"Ah ha."

"Yeah."

"That'll be the filtering," he said.

"Cor, bloody good stuff," said Seamus.

Another set of glasses were laid out. Jed talked while he worked, washing the glasses and pouring the drinks in a skilful, fluid motion.

"Now the Glenfiddich is a totally different cat, a single malt whiskey made from barley or wheat, with Highland spring water from the Valley of the Deer and gets its distinctive flavour from the Douglas Fir washbacks and the Spanish white oak barrels it's stored in. You'll be getting subtle pear traces from that fella," said Jed.

"Ermm."

"Yup."

"Yowza."

"You see the difference? The Tennessee and Kentucky bourbons are mellower, less acidic and not as dry as the whiskies. Which is best? Well it's all down to personal preference."

Yet more shot glasses were lined up.

The lads were in no hurry; they had 2hrs to go before a benefit gig in the Rialto Theatre behind Club Congress and had only come into the Tap Room to relax before the show. Jed had embraced them into his empty bar and was rejoicing in spilling not only free drinks but his entire knowledge of how they came to be.

"Now Vodka, or grain wine as it was known, was once made out of potatoes, as is the Irish Poitin, and is distilled up to as many as three times. It was originally a medicine and only fourteen percent alcohol, but today it's usually around forty percent. It was also once called 'The Burn' for obvious reasons."

The boys thought this a great game and egged Jed on to go through Gin, Rum and Tequila. Eventually sliding off of their seats, Tom endeavoured to try something different, he slurred "what's that blue stuff up there?" pointing to the Curacao.

"Oh that's a Laraha-based liqueur from the Dutch Antilles, usually an ingredient for cocktails; you wanna try some?"

But by this time they had to get going, and Seamus reluctantly put an end to the game. They thanked Jed for his hospitality and staggered their way to the theatre way drunker than was necessary for the beginning of a gig.

"Nice bloke that Jed, we should go in there more often," Tom managed to say.

The gig was poorly attended and went by in a blur and once at home, like a moth to a flame, Tom gravitated towards Holly's room, only to encounter the same scenario as the previous night, a lot of fumbling, and no open doors to the cupboard. He was confused, what was the problem? They were both unattached, gagging for it and were in a private place where nobody was objecting, apart from Holly that is. Tom was forced agonisingly to spend another night in just the company of his aching balls.

***

Macy Moore came to visit; she pulled up the drive in her cream Cadillac Brougham D'elegance sedan, bundled out of the driver's seat like a fragrant Weeble in white trousers and a tent-like cerise blouse. She bid the lads, who were idly clipping the Pyracantha hedge in front of the kitchen window, a high pitched sing-song good morning before trundling into the house via the open garage door.

The boys were nursing yet another yawn crowded hangover and melting, bare chested under the mid-morning grill.

Honey bees floated around, impossibly airborne, intent on collecting pollen from the tiny pink flowers of the shrub, pretty buds that were inexcusably being sheered off on the orders of Mr Berns, to turn the plant into a very unnatural green rectangle, trim and tidy, not a leaf out of place.

"They won't 'urt ya'," Tom insisted to his friend who was dodging bee flight like it was sniper fire.

"I'm not taking any chances, mucker, ya' know me an' bees don't get on."

"They're only after the pollen they're not interested in you."

"I … ain't … so … sure," Seamus managed to say bobbing between insects. "I'm going in t' get a drink."

Tom tutted at his friend's misplaced phobia and returned to mutilating the hedge. He felt an itch between his shoulder blades and reached round to relieve it with his grubby fingers, inadvertently squashing a bee into his back that instinctively reacted by projecting its sting into the assailant's flesh in its last act before death.

"Yeow!" shouted Tom in excruciating pain, "the bastard's got me."

It was pain beyond belief for such a small puncture wound, like a broken hypodermic needle left in the muscle.

Seamus came back out of the house clutching two large glasses of iced lemon tea, with a look of incredulity on his face. "Told ya'," he said self-assured.

Tom could only grimace and rub his back; the irony couldn't have been better timed. "'ope I'm not allergic like me' brother, 'e could die if 'e gets stung."

"If ya' start frothing at the mouth, I'll run ya' up the 'ospital mate," reassured his buddy. "Macy wants to see us in the 'ouse Ras'; she's been listening to our demo, I think she's got a proposition."

"As long as it doesn't involve the exchange of any body fluids, I'm all ears," said Tom.

Macy and Caitlyn were in the kitchen fostering a couple of soup bowl sized cups of coffee enriched with shots of brandy; they were giggling when the boys arrived.

"Look at me' back Caitlyn, I've just been violated by one of the natives," Tom turned and displayed his inflamed infliction.

His boss was on the case like a loose hair to a nylon shirt.

"Well there's no sting left in you, but I better put some antiseptic cream on it just in case."

She rummaged in a draw until she found some Germolene, then applied it to Tom's warm, moist, tanned young back, slowly and sensuously.

"I've heard your demo tape," snapped Macy, "I like it, you've got potential. What'll it take to get you boys on the radio?"

The lads were intrigued.

"Well," said Seamus after a pause, "we'd 'ave to 'ave a recording contract I s'pose and at least a single out, then we'd 'ave to promote it, get it in the shops and then punt it round the radio stations—"

Tom interrupted, "That's assuming a record company can see potential in us that is; you 'ave to be very lucky, ya' know, the right place, right time, unless ya' know somebody that is. We've been on that treadmill before."

"Is there another way?" asked Caitlyn.

"You can always make ya' own record and publish and promote it y'self."

"How much will all that cost?" challenged Macy.

Tom puffed out his cheeks, "'ow long's a piece of string? You can spend as much as ya' like on a recording in a decent twenty-four track studio; then it'll 'ave to be produced, mastered, pressed, the art work done and you'd 'ave to form a publishing company or get a licensing deal, then 'it the road and start bugging the radio stations to play it. It could take months and cost thousands. Why, d' ya' think that we're worth it Mace?"

"I sure do," she said with all conviction. "Where do we make a start?"

Seeing an opportunity Tom said, "Well actually the first thing that we need is another amplifier, Seamus 'asn't got one and 'e keeps nicking mine."

He'd expected a hearty rebuff, but instead received an innocent, "Okay, what else?"

Now his taste buds were really dripping. "Erm, then we have to find a recording studio 'ere in town. There's bound to be one that suits our needs."

Seamus remained silent, he thought this all too good to be true.

Caitlyn was bubbling up inside, she had to get involved as well.

"If you like Macy, you can take the boys off to a music store this afternoon and pick out an amp, and I'll go through the phone book and look for a studio, but you'll have to be back to go get Saul at four-thirty okay?"

Macy loved that idea, both boys to herself for the afternoon, a little one-upmanship on her pal.

Larry's music store in the Tucson mall off Oracle, specialised in Fender guitars and amps. After putting a few combo's through their paces, they decided on a hundred-watt Red Knob Princeton Chorus, it had a similar sound to Seamus' old Roland Jazz Chorus. Seamus was as pleased as a lion cub with a gazelle leg to chew on, He couldn't thank Macy enough.

"That's okay, maybe you'd come and look after my dogs for a weekend while I go away, as a favour in return?" she said projecting a fine filament of spider silk around the boys' waists.

"No problem," said Seamus, "only we can't do this weekend, we 'ave the dog show in Sierra Vista to go to."

"Ah yes, Caitlyn told me Tres Jolie was entering that," she smiled wryly to herself, knowing that the little bitch hadn't a hope in hell at winning a dog show. Macy bred Akitas and knew a thing or two about the business. "Well you'll have fun anyway," she said.

And that was all they ever wanted.

"'ow about the following weekend," asked Tom, keen to repay their debt with a bit of graft.

"Erm, maybe, I'll let you know," said their latest advocate.

***

After a superb dinner of ground turkey macaroni cheese casserole, a tossed salad with French dressing, and some garlic and herb flat bread, washed down with a couple of Heineken's, Kate Norton and the boys decided a walk over to the local bar across the dusty wasteland was in order.

Although only a few hundred yards away the lads had never ventured through its doors and didn't know what to expect. They knew it was a favourite haunt of the local indigenous folk and thought they might be treated as imposters, so always gave it a swerve, however tonight they were in high spirits and in local company. Kate knew many of the people inside and although they received a few glances when they ambled into the sparsely decorated joint, nobody bothered them as they shot some frames of pool, drank plenty of beer and had a right royal time.

The place had whitewashed walls, a green and white lino tiled floor, a simple bar, furnished typically with bar stools occupied by Yaqui tribesmen of varying ages, all of whom were a tad over weight and smoking heavily, giving the bar room its very own cloud.

In a corner next to a well-worn pinball table, idled a claw crane machine filled with five-inch-tall stuffed animals of various type and hue. Over-inebriated with the beer and seeing that it was only 25 cents a pop, all three of them took it in turns to operate the complexities of the grab, and amazingly managed to pull out armfuls of the gaudy coloured creatures before it became tedious not to win.

The boys loaded with toys, stumbled alongside Kate in the dark back to the hacienda where Tom indiscreetly burst into Holly's room to bestow on her the booty he had plundered. She giggled at the drunk Englishman and cradled her gifts like they were new born puppies before throwing a lilac rabbit at him as he proudly stood there, swaying with a glazed look in his eye. It hit him squarely in the face and as he swooped to pick it up, he fell over and rolled on the floor amongst the girl's discarded clothes, bundles of shoes and her dinner plate.

He struggled to his feet and said, "Good idea, I'll give this one to ya' mum." And with that he left the room and followed the corridor down to Kate's boudoir. The door was open so he just wandered straight in, to be stopped dead in his tracks as though walking into a force field wall.

Kate was on the opposite side of the room stark naked, and although she was a middle aged woman, nothing had gone south. Firm buoyant boobs, nipples facing front, a spare tyre around her midriff, heavy thighs and a 1970s dark bush made Tom feel unexpectedly aroused yet stunned senseless.

For at least a second the pair of them just stared at each other, before both simultaneously said, "Oh," and then Kate grabbed a robe to cover her virtue while Tom did an abrupt u-turn and headed back to her daughter's room.

He wanted to offload what he had just seen, but he couldn't, not to Holly, so that would have to wait for Seamus' ears. Right now he had only one thing on his mind; perhaps after his stroke of luck with the cuddly toy machine, this cuddly girl would let *him* have a few strokes tonight.

An hour, maybe two had past; they'd been through the ritual reefer smoking, groping and heavy petting, he'd ground into her so much that he felt like his cock had entered her, material and all, stretching her leggings inside her like a lycra tube, the ultimate condom. But then he'd managed to get her leggings off without too much of a struggle and for the first time in his coital attempts, there were only cotton panties between him and sticky delight.

He dry humped her some more, all the time kissing her face, her neck, her chest, breathing into her ears and nibbling her lobes, trying all manner of tricks but she still wouldn't yield. He was readying to give up; she was proving to be an infallible fortress.

Out of the blue she said, "What the fuck!" and reached down between her legs to rip her own panties in half at the crotch; she could take it no more.

A fanfare of trumpets sounded in the half light; he unzipped his shorts and pulled them down to his knees, taking his underwear with them. His chopper was so stiff he could have hacked down trees with it. He plunged it deep into her tight, sodden pussy, causing her to arch her back in sudden ecstasy. She moaned with pleasure, revelling in this first penetration; a moment she'd wanted for months, but was too proud to surrender to him.

It didn't last long; half an evening of foreplay had brought them both close to frothing over already and after just a few wild pumps the pair of them exploded in a joint orgasm that must have registered on the Richter scale.

He stayed inside her, their hearts beating in time, the pulse in their genitals prolonging the pleasure. He kissed her tenderly again, not wanting to let her go; she was the medicine he needed to get over Gretchen.

He was the dirty scoundrel that had voodoo'd her to love him and she was going to set him free; she just didn't know it yet.

***

Sierra Vista was a couple of hours away, South East on interstate 10 and then South on the 90 through Huachuca City towards the Mexican border. It was a typical Arizonan town, much smaller than Tucson and greener, the access to water must have been greater than its big cousin's.

They followed instructions given by Dr Sophie Kaminski, the breeder who produced Tres Jolie, on to Coronado Drive and then Tacoma Street, finally arriving at the community centre's soccer field, where the show was being held.

Tres Jolie's round, was set for 9:00a.m., in ring 3, so the boy's had got up at stupid o'clock in order to get there in plenty of time.

Miraculously they had made it and although it was hotter than the devil's Chimenea, Tom was required to wear trousers and a jacket and tie in order to parade the mutt around the ring.

Jolie thought it to be a tremendous hoot, with all these new smells and furry faces to look at; she was surely in doggy heaven.

The boys registered and tried to stay cool, seeking the shelter of an awning set up for grooming and watering the dogs; but it was like torture for Tom in his blue blazer and white heavy cotton trousers, and after a time Jolie was panting like a polar bear in Wadi Halfa. She was a pampered pooch, much more used to the confines of an air-conditioned lounge than the summer heat of a scorching sports field stuffed with other hounds. She lay on the grass at Tom's feet whining that she wanted to go home. This was going to be a disaster.

But persevere he must, for Caitlyn's sake; you never know, Jolie just might surprise them all.

She didn't, it was a struggle just to get her round the ring without sitting down every few paces and when it came to presenting herself, her tail kept falling to one side and she wouldn't stand in the correct position, just lolled her tongue helplessly from her frothing mouth and whimpered.

She was hopeless; they came 7th out of 6.

Disappointed not to be taking a rosette home for their trouble, and embarrassed by just being there, the lads melted away from the arena as discreetly as they had arrived. Evidently they really didn't fit in with this doggy crowd who were a unique breed of human, utterly committed to the show ring, its quirky protocol and its austere fashion sense amongst the dowdy spinster types and definite lesbian quota. Their fully equipped mobile kennel/grooming salon motor homes stocked every item needed for travelling the highways, bounding from one dog show to another. The men too, all seemed to be friends of Dorothy on this side of the valley, and as with every vocation, all they ever talked was business.

Tom removed his stuffy clothing at the nearest opportunity and drove back to Tucson in the Wagoneer relieved it was all over, but at least they did get to see another part of the State, which was refreshing.

Caitlyn and Saul were frustrated that the little bitch hadn't won a prize, but put her failings down to her being young and inexperienced; there was always next time.

The next time? Tom despaired.

***

Now the barrier to the Promised Land had finally been breached, Tom and Holly were at it every night; they couldn't get enough of each other. And although it wasn't officially announced that they were an item, it suited them both to be fuck-buddies rather than in an actual relationship.

Everyone around them knew what was going on, which was cool because they didn't have to answer to them or shower one another with gifts. They didn't even have to go out anywhere, though they did go to a few clubs and parties together as a group with Seamus and Rosita; however, they did a lot of shagging; in Holly's room, Holly's car, out in the desert, out in the garden next to the swimming pool, in the swimming pool, in Kate's car, in the local school amphitheatre, a precision made acoustic shell that exaggerated and carried every carnal sound, including the moans of a girl on cloud nine.

The conquests included the flat bed of the El Camino under a blanket of stars, in the toilets of the Purple Haze and around the back of the Circle K, by the dumpsters and the empties.

The arrangement was glorious for Tom, no ties and a bunk up with a warm, fragrant, cuddly 18-year-old whenever the opportunity presented itself; he couldn't be more at ease.

***

The following weekend Macy engaged the boys as promised in a spot of dog sitting. She was going away to visit her sister for two days and although the boys wouldn't be sleeping there, they had the run of the house for Saturday and Sunday.

But it came at a price; they had to feed, water, groom and clean up after six large beasts.

The Akitas didn't need walking; they each had a whitewashed kennel in a block house, individually with its own chain-link fence enclosed run. A pen that filled plentifully with mounds of dog eggs, discarded food bowls, and ripped to shreds play toys and stuffed animals.

Most of the animals were friendly enough, especially the females; but one male, a two-year-old dog called Reggie had a tendency to maul people to death.

Akitas are huge dogs with large powerful heads and you do not want to pick a fight with one, unfortunately Tom inadvertently did just that.

He was in Reggie's run clearing up the dog shit, raking the gravel and generally tidying up the scattered toys.

The dog was in his kennel eating a distractionary meal; however he had gulped it down and came out to investigate the clean up operation. Seeing that Tom had a hold of one of his favourite tug toys, a piece of rope, Reggie supposed it to be play time and lunged at the other end of the frayed thing. Growling commenced and a game of tug of war from which Tom couldn't possibly snatch victory, so he let the toy go, at which point Reggie took umbrage and reared up on his hind legs, placing his giant front paws on Tom's shoulders and bringing them snout to nose.

The dog was now taller than Tom, his snarling head was twice the size as the Englishman's and he had killer written in his squinting brown eyes.

Now Tom was a lover of animals and always got on well with dogs. He felt that he had some kind of affinity towards all things great and small but this beast hadn't attuned to that and was set to take his face off. This was it; he was going to be ripped to shreds and tossed about the pen like a saliva soaked crash test dummy.

"Good boy, there's a good boy," tried Tom, quaking in his boots.

It had no effect; the dog continued to growl and bare its fangs.

Tom's heart was rapidly beating; all the blood had drained from his limbs rendering him extraordinarily cold in the midday heat.

"Good boy, Reggie, alright, alright, there's a good boy, get down, get down," he said desperately trying to placate the dog in the softest most consoling voice he could muster.

Maybe it was magic or maybe Reggie just got bored, but for whatever reason, the dog suddenly lost all aggression, like a switch had been flicked, he got down and returned to being reasonable. Untroubled, the psychopath strolled off for a shadier part of the run and flopped down in the dirt.

Tom breathed a massive sigh of relief and tiptoed out of the cage, vowing never to go in there again.

Seamus was by the pool in the backyard skimming out some fallen leaves, "you alright mucker, ya' look like y've just seen a ghost."

"Nearly became one," he said and went on to explain what had occurred.

"Mate," said Seamus leaning on the long aluminium pole that was half submerged in the pool. "That could have ruined the weekend."

"And me' modelling career," replied Tom.

"What for … Airfix?"

Tom laughed. "Love the smell of that glue."

Macy came home on the Sunday evening and praised the boys for all their hard work even though they had hardly done a thing, and she insisted on cooking them a meal, despite the fact that she never usually lifted a finger in her kitchen as her maid always prepared the family meals.

The lads tried to wriggle out of the invitation but Macy wouldn't accept a rebuttal, she wanted them here for the evening.

Tom had refrained from eating red meat since the end of the previous year and Seamus had given it up out of respect for Tom's abstinence. Their benefactor cooked them a huge steak each.

It was an inch thick, the size of a dinner plate and tasted like candle wax. A host Macy certainly was, but she was no cook.

The lads put their morals to one side briefly and managed a few mouthfuls, before Tom spoke up, "Sorry, Macy but we can't eat this."

"Nonsense," she snapped, like stern mistress, "you eat it up!"

"We don't actually eat red meat anymore, Mace," protested Seamus.

"Oh fuddle, you eat it up," she demanded.

The boys looked at each other with resignation before cutting into the tough cows' arses once again. She had gone to all this trouble to entertain them and they didn't want to be rude. So they persevered with a few more dense chunks, chewing endlessly on the bland greasy lumps and swallowing hard, but after getting through only a quarter of the steak they had to surrender.

"Phew, that's enough for me, Macy," admitted Tom. "It was very nice, but I'm stuffed," he lied.

"Yeah, me too," said Seamus, "ya' wouldn't 'appen to 'ave any beer would ya' Mace?" knowing full well that she had a fridge full.

"Uh ha," she said sweetly, "would you both like one?" Her green eyes sparkled. Maybe she could get them both drunk and lure them into her *chambre*.

"Yes please, Macy," said Tom.

They talked for a while about recording studios. Caitlyn had contacted several and booked appointments for the boys to go and check them out, but all Macy was interested in was subduing her prey and like the predating spider she was, slowly wrapping them in her thread. The lads could only think of escape and after two beers they made their excuses and cut free. The warm evening air never felt so good on their skin as they made their getaway to the El Camino.

Macy squeaked her goodbyes from the porch then closed the door on them disappointed but swearing to claim at least one of them for another day.

On Monday morning Saul called them both into the kitchen.

"Did the fat fuck pay you guys for feeding her mutts?"

"Saul!" said Caitlyn.

He ignored her upset.

"She's paying for a recording session," replied Seamus, "in a studio in town."

Saul turned up one side of his mouth, "Ha," he barked, "she'll want more than just feeding the fuckin' dogs for that. She'll want ya' fuckin' juices."

Caitlyn cringed.

He went on to give them their mission for the week. Tomorrow they were ordered up to the Berns' log cabin at Pinetop in the White Mountains to give the garden a tidy. They could spend the rest of the week there, raking, hoeing, and trimming the trees. They could take the Lincoln and come back on Sunday.

They were amazed.

Caitlyn gave them detailed instructions on how to get there and in her usual officious manner, a list of do's and don'ts, where to buy groceries and places to visit, and 200 bucks spending money.

Tom and Seamus checked out the map in the afternoon. Pinetop was in the far North East corner of the state, close to the border with New Mexico and not a million miles away from some very alluring tourist attractions, they were going to make full use of this opportunity.

****

The White Mountains were roughly 260 miles away, a journey of around 5hrs. They set out North on Route 77 at 9:00 in the morning, full of cheer and excited expectation, taking Caitlyn's SLR and video camera along for posterity.

Pulling in at a gas station near Oracle, they stocked up on petrol and eats for the trip, then continued on their way, up to Globe where they turned right on to the old Route 60 and into the Tonto National Forest. This road wound its way to higher elevations and took them to a switchback canyon that crossed the Salt River at a spectacular scenic point above the rapids and fast moving current which then tumbled along beside the road until they reached a high flat top bluff reputably known as Geronimo's Look Out, where the gradient of the tarmac climbed away from the watercourse.

Rumour has it that the Bedonkohe Apache warrior chief hid out here with a small band of renegades, when they were on the run during the Apache wars in the 1880s. Being some 300ft above the road and riddled with caves, it certainly had an advantage over the surrounding barren landscape. Maybe it was true, maybe it was just folklore, but it was a great fantasy for boys brought up on Western movies.

Ascending from the canyon the elevation continued to rise as they travelled closer to their destination; they crossed Corduroy Creek and began to observe denser vegetation on the verges, mostly creosote bush, palo verde and mesquite at this level with a sprinkling of young pine, spruce and juniper. But as they neared the mountains the trees became taller and the forest thicker, and broadleaf trees such as Arizona walnut, sycamore and hackberry were making an appearance on the red hillsides amongst the more common slender pines.

The sky up here was an endless baby blue, contrasting with the rusty road surface that seemed like it rolled on forever, a brown ribbon sprawling out over troughs and brows that disappeared beyond the horizon. The lads passed the time away listening to the cassette tapes that Tom had bought from England; Simply Red, Hue and Cry, China Crisis and Tom's favourites, Everything but the Girl. China Crisis had a song quite apt for this land, a track called *The Arizona Sky*; 'the sky is big and flat, it took my breath away.'

They passed some dwellings, which were few and far between, but by the time they reached Show Low the landscape resembled something closer to what they had gotten used to in Tucson, only far greener and fresher. They were glad to see a Safeway up here.

Turning right onto the White Mountain Road they saw the first signs for Pinetop six miles away. From here on in, the streets approached something akin to suburbia that thinned and fanned out into gentle Alpine slopes and sporadic housing, and then a black dual carriageway which had been cut through thick forest with laser precision.

They passed Rainbow Lake and through the community of Lakeside and finally came to West Summer Haven Lane, where they took a right onto the dappled, heavy scented forest road, then meandered down its twisted length to West Yeager Lane, then right again onto the dense tree lined cul-de-sac of Apache Lane.

The log cabins here were spaced well apart in two-and-a-half acre plots of tightly packed lanky Douglas fir, Ponderosa pine and spruce groves, segregated by bright chain-link fencing or post and rail. Many were newly-built robust structures of traditional cabin designs in various sizes that creaked with all the mod cons for comfortable living up here in the woods. The Berns' property was at the end of the single track red dirt road, secured behind a padlocked five-bar gate. A pumpkin-coloured whole log rectangle with a pitched shingle roof, a porch veranda that wrapped around two sides and a stove pipe sticking out of the roof.

Seamus got out and opened the gate while Tom rolled the Lincoln in and crunched to a halt on the volcanic larva chip drive, beside the steps to the porch decking.

He got out and stretched his tired back muscles, breathing in a lung full of exhilarating unforgettable mountain air.

The place was eerily silent; a tranquil air, the type only a pine forest can produce, somewhat likened to being in an acoustically dead room.

A muffled dog bark announced their arrival followed by the crow of a cockerel.

"Wow this is something else," announced Seamus surveying the property.

A nostalgic chill stroked his bare legs, he had become quite accustomed to wearing shorts down in Tucson during his tenure, but the air up here was 30° lower, especially at night and it sent a bracing shiver up his underpants that reminded him of home.

"Fresh, innit?" observed Tom.

On the deck facing the front yard was the main entrance, a two seater couch and a couple of armchairs in a gaudy flower patterned fabric, which looked incredibly inviting to sit on and watch the sun go down. To the side, through a small gate, was a pile of cut logs that spanned the width of the cabin, and stacked to waist height. Interrupting the stack midway was a set of French doors, the preferred point of entry, and as instructed they used the large bundle of keys to gain access through these doors and into the open plan living area.

The overwhelming aromatic smell of seasoned timber embraced them as they ambled in. It was glorious and transported Tom back to the idle days of primary school when he was taught in a wooden prefabricated classroom.

It being mid-afternoon, the September sun was waning in the west and the dense forest cast a shadowy suppressed incandescence into the cabin that forced the switching on of some lights, before they were able to see the interior in detail. Immediately to their left was a pine table and six dining chairs, ahead of them a reasonably sized kitchen with the sink on the rear wall under a window overlooking the backyard.

To their right, a matt black wood-burning stove with an ornate glass door dictated the end wall of the living room, which was comfortably furnished with a three-seater sofa and a rocking armchair, both of which were strewn with rugs and throws. A coffee table rested in the centre of the room and an array of paintings festooned the log walls, the joints of which were sealed with what appeared to be white rope.

At the back of the house was a bathroom containing a separate shower, a bath and toilet, and two double bedrooms simply furnished with quilted waterbeds and pine wardrobes. An open-plan staircase ran up the dividing wall and led to an airy mezzanine bedroom that contained three single beds, simply attired, so all in all the place could sleep seven quite comfortably.

"This'll do Ras'," said Tom plonking himself down on the sofa spreading out his arms and legs.

Seamus was nosing around in the kitchen.

"Caitlyn said there was some Twenty-one bean soup in the freezer that she'd knocked up last time she was 'ere; I'm starving," he said rummaging in the frozen compartment. "'ere we go." He pulled out a large rounded oblong clear plastic storage container, showing evidence of something brown and bitty inside. "'ow the fuck we gonna cook this?" he asked. "It's like a massive Calippo."

Tom cracked a laugh and went over to investigate. "We'll 'ave to defrost it first," he said, "stick it in the microwave for five minutes, that oughta do it."

After fiddling with the pushbutton controls for far too long, the boys finally got the thing to operate and set it for 5min, while they retrieved their cases from the trunk of the Lincoln.

Expecting the soup to be liquid enough to slop out of confinement, they were amazed to find it still absolutely solid and reluctant to leave the bounds of the container.

Seamus laughed as he held the Tupperware box upside down releasing only a dribble into a saucepan on the hob. "This is gonna take a while," he said putting the thing back into the microwave and resetting the timer. "What d'ya' reckon, ten minutes?" he asked his buddy.

"I tell ya' what, we need some tasty bread to go with that soup and a few other bits, why don't we leave it to defrost and go back to the Safeway; it'll be done by the time we get back?"

"Let's go," said Seamus, "we can get some chips and salsa to 'ave as an appetiser."

In the store, which was a reasonable size for a backwater community like Pinetop, they picked up some toiletries, dairy goods, pumpernickel bread and enough treats to pacify a busload of kids on a school trip to Washington DC. They headed back to base.

The soup smelt delicious as they entered the cabin, but their error was immediately apparent as they looked dumbstruck towards the microwave. The broth had melted alright, but so had the container and soup was leaking under the oven door like a creeping estuary tide.

"Fuck," said Tom. "Quick—get a tea towel."

Seamus put his bags down and sprang into action, this was his dinner going to waste and his stomach would never forgive him.

He laid the towel down on the work surface under the door whilst Tom gingerly cracked it open, causing a surge of muddy bean water to glug forth and make its escape.

The top quarter of the container had peeled down like a giant rolled back condom, unleashing the upper contents, but miraculously the majority of the soup had survived.

"Thank fuck for that," said Seamus reaching in to grab hold of the now interestingly shaped vessel.

"Careful," warned Tom, but it was too late.

"Yowza!" screeched Seamus, "its fuckin' red hot."

"Funny that," quipped Tom. "Run ya' fingers under the cold tap." He got another tea towel and with the steadfastness of a bomb disposal expert, extracted the molten liquid and carried it to a waiting saucepan, where he deftly tipped out a large helping before resting the remainder back on the worktop. "'ave t' buy Caitlyn another Tupperware container I 'spose," he said staring mournfully at the sorry-looking vessel.

"Na, sling it in the bin," said Seamus nursing his broiled fingers in the sink. "She'll never know."

Despite a slightly burnt polythene undertone, the soup was magnificent, based on a chicken stock with all manner of whole beans; the lads polished off a huge bowl each and most of the black seeded loaf.

"Corr, delish," said Seamus sitting back in the recliner thoroughly satisfied.

"You'll be 'earing from me later," informed Tom, affirming the beans decomposition qualities.

Seamus lifted a butt check and made a fart noise with his mouth, "I've got gas," he said in a camp Southern accent.

"What shall we do tonight, Ras'?" said Tom, not relishing a night in without a TV.

"Why don't we go out and find a bar?" suggested Seamus. "I noticed a few on the way in, there might be some local birds that are real friendly."

"I hear that," said Tom. "Let's 'ave a shower, splash on some Brut and assault whatever's 'appening."

The Moonridge Lodge on White Mountain Boulevard was a dark wooden building with a low pitched roof set back from the road and canopied by thick pine trees.

Its warm sulphur glow beckoned a welcome and drew them in.

The place was anything but jumping. A lone drinker sat at the bar and a couple of tables were occupied by people having dinner. A young woman slouched behind the bar idly polishing beer glasses. She had a rustic look going on with a red plaid shirt and pigtailed blonde hair, this may have been her evening job, but she made a pretty convincing tree surgeon.

"What can I getcha?" she enquired unenthusiastically as the lads approached her station.

It was time for some fun, but how they were going to extract it in this barren hideaway was anyone's guess. The lads ordered a couple of bottles of cold Michelob, their accents sparked a modicum of intrigue.

"You guys passing through or ya' staying a whiles?" She placed two small square white napkins down on the shiny bar surface before landing the bottles of beer.

"That depends on the entertainment," said Seamus with a glint of mischief in his eye. He scoured the room looking for signs of life.

"Well, if ya' like silence and staring at trees, ya' gonna be thrilled, but failing that there's always Jack," she raised a glass of the unmistakable dark bourbon.

"I hear that," said the dude at the bar, ascending his 'in' acknowledgment.

Tom took a swig of beer. "Are we out of season, or just early?" he asked.

"Both," replied the girl. "Where ya'll from anyways?"

"Sweden," said Tom, tired of the question.

"Uh ha," responded the bartender somewhat confused. She went back to polishing glasses.

"Do you live 'ere, mate?" Seamus asked the guy on his lonesome.

"I do now," he said. "Retired from NASA two years ago."

This caught the boys' interest. He went on to tell them that he had worked on the construction of the space shuttle Atlantis and had stayed with the programme for a couple of years after its maiden flight in '85.

Tom more than Seamus was engrossed in the guy's disclosures and lost track of time as the bar slowly gained patronage around them. Seamus meanwhile had latched onto a group of 20-somethings that were rejoicing around giant pitchers of Budweiser and sinking Alabama Slammer shooters. Clearly this was more fun than listening to laments about space hardware.

"Why did you retire?" Tom asked the engineer who had labelled himself as Henry.

"Oh there's a lot of shit going on at NASA that's not in the public domain," he said taking another slug of Tennessee's finest.

"Like what?" pressed Tom.

"Let's just say, things aren't what they seem," said Henry woefully looking into his drink.

Tom's curiosity was piqued, but he felt the lure of a party going on over his shoulder and was missing out.

"I'm gonna do some slammers," he said to Henry, "wanna join in?"

"No, you go ahead, I'm too fried to play at that game, I'll just sit here and keep Jack company."

The Brit slid off of his wooden stool and sidled up to his mate who formally introduced him to his new best friends with great aplomb.

Jessie, Tyler, Jan and Megan were up from Mesa for a week and had rented a cabin in Lakeside.

The ladies weren't stunners by any stretch of the imagination, but as the evening wore on and the alcohol took over, the girls gained a certain appeal, especially Jan who had a passing resemblance to Lindsay Wagner, the Bionic Woman.

"So you guy's partying back at your cabin?" asked Seamus.

"We sure are," slurred Jessie. He slapped Jan on the arse causing her to yelp with surprise.

"Alright to tag along?" enquired Seamus pushing his luck.

"No way man, this is a private party," said Tyler with a glazed smile, wrapping his arms around Megan.

"Sharesies?" prompted Seamus.

"Cher's what?" replied Tyler perplexed.

"Sharesies, it'd be rude not to share."

"Are you guys swingers or something?" said Megan with a half smile.

"I like a bit of jazz, but I'm more of a Beatles fan," conceded Seamus.

"No, no," Jan laughed, "do you like to swap partners?"

"I've swapped a few marbles in me time," said Tom.

The Americans looked baffled.

"Oneers and twoers," continued Seamus.

"I had a ninety-sixer once," exclaimed Tom.

"A ninety-sixer," laughed Seamus cynically.

The two couples looked on wondering if they were witnessing a foreign language exchange.

"So can we come round then?" Seamus asked unabashed.

Megan smiled, amused at the Englishman's tenacity. "We've had a good night," she said politely, "but no, we have to say, it'll be just us four."

"Only joking," said Seamus excusing himself. "You 'aven't got a spare fag 'ave ya'?" he said to Tyler.

"A fag?" quizzed the all-American.

"Sorry, a cigarette," said Seamus correcting his noun.

"Oh," said Jan, "a *fag* means something completely different where we come from, a fag is a homosexual."

"Poovery," said Seamus in his campest voice, which wasn't very convincing.

The Yanks laughed nervously.

"Sorry, sorry," said the inebriated Seamus, "a cigarette."

Tyler gave him a Marlborough Light and the group turned to leave.

"You 'aven't got a light 'ave ya'?" Seamus persisted.

Reluctantly Tyler obliged.

After they had left, Tom quietly amused by his friend's cheek, realised that they were once again alone in the bar, with just the lumberjack washing glasses and wiping down the sides.

"Tell ya' what Ras', I'm starving, let's go and see what's open," he said.

"I'll drive," said the smoking one.

The only building with any resemblance of being functioning at this time of night was McDonalds. Seamus pulled up to the drive-through, lowered his window and bellowed to the uniformed girl inside, "Chips please!"

"Excuse me?" she drawled.

"Chips please," Seamus repeated and stifled his amusement.

The girl leant on her mop handle and starred at the enigma in the car, open mouthed.

"Chiiiiips! Chiiiiiips!" bellowed Seamus.

"Er, I'm sorry sir we are closed," said the paper hat-wearing numpty.

Seamus mustered his best Queen's English, "Then I shall put in a full letter of complaint to Ronald, you haven't heard the last of this young lady," he announced before the screech of tyres signified the boys' departure.

"Fried egg sandwich it is then," said Tom reverently.

Tom woke the next day confused as to his whereabouts, in an unfamiliar bed, confronted by alien smells and utter silence. It took a split second to realise his surroundings.

Unsteadily plodding to the toilet to drain his lizard, a sharp chill wafted in through the open fan-light and bristled the hair on his naked arms; he hadn't felt that in a while. He rubbed down his goosebumps and continued into the bathroom.

Seamus was still unconscious so Tom dressed, including throwing on a jumper, a discipline that seemed weird these days, and then fixed himself some cornflakes. He ventured to the veranda and sat on a dining chair in the monastery like stillness and watched ruby throated humming birds drinking nectar from stylised bird feeders strung up to the joists. They were so used to human presence that he could get to within a foot's distance of the birds to witness their brilliance in detail before they would retreat.

A dog barking at the chain-link fence bordering the next property ended Tom's twitcher moment and brought Seamus into the day, lumbering out onto the porch in his underpants, a sight not for the faint-hearted.

The dog was called Shalimar and belonged to the neighbour Van Van den Berg, a grey haired bespectacled retiree with a guarded demeanour and a dubious history.

After a brief introduction, the boys were left with the distinct impression that not all was as it seemed with Mr Van den Berg, and they fantasized that he may well be a fugitive of some sort, hiding up here in the mountains from the government. He had a wife with him and a son down in Tucson; a private detective apparently. The lads said they would look him up when they got back and give him Van's regards, but they really didn't expect to get involved with the guy, it all felt a little too clandestine for comfort.

The chores for the week were simple; rake the entire forest floor of pine needles; depriving the trees of their natural source of sustenance, mow the lawn in front of the cabin, cut down any bullshit branches and burn anything that isn't attached to its parent or model perfect.

This lasted for most of the day, until they considered it to be bollocks, then copious amounts of Budweiser was consumed whilst a plan to 'fuck the work' was hatched and instead to go and explore the rest of the state.

***

Unimpressed with the local attractions, the tranquil Hawley Lake, McKay Peak fire look-out tower (elevation 9,000ft) and Sunrise Peak ski area, they decided that it was quite reasonable to take the Lincoln Continental farther afield.

Armed with the camcorder, the Canon SLR and a suitcase between them, the boys locked up the cabin whilst Van and Shalimar hovered on the veranda. The German Shepherd was happy to chase Tom around the car and quite willing to be photographed, but Van was elusive, shying away suspiciously from the lens, adding more weight to the theory that he was one of America's most wanted.

The camcorder rolled, Tom hammed it up, loading his suitcase into the trunk. He spoke like a BBC news reporter, "There is a different point of view up here in Pinetop, so different in fact, I'm leaving." He slammed shut the trunk lid.

"Ha," snapped Seamus behind the lens.

They said their goodbyes and headed north, stopping for breakfast at a café in the infamous small town of Snowflake, the home of alien abductee Travis Walton, the subject of the film Fire in the Sky. At this point in time neither of the lads had heard of that story.

Tom reached across to another table and retrieved a lonely newspaper. On the front page was a story of a fatal car crash back in Pinetop.

"That's 'im," he said.

"Eh, who?"

"That bloke from the bar the other night, fuckin' 'Enry, that fuckin' NASA engineer we were talking to, 'e ran 'is motor into a fuckin' tree, dead on impact it sez' 'ere; fuck me."

"Poor cunt," said Seamus. "You could tell 'e'd 'ad enough … probably did it on purpose."

"'e was talking about some dodgy shit going on at NASA, I wouldn't be surprised if 'e was silenced."

Seamus was deep into the menu, "Well 'e's quiet as a mouse now; what you 'aving Ras'?"

"Eh? Oh, I'm just gonna 'ave a couple a' fried eggs, 'ash browns, beans and mushrooms, an' a cuppa tea."

"It's the chicken mountain melt for me. Montgomery by name, Mountain by nature."

They journeyed on passing through Holbrook and Winslow on interstate 40, the world renowned 'Route 66', turning left and traversing down along Meteor Crater Road.

The landscape here was positively Martian; rusty brown, flat, rock strewn and appearing lifeless for 10s of miles in either direction, all except a slight rise on the horizon, apparently their next stop.

Arriving at the car park of the visitor centre, Tom and Seamus were still clueless to the spectacle waiting to unfold, all they could see were a few single story buildings ahead of the black tarmac where a steady stream of tourists were heading. They followed suit and got in line, paid the entrance fee and pursued the herd, chatting liberally as they went.

It wasn't until they passed a huge plate glass window that they got a glimpse of the massive impact site for the first time. The vision stopped them in their tracks; it was jaw-droppingly immense, and silenced them immediately. Slightly higher on its southern rim, it gave the appearance of a giant pebble having been lobbed into a monstrous mud pool at a 45° angle, causing a splatter mark banked favourably where it halted.

Tom read the information board that presented itself after the window in numb solitude.

Once known as Canyon Diablo Crater, and scientifically as Barringer Crater, Meteor Crater lies at an elevation of 1,740 m above sea level. It is roughly 1,200 m in diameter, some 170 m deep, and is surrounded by a rim that rises 45 m above the surrounding plains. The centre of the crater is filled with 210–240 m of rubble lying above crater bedrock.

The crater was formed around 50,000 years ago during the Pleistocene epoch when the local climate on the Colorado Plateau was much cooler and damper. It is the world's best preserved meteorite impact site. At the time, the area was open grassland dotted with woodlands, inhabited by woolly mammoths and giant ground sloths. It was probably not inhabited by humans; the earliest confirmed record of human habitation in the Americas dates from long after this impact.

The object that excavated the crater was a nickel–iron meteorite 50 m across, which struck the plain at a speed of several kilometres per second. Impact energy has been estimated at about 10 megatons. The speed of the impact has been the subject of some debate. Modelling initially suggested that the meteorite struck at a speed of up to 20 kilometres per second, but more recent research suggests the impact was substantially slower, at 12.8 kilometres per second. It is believed that half of the impactor's bulk was vaporised during its descent, before it hit the ground. The meteorite itself was mostly vaporised upon impact, leaving only 10% buried in the crater.

"It's nearly a fuckin' mile across," spluttered Tom after some length.

14
Reverie

They stayed for an hour, skirting the accessible parts of the rim, mostly in humbled silence, as were the majority of the visitors scattered along the metal railed walk ways. It was a still place, a barren place where barely a leaf grew, just rock and earth and baked concrete. The scale of the impact was belittling, the force and devastation impossible to imagine, the possibility that it may happen again at any time without warning; terrifying.

"I'm fuckin' staving Ras', shall we get going?" beseeched Seamus.

Tom gave him a look as if to say, is that all you think about? "We'll grab something from that Subway out front, it's not the best grub in the world but it'll fill an 'ole."

"Good, 'cause me' got an 'ole as big as de crater."

"I can see that," said Tom monitoring Seamus' belly.

They bought a couple of subs and drinks, then got back on the trail, up to Route 66, where they turned off and headed for Flagstaff. At Winona they veered right, then picked up Route 89 and headed North. Before they reached Hanks Trading Post, they saw signs for the Wupatki National Monument, a site of ancient Anasazi Indian ruins.

"Shall we?" enquired Tom.

"Lead on," concurred Seamus.

The Anasazi disappeared as a race sometime in the 13th century, theories over their demise range from climate change to inter-tribal wars, or perhaps simply merging with other pueblo peoples whose ancestors still live in Arizona and New Mexico today. Folktales of cannibalism due to evidence on some unearthed remains may have been in-house, but just as likely to have been performed by raiding parties from rival tribes.

This place was highly spiritual, nestled between the Painted Desert and the Ponderosa Highlands, Wupatki is said to be a landscape of legacies. Ancient pueblos dotted amongst red-rock outcroppings across miles of heat shimmering, leeched, scrub prairie, where food and water seem impossible to find, yet people built these dwellings, raised families, farmed, traded, and thrived for 700 years.

Some say that if you linger and listen long enough, you'll hear the whispers of the ancients on the wind. There was a light breeze, but the only voice Tom could hear was Seamus reading from the information plaques and struggling over the pronunciations.

"Ana, Anazeezee, Aneasy …."

"Not for you it ain't!" bantered Tom.

The flat, red-rock dwelling in front of them resembled a bomb site; no roof, tumbled walls, with the occasional square window opening. A path led the visitors around the site leading to other buildings of a similar state; it was as dull as dishwater. Lucky for them, the boys had brought along the camcorder and had shot some footage of them larking about throughout the journey. Here was another opportunity to liven up their tame surroundings, so they concocted the 'Singing bush' scene, where Seamus concealed himself behind a reasonable sized Creosote bush, and sang *'You take the high road'* in a falsetto voice, shaking the plant like it was resonating with joy.

Tom approached with the camera, commentating like he had witnessed a miracle and asked the bush if he did requests, opting for *'All over now'* by The Rolling Stones.

The bush duly obliged.

They got back on the road, still travelling north on the 89 which steadily climbed in altitude. Before the town of Cameron they turned left onto the 64, Desert View Drive, which ran parallel to the Little Colorado River Gorge. There were stopping points along this route, photo opportunities for the gorge itself; they stopped at one, they weren't impressed, it seemed highly inadequate, they moved on.

As they continued to climb the scrub became forest, stumpy Mesquite, Sagebrush and Manzanita soon gave way to taller pine, juniper and Douglas fir. They passed The Desert View camping ground on their right and carried on. A few 100m up, they stopped at Navajo Point and got their first glimpse of what they had come for, one of the seven natural wonders of the world; The Grand Canyon.

Anyone who tells you the Grand Canyon is just a big hole in the ground is inherently stupid and seriously misinformed. No picture or television screen can come anywhere close to showing you the sheer scale and breathtaking enormity of it. The vastness of its expanse belittles the beholder and leaves one dumbstruck. Being 10 miles across at its farthest point and a mile deep, this multi-hewn water-carved wonder is so inextricably more than just a hole in the ground.

The camcorder rolled, the wind buffeted the little onboard microphone, but not a human noise was made as Tom panned from one extreme to the other. Eventually Seamus asked "What d'ya' think Ras'?"

"I'm in awe," was all that Tom could muster.

He imagined the jaw dropping moment when the first conquistador came upon this spectacle on horseback at the rims edge, without any pre-knowledge of the canyon's existence, no postcards or magazines to prepare him; he must have fallen to his knees at the splendour of its enormity.

They stayed a little longer, soaking up the reverence, but there was so much more to see, so they put the camera away and got back into the air-conditioned Lincoln, stopping at Lipan Point where you could see the emerald green Colorado River snaking its way through the massive pink and fawn layer cake ravines, and again at Grand View Point, before finally arriving at the Grand Canyon Village, parking by the famous El Tovar, the first hotel to be built on the rim.

If you throw a stone across a gorge or ravine, a strong adult can make some distance, maybe reach the other side. If you throw a stone out into the Grand Canyon void, it falls at your feet; it's a physical anomaly, it goes nowhere, such is the vast volume of space between you and the other side, it's like some sort of illusion, and the boys revelled at it a couple of times each. The treeline on the North rim looked nothing more than a dark green carpet atop a phenomenally distant wall of wind-carved rusty horseshoe formations, eerily drawing one in, beckoning you down into its vast empty cavity, a pull that Tom felt physically.

Another spectacle immediately apparent was the hazy filter hampering a clear view and interfering with the massive panorama. This optical annoyance turns out to be air pollution, mainly sulphates from nearby civilization, but also light absorbing dust and water particles carried on the wind. It didn't ruin the view to much extent, but it did make you question your eyesight.

The lads fooled around on the perimeter wall for a while, went inside the Hopi House, then sat on the rim and perpetrated the forbidden act of feeding the squirrels, which were very grateful and extremely tame. The big no-no being that the wee fluffy Kaibab got so used to being hand-fed, that they perished in winter due to a lack of visitors and scant knowledge of how to forage for themselves.

Before long, Tom and Seamus decided it would be a great idea to descend the Bright Angle Trail, just in the attire they were wearing, shorts, vests and trainers with no food, water or camping gear.

Through the hole in the rock and a half mile later, they reasoned that this was a bad decision. Apparently it took a seasoned climber half a day to reach the canyon floor and then another day to walk back to the top. And it gets cold down there too; you need sleeping bags, a tent and overnight provisions, not just a pair of Ray Bans.

There were organized mule trips, but that took planning and forethought, two things the boys were short on today, well most days really.

The views were spectacular wherever you looked, but what they wanted to witness without doubt, was a sunset in this magical place and to capture it on film.

They ventured along the rim again to a broad spot where they could clamber over the barrier and stand right on the edge, taking it in turns to use the camcorder or the SLR to film themselves in various poses, then they settled down to record a message each, to send back home to their families.

As the day drew to a close and the shadows grew longer, the colours of the rocks intensified. From dusty blush to red to crimson and burnt ochre, from cream to yellow to brilliant gold and then a dirty orange. The spectacle was transcendent and repose fell about its witnesses. Night brought with it a chilled air at this altitude and sent the visitors back to their cars or accommodation in a hurry. The lads were no exception; their bare arms shuddered from a forgotten type of cold. It was inky black away from the visitor centre, but the path back to the Lincoln was lit by low level lighting that was kind enough to show them the way.

Now the task was to get down to Flagstaff before the early hours and book into a motel. Seamus elected to drive, a long laborious plod down the 180 through low level pine forest, past Humphrey's Peak and the Lowell Observatory.

They found a budget motel on S. Milton Rd called The Arizona Hotel and checked into a twin room that hadn't been decorated since the 1970s and smelt particularly mildew. It was the usual affair, two kingsized double beds made up with sheets and an eiderdown quilt, flowery wallpaper, a decrepit TV and a bathroom at the far end, but it didn't matter, they just needed to get some rest and it was cheap at $23.50 for the night.

Sunday morning was bright and cooler than anticipated; Flagstaff is 2106m above sea level, but still warm enough for a couple Brits to don shorts and T-shirts. Tom left Seamus rattling on his back and went to a gas station to buy some doughnuts and coffee. After breakfast they filmed a little more before setting off again.

Tom came out of number 15 and spoke to the camera. "As you can see, we have spent the night in the Hotel Arizona—"

Seamus panned left to the busy roadside sign. "And as you can also see," said Seamus, "the price has dropped six bucks since we booked in."

Tom smiled and nodded in agreement. It had indeed; the black magnetic letters and numbers had been freshly re-arranged that morning.

"They must have seen us coming," declared Tom.

The record button was thumbed off and they hit the road once more, heading for the picturesque and location happy town of Sedona, famous for its brilliant dusky red rock formations and mountains.

A good while later, down the 89A they stopped beside the beauty spot of Oak Creek Vista, a pretty little canyon of gray and pink rock, littered with pine and broadleaf hardwood trees. The temperature here was perfect in the mid-morning sunshine; they stayed for a bit, took a few pictures, then went on their way again.

The farther south they drove, the pinker the rocks became while the trees were shorter, scrubby and more thinly dispersed. The road was a valley floor with the Oak Creek running to their right and hemmed in on both sides by red and orange sandstone buttes known as the Schnebly Hill Formations, which had the appearance of being separate layers plonked precariously on top of one another, enormous pebble towers, ill fitting shapes built in a hurry and easy to tumble. Here was the backdrop of so many Western Cowboy movies made in the mid-1900s, and Tom was excited to be amongst it.

Passing Slide Rock Park, the creek passed under the road and switched sides, the rocks became ruddier and houses started to appear sporadically along the highway, cut into the landscape, partially hidden by forest. Sedona was fast approaching, a vibrant artist community with New Age shops, spas, galleries and a very agreeable climate.

Several miles before the town itself, the valley spread out making the buttes and canyon walls more apparent. Passing formations with apt names like Snoopy, Rabbit Ears and Cathedral Rock, each one a wow, Seamus took to naming his own summits, picking out three suitable specimens and calling them Tom, Dick and Harry. Tom's namesake didn't resemble him in the slightest.

Through town, the camcorder rolled on.

"As you can see …." an overused introductory line. "…we are in Sedona, Arizona." Seamus leant into the steering wheel so that Tom could get a decent shot of the mountain framed by the driver's side window.

"We are at an elevation of four thousand, three hundred and twenty-six feet and a long way from 'ome." He then started to sing *Show Me the Way to go Home*, before cracking up with laughter.

"Shall we pull in for refreshments old bean?" suggested Tom.

"Feed me Seymour," quoted the driver.

After a club sandwich apiece at a pavement table café served with complimentary potato chips and a long neck glass of beer, the chaps were ready for the big push back to Pinetop.

They stopped once at Midgley Bridge for some breathtakingly beautiful scenery shots and film footage with customary tomfoolery thrown in, then hit the road big time, wanting to get back before the early hours of Monday morning.

Passing through the fructosely-named village of Strawberry, famed for having its illegal distillery smashed to bits by federal agents in 1931, who spilled 700 gallons of 'Mountain Whiskey' onto Sandrock Canyon then through Star Valley on Route 260, famous for not having any stars living there at all. The unremarkable yet oddly named Heber-Overgaard followed, then eventually Show Low, by which time it was pitch-black and getting on for 1:00 a.m.; the boys were extremely tired. To make haste for home Seamus put his foot to the floor—big mistake. Rounding a bend on a desolate stretch, red and blue lights ignited in his rear view mirror. He had no alternative but to pull over and face the consequences.

A rotund highway officer slowly waddled up to the driver's side window and shone a blinding torch beam into the Lincoln.

That's it, thought Tom, the games up this time.

Seamus rolled down the window. "Evening officer—" he began.

"Stay in the vehicle and keep your hands on the wheel where I can see 'em," drawled the policeman.

Seamus complied.

"Drivers licence," requested the cop lazily.

"It's in me' shorts pocket, is it alright to reach for it?"

"Slowly, use your left hand, buddy. Say, are you from England?" The highway patrolman had a reluctant manner about him like he'd been in the job way too long.

"Born and bred," said Seamus turning on the charm.

"I was there in forty-four, sailed out of Weymouth harbour for the D-day landings, worst sea crossing of my life, I was sick as a dog."

"Wow, you made it off the beach then?" deduced Tom.

"Was back in Britain in the afternoon, took a round to the side of my head before I'd even left the landing craft at Omaha; knocked me clean out. I woke up two days later in a hospital in Portsmouth. The doctor said another quarter of an inch to the right and I'd have been in a body bag."

"Cor, you were lucky," said a weary Seamus.

"If you can call going to war lucky. I lost a lot of good friends that day." Officer Bradley stood upright, his mind back in 1944, reliving the shit that went down. He flicked his torch over the Brit's licence card, all seemed to be in order.

He asked them what they were doing here in the States and whose car it was. They gave him a cock and bull story about Saul Berns being their uncle and that they were on vacation for 3 months.

Seeing that they were now on friendly terms Tom asked the man if he had ever had to use his revolver whilst on duty.

"Thirty-five years as an Arizonan Officer, and I've never had to use this gun once," he proudly announced.

Tom was genuinely impressed. "Wow, that's some achievement."

"Sure is," said Bradley gently patting his side arm. "Well, you have a safe journey back home now fellas, it was nice meeting you."

"Nice meeting you too," they said in harmony.

"And Seamus, slow that Lincoln down, buddy," advised the friendly official.

"Uh, will do, officer, will do." acknowledged the Brit winding up his window, "Good night."

The dark blue Continental peeled away from the dirt shoulder and purred off into the night leaving a satisfied traffic cop to stroll back to his car; he was retiring in 5 months' time and wanted the least amount of paperwork as was humanly possible to do between now and then.

Seamus puffed out his cheeks, "Got away with it again," he mused.

Tom turned under the duvet; the pleasing smell of cured lumber peeled away his dream and anchored him to the here and now. He sat up, causing the oak-framed bed beneath to creak with resentment, and swung his legs over the edge, taking a lungful of cabin goodness as he headed for the bathroom. From the hall he noticed the French doors were wide open, a cold alpine zephyr made him shudder before he stepped naked into the warmer air of the water closet. Surely we didn't leave those doors open all night? He wondered.

They hadn't, Seamus had woken up even earlier and had decided to go native. The fresh morning and the freedom from any kind of conformity, combined with the isolation of their predicament, had a primal effect upon him, drawing him outside to go prancing starkers upon the Pine needles amongst the trees.

Tom studied his pal from the dining room window, amused yet bewildered as to why this was happening, and it occurred to him that Seamus' little acorn had shrunk to even smaller proportions than on the odd occasion he had happened to glance at it in the past. Evidently, going tackle-out at this elevation had its disadvantages.

Tom wasn't a practising naturalist by any stretch of the imagination, though he had been known to perform the occasional streak when 'slaughtered' at parties, much to his mum's embarrassment, but today it just felt like the correct way to proceed.

Seamus cracked up on seeing his bare-arsed buddy join him. "Yambozie!" he said in a baritone voice. His feet were caked in muddy clay, where he'd squelched in a bog-like area near the tool shed.

"Aren't you cold, Ras'?" Tom beamed.

"Refreshed and ready for the day," announced the chubby one. The chances of Seamus being ready for a days work were remote.

Soon the pair of them were frolicking like fledgling wood sprites, high on morning dew, charging through misty sunbeam lances on a golden brown dappled stage.

It felt ludicrously normal, yet radically anarchic to be amongst the Ponderosa Pine with nothing but your body hair for protection, and what if Van Van den Berg was to be out for a stroll? The sight of the two odd neighbouring Englishmen cavorting next to nature might raise his bushy grey eyebrows an inch or two. He was already a suspicious bloke so this could push him into thinking he had a couple of woolly woofters in the vicinity.

Caitlyn's camera was retrieved from inside and a series of staged photographs produced that would come back to question them years later.

This started a tirade of antics that occupied most of the day, clothed by now. Using the camcorder they acted out some ad hoc comedy sketches which included Tom as a chainsaw wielding Michael Caine in hot pursuit of the cameraman. The chainsaw, a real thing, was actually running and it could have gone horribly wrong, but fortunately didn't.

Seamus' climbing and falling out of a tree act and Tom on the veranda, playing the leaf-rake like a guitar to the backing track of Brian Adams and Tina Turner's *'It's only Love'*. This inspired Seamus to act as Hughie Lewis the estate agent, to show Tom the perspective buyer, who was married to a very large Iguana, around the cabin, highlighting several rooms and their features while constantly changing his appearance.

Proceedings came to an abrupt end during the filming of a dance routine late in the day, out on the front lawn. A static camera positioned on the porch captured a choreographed step pattern hop to the soundtrack of Pink Floyd's *'Money'*. Seamus and Tom, adorned in shorts and vests and sharing two pairs of ill-fitting boots romped around like a couple of poorly-attired Morris Dancers on their first day, appearing in and out of shot, coming together to either slap hands or kick each other's boots, when in mid-flow Seamus turned his ankle in a grass rut.

The sickening crack was audible on film as Seamus went down in agony clutching his ruptured tendons.

Tom doubled up with laughter, mostly out of mirth for the fuck up, but partly due to the sadistic enjoyment installed in all of us labelled as *schadenfreude*. Why we laugh at another's misfortune is something for psychologists to debate, but it may be a release of pent up energy, or a response to oneself feeling better off than the afflicted, or just a confused state of mind. Anyway, it took a while to sink in that Seamus was actually badly injured and when his laughter gave way to a serious gaze, Tom bizarrely dived to the camcorder first to switch it off before tending to his prostrate friend. Perhaps it was an instinctive reaction in order to not record any evidence of them abusing their posting.

Seamus was groaning and clutching his ankle.

Tom bent over his buddy. "Shit Ras'' that made some crack, d'ya' think it's broken?"

"Fuckin' 'ell mate, it could be," Seamus managed through gritted teeth; he was in the foetal position, eyes closed.

"Can ya' move it at all?"

Seamus tried in vain.

"I'll 'elp you up mate, get on ya' knees."

After a struggle Seamus managed this. Then Tom got his shoulder under Seamus' armpit and hauled him upright. The agony was etched on the big lad's face.

They limped back into the cabin like a very lame three-legged race and Seamus was duly dispatched to the sofa where he could rest his leg up on the coffee table.

Tom graced it with a bag of frozen vegetables wrapped in a tea-towel and got his friend some cold water to drink.

"Can ya' wiggle ya' toes mate?"

The toes moved a bit.

"Good, so nothing's broken then?"

"Fuckin' feels like it," Seamus grimaced, "I think I better go to the hospital."

"'ow we gonna pay for that, it'll cost an arm 'n a leg?"

"It's already cost a leg."

"True, but I now think that it's a case of lost limb limitation, better 'old on to what you 'ave got and be grateful."

Seamus gave him a disapproving look.

"Let's see 'ow it is in the morning, then we'll decide what to do about it," delegated Tom.

"Saul's gonna 'it the roof."

"'e might 'it the pair of us if we 'fess up to 'ow it 'appened, best we come up with a story."

The boys ceased talking for a while; both visualising a sinister outcome. There was also Caitlyn to consider; they didn't want to lie to her, she'd put her trust in them both to do a decent weeks work up here, not piss around at their expense.

"We'll tell them that you fell off a ladder whilst lopping off some branches from a tree, that way we're covered and they'll feel responsible. That's believable," said Tom.

"Okay, but what about the film evidence, we'll 'ave to erase that."

Tom didn't want to; they had some gems on tape. "We'll copy the whole thing onto video when we get back 'ome, then erase what's on the camcorder," he said in a lightbulb moment.

"Brilliant, now 'ow about some dinner? I'm Hank Marvin?"

Tom reached for his manservant uniform and wandered to the kitchen humming The Shadows song *Apache*.

Saul sounded subdued on the telephone, maybe he was sceptical, maybe he had other things on his mind, he just quietly told them to come back home.

After a detour back to the hacienda to destroy the damning truth, the lads headed up to Orange Grove to face the inquisition. It was surprisingly soft, Seamus was obviously in a lot of pain and unable to bear weight on his foot, and their story seemed utterly plausible.

Caitlyn fussed around like a doting wet nurse and insisted that Seamus go straight to a medical centre; she drove him, while Tom returned to work in the garden. There was a lot of dog poo and leaf litter to pick up, and many plants to water.

Two hours later, the wounded soldier arrived back complete with an air-cast and crutches. He'd torn a ligament in his ankle and would be incapacitated for a couple of weeks.

Wonderful, thought Tom, guess who's got to carry the load for a fortnight?

And it was exactly that. Whilst Seamus kept his leg elevated, gorging on painkillers and weed, and playing guitar all day, Tom went to work, toiling under a baking sky, well partially anyway. He was now driving Saul to and from his office every day and spending more and more time inside the house with Caitlyn who was finding him the most menial of tasks to do and insisting on feeding him breakfast and lunch.

It was at this time that Saul took possession of a brand new Cadillac, a cream coloured Brougham d'Elegance. With its V8 5-litre engine, plush walnut and velour interior, it smelt and felt utterly regal.

Tom handled her like a kitten, wanting to give his boss the smoothest ride possible; he nursed her over every bump in the road, every corner and eased her to a stop with just a gossamer touch of the brakes.

After a few days of this, travelling down Oracle, Saul did a life changing thing, an ordinary thing really, but coming from

Saul it was an event, an exchange, an offering, a welcome to the fold, a bonding show of acceptance that opened doors and glowed in Tom's heart, a moment that would remain etched forever in his memory.

Saul turned his wrist towards his driver and said, "Gum?"

Although astonished at this first showing of palliness of any kind, Tom didn't hesitate and drew a stick of peppermint from the pack.

Not another word was spoken, just the sound of smacking lips from a man deep in thought and the effortless purr of a 140hp engine.

I'm in, realised Tom.

On Friday, he was asked to wear something a little tidier than his usual work clothes, the day was going to be a bit different. It was way too hot for trousers, so he put on a beige pair of Lacoste shorts and a dusty pink Ralph Lauren polo shirt, finished off with some canvas deck shoes; he even had a wash and splashed on some Tabac before leaving the house.

Caitlyn concealed it well from her husband, but Tom sussed that she was beaming with pride at the way her plaything had scrubbed up.

"We gotta go out to a parcel and take on the deeds," informed Saul, hovering over his grapefruit breakfast.

Tom was wide eyed and enthusiastic, "Okay, where's that?"

"Caitlyn's got the details, she's written them all out."

The dutiful secretary handed Tom a very precise route explanation and a printed area map. They were heading South of the Coronado National Forest, near a place called Elgin, to look at a 300 acre plot offered by an unsuspecting landowner. Tom was to accompany Saul in the capacity as driver and nothing else.

The land was a sprawling emptiness of scorched grass hillocks sprinkled with the occasional patch of scrub, rusty unmade roads and single strand barbed wire boundaries.

The Englishman couldn't see the potential here, but then again he wasn't the ruthless criminal-minded genius that had a million dollars in the bank.

The poor schmuck who handed over the deeds appeared to be just a regular guy, mid-50s, slim, grey haired and balding, he had no idea he was dealing with the devil. They even shook hands before the Cadillac left him clouded in a whirl of tyre dust, wondering if he'd done the right thing.

"We're going to lunch with some associates of mine," revealed Saul, "At Condelli's on Broadway, they do a fine fuckin' veal."

Tom grimaced inside as he thought of small calves kept in the dark and fed on nothing but milk; appalling. As long as they served up a drop of seafood pasta he'd try and ignore what everybody else was devouring.

Inside Condelli's, apart from the white linen tablecloths, it was dark, dimly lit and sporting miles of mahogany furnishings, the ambience firmly set in the 70s. Paul was here, Saul's right hand man who took care of everything at the blunt end of the business. He was accountant, secretary and lawyer rolled into one, an extremely amiable bloke, mild mannered and as bald as a coot. Paul was turned out in his usual attire of a short-sleeved cotton shirt and slacks.

Also joining the party today were two fellows that Tom hadn't met before, who typified a couple of hoods from a Martin Scorsese movie. Unsurprisingly their names were Joey and Cheese, their overindulgence loosely disguised with ill-fitting expensive suits. They considered Tom with sceptical probing eyes, any newcomer would have received the same consideration, but because he was English he was even more a square peg in a round hole and the goons were overtly on guard and cautious as a result of his presence.

"Any problems?" probed Joey.

Saul was measured in his response, "Nope, that guy's fuckin' clueless."

"You got the papers?" asked Cheese, it seemed like an effort for him just to talk.

"We wouldn't be here if I hadn't." Saul stated the obvious.

Tom tried to zone out and concentrate on the menu, but he could feel the unease coming from across the table.

"Your boy here, is he kosher?" said Joey at length.

Saul looked disappointed. He peered over the top of his reading glasses and raised a crooked finger to the ceiling. "Did ya' mother squeeze ya' fat head out of her stink hole?"

The idea of a pleasant lunch had become severely tenuous.

"I was just saying …." shrugged Joey shaking off the insult like he was brushing away crumbs.

"Well don't," barked Saul. "He's with me."

It was all the reassurance that these two gangsters needed and highlighted who was paying the wages. No more was said on the subject, although it being cowboy country the Brit was still a novelty, so they did quiz Tom on his hometown.

"… London, eh," said Cheese. "I went there once back in the sixties. Couldn't get a fuckin' thing to eat on a Sunday, everything was shut up shop, and it wouldn't stop fuckin' raining, it drove me nuts."

"Things have changed a hell of a lot since I was a lad, there are corner shops everywhere now, they nearly never close, and we do have some warm summers, especially back in seventy-six … it was almost as dry as it is here."

Saul sat back listening and grinning like the proud owner of something desirable.

Tom thought to reciprocate Cheese's line of enquiry. "So where are you guy's from?"

"You don't need to know." It was Joey's curt reply, and that was the end of that. It seemed that being rude to one another was not only customary, but expected.

Tom got on with a delicious Linguine ai futti di Mer, washed down with a glass of Malvasia Istriana and some water. Saul's command of, "You can have one fuckin' drink." still rang in his ears.

The crux of the meeting was to supply a fictitious bill of sale, have it signed with the vendor's forged signature and put an official stamp on it. Joey turned out to be a crooked notary often in Saul's employ; he had all the equipment in his car. Cheese, a dab hand at forging signatures, supplied the necessary ink. It was all done in a matter of seconds, an envelope changed hands in the car lot and the men parted company.

Tom resumed his chauffeur role, musing over the forger's name. "Why is he called Cheese, Saul?"

His boss gave a deadpan response. "Coz he likes fuckin' cheese."

They proceeded downtown.

City Hall was an impressively ornate, pink blend of art deco and Moorish architecture with arches and a round central tower topped with a copper green dome, intricately painted with a blue and yellow seamless zigzag pattern, interspersed with yellow and orange spots. It wouldn't be out of place in Tunisia, but was instead down on Alameda Street.

All that was required to make the land Saul's, was to have the documents micro-photographed and registered with the clerk. It was a breeze, it was incredulous; Saul was as blasé about it as if he were buying a newspaper. He allowed himself a smug little grunt of a chuckle as they walked back to the car, just for Tom's benefit, who right now was suffering from a mixed sack of emotions like wrongdoing, apprehension and sympathy for the rightful owner of the land. It hung like a bag of rocks around his neck, because at this point in time the vendor didn't have a clue that he'd been well and truly shafted.

When Mr Watson came to legally try and sell his chunk of real estate, he would find that not only had he already sold it for a nickel, but the land had been split into smaller parcels, each owned by separate companies that were subsidiaries of Saul's parent company, each registered in a different state. After he got over his heart attack and dragged himself out of the hospital, if he had the resolve to fight the court cases, he would have to file a legal challenge in every single state, including one in Puerto Rico and one in Grand Cayman, which meant physically going to those places to do so.

Past victims had simply given up; lacking the funds or the determination to see through such a lengthy process and Mr

Berns had simply got away with it. "Those cocksuckers can blow it out of their ass." He would delight in reflecting.

Saul's game of taking his parcels of prime real estate, ideal land on which to build small developments, to his numerous banks to acquire loans on the titles, was what he was living off, and if he never paid a cent back to the bank. What the hell, they'd take possession of the land and Saul would go and obtain some more. This crime had just been committed, and Tom had played a role in it.

When they arrived back at Orange Grove, Caitlyn was effervescing. Her son Jamie was coming back to Tucson.

"He ain't fuckin' staying here," announced Saul before marching off to the lounge.

Caitlyn hid her deflation by asking Tom if he had a good lunch.

"Really nice," said Tom cheerfully; he could tell it was time to depart, a storm was brewing within these walls and he didn't want to be party to it.

He bid Caitlyn a good weekend and scurried away. Off The Scale had a gig to do at the U of A mall, a student radio task force concert supporting River Roses, Pollo Elastico and Johnny Law. It was high time he and Seamus had a blow-out; he had money in his pocket and a tale to tell, but they had to be back in town for 5:00 p.m. A tight call for it was now 3:30.

Arriving home around midnight, drunk and full of vigour after some decent shenanigans, the boys burst into the living room. Holly was sat on the couch with her feet up, knees to her chin, painting her toenails. She shot a short glance at them, giggled through the copious blonde curls veiling her face, and went back to polishing. MTV was blazing as per usual, a leather clad, bandana wearing Axle Rose gyrating out the lyrics of *Sweet Child of Mine*, shot in a grainy black and white video. A classic, timeless rock anthem that didn't appeal to Tom's senses at the time, but Holly dug it.

He flopped next to her. "Whatcha' doing?" he foolishly asked.

"Punching you in the throat if you make a mess of my toes,"
she warned.

"Sorry, gravity has a firm grip on me tonight," he slurred.

She giggled again, "Get away from me you hooch."

"I'm a Hooch?"

"You smell of it."

"I'm the hoochie coochie man, everybody knows I'm here
…." sang Seamus.

"You're a gypsy alright," laughed Holly, "Never in one
place for long."

"Talking of which, I'm outta here," Seamus said turning on
his heels and heading for the bedroom. He had a desire to roll a
fat one before crashing on his cot. "D' you have any herbage
that we might partake in, sweet child of mine?" Tom enquired
gingerly.

Holly giggled yet again; she loved it when Tom spoke to her
with an exaggerated British accent.

"Let's go outside, my mom's still mooching around, I don't
want her to know."

Along one side of the hacienda, Kate had parked her old
gold Cadillac Coupe De Ville; it was a two door machine, so
they had to fold down the passenger seat in order to get onto the
back seat.

It was a mellow evening, the spliff was heady, the two of
them rampant. In a haste to kick off her black leggings Holly
inadvertently hurled the loosely hinged driver seat forward with
her feet, punching onto the steering wheel and sounding the
horn.

Tom sprang into action, quickly retrieving the offending
back rest. They waited in the dark, motionless, like naughty
children, fully expecting Kate to round the rear corner of the
house and catch them at it. A full minute passed, no sign of
mother.

"Everybody, stand and sound your funky horn," said Tom
reciting a KC and the Sunshine Band lyric.

"I'm gonna blow yours," said Holly giggling as she
disappeared into the footwell.

As her warm, soft, wet mouth encased his throbbing stick shift, he couldn't help but ponder the enthusiasm of youth, and finding with it not a fault.

In the morning when the boys were sat at the breakfast table necking some Cheerios and planning their day, Kate came waltzing through the dining room in a bathing costume shrouded by a colourful chiffon shawl en route to the pool. She took great pleasure in reciting a popular bumper sticker message of the day, purposefully letting Tom know he'd been busted. "Honk if you're horny, eh!" She chuckled, slipping from shade into full sun; she was so cool.

***

On the menu today was Pete and Maisy's wedding; they had been living together as man and wife for a number years, but had decided at last to jump the broomstick with a pagan ceremony administered by a Druid high priest, in their backyard which had been appropriately festooned by friends of the fold.

Tom and Seamus were not only guests, but also the entertainment and had to be on site mid-afternoon for the knot-tying, guitars in hand.

This was easier said than done when you've been up half the night, off your face, and one of you had a partiality for inconsequential timekeeping.

Kate came back in from her daily ritual float, initialling the linoleum with wet foot prints as she passed, and drying her matted hair with a small towel. "Are you boys coming with me, or making your own way?" Her words faded down the hall.

"We'll follow on behind," said Seamus. "We need to shower and stuff yet."

"Okay," yelled Kate from her room, "but don't be late, you've only got an hour."

"We'll be two … two shakes of a lamb's tail," promised Seamus.

Tom knew better.

Two hours later the boys were on the road.

"It wasn't my fault—" insisted Seamus in high pitched defence.

"What do ya' mean; it wasn't your fault? Who went back to bed after breakfast for an hour before spending an eternity in the bathroom?"

"I needed some more Zs and then the three Ss."

"We're gonna look like a couple of Cs if we miss the ceremony," protested Tom.

"It'll be alright Ras', trust me, weddings always run late."

"I'd 'ave more faith in a one-legged man at an arse kickin' contest. Trust you? You're always fuckin' late."

Seamus laughed, "No 'arm will come, Rasta'," he said in his best West Indian.

Incredibly the chubby one was right, but it was close. They weaved their way through a sea of groovy people decked out in their finest summer clothes; light frocks and suits in hues of cream and white, hats and parasols abounded in a garden adorned with flower arches, garlands and wreaths. Jennifer and her crew had transformed this little patch of abandonment into a verdant Eden in less than a week, she deserved a medal.

The lads were introduced to a large plastic chiller chest where they deposited the bottles they had brought and each received a flute of the finest bubbly. Today was champagne only day and one couldn't grumble at that.

Maisy was resplendent in a white, fitted vintage number; someone had fashioned a circular Celtic plait on the top of her head and woven little daisies into her flowing locks, she looked like a proper Iron-Age bride. Pete hadn't quite gone that far back in time, opting instead for a cream linen 1930s style colonial suit, cravat and Panama hat.

Maisy had done her research well, the blessing and vows were in Gaelic, beautifully incomprehensible, yet admired by all and sundry, some of whom were moved to tears. Love was definitely in the air today and it seemed that for love, language held no barriers.

Confetti and kisses dealt with, the party began in earnest. Lobster tails were the main source of nourishment accompanied with a pot-luck approach to breakfast, guests having brought their own fare; it was both eclectic and fun. Seamus piled his plate high and parked himself by the chiller, while Tom mingled with the multitude, plate in one hand, shampoo in the other.

Before long the boys found themselves on the patio, lofted onto chairs and behind guitars; singing classic love tunes to an audience of highly inebriated well-wishers. Pete and Maisy had retired to the bedroom right behind them, consummating the marriage apparently, and everybody knew.

The boys sung a rendition of the Temptations *My Girl*, followed by Bob Marley's *Is This Love*, which had the whole room in deep amour, especially two young ladies who were deeply in amour with the English boys, well just for tonight anyway. The boys then ad-libbed a song involving what may be going on in the bridal suite behind, much to everyone's amusement, even Pete and Maisy who eventually leant through the open window with smiles that confirmed all suspicion.

After their performance Seamus was engulfed by an extremely sexy, streetwise chick called Clarisse. They disappeared after a while, to where Tom had no clue. He by comparison had been caught by a vivacious brunette 30-something, apparently an actress, who called herself Lucy Brahms.

Now what took place next was a bit of a blur, so dreamlike that Tom felt like he may well have been hypnotised, for Lucy wasn't that attractive in his eyes. She was a few years older than he, not particularly pretty, but she had a commanding presence, was overtly intelligent and exuded insatiable lust.

In his inebriated, elevated, loved-up state, he may well have been bewitched, because he found himself being whisked away to a psychedelic lounge bar somewhere in town, plied with more alcohol then driven back to Lucy's apartment where he was flopped on her bed, stripped naked, sheathed like lightening with a condom, and then sat upon and rocked like a rodeo Mustang until the volcano erupted, swiftly followed by unconsciousness and a deep sleep until daylight.

At least the witch had a good body he thought, watching her heading starkers towards the bathroom. Dressing rapidly while she was out of sight, he sang her a line about having an early rehearsal and had to get going, that she was more than willing to accept, showing no eagerness to keep him entrapped whatsoever. A most agreeable mutual understanding passed between them and they'd never meet again.

Seamus phoned Tom at the hacienda sometime in the afternoon. He wanted to be picked up from Clarisse's house on 6th Avenue. His buddy was chilled enough to accept the plea; they could have a beer and a spot of early dinner at Rosa's cantina.

"What a tidy little fuck ...." announced Seamus entering the El Camino.

Most people greeted each other with a *hello* before launching into a diatribe of their carnal conquests. But this pair knew each other so well, that sort of formality was no longer necessary.

15

Sweetcorn

Tuesday night, 6th September, after their third and final Eat to the Beat gig in The Cellar Bar; the money did not justify the effort. Tom, Seamus and Chad occupied some concrete bench seats and a table resembling street furniture from a Flintstones episode, outside a shabby little joint on Speedway that boasted stone-baked authentic Italian pizza. The slices were monstrous and worthy of the marketing.

They were sharing a pitcher of beer and having a good time, the light had faded, the cicada bugs had turned in and the passing traffic was a lethargic patchy affair.

Out of the shadows a rough sleeper honed in, following his nose.

"I could really do with a slice of pizza," he burred, obviously stupefied by the drink. The inflection came through long lifeless hair, from ulcerated lips on a sullied sun-torched face.

Chad was wary, his nervous smile twitched.

Tom thought the bloke was a cheeky fucker, but probably harmless.

Seamus welcomed him in as one of the family. "'ere, help ya' self mate," he said offering the tramp a wedge.

His grubby fingers latched onto a triangle and funnelled it straight into his stubbled mouth.

Seamus attempted conversation, "Where you off to then, mate?"

"I could really do with a beer," was his reply.

Now Tom knew that he *was* a cheeky fucker.

Seamus found it amusing and poured him a glass, which he downed in one, licked his scabby lips like a frog cleaning its eyeballs, belched and then incredulously said, "I could really do with a stogy."

"Fuck off!" the boys said in unison. The hobo obliged.

                                  ***

Jamie's introduction was a mellow affair; no trumpets or ticker-tape parade, just a welcome call into the kitchen from the mid-morning heat. Caitlyn had fetched him from the Amtrak station downtown; he was now standing in the Berns' house, a place he had been exiled from some time ago and as far as Saul was concerned, was still out of bounds. Jamie was tall and stocky, had close cropped light brown hair and the beginnings of a beard. Dressed in a white T-shirt and jeans, he was typically American, although somewhat remote, guarded and tinged with scepticism; definitely living on the fringe of Disturbia. The presence of the boys occupying what should have been his domain was obviously having an effect on him. But Caitlyn either didn't notice or was pretending that everything was just fine.

"Jamie and I are going out apartment hunting and will be gone all day. Help yourselves to lunch, there's ham and cheese, bread and eggs, and the freezer has some mini pizzas and things; just clear it all up before Saul gets back. Would you like a coffee now?"

"If you wouldn't mind Caitlyn, a little something to rev up the old engine this morning wouldn't go down too, too bad," decided Seamus.

"How about a shot of whiskey to add a little zip, we used to do this in San Francisco all the time," she offered suggestively.

"It'll warm me' cockles," advised Seamus.

"Cockles?" Caitlyn reached for the Johnnie Walker with a mischievous smile.

"Cockles of me' 'eart," explained the cheeky Brit.

"As long as it's just your cockles," she replied full of innuendo.

Jamie walked away unwilling to listen to the flirtation taking place with his mother; he was disgruntled enough already.

Caitlyn and Jamie out of the way, the boys had their work set out for them. They were to cut down the ripening dates from the palms that lined the drive and lay them out to dry in the backyard. This sounded straightforward enough, but of course, as usual it wasn't. Having little idea about the techniques of date harvesting their course of action was to place a ladder up against a tree, hack off the fruit baring fronds and cart them off to the rear of the house where they laid them out on the slabs near to the pool. The fronds were heavy, protected from predators by large needle sharp spines and, due to their length and bulk, awkward to transport. Also, the needles, secreted an irritant that bubbled up the flesh immediately when penetrated.

By the time the lady of the house came home the boys arms looked like they had contracted chicken pox. Her buoyant 'pleased to see you' face soon melted when she saw their injuries.

"Oh my God, did you get that from the palms?"

"Yes Cait, the buggers fight back," said Tom with mirth.

"With swords and lances," added Seamus.

"Does it hurt?"

"They itch a bit that's all."

"*Quelle horreur*," she emphasised. "You better quit doing that now, come inside and I'll bathe those wounds with some lotion."

The boys complied and while she dabbed Calamine onto their spotty limbs, she told them that Jamie had been installed in a furnished apartment block called La Mirada over on E. Grant Road. She had stocked up on groceries and utensils, and he was all set. The only problems the boys could envisage were that the bloke was alone on the other side of town, without transport or a job, and solely reliant on his mother who was in turn solely reliant on Saul, who hated his stepson's guts. Jamie had wanted his jeep back, but that little luxury had also been denied. The English lads didn't know what Jamie had done to piss off Saul so much, but they could see the lad was a pressure cooker waiting to explode.

***

Letters from Lela had fizzled out to nothing now and Tom was having the time of his life, yet the residue of her spell still lingered like a dim light hovering just out of reach above and in front of his forehead, like an angler fish's lure. It was this faint aurora that drew him to the mailbox each morning.

He received regular mail from his family and a couple of friends that had kept in touch, almost a daily occurrence in fact and today's inquisitive mosey started off no differently. He traversed the few steps across sandy soil and tufts of hardy Buffelgrass to the roadside aluminium box barefoot, cracked open the door and grabbed a handful of junk, simultaneously obtaining a searing injection of pain into the middle toe of his right foot. Grimacing, he shot a glance down to see a small black ant making a casual retreat into the subsoil. The pain was intense, burning and growing in strength as it spread along the extent of his foot.

"Jeez!" he hissed, before hobbling back into the hacienda on his heel.

Making for his bed, he laid down as the poison crept further up his appendage. Within half-an-hour the whole limb had gone numb and paranoia was taking hold. Nobody was home, where were they all anyway, he thought? He'd have to face this alone. His heart was racing, he was being paralyzed, he feared he would go into shock and die from a seizure; killed by an ant! His father was right; he was stabbed to death, knifed by the mandibles of a Formicidae.

He felt giddy and breathless, helpless. He laid there accepting his fate in his darkened dusty room, in the sweltering desert, 5,000 miles from home. Blackness came over him, a cold veil pulled slowly up from his feet to his head, and an icy chill that lanced his side, stalled his repose like the shuttered movements of a flu infection.

The front door opened and in spilled Kate and Holly laden with shopping bags from Walmart.

Kate caught sight of the stricken Tom through his open bedroom door.

"Hangover again, Tom?"

It was all he could do to roll his head their way and feebly utter, "No I've been bitten!"

Kate's mouth dropped in horror; she studied the stricken Englishman for a nanosecond contemplating his survival chances. "Was it a black ant?" she asked frenetically.

Tom nodded weakly.

"Harvester ant; hurts like a bitch don't it?" she affirmed, before waltzing off encircled by Fonzi and Arnold eager for a handout. Holly giggled and followed her mother down the hall, without sympathy forthcoming; evidently he wasn't about to expire after all. Five minutes later he was back on his feet.

It was a Saturday, Seamus and Chad had gone out for some takeaway beers and were now back and buzzing. The lads were eager for a jam session in the small room next to their bedroom. Tom relayed his near death experience to his band mates who were unfazed, they had little idea of the amount of grief a tiny insect had caused; in fact Tom's inarticulate account seemed implausible and inane. He stopped talking through fear of ridicule, and wandered off to the kitchen for some water.

Kate eyed him up and down. "How's your toe?"

"It's completely gone away, amazing; I thought I was at deaths door."

She chortled, "So much trauma from one little critter eh, they're small but they pack a mighty punch."

"I was only bringing in the mail, next time I won't go barefoot."

"He was just defending his territory; you have to go in fully armed if you wanna survive the desert man." She was still smiling her toothy grin.

Tom felt venerable; his landlady was well in tune with the land of which he knew so little. He changed the subject. "'ow's Alfonso?"

The Pascua Yaqui Indian chief hadn't felt too well of late and Kate had spent the night with him.

"Oh we had the most wonderful night, we were lying in bed staring at the stars and deer spirits were walking all over the roof. They came down the walls and kissed Alfonso on the forehead. They have such healing powers and he felt so much better this morning he's gone to chop wood."

"Isn't 'e like sixty-six or something?"

"Sixty-seven, but with the passion of a twenty-five year old," she said with mischievous sparkle.

Tom didn't want to picture that scene. He contemplated the ghosts of dead deer kissing the old boy on the head and wondered if they were cold kisses, icy white wisps planting smackeroos on warm brown skin in a roofless box under a star spangled sky. Then he wondered what kind of drugs they had taken before they went to bed.

Back in the ad hoc rehearsal room they cranked up the noise, two guitars and a drum kit, jamming riffs and chord progressions. After a couple of hours they had the bones of two new tunes that just needed lyrics and structure that would come later; right now they had some beer to drink and a swimming pool to play in.

A storm came in that night, a hot and sticky torrent with raindrops as big as broad beans and the roots of heaven sparking down in the guise of fluorescent forked lightening.

Kate had gone off to the Res', Caryn was back in town again, Seamus had taken the El Camino and gone over to see her. Chad was in his room, which just left Tom and Holly sitting on the couch with Buster stealthily creeping along the backrest to inflict damage.

"Ah ya' little bastard," yelled Tom taken by surprise yet again. "If 'e does that one more time I'm gonna tape up 'is beak."

Holly giggled, "Ah ya' big baby, he's only playing, if he wanted to hurt you he could take your whole ear off."

"It might be funny to 'im, but it's fuckin' annoying. 'ow about we go for a drive and watch the lightning?" He swung his mood.

"No, I'm all cozied up here; I don't wanna go storm chasing."

"We could test the springs on your AMC," he said with a hopeful grin.

It didn't take long for her to change her mind, the thought of a rump on the back seat of her new set of wheels, in the middle of a storm was suddenly a real turn-on, they were out of there in two minutes flat and heading up to Starr Pass Trailhead in the Tucson mountains. It had brilliant uninterrupted views down into the Southern part of town.

The rain beat down on the roof of the old car like multiple fingers drumming out an irregular rhythm, the tempo inside however kept time like a kick drum, four on the floor, steady, intense. Holly was vivacious, clamping down Tom with super-human strength in her legs wrapped around the back of his knees, drawing him in as deep as any man could get without being devoured.

Thunder shook the brown Ambassador, thunder rolled on the rear vinyl seat, and electric high voltage discharge illuminated the pitch black interior as Tom shot a shuddering climax into the depths of Holly's velvet purse making her come on impact. Breathing heavily like a rutting moose in a glen and damp with perspiration, Tom looked down at his dishevelled teenage lover who was glowing with flushed exuberance. A single condensation rivulet ran down the clouded interior side window above their heads, as providently a Tina Turner song struck up on the radio; *Steamy Windows* would forever mark this night.

***

The Havasupai people or 'The people of the blue-green waters', have lived in and around the Grand Canyon area for more than eight centuries. In 1882 President Chester A. Arthur issued an executive order that all land on the plateau of the canyon, which was traditionally used for winter homes for the tribe, was to become public property of the United States. The order in effect relegated the Havasupai to a 518 acre plot of land in Cataract Canyon, taking almost all of their aboriginal land for American public use.

The loss of most of their territory was not the only issue the Havasupai were contending with. The increase in the number of settlers in the local region had depleted game used for hunting, and soil erosion (a result of poor irrigation techniques) touched off a series of food shortages. Furthermore, interaction with the settlers sparked deadly disease outbreaks amongst tribe members who were ravaged by smallpox, influenza, and measles. By 1906 only 166 tribal members remained.

President Gerald Ford passed a law on January 4th 1975 that granted the Havasupai a trust title to approximately 185,000 acres and another 95,300 acres that were designated as "Havasupai Use Lands," to be overseen by the National Park Service, but available for traditional use by the indigenous people.

At present the tribal population stands at around 650 and is flourishing, taking advantage of the beauty of its land by turning it into a tourist destination for visitors to the Grand Canyon, and The Havasu and Navajo Falls. But in 1988 the tribe desperately needed money and one way to achieve this was by hosting benefit gigs within the state. Off the Scale were lucky enough to be invited to play at one of these benefits, held at a venue they had been eager to play in, Gracious Bob's. Supporting Mystic Lights, Rainer and River Roses, this would be their foot in the door, and raise a few dollars for the Havasupai conference in the process.

The gig was a Sunday afternoon start and the venue was buzzing. All of their friends were in attendance. Caryn introduced a couple of *her* friends to the boys, a scrawny ringlet haired LSD fiend called Bom and José a blind piano player.

"Bom?" asked Tom. "Do you 'ave trouble at airports?"

Bom laughed through a gigantic smile that practically occupied the room. "No," he said happily, "no trouble."

"Did ya' cause havoc as a kid when ya' got lost in the mall, and the announcement came over the system 'we 'ave an unattended Bom in the building?"

Bom kept on smiling unused to such wit.

José was expressionless; his eyes were rolled back into the top of their sockets, like a zombie automaton waiting to be prompted.

"That's an unusual name Bom, where did it come from?" searched Seamus genuinely intrigued.

"Oh my parents were backpacking through Asia in the early 60s, apparently I was conceived in the Chittagong hill tracts of Bangladesh, the people who live there are the Bom, so I was a Bom too, right?"

Seamus flourished. "Cool, cool, my name is Bom, Bom and gimme some." He sang

Caryn rescued her friends "You guys. Listen Bom's a teacher but he plays guitar also, it would be really cool if you got together for a jam round at his place, José could drop in on keyboards, it'll be fun right?"

"Mmm," delighted Seamus drawing on his cigarette, "we could come over tomorra' night."

"I'll stoke up a bong," Bom grinned.

Tom couldn't help another quip. "A Bom bong, sweet."

The gig was a major success. Off the Scale got a warm reception, Gracious Bob's manager was impressed enough to offer some Friday and Saturday night slots. This was excellent; a popular venue bang in the middle of the university campus offering regular paid work. The ball was starting to roll in the right direction and straight through a plethora of college girls.

Mystic Lights played their usual fusion of Pop-Reggae. River Roses stirred the crowd with a set of Rock-Americana and Rainer finger-picked and slid his way eclectically through Blues, Acoustic, Contemporary folk and American Primitivism. He was truly captivating, destined for a higher plane; Seamus was particularly inspired and went on a mission after the show to get to know him better. An impromptu gathering back at Jennifer's gave him just the opportunity.

The Champagne flowed and the Nose Candy funnelled and before you knew it, the clock struck two in the morning. Tom was hanging and wanted to leave, but as usual Seamus was squeezing every drop of life out of the situation. He had to be prised away with a wrecking bar, or the threat of one, before he would leave and then promptly fell asleep in the passenger seat on the way home.

Chauffeur Tom was not amused.

***

Monday morning is a struggle at the best of times, but driving to work with your eyes closed is a challenge not recommended at all, and when you have to drag two dehydrated spent bodies to work, the effort can be testing.

What the boys didn't need this morning was Macy on a high, flitting around them like an over exuberant kitten and posturing over Caitlyn's new car.

Out on the drive gleamed a spanking new Antelope Firemist Cadillac El Dorado, with just seven miles on the clock. The boys stopped to admire it with all of the lustre they could manage, using refracted light through aching eyeballs into blancmange brains.

"Beautiful car, Caitlyn." Was all Seamus could muster.

Saul stood in the shade of the open garage, "Wants to be at that fuckin' price."

"Saul, don't be such a sourpuss, we needed a new car, that old burgundy Lincoln was like driving a bus." Caitlyn defended her new toy like it was a necessity, not the prestigious accessory it certainly was.

Macy grinned, "It was rather a large car for a lady, Saul."

The man of the house stayed in the shade smacking his lips chewing his gum. Macy's little dig didn't go unnoticed. "Some ladies need a bigger car," he retaliated, performed a short 'ha', turned and then sauntered into the house.

Caitlyn embarrassed, turned to her friend. "I'm so sorry Macy, Saul has whiplash mouth today, I don't know what's upset him."

"Today? He has whiplash mouth every day," she recoiled.

The boys stood in the full heat of the morning failing fast; as much as they'd like to paw over the new Cadillac, they needed an excuse to head off for the shade of the tool shed and get some much needed iced water from their fridge. But it wasn't to be, Macy had a newsflash for them.

"I've got some studio tours booked for this afternoon, its okay with Caitlyn for you to take the afternoon off, but we'll keep it from Grumpy in there, he doesn't need to know.

Seamus yawned, "Sounds good Mace, what time we leaving?"

"Am I keeping you up?"

"Someone needs to," Tom inputted.

Macy cackled a laugh, showing her missing teeth. "I'll pick you up at one-thirty, after lunch, be ready," she warned waggling a finger in their direction before tramping to her car.

At last the boys could be off.

"Seamus … Tom," barked Saul from the back gate, he had alternative plans for them today.

They begrudgingly filed past the tool shed oasis, through the wrought iron side gate and followed Saul up the garden path towards the back 40 like a line of desiccated camels in a sea of sand. The very rear of the yard, behind the block wall, against the chain link fence that bordered the scrubland beyond and an apartment complex to the right, was a shady row of palo verde trees. The large fat white larvae of the palo verde beetle spend up to 4 years underground, and who could blame them in this heat, dining on the succulent roots of the tall smooth green barked sheltering trees, which if left unchecked, could cause an untimely demise for the plant, and at the very least wreck the chain linked fence for the boss.

"Y'take a metal bar and hit it with a fuckin' hammer, y'put fuckin' holes all around the tree. Y'pour this poison into the hole .…" Saul held a green plastic bottle in his hand. "Y'kick dirt back into the fuckin' hole, we don't want the fuckin' dogs eating this shit, it'll fuckin' kill them as well. Wear gloves then throw 'em away; this cocksucker will kill *you* too. Here." He handed Tom the bottle. "Read the fuckin' label. When y'done that, clean up the pool, the pool furniture, wash all four dogs and water all of the fuckin' trees, they ain't been done for a week."

He strode away leaving the boys wondering how they were going to fit all that in this morning.

Tom who was adverse to killing any kind of wildlife, would rather let nature take its own course and felt sick at having to murder these innocent grubs, but orders were to be obeyed if he wanted this cushy life.

"Better get a 'wiggle' on," he suggested.

"Just gonna wiggle to the shed," said Seamus, "I'm dryer than a duck in a wetsuit!"

"I'm coming with ya'."

Seamus had just got back from driving Saul to work when Caitlyn decided to compound the time shortage further by demanding they both come in for some breakfast.

"Oh I'll take care of the grove while you're out with Macy; you can clean the pool when you get back."

Just then a white Ford Murker XR4 with tinted glass windows and biplane spoilers rolled up the drive and out popped a blonde haired couple in aviator shades and ill-fitting denims.

"Charles and Leica," squealed Caitlyn upon seeing her brother and his girlfriend.

Tom was intrigued. "Leica?"

"Oh she's Swedish, and such a sweetheart, come and met them."

As if time wasn't short enough, the Brits now had a lengthy meet and greet to endure. They followed Caitlyn out into the dazzling daylight.

"Leica," whispered Tom to his mate, "Like 'er?"

"Me like," Seamus replied.

Charles was facially, uncannily like his sister, only of slighter build. He was extremely cocksure, straight-talking and jingoistic. He'd had this imported German car for just 6 months and she was ridiculously precious to him.

"Nice set of wheels you 'ave there, Charles mate," complimented Seamus.

"One of only two thousand in the country Seamus, five-speed stick shift, one hundred and thirty miles per hour, and naught to sixty in just seven seconds."

"Gives the old El Camino a run for its money then?"

"Hell yeah, she'd leave that old lady in the dirt."

"I dunno what the El Camino does, the speedo's broke," lamented Tom.

"Y'all not fixed that yet? Shit, that's a ticket right there."

"We like to live dangerously." Seamus laugh-whistled as he blew cigarette smoke through his pursed lips.

Charles' blue bug eyes made scant recognition of what the Englishman had just said. Leica, who up until this moment hadn't uttered a word, suggested they get out of the burning sun. She seemed shy and reserved, yet covertly in command, and happy to let her man posture himself while she got on with the important things in life like health and wellbeing.

If Charles had a sense of humour it hadn't reared its head yet. As Caitlyn fixed drinks he proudly told the scantily clad Brits that the US of A had the best goddamn army in the world. The boys humoured him; they hadn't the energy to indulge in conjecture.

Hurrying their whiskey-laden coffees and getting back to work was an oddly welcome pursuit, at least from Captain Staid anyway. In an attempt to get something done before Tom's hefty suitor came back they decided to split the workload. Seamus washed the dogs while Tom annihilated infant beetles. He'd rather the roles were reversed, but he knew this was a more productive plan.

The insecticide had to be diluted 10-1 within a watering can, it smelt wholly insidious and as each borehole filled and overflowed with milky fluid Tom couldn't help wonder if he was doing more harm than good, man's intervention of Earth's natural path, once again; more poison into the soil. He was disgusted with himself and with Saul for his ignorance and lack of understanding.

By the time lunch arrived the boys had also managed to clean the pool furniture and were suitably dirty and fragrant. Jamie had caught a bus over to see his Uncle Charles, so the kitchen was uncharacteristically teaming with life. Gracie was mechanically ironing shirts in the dining room and a spread had been prepared on the kitchen table. Caitlyn was in her element shrouded by her people and entertaining.

Tom and Seamus barely had time to wash their hands and faces, grab a tortilla wrap and some lemonade before Macy added to the number. Tempted though she was to get stuck into the delicious looking cuisine, she had no time, so whisked the boys away for the first appointment, Jim Brady Studios on E. Glenn.

"She ain't gonna water them trees this afternoon," imparted Seamus as they slid into Macy's Cadillac.

Tom concurred, "It'll be a miracle if she does."

"What's that?" chirped Macy.

Tom explained.

"Oh don't worry about Saul, he won't even notice; just concentrate on the studios. I've also got a breakdown on the cost of making a video for one of your songs from a company called Rose Robbins Productions. A four-minute film comes in at just over eleven thousand dollars."

Seamus and Tom raised eyebrows at each other, was this really happening?

Jim Brady's was a large square block of a building painted the colour of sandstone. Out front the landscaping was minimal and easily had parking for 6 cars. It had the austere resemblance of a doctor's surgery. Established 4 years ago, it boasted previous prestigious clients such as Kenny Rogers, Linda Ronstadt, Neil Young and Wishbone Ash.

Jim was a slim strait-laced fellow with combed back moulded hair. He welcomed the trio into the cool dark control room that was lined entirely with antique pine panelling with a leaf green carpet. It was typically equipped with a large 24 track mixing console beneath the glass window through to the live room and a plethora of speakers, racks of outboard machines and tape decks. The strict no eating, smoking or drinking policy in the studio was tantamount to a no fun order; indeed it was the cleanest control room the boys had ever been in. It felt clinical.

The 'live' room was easily 3 times as big, and had been acoustically designed with angled wave like panels on the ceiling, timber acoustic constructs lining the walls, some triangular, some square and others curved like waves. It housed a grand piano, a wooden cased dual keyboard organ, movable sound panels and a fair collection of mike stands huddled together like a group of skeletal rockers forgotten in the corner. The sound in here was dead, not an echo to be had; Tom clicked his fingers and the noise ended almost before it began.

Macy spoke, "Well what do you think boys?"

"Mmm, it's like Abbey Road in 'ere," Seamus responded.

"Only without the 'istory," informed Tom.

The price for 100hrs studio time and 3 reels of 15-minute 2-in tape, plus 3 reels of half-inch tape would be $5,690; pocket money.

They thanked the puzzled slim Jim and said that they would be in touch if they were interested, then swiftly left for the next appointment at The Sound Factory on S. Highland.

Outside you would be mistaken for thinking you were entering through the emergency exit of a Mechanic's shop; just a plain white door in an oblong red brick wall, totally unassuming and bland. This studio was small by comparison to Jim Brady's; 2 rooms of a sauna like quality, rammed to the gills with equipment. One of the engineers, Steve English, welcomed the party. He probably had a face under all that hair, beard and baseball cap, but it was hard to discern.

Relaxing into a padded office chair in front of the mixing console, his tall slender frame was reminiscent of a hirsute praying mantis.

"What can we do for you folks?" His voice had a soothing resonance, a calming tone.

The boys explained they wanted to record 2 tracks to release as the A and B sides of a single, and they were planning to put the music to video, distribute and promote it themselves around the country, funded by Macy's deep pockets; then hopefully catch the attention of a mainstream record company or at the very least a publisher.

Macy sat at a distance smiling, proud that her boys had direction.

Steve turned down his mouth and nodded slowly; he'd heard it all before, but never from a pair of Brits.

"So you're from England, huh?"

"Yeah, North of London, you ever been?" asked Tom.

"Despite my tenuous connection, regrettably I've never had the opportunity, but I'm a huge fan of British music. I've always loved the Stones."

"Great band," agreed Seamus, "Ron Wood's made an excellent addition."

"That guy's a versatile musician, compliments Keith's style exquisitely. So what you looking for, a hundred-hour slot with a finished two-inch master?"

"Yeah and maybe a quarter-inch master and some cassettes as well," said Tom.

"Of course, of course."

The studio had an automated board which was like wizardry to the lads, the faders remembered their last saved position, and if moved at all would effortlessly slide back to that point with a touch of a reset button. Magic. The price for studio time here was almost the same as Brady's, just $30 less for the same deal. The rooms were small, but the atmosphere was easier and they liked it.

Steve was keen to move on, "So does the studio meet your requirements?"

"It's perfect," replied Tom, "but we 'ave to talk to the boss first," he indicated towards Macy. "We'll get back to you."

Steve had heard that one before as well. He nodded knowingly and showed them to the door. You win some, you lose some, he thought.

Westwood Studios was one of 10 units in a strip mall on W. Grant Road. The building resembled a line of motel rooms, sterile and uninteresting.

The trio pulled into the plaza unimpressed.

"We gonna shop or book a room for the night?" Tom's sarcasm underlined what each of them was thinking.

They exited the car onto blistering tarmac and speedily sought shelter under the terracotta tiled front canopy. The afternoon was atrociously hot.

Number 964, had blackout glass windows and a large sea-green wooden front door; it was locked. Rapping on it several times produced nothing. Tom suggested he go round the back to see if it had a rear entrance while the others wait. The back of the block was blander than the front, tarmac up to a plain roller shutter door, this too was locked. That was that then, they didn't need the business.

"'ow rude," remarked Tom once he had circumnavigated the block.

"Perhaps they forgot we were coming," reasoned Macy.

"Bad business," announced the Englishman.

"Their loss," concluded Seamus. He was desperate to get back to Orange Grove and some more refreshments; last night was punishingly weighing him down.

"Let's not waste any more time, Mace, we need to get back and finish off our chores anyway, it'll soon be time for Seamus to go get Saul."

"Okay, it's very disappointing to be let down like this; I shall be calling them up first thing tomorrow to give then a lick of my tongue."

Tom couldn't imagine anything worse.

"Well, you have two choices, Brady's or the Sound Factory; which do you prefer?"

They got back into the roasting Cadillac.

"Sound Factory, definitely," they both agreed.

Macy shot them a glance. "You don't seem very enthusiastic."

"Oh we are Mace, we're just 'knackered' and parched," pleaded Tom.

Seamus concurred. "A late night on the tiles, Mace, too many 'sherbets'."

Macy was confused; she started the car and drove off without a word.

Back at headquarters, the boys found they had been right; Caitlyn had not lifted a finger to help with the chores. However she had delegated, and as they rumbled up the drive they were greeted by Charles and Leica brandishing hosepipes in the groves whilst Jamie was begrudgingly netting debris out of the pool. Tom embraced the poise of Lord of the Manor for just one second, "The staff have done a superb job in our absence Monty; quite remarkable."

***

And so it was decided, Off the Scale's first single would be recorded at the dishevelled block of a building on South Highland. Seamus and Chad thought it appropriate to celebrate the landmark occasion with a few beers in town at Geronimo's. After all, they had black gold on tap and excellent pizza. Tom agreed, they'd meet the other two there. Jules was beside himself with anticipation, like a puppy out on a leash for the first time. But Bryce couldn't be contacted.

"Cheers, cheers, cheers, cheese."

Four glasses of the Irish good stuff clinked together above a section of the long bar. The wait for the slow pour was worth it and four thirsty mouths made contact with the rapidly condensing pint jars. The dark stout wasn't everyone's cup of tea and Tom really had to be in the mood for it, but now and again when the thirst was particularly on, it was an outstanding beverage to neck at the end of a days toil.

The question was, which song did they think was their most commercial to have as an A-side? Chad wanted to re-record

Rosa, Jules preferred *Be Mine*, while Tom and Seamus wanted to record something new. Tom's notion was a song they been perfecting for a while, *Tell all the People*, another song loosely based on *Lela*, it had a good hook and melody and was bouncy enough for the pop market. Seamus wanted to write something brand new, which in itself was appealing, but did they have the time? After all, masterpieces didn't grow on orange trees, and days or even weeks in rehearsal couldn't guarantee a hit tune. They would see what creative juices leaked out of them over the next few days.

There was also the video to consider; Caitlyn had been in touch with Rose Robbins Productions, evidently a film company of some repute. They wanted a little input up front, a basic outline, a storyboard, ideas, the song title and length of time. Professional, responsible deliberation was called for, contra to the boys' career mandate thus far. Their conscience said they should knuckle down and focus, their hearts pulled them elsewhere. There was a bong waiting for them at Bom and José's house.

***

Toward the end of the week, Saul had taken it upon himself to rearrange Tom's weekend. The lad was to take four ladies up to Pinetop for a bit of R&R. It transpired, he had no great plans anyway.

Saul's 15-year-old first cousin Lilly, Oren's daughter, was flying in from New York and he wanted to show her his empire, so Tom had been designated driver to escort Caitlyn, Macy, Lilly and Annabel the ginger misery, up to the cabin.

"Four 'ens, one cock, have thee the stamina Rasta?" Seamus' slightly derisive comment didn't go unnoticed. He was joking of course, but he would have preferred to be the one heading off to the mountains in the Wagoneer. Tom pulled a look of disdain.

"The stamina yes, the intent no. Now 'ad they been four twenty-year-old pole dancers from TD's, they might 'ave been in trouble."

Seamus laughed, he didn't hold a grudge for long, there were many stones to be unturned still, right here in town; you just had to reach down and flip one.

"When ya' going?"

"Friday night, I can 'ave a shower 'ere after work, so you can take the car home, then I'll bring the Wagoneer to the hacienda on Sunday and we can drive both in on Monday."

"No problem. What's this Lilly like anyway?"

"She's fifteen mate."

"Ah, 'nuf said."

Lilly had taken the red eye from JFK to arrive at Orange Grove mid-morning Friday. Caitlyn wasted no time in introducing her to the boys who were scrubbing the flagstone paving in the backyard with detergent and yard brooms. They were suitably glistening with perspiration even under the shade of the towering palo verde, toned and tanned and practically naked, a flame to the torch paper of bubbling adolescence.

She tried to mask the incendiary within, by being coy; she owned a quiet assurance but lacked the experience to pull it off. Her dark chocolate eyes couldn't hold the lads' gaze and her soft handshake lingered a little too long. Lilly was, at a guess, 5ft tall, had short raven black hair, small facial features, good lips and great teeth, a small amount of puppy fat, but nothing she wouldn't shake off in a few years. Caitlyn saved the girls blushes.

"Lilly's down with New York City and wants to see the country for a while. We are going to the mall after lunch, is there anything that we can get you boys while we're out?"

"A cool breeze and a winning lottery ticket will do for me, Caitlyn," jibed Seamus.

"I'll take a dozen quails eggs, two yards of emerald green Bivoltine Mulbery Silk, a pound of saffron and the tears of a rainbow leaf beetle," requested Tom. His outrageous list stunned the ladies into silence. Caitlyn's full bottom lip hung agape, a gleaming beacon of dazzling red lipgloss akin to the flower of an Anthurium plant.

"I'll try JC Penny's." she said with a wry smile.

***

The Jeep Grand Wagoneer cruised effortlessly along the tedious straights, negotiated the twists and turns through the Salt River Canyon and ascended into the White Mountains like a purring cougar. She was a luxurious comfortable ride, yet had the power and the versatility of being a 4x4 should they need to go off-road, which they wouldn't. His passengers made more noise than the 5.9 litre engine but Tom didn't care; he had zoned out in climate controlled armchair soft leather upholstery most of the way, and when he hadn't he felt slightly masterful for being at the wheel and in command of a gaggle of hormonally charged dependants.

They stopped at the Safeway in Lakeside to ram the jeep with groceries. Tom attempted a joke on the way in, "I 'ear they are selling condoms now."

"What?" snapped Macy.

"Safeway's—"

She just grunted in reply; his humour was wasted on these girls.

Fully loaded for the weekend they set off once again in the panelled, wood effect, mobile for the cabin. It was great to be back, that distinctive heady pine aroma smacked Tom right on the nose as he stepped over the threshold, it was like being swamped with nostalgia.

He got a fire going in the wood-burning stove whilst Caitlyn and Lilly made dinner. The nights were cold up here now and a good meal and a hearty chat around a log fire were exactly what they all needed.

Caitlyn was a genius in the kitchen and in what seemed like just minutes, with limited ingredients, she produced chicken kebab skewers, lobster tails, home fries Louisiana style and corn on the cob, washed down with a couple of bottles of Sauvignon Blanc, various beers and then the perilous José Cuervo tequila.

Tom limited himself to just one shot, he didn't relish being ill in front of this lot, and the way these vixens were livening up he had to keep a modicum of sobriety, although he could feel himself losing his footing on that slippery slope.

Macy on the other hand was knocking them back like a woman relishing her last request, sitting next to Tom opposite Caitlyn and Lilly who was wrinkling her brow at the older woman's increasingly embarrassing demeanour.

Annabelle was her usual sullen self and hardly said a word; Caitlyn was falsifying a smile, but the trepidation in her eyes was akin to someone grinning while diffusing a suicide vest as she could sense impending doom.

"Have you chosen the songs that you want to record yet?" slurred Macy, her chin was almost touching her chest as she bobbed back and forth on the couch. She took another sip of Tequila.

"The jury's still out on that one Mace, although we 'ave a short list."

"A short list, but a long dick!"

Audible gasps came from across the room.

"Oh my God," whispered Caitlyn.

Tom quoted Marvin Gaye, "Believe none of what you hear and only half of what you see Macy."

"I wanna see all of it!" she announced clearly out of control.

Lilly's embarrassment glowed in her cheeks while Annabelle took this quote as a cue to turn in for the night, which was in one of the single beds up on the mezzanine floor above the lounge.

Caitlyn hoped to change the subject. "There's a dog show coming up in Las Vegas Tom, we'd like you and Seamus to take Jolie up there, see if we can do better than last time," she giggled.

Vegas! It was like being told he'd won an all inclusive holiday.

He kept his cool. "Absolutely Caitlyn, when is it?"

"Oh it's not until next year, April I think, we've got plenty of time to get Jolie into shape."

"That dog will never be in shape," drawled Macy, "she hasn't got the temperament and doesn't respond to commands. You've spoiled her, she's a pet, not a show dog."

The drink had definitely diluted Macy's restraint and the brutal truth came spilling out unreservedly.

Caitlyn masked the hurt well. She knew that Jolie would never make a champion; still, she had to pursue her castle in the air. "We have time Macy, she's a very bright girl."

"Ha," said the inebriated one, "disobedient more like." She swigged yet another dram of Mexican mouthwash. "Tom and I are going to make sweet music together."

Tom crinkled in disbelief.

Macy leaned into him and whispered with feted breath, "Let's go and make love."

The English boy had never sobered up so quickly. He sat bolt upright as if suddenly he was the only adult in the room. "I think it's time we put you to bed Macy." His boss came over to lend a hand and between them they hauled the big lady into one of the rear bedrooms. As soon as her head hit the pillow a thick spray of projectile vomit launched sideways with some vigour, decorating the duvet with a coat of sweetcorn studded beige mush.

It had been one of the greatest of escapes. Had Tom been less than particular in the carnal department, then that sweetcorn relish would have garnished him.

Caitlyn despaired, she enlisted Lilly and between the three of them they cleared up the mess, changed the sheets and the unconscious Macy and tucked her in. The woman had behaved disgracefully, but they hoped that by morning she would have forgotten more than she could recount.

Tom however, would never forget.

16
Late

At the beginning of October, it was still 90°F at ground level, rubber sole meltingly intense. The air was element hot, like inhaling the exhaust from a hairdryer. Up in the orange trees however, at least the boys were afforded shade and slight respite. Even so, this operation with which they had been tasked came fraught with hostilities, as delightful as inch-long thorns, sharp dead twigs and stinging insects.

Their bare backs and arms were a map of scratched abrasions, and their hair was full of irritating detritus. As the boys worked cautiously to avoid further maiming, the pruning task became infectious and hypnotic. They wanted to clear the trees of dead material and unwanted growth, and couldn't leave a specimen until it was tidied, and there was a lot of tidying to be done, as this process hadn't been carried out in a while. Taking breaks on the hour in the relative cool of the tool shed, they drank gallons of scorched hair smelling well water.

"Jesus, Rasta', what on earth made people want to settle 'ere in the first place? Imagine what it was like before air-conditioning, it must 'ave been 'orrendous. I mean, it was 'ardly a lush green idyll that prospectors 'appened upon and were too enthralled to leave was it? There's no gold 'ere, no rivers—"

"Snow birds Ras'," blurted Seamus.

Tom shot his pal an inquisitive glance. "There was no such thing in the 1800s mate, that's only a recent indulgence. Imagine that, taking a stagecoach from New York to Tucson, it'd take ya' at least 2 months to get 'ere, if the Indians didn't savage ya' on the way."

Seamus started singing 'Three wheels on my wagon'; his baseball cap had darkened considerably, sodden with perspiration.

"We'll 'ave to ask Caitlyn why people came 'ere, she'll know," continued Tom, "There's no industry 'ere, just an airbase and the Uni, everything else is services and shops as far as I can make out."

"An' reggae music Rasta.

"True 'dat', the music is the warmth you are feeling," Tom quoted a saying from their days gone by.

His mate looked like he was melting. It was lunchtime so they went inside.

"Why on earth did people settle 'ere Caitlyn? Seamus and I were just saying 'ow unpleasant it must 'ave been back in the day."

"Gold, mostly," replied their beneficiary, extricating some gold of her own making from the fridge. She'd knocked up a couple of large Tequila Sunrises for the boys and furnished them with clear plastic straws.

Tom showed surprise. "I didn't know there were goldmines 'ere."

"Not in town, but there are small deposits to be had in the territory, I've read a little about it."

Seamus was halfway through his cocktail already with one elongated draw. With his cheeks sucked in, he almost looked skeletal. "Corr, lovely drop of squash that Caitlyn."

"Not so fast Seamus, there's powerful voodoo in that drink."

"Will it magic me home to me' bed?"

She laughed, "More than likely."

Tom took a much needed swig of the ice cold beverage; it was heaven sent. "So, what year did the prospectors start coming down 'ere then Caitlyn?"

"Well as you know, there have been native American people in the area for thousands of years, the Tohono O'odham mostly, but they had no use for gold. It was the Spanish, as far back as the 1500s who searched for cities of gold, like they found in Mexico. Have you heard of Vázquez de Coronado?"

"No."

"They named the Coronado National forest after him, amongst other things. Well he led an expedition up from

Mexico in search of the fabled city of Cíbola, a kind of Shangri-La; it took them way out North East as far as Kansas and West to the South rim of the Grand Canyon—"

"'e discovered the Grand Canyon?"

"Well I think the Hopi Indians might have something to say about that, but a party of Coronado's men certainly were the first Europeans to gaze upon it."

"Jeez, that must 'ave been majestic, it's jaw dropping enough when ya' know about it and see it for the first time, imagine if you 'ad no idea," offered Seamus.

Tom concurred, "Phenomenal."

Caitlyn continued, "However, after two years of exploring they found little more than simple pueblos, herds of buffalo and dozens of differing tribal people, some of whom they fought with, but scant in the way of precious metals."

Seamus was confused. "So who discovered the gold then?"

Caitlyn smiled, "You really wanna know, huh?"

"It weren't Indiana Jones was it?" quizzed Tom.

"It's funny you should say that. In the film *Indiana Jones and the Last Crusade*, there's a golden cross called the 'cross of Coronado'. Anyway I digress. No, the San Agustín de Tuquison, the Tucson Presidio, was founded in the mid-1700s along the banks of the Santa Cruz river, when it still had flowing water, by a group of Spaniards led by Juan Bautista de Anza, travelling up from Nogales. It was just a camp then; they were on their way to San Francisco, they knew where it was at." She smiled remembering her frivolous youth. "Anyway along the trail that took them close to the Santa Catalina Mountain foothills, gold was discovered near Oro Valley—"

"What, on the way to Pinetop?"

"The very same Seamus, just up the road a little; Cañada del Oro or Canyon of gold. It's found in veins of quartz, which is abundant around here, there was even an Oracle mine, hence the road name.

Anyway, the Spanish took most of it away, back to New Spain, Mexico, and the town didn't really grow much at all apart from the Mission San Xavier Del Bac which was built by

Jesuits and the Tohono O'odham, until after the Californian gold rush was over and Americans descended upon the Old Pueblo in the 1800s hoping to resurrect the mining industry.

Find it they did, not just gold, but silver as well and copper. Copper is huge in Arizona now, not so much here, but in Bisbee and Ajo and other open mines; we produce sixty percent of the country's copper. After the metals were rediscovered, the inevitable railroad and road networks were built in earnest and that's when the town really took off. By 1867 it had become a city and the territorial capital."

"But they 'ad no air-con then right, it must 'ave been unbearable in the summer."

"I think that the people back then were made of sterner stuff Tom. There's a poem written about the Devil making Tucson a home from home, I think it ends like this; And now, no doubt, in some corner of hell He gloats over the work he has done so well, And vows that Arizona cannot be beat, For scorpions, tarantulas, snakes and heat. For with his own realm it compares so well, he feels assured it surpasses Hell."

Seamus' straw gurgled in the dregs of his drink. "Imagine 'aving no ice for ya' cocktails Caitlyn, they wouldn't be 'alf as good."

The woman smiled at Seamus' naivety. "I think that whiskey was the order of the day back then … much safer than water."

"Why was water unsafe?" Tom was considering the weird smelling well water.

"Before proper sanitation and the invention of sand filtration, oh and adding chlorine, water sources would be infested with diseases such as Cholera, Typhoid or Dysentery. People died in droves and it was really quite late in history, early twentieth century I think, before these systems were in place. So whiskey and beer were quite normal beverages of the day."

"I hear that," replied Seamus.

The boys relished Caitlyn's little tutorials; they ate up a good portion of the day and kept them out of the sun.

"'ave you 'eard from Macy at all Caitlyn, she 'asn't been in touch about the funding for the recording sessions, we'd like to get something booked."

Tom sat at the kitchen table eagerly anticipating a lunchtime delight. Caitlyn rescued some vegetable Samosas from being cremated in the oven just in time.

"Oh darn," she said, "I almost forgot these. No, I haven't, I'll give her a call this afternoon, she may still be a little embarrassed over the incident." She served up the crispy pastries with some warm curried rice, it was superb.

"Beautiful, beautiful," concluded Seamus.

***

Macy got in touch a few days later; she wanted the boys to take a sample of Reggie's sperm down to Doctor Sophie for testing on Saturday. The vet lived in Green Valley; Seamus and Tom could take her Cadillac if they wanted, Macy had to be somewhere else. They arranged to be at her house at 10 a.m.

They arrived at 10:30 keen for the experience. The front door was opened by a pretty 18-year-old girl with extremely long, straight light brown hair, and an elfin figure. She offered a graceful hand.

"Hello, I'm Kimberly, Macy's daughter, we haven't met."

The boy's were stunned, how did this happen?

A lad of possibly 15 trotted out of the kitchen and into the hall, he had a soccer ball under one arm and a sandwich in the other. He too was a good looking individual, raven haired and athletic. He introduced himself as Kim's brother David before disappearing into the rear of the house. The lads were both wondering the same thing, had Macy just bought these two from somewhere, after all they looked nothing like their mother. It turned out they had been staying with their father for a while, but were now back for good.

"Mom's out in the kennels, I'll let her know you are here."

Kimberley wiggled away; two pairs of eyes watched a perfectly formed bottom fade from view.

"Fuckin' 'ell Ras', she could take a sperm sample from me any day of the week."

"Rather old boy," replied Tom in a Leslie Thomas sort of way.

The mother came back alone, which was disappointing, she was peeling off some latex rubber gloves as she thundered along the passage. A picture of her bent over wanking-off the dog appeared in Tom's mind; he nearly retched.

"You're late!" she bellowed, "can't you ever be anywhere on time?"

"Sorry Mace, 'ad a touch of the old 'Deli belly' this morning, must 'ave been that 'Ruby' we 'ad last night," Seamus lied.

She had no idea what language he was using. Pulling a small polystyrene box out of her lab coat pocket she handed it to Tom. "Here, take this straight away to Sophie; the keys to the car are on the side in the kitchen, with directions, you've got an hour before this stuff goes bad, so hurry, but don't break my car."

Tom didn't want to touch her or the box; reluctantly he swallowed hard and took it gingerly.

"I'll drive Ras'," Seamus grabbed the initiative, "you keep the swimmers warm."

Walking to the car Tom said, "Imagine 'aving that as occupation on ya' passport."

"What?"

"Dog wanker."

Green Valley was 20 miles south on the I-19; it was unlike Tucson, cleaner, pristine in fact, a model town. They passed signs for a Pecan grove and the Titan missile museum, then turned off onto Nogales Highway, then Abrego Drive. With a name like Green Valley, they were expecting everywhere to be lush pasture and verdant farmland, but what they got was a dusty car lot of scrub and cactus in front of a whitewashed block of rectangles with flat roofs, it was hardly impressive.

Sophie Kaminski was a busy lady, not only a vet, but also an American Kennel Club Judge and a breeder of Timberline Akitas. She was shortish, with a blonde Bob, bushy brown eyebrows and wearing veterinary scrubs. Her house was next to the animal clinic which was seeing a high turnover of visitors today, so she didn't have time for chit chat. She was obviously a professional and overtly pragmatic, taking the sample and telling the boys that she would be in touch with Macy when the results came in, then whisked herself away behind closed doors.

"Okay, bye," Tom said to the wall.

They left, grabbed some lunch at Denny's on the way out of town, then moseyed up the I-19 at a leisurely pace. It was a glorious afternoon, the boys hadn't a care in the world. They were cruising in a new Cadillac, windows down, in no particular hurry; in a great country and being cared for by people with pots of money. Free as birds, they felt blessed. Taking one look at each other they just burst out laughing, instinctively knowing what the other was thinking; this was ridiculous, but glorious, what were they doing here? Penniless millionaires.

"D'ya' think Macy's gone cold on fronting the cash for the recording?"

"It's 'cause you wouldn't fuck 'er."

Tom frowned, "I couldn't mate, I've got standards ya' know."

"Can't ya' just take one for the team mucker, it'll wash off."

"Yeah, but I couldn't erase it from me' mind, besides I couldn't even get an 'ard on looking at that; she must be as old as me' mother, it'll be like punching smoke."

"Ha," barked Seamus, "what about Saul's favourite, the mother-daughter act?"

"I don't think that's on the table Mush, but it would sweeten the deal; why don't *you* give it a go?"

"It's not my beans she's after mate, 'tis only you can tickle 'er fancy."

Tom perished the thought.

"We gotta give 'er something else Ras', string 'er along, or we can kiss that single goodbye."

***

Midweek rehearsal was marked by Bryce's absence, he couldn't be reached by phone and no-one had seen him. Chad would make enquiries at college, surely he was attending class? They tried out some new material, a few originals, *Hollow Heart* and *Halfway Woman*, both about Lela of course, and *I Wanna be Known*, a tune that they'd had for a while but decided to revamp in a Power Station style and tag the hook line of Bros' *When will I be Famous*, on the end; it worked well. They also incorporated the cover tunes *Private Number* by William Bell and Judy Clay, and the Temptations songs *Get Ready* and *Ain't too Proud to Beg*.

Bryce hadn't been in school either; the mystery was deepening. On the day of the next gig, Seamus and Tom went to his house to see what was up. They found him in a state of severe anxiety; he couldn't keep still, flitting from room to room, talking incessant bollocks. It was shocking to see, his face was gaunt and the dark circles around his eyes were like bullseyes of mud.

Tom noticed a distinct lack of woodwind. "Where's all ya' instruments gone Bryce?"

The sax player had his wig back on, but it sat at an unnatural jaunt. "I'm afraid I've got some bad news guys. Due to some err, unforeseen financial difficulties, I've err, had to hock all of my gear, err, temporarily of course, just for the time being, until my next paycheck comes in. You know, I got bills and shit, so I err, won't be able to play tonight, you know, goddamn shame, I was really looking forward to it, god damn."

Seamus looked on, whistling smoke through his lips. "Couldn't ya' borrow a sax from school or something? You'll get money tonight."

"School huh, err, no, I err, school, err, I haven't been to school of late. Not sure if I err, have a job there or not …."

Bryce's pacing was dizzying. He was obviously in a lot of trouble here; the house was a complete tip, which was hard to discern seeing that it was such a dump before. He needed help, but the boys didn't know who to call.

"Seamus, are you carrying at all?"

The question was puzzling, Seamus patted his stomach. "A couple of pound Bryce, nothing that a good run wouldn't sort out!"

That stopped the American in his tracks, he had no idea what Seamus was referring to. His dead eyes pondered the statement. "Snow, man, Bump, Blow …."

Seamus twigged. "Oh, Toot, no man, I've got a little green, d'ya' want me to roll ya' a one skinner?"

Bryce nodded feverishly and carried on stomping the floor.

Tom was heavily disappointed; the band had been sounding great, now this coke head was fucking it up. He tried diplomacy. "Is there someone ya' can call to 'elp ya' out of this mess mate, someone ya' want us to call?"

"No cops man, don't call the fucking cops on me."

"I wasn't, I wouldn't … I meant friends or a relative that could maybe loan ya' some cash."

"Friends, no friends, no friends, relatives no, no, no relatives …." He picked up a giant open bag of pretzels and proceeded to stuff his face with gusto.

Seamus handed him the slim tailored reefer, the drug had a brief calming effect on him, before he was off pacing again.

It was time to go; the boys were on a lost cause here and the evening was drawing in. Maybe he'd sort himself out and come back to the band, maybe he wouldn't, but they would have to press on regardless. Seamus didn't seem as bothered as his mate, but Tom knew they'd lost a real asset, a competent musician with ideas and talent; it was such an utter shame.

On the way to Rosa's Cantina, Tom spoke with certainty. "We ain't never gonna find a sax player as good as 'im, that'll wanna play with us, not for no money."

"What about a keyboard player?"

"They're rarer still; it'll be like looking for jam in a pot of mustard."

"What about José? 'e's a good little player."

"Yeah but 'e's such a fussy fucker, d'ya think 'e'll wanna lower 'imself?"

"I'll ask 'im, we can go round there tomorra'."

Both Chad and Jules were flattened by the news of Bryce's departure; it showed in their performance, but they survived the Haze gig sax-less, Seamus had to work doubly hard to make up for a lack of instrumental versatility. It was also a mismatched affair; supporting the very energetic rockabilly band Train of Thought, who had by far the larger audience.

A funny thing happened after the show; Chad's mate Dave approached the lads with excited eyes. He told them he'd heard one of their songs on the radio being played by another band. Plagiarism was insinuated and dollar signs visibly appeared in Tom's eyes.

"Oh yeah, what song was it?" he asked the beaming American.

"*I Wanna be Known*, you know that end section." He started singing "When, will I, will I be Famous …."

"It was Bros mate, it's their song we nicked from them." Tom said ruefully.

Bom's bungalow was on Euclid Avenue, not far from the U of A, a brown affair with a jungle of a garden. Its long living room was a perpetual jam session littered with instruments and drug paraphernalia, in the centre of which towered a red Perspex bong, a yard and a half high. The homeowner sat cross legged beneath it like a snake charmer enticing a spitting cobra from a basket, loftily stating his position as keeper of the bong. Tom didn't want some anyway, it wasn't the time or place.

Well it was the place, just not the time. Seamus of course had other ideas and asked for a hit immediately.

"Sure, man," said the unmovable Bom, "help yourself."

Seamus leaned in and covered his mouth with the tube, placed his thumb over the kick hole and sucked like his life depended on it to get a glow going on the hash embers in the bowl. Once the fumes had bubbled through the stem and into the water in the tube, he took the pressure off of the carburettor which allowed the pall of smoke to rise up to his lungs. He took in as much smooth exhaust fume as his respiratory system could take and held it there for a good 15 seconds before it bust back out of his gob like a ruptured gas main leaving Seamus coughing, spluttering, and pomegranate red in the face.

"Whoo, that's got some fuckin' balls on it," he said when he finally got his breath back.

"Finest Lebanese," said Bom with a smile so wide you could have forded rivers with it.

"D'ya' mind if I have another bash?"

Bom laughed, "Knock yourself out guy."

Seamus probably would, this was going to be a long night.

José meandered through the hazard strewn living room without a hitch; the layout must have been programmed into his Hippocampus. Tom fixated upon the black bum fluff above his upper lip, languishing like the poor camouflaged comb-over of a balding man. He plonked himself behind his Fender Rhodes, set up in one corner, and started to tinkle the opening riff to Steely Dan's *Peg*.

"Mmm, mmm," mumbled Seamus, short on air. "Keep it going José."

He got out his Strat and plugged into a nearby amp. Bom held his position steadfastly on the floor but managed to reach over and retrieve his acoustic from off the couch; they joined in.

Tom pulled up a stool and tried to conjure up the lyrics, but not being an ardent Steely Dan fan in the past, he fell short of most of it. Luckily Seamus had a better grip on the words and so took the lead. It grooved; José could manage the bass line with his left hand and the lead lines with his right, he was a decent player, it just seemed like he was dead from the neck up. After that tune they jammed *Believe It All* for 20 minutes; at last it had some soul. It was a song written on a keyboard and it had missed one.

They stopped for a bong break. It was an apt time to ask José if he wanted to try out for the band. To Tom's amazement he said he would come along to the next rehearsal and meet the rest of the crew; he could do with the experience of live work, but, and there's always a but, he would have to be picked up and dropped off home. Bom couldn't always be on hand to ferry him. Seamus said that it would be no problem. Tom could see it becoming one.

The night rolled on and so did the tunes. By 2:00 a.m. one wasted rotten, and one spent Englishman fell out of the front door and into their El Camino; it was home time.

***

Seamus exercised a proper Professor Yaffle yawn. "Mondays should be illegal Ras', I need a weekend to get over me' weekend."

Tom glanced his way. Seamus was flopped in the passenger seat, head lolling between the back of the seat and the door jamb, his eyes closed and his sticky hair pushed around by the air influx of the open window.

"You'd only fill it up with more 'yahooing'."

"Life's too short Ras', and work's purely an interruption."

"Ah, a philosophical fucker, try that one on Saul."

They rumbled onto the drive on Orange Grove and crunched to a halt by the new compost heap.

Tom levered his sunglasses up onto his hair, "Let's see what delights our leader 'as in mind for us today," he said sarcastically.

It turned out to be staggeringly tedious. They were to clean, prepare and oil the teak garden furniture, all 16 pieces of it. The prospect of doing it was like turning off all the lights in Tom's head. At least he would get a respite cup of coffee while

Seamus drove Saul to work. He took the opportunity to probe Caitlyn on the burning question of why Jamie was banned from the house.

The lustre fell from Caitlyn's cheery face. "Well that's a long story Tom, come and sit down."

They settled on the edges of the wicker chairs in the kitchen, mugs of Tia Maria laced coffees in hand. Caitlyn's eyes rolled up to the ceiling as if picturing the past in the plaster.

"One time, when Saul and I were away for the weekend, Jamie threw a party. He was only seventeen and he invited half the school to come along; they absolutely trashed the place, smashed windows, broke ornaments, threw up everywhere. By the time the cops arrived there were naked girls running amok and Jamie and his pals were firing guns off in the backyard; it was bedlam."

"What … firing live rounds?"

"Yes, Saul's guns."

"What were they firing at, not each other?"

"No, no, some cans lined up on the back wall."

"Christ, the bullets could 'ave gone anywhere."

"Exactly, but no-one got hurt, luckily. The cops charged Jamie with causing a disturbance and they caught two of his friends in possession of class A drugs, cocaine and marijuana, so arrested them for supplying to minors."

"Did ya' come back to a wrecked 'ouse?"

"We got a call on Sunday from the Tucson Police Department and had to get an early flight back from Florida. Saul was livid, you know the last thing he wants is to have cops crawling all over the house. We had to put up ten thousand dollars bail money to get Jamie out of jail. Saul was so pissed; we had to have the whole house redecorated."

"Jeez, no wonder he's not allowed back."

"Oh that's not it, that's not what got him thrown out, that was just the start of it."

Caitlyn's sedate recount weighed her down heavily; she was regurgitating a family history of which she wasn't too proud. The intrigue in Tom's face prompted her to continue.

"Jamie towed the line for quite some time after the party, or at least we thought he did. We bought him the Jeep and allowed his girlfriends to stop over, he was doing okay at school. Then he started to stay out all night, sometimes go missing for a day or two, I knew he was into drugs but I just didn't want to admit it. He was hanging with a different crowd; older guys that didn't seem to have jobs yet they had expensive cars, Saul can smell a rat a mile off and he warned Jamie to stay away from these guys, but he didn't listen; Jamie knew best...."

She paused, staring into the middle distance, recalling the nightmare. ".... Then we got the call, not from the cops this time, it was Border Patrol, they had Jamie locked up in Wilcox. They'd caught him and his friends running Mexican migrant workers up from the border in hired vans—"

"People trafficking?"

"Human smuggling yes, this was serious. They weren't actually bringing them across the border, just meeting them on this side of the wire and ferrying them into town but it's still classed as aiding illegal immigrants."

Tom puffed out his lips, "What 'appened?"

Caitlyn's eyes were glassy and bloodshot, tears were on the horizon. "Jamie was looking at a mandatory jail sentence of up to ten years, Saul was ready to let him do it; teach him a lesson, he said, but I pleaded with him to do something and eventually he did ...."

Tom waited, her sombre tone was deathly.

".... This doesn't go beyond these walls Tom, or we all go to jail."

Tom shrank into the folds of the chair. "Absolutely," he said meaning it wholeheartedly.

"Saul bribed the judge not to put Jamie away. Cost us a hundred thousand dollars. Because there was some confusion over who was actually driving the trucks, our lawyer made out that Jamie was just a passenger and under the influence of the older guys who were grooming him. The judge played along, he had to give Jamie something though or else it would look too suspicious, so he handed him thirty days in Juvi, six months of probation and a five thousand dollar fine. He was out after two weeks, it shook him to the core. And that was it; Saul washed his hands of my son and he was never to set foot in this house again. Not so much for being a criminal, that'll be the pot calling the kettle black, right? No, for bringing the law down onto us, into our business; to Saul it was like breaking the Ten Commandments."

"Is that when Jamie went up North to college?"

"He went and stayed with Charles for a while, even though Charles only has a one bedroom apartment; until I could find him a place at the University of Alaska in Anchorage. That cost me a packet too, I'm still paying that off."

"Jesus, Jamie must 'ave been paid a lot to risk 'is liberty like that."

"Oh yes, it was very lucrative operation, but also very stupid, and the last thing on earth that Saul wanted to have to deal with."

Tom suddenly considered his and Seamus' own status. Weren't Caitlyn and Saul also harbouring a couple of illegal aliens? He pushed that reality gently under the carpet with a bare toe.

***

Mid October; rehearsals were running smoothly, José complimented the band well. He was hard work though, obnoxious at times and stubborn, but made up for it with his ability to play. The first gigs proper at Gracious Bob's were coming up at the end of the month and they needed to insert a few more cover songs into the set to appease the audience. Maxi Priest's *How Can We Ease The Pain*, UB40's *Please Don't Make Me Cry*, *She Drives Me Crazy* by Fine Young Cannibals and *Cherry Bomb* by John Cougar Meloncamp, were drafted in along with *Get Ready* and *Ain't Too Proud To Beg*, by The Temptations.

The group sounded reasonable, good enough to make an audience dance at least. There was still no word from Macy about the funds for the single, and the buzz for that likelihood had dwindled.

Seamus reasoned that all Tom had to do was go round and give her one, and they'd be set up for life. They'd be set up for life, but Tom would have to do the dirty work, bury the sausage, in all that mashed potato.

The idea turned his stomach. Could he do it? Become a kept man to a sumo-sized Cougar? The lifestyle was appealing; he wouldn't have to work a day anymore, feet up by the pool, sports car on the drive, pretty girls on the side, music as a way of life. Fantastic, he'd just have to fuck that!

Tom was staring at Macy's daughter Kimberly across a crowded room at a barbeque they'd been invited to. Now if she was the ticket to Utopia, he'd have been in there like a shot. She caught his eye and came over, her slim body swaying through the room like a satisfied cat. Leaning back on a door jamb, sipping her Mojito through a straw, she spent the next half hour rabbiting about nothing in particular while Tom delved into her hazel eyes, hoping his gaze would help him delve into her knickers. It didn't.

A few days later in the Berns' kitchen, Caitlyn offhandedly remarked that Kimberly thought Tom was in love with her.

Seamus, immediately jumped to his mate's defence. "Bleeding cheek, she should be so lucky; Tom's way out of 'er league, what audacity."

Tom was surprised by his friend's gallantry, chuffed by the show of solidarity, but also slightly guilty because he had tried to seduce the girl with wanton puppy-dog appeal. But he certainly wasn't in love, not with *her* anyway.

"Just 'ad a chat with 'er the other night, that's all, I dunno where she got that idea from," he fibbed.

Caitlyn seemed buoyed by this recount; she smiled and trotted off, leaving the boys to finish off their mid-morning Irish coffees in peace.

Seamus licked away his cream moustache with some enthusiasm. "You're not are ya'?"

"Leave it out, I was just testing the water. It was cold."

***

Chad had a friend at college, a female friend, whose best mate was getting married this Saturday. The boys weren't officially invited, of course, but they were going anyway. All three of them bundled into Chad's VW camper van in their best togs and headed into town. They were to pick up Chad's friend Alana and then go on to the church for the service. Of course they were running 10 minutes late and even Chad putting his foot down couldn't make up the time.

Alana lived with her parents on the Eastside, near the Oxford Plaza on Grinnell Avenue. It was a pleasant neighbourhood with tree-lined sweeping roads and well kept brick built bungalows. They stopped outside a house with the Stars and Stripes proudly fluttering atop a 20ft white flagpole in the front yard with a collection of mature coniferous trees offering supreme shade. The boys exited the van and walked the paved path to the white iron-barred front door; it was opened by Alana standing in front of her mom and dad.

Even though they were running late, American etiquette demanded that the guest be welcomed into the home, and so they were led into the living room for a brief meet and greet. An hour later after drinks, nibbles and the inevitable inquisition about the UK, Alana was appearing rather tense. Her dad, Clark, an ex-diplomatic aide for the Ford administration, of vast experience, was infinitely interesting. He had visited every country in the world bar one; to his great regret he was yet to experience Tajikistan, a soviet republic.

Despite Alana's obvious anxiousness to leave, Seamus still wanted to know more. "Bet ya' know some secrets then Clark?"

The man gave a measured response, "The thing is with secrets Seamus, they don't stay secret forever; they just become facts. Most of the things that I was sworn to secrecy are now in the public domain, the rest; well you'll have to fight me for those." Clark half smiled provocatively.

"Special are the promises in the secrets that we keep," quoted Tom from his stock pile of lyrics.

"Indeed," said Clark, "Well I think that Alana is itching to go. It's been a pleasure to meet you all, have a wonderful afternoon."

They shook on it, and the four of them left, heading for St Paul's church on Broadway at breakneck speed. Too late, the ceremony was over and the wedding party had hightailed it.

Alana must have been distraught; missing her best friend's big day was obviously devastating, but she masked it well. She was too dignified and excruciatingly polite to let it show, with just a weak smile in response to the boys' profound apologies.

The girls had spent years meticulously planning their respective 'big days' and at the very knife point of her friend's ultimate occasion, Alana had blown it, or rather it had been blown for her. There was always the reception.

Not far from the church on E. Scarlett St, a neatly manicured bungalow had been decorated with pink and white balloons tied with white silk ribbons to anything resembling an anchor. The same theme of bunting had also been draped from pillar to post, unmistakably indicating that this was it; the place to be. Another hint they had arrived, was a white Toyota Supra festooned with more ribbons, balloons and spray foam information, alerting the public to the fact this car belonged to some newlyweds. It even had the classic assortment of tin cans hastily tied to the rear bumper. The final clue of affirmation was in the form of an arch of pink Chrysanthemum letters nailed over the double carport out front, linking the bridal couple's names Carter and Marta; they were made for each other.

The house was rammed with guests who paid little attention to the boys' arrival; Alana quickly disappeared on a mission to apologise to Marta for missing the ceremony. The lads meandered through the rooms in search of the buffet table; they discovered it lurking in a heaving back room, and naturally loaded up a plateful each, helped themselves to a flute of bubbly, and settled down to enjoy some much needed din dins.

Unexpectedly, a microphone burst into life over the stereo speakers announcing the bride and groom; evidently they were entering the house via the back door and one was expected to stand up to greet them, which meant reluctantly, putting your lunch plate down. Disconcertingly, the backing track to Atlantic Starr's *Always*, struck up and in wandered the shackled pair, bonded arm in arm and holding a microphone a piece. Apparently they were going to sing their own wedding song.

Carter began, pitifully nervous and dramatically out of tune, "Girl you are to me, all that a woman should be …."

Marta was equally as nerve grating, so; thus far they had a lot in common. It was excruciatingly awful, yet they sung into each other's eyes like they were heavenly seraphim drenching each other with sonic love.

Tom found it extraordinary; it was painful and uncomfortable to watch, yet brought rapturous applause when the noise stopped. He mouthed the word "Fuck," to his buddies who were doing their damnedest not to laugh.

Alana had tentatively followed the duo into the house, but was keeping a nervous distance; obviously Marta wasn't happy with her friend's absence from the ceremony and was openly ignoring her, making Alana feel surplus to requirements.

After the mind-numbingly boring speeches which the boys could not relate to at all, the party actually picked up pace. Tom and Chad got into light frivolity with a couple of the bride's friends; Alana brought Marta over, who was curious to meet the antagonists who broke her friend's heart.

"Marta this is Chad and Tom; Chad, Tom; Marta." Alana's introduction was almost resentful.

Chad creased one cheek with his crooked smile, "Tom, Marta, maybe you guys should have got married; it would be a great sauce of entertainment."

"Huh?" Marta's forehead wrinkled in bemusement.

"Come on Marta … ketchup."

He waited.

She stared. She walked away.

Across the room, under a doorframe, Seamus entertained one of the bridesmaids.

Tom could see from several glances towards his mate that the woman had fallen for his outrageous charm, giggling and folding up at his antics. Within an hour their presence was notably missed by their absence.

Any bedroom will do in times like these, whatever necessitates; it just happened to be the master bedroom. Seamus was rampant, he wasn't sure if it was the pink satin dress roused up around her tits, the decadence of shagging in the afternoon in someone else's house, or that he just liked weddings, but he was drilling her like a road worker with a jackhammer; holding her legs up with one hand, her back supported by the bed, him stood beside it, trousers round his ankles and his other hand raised like he was conquering a feral horse, his white arse a blur in the shuttered light of the room.

The nameless girl was squeaking with every pump like a rubber toy in the mouth of a Border Terrier, loud enough to be heard above the music downstairs. The noise, humoured Seamus, prolonging his act and heightening her enjoyment. At last, just when he thought his heart might give out under the strain, he reached climax, at the exact moment Marta's dad, alerted to the carnal depravity occurring in his room, burst through the door.

Seamus, in shock, pulled out and turned rapidly to face the intruder, clutching his weapon with both hands and simultaneously ejaculating into his palms. The embarrassment was intense, the coitus definitely interrupted and the dad furious. The bridesmaid recoiled further onto the bed, deeply ashamed of herself, and gathered her dignity as best she could. A small posse lingered on the landing outside, necks stretching in to see what was going on. Seamus stood there, bare legged, cupping his sticky mess while he got the berating of his life.

"What the fuck?" shouted the man of the house, "you turn up here late, making Alana miss her best friend's wedding—"

"Ah that wasn't exactly our fault, y'see—"

"Can it buster, I don't want any of ya' lame ass crap. You think we're a push over huh? Think ya' can turn up and drink our wine, eat our food and fuck my relatives in any place of your choosing? Well, think again shithead. Get your things and get the hell out of my house, and take your fuckin' buddies with ya', you fuckin' roué!"

Seamus feigned remorse and appealed in vain to the man's empathy. "Sorry," he said repentantly, "I don't know what came over me."

17
Gone

A glint of red and blue in the rear view mirror caught his attention, a flicker animated by the glow of a passing street light on University Boulevard. He double-checked. Yep, no doubt about it, the dull presence of a dormant polycarbonate light bar, atop a City police car on his tail. Despite his inebriated state, Tom's instinct manifested quickly. He'd been followed by the cops on many previous occasions, drunk and otherwise; this was nothing new.

Stiffening as the anxiety leeched the blood from his extremities, it somehow aroused his sensibility, and the dread that if he got 'nicked' for drink-driving now, it would definitely be the end of his jolly. Daring not to panic, he willed himself to act casual, angling his elbow out of the gaping window and trying his utmost to appear like the average sober Joe on his way home from work, despite it being beyond midnight and he wearing an overtly fancy patterned shirt.

Cruising down North 4th Avenue, he was suddenly gripped by the uncertainty of the speed limit, was it 25 or 30 along here? He couldn't remember so would like to keep it somewhere in between, but seeing that the car's speedometer was crippled, this was going to be some task. There were few other vehicles on the road just now to mimic, so he nursed his motor along just above tick over, barely touching the pedal and hoping for the best. Determined to remain calm, alert and assumed control of the vehicle was all that his dull brain could cope with. The tension in his right arm welded to the steering wheel, was akin to a steel vice clamped on a wrecking bar, his brow furrowed in concentration, resembled a quizzical Shar Pei puppy.

A bundle thoughts rampaged through his mind, lies he could tell to the police to avoid being deported, ways of fooling a breath test, making a run for it. He cursed his idiot self for drinking too much and pondered the thought of losing all he had gained. A brilliant life in the sun, a great band, a good job, a potential record deal with Macy's backing, a warm rampant girlfriend waiting for him back at the hacienda.

The prospect of a cold cell made him shudder. "If ya' can't do the time, then don't do the crime," he whispered the old adage his Uncle Dave once taught him. So far in life he hadn't committed to the advice.

At the junction of 6th Street he got a red light and eased to a halt, the patrol car did likewise behind him. "Turn off, turn off," he mouthed without moving his lips, praying they would go away. Green light, they didn't. Through the tunnel below the Amtrak the police stayed close. He considered maybe they were just going his way and he was fretting over nothing. Between the Rialto and Congress Hotels he indicated and got into the outside lane ready to turn left onto 6th Avenue; the cops followed suit, they were definitely stalking him. If they were going to pull him over it would be soon, he'd given them enough time to check him out. He was handling the El Camino like it was his driving test, hyper-sensitive, the veins visibly throbbing in his neck, yet the night air was fantastic; a dreamy juxtaposition.

The Ford Crown Victoria stayed with him from downtown all the way out to the crossing on 22nd Street, one corner of which was monopolised by the pristine white reverence of the Santa Cruz Catholic church in all its sanctity. Here the boys in blue slid into the left hand lane and halted alongside him. A blonde moustachioed officer casually peered into the cab of the pick-up giving the driver the once over.

"Don't look, don't look," Tom said to himself. He looked, glancing back lazily, pretending not to care, he gave the cop an upward nod, before resuming his transfixed stare up ahead, feigning a relaxed air. If a casting director could see him now, he'd piss all over the competition.

This was it surely, those red and blues were going to light up, and with a single pulse of their siren he was going to be directed towards the sidewalk. But no, Tucson's finest peeled left and slowly faded into the night like a bad smell on a breeze. Tom, mightily relieved, melted into his seat and inhaled deeply before accelerating gently down 6th. He puffed out his cheeks; squeaky bum time was over. Well at least he was awake now so it would be a far safer ride home.

It was the end of the band's first 2-night booking at Gracious Bob's; a meagre success with a receptive audience and some customers dancing. The band was smooth, they'd had a free meal and enough beer to bathe in, and on top of that they'd been paid cash, $400 split 5 ways. Chad and Jules had gone on to the Racquet Club for a late one and Caryn and Seamus were taking José home before heading back to hers; so Tom, three sheets to the wind, was taking himself back to Rocker-baby, a pet name given to Holly by her godmother Katie Pirelli.

***

At the start of November, the boys had been introduced to Saul's cousin Oren Kirsch, a hirsute, thick set New Yorker who apparently lorded over a porn distribution business. He was smug, self-assured and circumspect over the English guys in Saul's kitchen. He was Lilly's father; glitteringly shrewd with a minatory smile.

Saul gesticulated with his breakfast fork, launching a morsel of scrambled egg onto the tiled floor, Fonda was the first responder. "Cait, Oren and me are going to Florida for the weekend, you guys gotta look after the house."

"Sure, sure," Seamus replied, "a little 'oliday is it?"

"Business," grunted Saul cutting off any line of enquiry; then continuing to eat.

Oren offered a lopsided smirk and nodded rhythmically.

Caitlyn, forever gracious piped in. "Oh we're just going to visit Uncle Albert, that's all; we'll be back on Monday if that's alright with you guys, if you haven't made any plans or anything?"

"No, no plans this weekend Cait, we were just gonna do 'penny for a guy' outside the pub to get some money for some sweets."

"What?" snapped an uncomprehending Saul.

Tom tried to explain the English tradition of children building an effigy of Guy Fawkes by stuffing old clothes with newspaper and using a cardboard mask for a face, collecting spare change from drunks leaving the pubs, then burning the 'Guy' on a bonfire on firework night, November the 5th. The concept was a foreign nonsensical thing to their boss. "There'll be no fuckin' bonfires here; you'll burn the fuckin' neighbourhood down. What are ya', twelve?"

Seamus thought it wise to defend himself, "Only fooling with ya' Saul."

"I'll fuckin' fool with you in a minute," said Saul in all seriousness.

Oren was choking back a laugh.

"Now get back to work, that fuckin' dog shit ain't gonna pick itself up."

Caitlyn tried to veil her embarrassment, "Don't be so hard on the boys Saul, they're only trying to explain some of their culture to us. I find English tradition fascinating."

Saul ignored her. "Now here's the fuckin' rules ...." he peered over the top of his horn rims. "No fuckin' in the house. You find a whore, you bang her some place else. And nobody goes into my room period. Unless you need a gun to blow a hole in some motherfucker intent on stealing my property! You know where they are ...."

Oren had a fist to his mouth and was concentrating hard on the tables surface.

"And another thing, if anything happens to my dogs I'll put you two on a fuckin' bonfire."

"We'll treat the 'ouse like it's our own Saul," assured Tom.

"That's what I'm a-fuckin-fraid of." Saul gave them the Odessa death stare.

They flicked eyes at each other, turned, and walked out via the garage door leaving behind a burst of repressed Brooklyn laughter.

***

The camcorder focussed on Caryn Ventura's tiny frame, beleaguered by a frail one piece black bathing costume, carrying a silver tray in one hand, transporting a glass of milk up and around the top end of the pool, to a white plastic sun lounger occupied by a prostrate gentleman hidden behind a sprawled broadsheet newspaper. The individual was bedecked in a dinky pair of Union Jack shorts, a knotted white hankie on his head and a pair of Caitlyn's white cat-eye sunglasses, which didn't do him any favours.

"Your beverage, Sir," she announced, as per the script.

"e' thanks, chuck," responded Tom in a Yorkshire accent.

"You're welcome, Sir." She turned and wiggled away.

He dropped his shroud and said, "Beats Scarborough any day."

Seamus with his eye to the viewfinder blurted out a hollow laugh, "Bloody luxury," he said and then followed the love of his life with a slow zoom as she retraced her steps, covering her butt with the glinting silver tray.

"Doh-hon't," she protested.

Tom folded the paper away and turned to the camera, "Don't worry," he said covering *his* arse, "It *is* lunch time."

Seamus ruined the ruse by saying that is was in fact half past two.

Caryn came around in front of the camera "I'm going to sit next to Tom."

The tall olive green Saguaro she passed complimented the baby blue sky reverently, epitomising the sunset state to perfection. In years to come whenever Tom closed his eyes and thought of Tucson, the green on blue would be the first thing that came to mind.

She'd stopped at a white wrought iron table festooned with plant fronds. "What are these?"

Tom looked her way, "Oh they're dates. We were trying to dry them out in the sun."

"You've failed."

"Yep!" He got up exposing his full attire. Kitted out in his working boots with his feet at ten to two on the margins of the pool, he addressed his audience through the lens. "Welcome mums and dads, 'ere I am dressed as a traditional Brit abroad, it's November the 7th. I come to you dressed this way in need of some sympathy. Yes while you are all invigorating in a crisp two degrees Centigrade, we 'ere in the States 'ave to endure a roasting eighty degrees Fahrenheit. And I can tell you it is torturous."

"Awful," agreed Seamus panning to the pool water. "Are ya' going to go in?"

Tom reverted back to Yorkshire. "Not bloody likely. That water int' pool is as cold as an iced bath, you'll not get me in there."

Caryn was crouching by the bubbling jacuzzi, teasing the water with one hand, "This isn't getting warm," she lamented.

Tom switched his accent to upper crust, "The maid is looking particularly fine this afternoon."

"She certainly is," Seamus concurred.

"We'll have to get a couple more of those," concluded Lord Snooty.

The scene changed, Tom held the camera, focussing on Seamus decked out in just his big baggy navy shorts, constructing some courage at one end of the pool by rocking backwards and forwards on alternate feet and clapping and rubbing his hands together a half dozen times, whilst repeating the words "right then," once too often.

Then after his sixth approach he finally completed the legendary Montgomery legs bent dive, a technique he has yet to tire of. Seamus swam the length of the pool underwater with his shorts halfway down his arse, framing his lily white cheeks for posterity. Bobbing up in the shallows exasperated, he took several gasps of air and tightened his torso, "whoo, whoo, that's fuckin' freezing."

He shuddered before sinking beneath the water for more punishment, coming up by the steps where he exited the pool like a dripping bi-pedial Beluga. He ran to the diving board and performed a classic tucked bomb, soaking the flagstones and his girlfriend.

She sprang to her feet, hopped onto the diving board and completed a perfect plunge, slicing through the water like a raven Marlin, surfacing next to Seamus to justifiably duck him with two hands placed on his saturated skull.

Tom kicked a tennis ball into the pool which was swiftly followed by Fonda the Retriever, who relished rescuing spherical objects in distress. Her swimming prowess was not unlike Seamus'. The camera curved right and picked up Reina sun worshiping with her tongue lolling out.

"Will you be partaking in the water aerobics today?" questioned Tom.

The plump strawberry blonde slow-blinked a response.

"I guess not."

When the frolicking dissipated, the nipple hardened pair joined Tom on the pool furniture to dry off.

"What do ya' fancy doing tonight Ras'?" enquired the big lad.

"Well there ain't no firework parties to go too, so why don't we 'ave our own?"

"Where we gonna get any fireworks?"

Caryn piped in, "Unless it's the 4th of July or New Year's Eve, the only fire works you'll be able to buy would be sparklers; some party you guys."

"What ya' can't get rockets and bangers?" protested Seamus.

Caryn laughed, "No, and if you did and set them off, there's a heavy fine for that sort of thing."

"What rotters," rued Tom.

"Let's knock up a big dinner and invite the lads round for a jam."

"Fuck off, Saul'll go nuts if 'e finds out."

"Well I won't tell 'im." Seamus lit the spliff he'd been rolling.

"Come on it'll be fun," encouraged Caryn.

Tom considered it for a moment, "Okay, but everyone has to be on their best behaviour, no getting pissed and fuckin' breaking something."

"As if …." reasoned Seamus.

The smell of pizza reaching the point of perfection wafted into the lounge signalling the end of the rehearsal session. The boys' new found culinary love was ready made Bobbly pizza bases, a delicious blank canvas on which to experiment. Tom had invented his own tomato and garlic passata, he topped a couple of bases with an overload of grated mozzarella, green pepper, mushroom, onion and black olives, while Seamus knocked up two tuna, sweetcorn and red onion numbers that resembled two of the Galapagos islands. Caryn tossed up a huge green salad while the group were playing and laid the dining room table.

Bom, who had driven José over had done nothing apart from sit on the big white couch and line up three fat spliffs, and was currently stoking a bong for afters.

Seamus took charge of slicing the steaming hot disks as they came out of the oven.

"Corr, look at that, look at that," he said burning his eager fingers, before wrist-flick snapping them through the air.

Jules was hovering, keen to tuck in, "Seamus, you're quite a cook there, guy."

"One tries one's best."

"Take a seat guys," commanded Caryn, "Get it while it's hot."

Tom retrieved a bunch of Budweisers from the fridge and bought them to the table, "'elp yourselves guys, the milky bars are on me."

"This is a spectacular house, guys," remarked Jules spooning a large helping of herbage onto his plate.

"Just our little weekend retreat, when we like to get away from it all."

Seamus declared, "Highly salubrious," he informed his guests, not quite knowing what that word meant.

"I'd love to see it some time," Joked José, his ultra dry sense of humour rising above the parapet.

Chad remained suspiciously quiet, as he had been all evening.

Tom noticed, "You alright there Chad, you're not eating much?"

Chad cleared his throat, "Actually guys, there's something I've been meaning to tell you .…"

Everyone stopped chewing to hear what Chad had to say, apart from José who ploughed on.

"Um, I'm, moving back to Fort Worth in a couple of weeks .…" He pulled his crooked smile and looked down at his plate. "I've been offered a job at a stage lighting company, and it's a really good opportunity, da, da, da, dar .…"

Seamus felt like he had been punched, "What, Texas?"

Jules was astonished, "Gee guy, what about college?"

"Well I'm kinda bummed with college right now, it's not all what I expected it to be, you know sleep deprivation is interesting 'n all, but as a career, it kinda sucks."

"Fuck college, what about the band man?" said Tom losing his appetite.

Chad was visibly deflated by his decision, "I know guys, I feel like I'm really letting you all down; the band sounds great just now and it breaks my heart to leave you all, but I gotta do what I gotta do right? I'll help you find a replacement, we got a couple of weeks."

It was like a giant had dropped his napkin on the evening. The end of the ride.

This was hard to digest; Chad was the backbone of the band.

"Can I use the bathroom?" asked José seemingly unperturbed.

"Yeah it's just through there, mate," pointed Seamus discounting the keyboard player's affliction.

"I'll take him," said Bom. They went through one of the arches and across the hall, José's hand on Bom's shoulder.

"Fuck man, what a bummer, 'ow we gonna replace you?" Tom pleaded with his eyes.

Chad tried to make light of it, "Hell you'll be alright, there's plenty of Muso's in town."

"Yeah, for Rock or Country, not with your feel Chad, you understand us."

"I'm sorry guys, it's just something I gotta do, you know, no disrespect an all, but playing in Tucson bars for beer money, just ain't gonna pay the rent. If the thing with Macy would have come off, then that would be different, but you know I gotta think of a career."

"Yeah, Tom, all ya' 'ad to do was slip 'er a length," Seamus added.

"What?" Caryn pricked up her ears.

Tom gave Seamus a disparaging look. "Ya' can't blame me for that, mate, that would 'ave been a right old mess, and besides I've got benchmarks."

"Forget benchmarks, Deutschmarks are what we need!"

Jules laughed, "Tom, you could have taken one for the team, guy."

Tom shook his head.

"She wanted to sleep with you?" Caryn's eyebrows looked like they wanted to retreat into her hair.

"Apparently so," acknowledged Tom.

"No biggy," said Seamus burning his bridges way too lightly, "We'll just have to poach Carl Strawberry from Mystic Lights, 'e'll do."

The meal over with, everyone got invited out into the garden for a smoke, but Chad felt awkward and wanted to get going, he also had to drop Jules off on the way home. They packed away their gear and before Jules departed, he told the boys that he might know a drummer at school who'd be willing to audition, he'd let them know.

Midway through Monday morning the Berns came home. The house had been given a going-over that a professional cleaning crew could have put their name to, they had worked hard on it all Sunday afternoon, everything was spick and span, nothing out of place; well at least they thought there wasn't.

Through the still languid air came a melodious shrill from the darkness of the rear patio door, "Seamus-Tom."

They downed tools.

"Coffee break?"

"Quite possibly."

It definitely was not. Saul was leaning one handed on the kitchen table with annihilation etched into his features.

"Who used my room over the weekend?" His words were like acid rain.

The boys were equally confused, neither of them had.

"Nobody," they said in unison.

Saul's eyes were slits in a castle walls.

"Nobody … Did nobody leave a great stinking turd in my bathroom and not use any paper to wipe their ass?"

Perplexed at first, it dawned on them simultaneously; José and Bom had wondered off during the meal, it was one of them dirty bastards, perhaps José couldn't find the flush, but the loo roll?

Seamus was quick to react, "It could have been José."

"What … who the fuck is José?"

"'e's our keyboard player, 'e's blind, 'e came over for lunch on Saturday. Come to think of it 'e did ask to use the toilet."

Saul exploded, "Ya' dumb fuckin' shits, do ya' think I'm stupid? Do ya' expect me to believe that a fuckin' blind man came over here and shit in my toilet, do ya' think I was born yesterday?"

Tom offered some explanation, "Oh 'e didn't come over by 'imself, 'is room mate drove him."

"What fuckin' part of, don't have anyone over, do you guys not fuckin' understand?" Saul fumed.

"Sorry Saul we thought you meant girls, for the night." Tom feared for his job now.

"Nobody means fuckin' nobody, you fuckin' schlemiel."

The lads stayed rooted to the spot, not knowing what to say in their defence.

Saul sauntered round to the worktop where the mail had been placed. "You can kiss goodbye to any more trips to the cabin, that's for sure."

Caitlyn considered it appropriately safe to butt in now, "Oh honey, don't be so hard on these guys, apart from that little incident they have kept the place safe and sound, and remarkably clean, I must say."

Saul's attention was drawn away to a particular letter on the side, so much so he lost impetus on his rant.

"Huh, right," he said. "Get back to work the fuckin' pair of ya', and no more fuck ups, ya' got it, nobody shits in my toilet, period." He wandered off to his bedroom.

Caitlyn winked at them triumphantly letting it be known that everything was okay.

***

A week later Tom received a phone call from his mum telling him that his grandmother had died, his dad's mum. She was the closer of his two nans, and had succumbed to stomach cancer. Tom was naturally upset and spent a couple of days agonising over whether to go home for the funeral. He reminisced some of the happier memories he'd shared with her. His grandparents had owned a sweet shop in North Watford and his brother, sister and he had spent many Saturdays in there helping themselves to the sweets; old fashioned stuff that is no longer in existence like sweet tobacco, Bazooka Joe's and Lord Toffingham ice lollies. He also relished the times spent above the shop in the storeroom playing, and, to his shame, pilfering, the Tempo toy soldiers and Cowboys and Indians; it was Utopia to a ten-year-old boy, and the smell of the place reclaimed his senses.

Other memories included his nan's cooking; she always seemed to be making some kind of pudding, kneading pastry or dough in a big stone bowl. A cigarette would be stuck in the corner of her mouth, the long ash threatening to collapse into the mixture at any moment. And glorious things, such as picking granddad's runner beans and peas in his back garden, fresh for the Sunday roast; the smell of mint and the aroma of their creosote fence.

His grandparents went away for 4 years to live in Australia with Tom's aunt; he was then a spotty teenager who thought he knew everything, but somewhere along the line he'd lost a little humility. His remorse over one incident would forever stain his conscience, and he had scant explanation as to why he said the things he did, they just fell out of his mouth for no reason.

He'd come home from somewhere, and went in through the kitchen, with a carrier bag swinging on his arm, he couldn't even recall what was inside, but it must have been something precious. He passed through the living room on his way to the stairs, where his nan was having her hair set by his mum. She asked Tom offhandedly what he was carrying, "A bag of shit!" he snapped, instantly embarrassed by his outburst, he headed off to his room ashamed.

She wasn't ill when he had departed from England, or at least he had no knowledge of the fact, and now she was gone, never to be insulted again. His angst over what to do tormented him for a few days. In the end he sent flowers, reasoning that she would have wanted him to enjoy his life and not waste time and money on showing his respects to a loving grandparent at a freezing cold dreary funeral; his family would understand, surely, he had spent $80 on a wreath!

***

Tom was having one of his recurring theme nightmares, the ones in which his inner psyche was trying to convince him that he'd never amount to much, manufactured by his lack of confidence. He was trying to catch a bus, it was raining, and each time he'd get on the 'Routemaster', he had no money to pay for a ticket. He would get off, back into the downpour to find a cash machine, withdraw a 'tenner', get back on a bus, only to find he still had no money. So it went on, underlying the frustration of not being able to get to where he wanted to be.

His mum was outside on the pavement yelling at him, "Tom, Tom," only it wasn't his mum, it was Kate Norton and the yelling became an elongated, "Taaarm, Taaarm."

He woke in the solemn light of his bedroom and opened one eye. "Yeah?"

"Telephone."

"Okay, thanks."

Peeling himself off the single mattress, Tom pulled on some shorts and plodded out into the office.

"Hello,"

"I didn't wake you guy, did I?"

"Yes Jules, but it doesn't matter, what's up?"

"Are you guys busy today?"

"Er … no … I don't think so."

"Well you know that drummer I was telling you about, from school?"

"Yeah."

"Well, he wants to meet you guys and have a jam at his house."

Tom plonked his arse down in the big comfy office chair. "What's 'e like?"

"He's a really cool guy, very popular, I've never heard him play, but he's saying all the right things."

"Where does 'e live?"

"Up in the Catalina foothills, Alvernon Circle he says, there's some pretty cool houses up there."

"What time?"

"Around two o'clock."

"Ah that's good, give us some time to get human. Do you need picking up or can ya' make ya' own way?"

"Oh that's okay; Diana can give me a ride."
"Whoa ho, ho, Jules, who's Diana?"
"Oh she's just a friend."
"I see, just a friend, eh?"
Jules giggled.
"So what's 'is 'ouse number mate?"
"4017."
"Got it, see you there."

It took three quarters of an hour to travel across town; Alvernon Circle was off Skyline Drive, not too far from Macy's place. The housing out this way was upmarket, the streets were spotless and the gardens manicured.

A distinct line brokered the border between concrete road and tarmac drive as Seamus ushered the El Camino left amidst whitewashed low brick walls and a couple of lantern topped pillars. He was forced to give the accelerator a nudge to cope with a sudden curved gradient lined with white boulders, squat mesquite trees and agave plants. At the top of the drive, Jules was waiting in the passenger seat of a shabby cream-coloured hatchback, driven there by his new friend Diana. Why they hadn't gone inside already was a mystery.

Chester's cream painted house garnished a small rise, affording it uninterrupted views of the Catalinas and the sprawling hazy vista beneath. There were a couple of 1960s Ford Mustang convertibles up by the porch, a red one in pristine condition, top down, glinting in the afternoon sun. The other, a yellow one, was in need of some attention. There was probably room for 10 cars in the lot; Seamus parked along side the red Mustang, so close that Tom couldn't get out.

"'ave ya' brought a can opener?" He said sarcastically.

"Sorry mate, sorry." Seamus reversed without looking behind and almost ran over Diana, who had departed her old banger and was strolling up to meet them.

"Sorry, sorry." He held up a hand in surrender, before driving forward again, this time giving Tom plenty of berth.

Jules was laughing his nervous head off again. "Guys, I'd like you to meet Diana."

She had shoulder-length auburn hair, unimpressive features, but a tidy figure beneath her tight fitting jeans and white T-shirt.

"Diana, Diana, sorry, sorry, I didn't see ya' there, you were nearly roadkill." Seamus presented his hand, she took it delicately.

"It was almost over before it had begun," she mused, a wicked smile smudged across her face, rendering her less than ordinary.

"'ello I'm Tom," he said offering a paw.

"So you are," she gushed taking his golden mitt. The contrast of her milky white skin was remarkable; she definitely didn't do manual labour.

"Shall we?" Jules gestured toward the heavy oak front door.

"Lead on, dear boy," conceded Seamus.

After a short wait the door was opened by an attractive elegant lady in her 40s, she introduced herself as June, Chester's mum; she'd been expecting them and was overjoyed. She was dainty, had the demeanour of a Hollywood star and appeared to walk on a cushion of air. Her long blonde hair was bundled up loosely atop of her head, and without a hint of makeup she radiated beauty.

Introductions over, she led them through the spacious bungalow to a converted garage, now games room, that was walled to the front with smoked glass patio doors and floored entirely with mustard coloured ceramic tiles. It had a multi-gym in one corner and a rather over indulgent cherry red drum kit in the centre against the white rear wall. It boasted 2 bass drums, 7 tom-toms and an equal amount of cymbals. It was like Neal Pert's (from Rush) baby kit, and it was surplus to requirements for this outfit and also impractical to transport in a Mustang.

Chester Belew III entered via a back door, looking like he'd just jettisoned a surfboard, wearing a black one piece Spandex lifter suit, which left nothing to the imagination. He was tanned, toned and devastatingly handsome, with a shoulder length, dirty blonde mullet and as confident and charismatic as a person could get; witty, intelligent, charming and gracious, but without a hint of conceit; a genuine babe magnet.

He had all these attributes and he knew it, yet he wasn't in the slightest bit arrogant or big headed, he was going to use his arsenal to achieve great things; he'd already been in a teen movie and was destined for further notoriety. June was a casting agent and could shin him up the ladder quite comfortably, after he had graduated from college that is.

"Hey guys, what's going on?" He had an overbearing handshake, meaning to portray dominance. "Sorry I didn't hear you come in, I was out by the pool topping up the old tan."

Seamus thought he had the measure of the bloke already. "Nice place you've got 'ere Chester."

"It's pretty cool isn't it; my old man's got a good job."

Tom was wide eyed. "What does 'e do?"

"Oh, he's the mayor."

Jules' jaw nearly hit the floor. "He's the mayor of Tucson?"

"Just kidding, he's at city hall, he's in planning." So he was a comedian as well. "Why don't you guys haul your equipment in while I go and fix us some drinks? You can use the patio doors there to come and go, save ya' pulling it through the house."

By the time the amps had been set up Chester was back with a huge glass jug of home-brewed lemon iced tea; it was sorely needed, the boys had a sweat on now.

Seamus held up his glass, "your 'ealth, Sir," he said before downing it in one swoop. "Corr, that tickled me trachea."

Jules laughed.

Tom took a gulp; it was nice but not as sweet as the bottled stuff off the shelf. "'ow d' ya' make that then, Chester?" he enquired earnestly.

The question tickled Chester; it was such a common thing to do in this part of the States, but he was happy to explain. "Well you just take some Lipton's tea bags, throw them into a glass jar, add some water, some lemons and some sugar, and put it out to brew in the sun all day, then bring it in and place it in the refrigerator till it's cold."

"As natural as that?"

"As natural as that."

Chester also possessed a small PA system, mikes and stands, which were a godsend, but he played so loud the amps had to be cranked, and as Seamus had suspected, the array of toms and cymbals proved too much for the lad who was struggling to keep time, yet insisted on playing every single piece of kit. And although Chester took control over the jam session, it was evident that a heavy cull of percussion would have to take place if the pretty boy was to join the band.

Tom and Seamus stayed humble despite the audition sounding a complete mess; Jules looked highly uncomfortable and wholly embarrassed while Diana sat quietly throughout, content it seemed, just to be there.

If Chester had played in a number of bands in the past, they must have all been rock bands. He had limited knowledge of styles and was a mile away from Chad's skills, so it was going to be hard work to pull him into shape. The boys had the time, but did they need the hassle? If Chester came on board they'd be taking two steps back when they wanted to go forward.

At the end of the session he asked them what they thought. Seamus was disingenuous as usual. "Yeah, yeah, not bad, not bad Ches', I thought you 'ad three feet there for a second."

"Nah, just the twelve inches," he smiled earnestly patting his bulge.

"I think we can all see that," joked Seamus.

It was decided that the boys would come back Tuesday and Thursday night and take it from there. They all departed after a flurry of sweaty hand shakes.

Tom drove the car back home. "Well what d'ya' reckon?" he asked his slouched passenger.

"She's got a lovely arse."

"Not fuckin' Diana you 'pranny', Chester."

"'e's gotta lose 'alf that fuckin' kit, it's ridiculous, 'e's all over the place."

"Ya' not wrong, but 'ow we gonna tell 'im?"

"By great stealth Ras', watch me, watch me." Seamus closed his eyes and fell asleep for the rest of the journey, his bare feet up and out of the window.

At Tuesday night's session Chester introduced the lads to a friend who'd come along to listen to the jam. Her name was Rachael; a slim, obsidian haired beauty, marred only by a feint moustache on her upper lip. Also joining the audience tonight was the family dog, a white Alaskan Malamute called Kiku, and Chester's dad, Chester Belew II. He had short, thin, sandy hair with a side parting and a ruddy complexion, pointing to a fondness for strong liquor.

Chester senior occupied a comfy position in a well cushioned chair close to the band, a glass of something golden in his hand and Kiku, who was reputed to be profoundly deaf, lying on the floor by his side. He listened contentedly for some time, remarking that their song *Be Mine*, one of the originals the band had recorded at the U of A, was their best material, and that "you could really do something with that."

He had the aura of a well respected member of the community and the presence of a wise sage about him. He oozed respect and was himself a very confident man, so every comment he made was duly listened to and appreciated, until at the finish of a song he imparted a gem.

"I gotta say it guys, the band sounds fucking great, there's just one thing you could do to improve things."

The lads waited with bated breath, expectant of some life changing sapience.

"You gotta lower that cymbal, Son; the girls can't see ya fuckin' face."

Initially stunned, the lads said nothing, yet a pearl of wisdom it might have been, after all Chester was a very good looking chap, and if girls came to see him, they were coming to see the band, and girls attracted blokes. Hey presto, an audience; so maybe it wasn't just an inebriated piece of monkeyshine after all, maybe it was marketing.

Chester junior was having trouble with the reggae beat on UB40's *Please don't Make me Cry*. The rhythm was totally alien to him and once more he was filling all the gaps with unnecessary rolls.

Seamus stopped the song. "Ches, all it needs mate, is kick drum, snare and hi-hat."

Chester tried to justify his technique with implausible excuses, "Oh but it felt a tad empty, I thought I'd jazz it up a little."

"But it's not jazz mate, it's reggae, it's all about the groove, bah, bah, bah, bah, tat, bah, bah, bah, bah, bah, bah, tat, that's all ya' gotta do."

The drummer looked slightly wounded. "Oh, okay, we'll give that a go." He counted the song in again.

The same thing happened once more.

"'old it, 'old it, 'old it," Seamus called. He took off his guitar and moved in behind the kit, to Chester's indifference he moved a section of toms and a couple of cymbal stands to one side. "Try playing the song without this lot, simplify the I," he said with added Jamaican.

Reluctantly Chester conceded, and as if by magic, with fewer toys, the rhythm improved dramatically.

"Sim say?"

"Yes I," concurred Tom.

This was going to take some perseverance; Jules obviously wasn't into the new flavour, but what choice did they have? A gig was looming and they needed to honour it or lose momentum and standing. Chester would have to get up to speed or else they were going to lose a bass player as well.

Thursday was a similar affair, only with a different girl on Chester's lap, Danielle a bubbly blonde who was keen to add her expertise to the session. Tom kindly gave her his tambourine hoping that it might prove entertaining, a mistake that he regretted after just a few bars; she played infuriatingly out of time. The other distinction tonight being that Chester had removed one of the kick drums from his set up of his own accord. Seamus' influence was evidently taking effect.

"That's better Ches', you'll play tighter like that."

"You know what, I messed around a little with it and it feels more comfortable."

"And you've lowered that cymbal," quipped Tom.

"Gotta listen to the old man right?"

"Sometimes."

"Speaking of which," said Chester, "it's my Dad's birthday this Saturday and we are throwing him a surprise party. I was thinking that the band could set up, throw down some songs, invite people up, have a few drinks, you know, it'll be really cool, a chance to show off the band to a great crowd, what do ya' think?"

They thought it might be a car crash and a bit presumptuous of Chester to regard himself as one of the band already, seeing as the jury was still out on that one, but a party up here in the hills and a chance to make a few acquaintances; well that sounded like a cracking idea.

Chester invited Tom and Seamus round early on the Saturday so they could go for a ride in his Red Mustang. He needed to drop something off at college and the day was perfect for a jaunt in an open topped classic sports car. An introduction to Stevie Ray Vaughn's *Couldn't Stand The Weather*, strutting through the ether was a revelation, despite the lyrics being in complete contrast to the Wedgwood blue crystalline sky and the 75° heat, the groove was an impeccable compliment.

Gorgeous women were out *en masse* today; the car turned many a pretty head, making the boys feel glorious, like they were exactly where they were supposed to be.

"Where's Danielle today Ches'?" enquired Tom.

"Who?"

Seamus barked a laugh, "You deleted her already mate?"

The driver feigned arrogance "Ah, find 'em, fuck 'em and forget 'em, there's plenty o' fish in the sea, and you're a long time dead."

Two idioms in succession thought Tom, only the very handsome can afford to be so flippant, lucky bastard.

Chester's golden locks fluttered in the slipstream; with his trendy sunglasses and vest top, with one hand on the wheel, he could quite easily be the focus of a music video. He posed a question that suddenly came to mind. "So do either of you guys have girlfriends right now?"

Seamus told him about Caryn, and Tom said he was seeing Holly on a casual basis.

"Do they take it up the ass?"

It had never crossed Tom's mind, the act was rather Homoerotic wasn't it?

"Never tried it mate," answered Seamus.

"Girls go fucking crazy for that shit," informed the expert.

Tom raised his eyebrows. "What … every girl wants to be fucked up the arse?"

"After some gentle persuasion, a little coaxing; yeah, you have to start off real slow, ease it in gently, and you're good to go."

Tom wasn't convinced; it didn't seem natural.

Seamus on the other hand appeared interested.

The slow drive around the university campus was a rubbernecker's paradise, for the English dudes at least.

Chester remained unaffected. He cruised into University Boulevard and parked idly outside one of the red brick buildings, disappearing through a shaded doorway with a bundle of books in his hand and a, "Be right back, guys."

Had he not parked under the shadow of a giant Eucalyptus tree, Seamus and Tom would have fried in that tin can. Chester came back 15 minutes later with a girl on each arm. They were both stunning. "Guys, this is Sheri and Cherry, they're coming to the party tonight, and guess what, they're bringing friends! Holy Mary Mother of Christ, there is a God."

The ladies couldn't have been older than 19, they both laughed at Chester's charm offensive, each one kissed him on a check, gave a resolve destroying little wave to the lads and said, "See you later, boys," before strutting off arm in arm down the palm-lined avenue.

Chester jumped back into the Mustang exclaiming "God bless the USA."

I think he has, thought Tom.

Back at Alvernon Circle, preparations were well underway for the nights shindig; a warehouse of booze had been wheeled in and the kitchen was a hive of activity. The boys were introduced to Chester's younger brother Spencer, tall and lean with a nervous smile, and his sister Rochelle, blonde and gorgeous, her looks residing on her father's side. Her husband Dante was also here, setting up the keg under the pool veranda; he had a kind smiley face and welcoming aura.

Bom brought José and Caryn over; it was the first time for all three at Chester's. Jules and Diana rocked up around 6:00, and they got down to a sound check, causing all the people there, apart from June, to down tools and listen to a protracted version of Sting's twelve bar blues number *Down So Long*, a rendition with way too many guitar solos; still they got a round of applause at the finish.

KP, Glen, Jennifer, Jack, Freddie, Kate Norton and Chad all turned up together around 7:30 just as the light was fading. Holly didn't wanna come, social gatherings with people she didn't know weren't her thing; she'd rather hangout with her dogs and a couple of fat Doobies. Stu and Fenella put in an appearance, bringing with them Kris, Randy and his wife; it was unexpected but fair, for the boys had crashed and nearly ruined one of their parties.

As promised Sheri and Cherry found their way accompanied by six other delightful valley girl stereotypes, it was like a Chester fan club, all vying for Alfa female; Tom found it a hoot and empowering to be around. Rachael came along, as did surprisingly, Carl Strawberry's ex-girlfriend Poppy, of course she was a friend of Chester's as well.

The lads were amazed to find that Chester also had some male friends, a few of whom were here for the beer, and along with a mixed bag of his parents' buddies', the house was nigh on bursting at the seems.

The conversations rumbled, the beer flowed, the party food laid out, the jam session began, kicking off with a trio of Temptations numbers, which should have been polished by now, but were a woeful mess. Probably due to the occasion, Chester's timing was all over the place which was frustrating and left Seamus overly embarrassed.

The jam needed rescuing; a number with a less demanding beat and Seamus called it, a pair of Beatles tunes with *Mean Mr Mustard* segued into *Come Together*. That worked; familiar ground and simple. They followed those up with George Michael's, *Hand To Mouth*, an easy groove, before Seamus invited Hot Pot and Kris up to join them. Jules reluctantly gave over his axe to Stu, and Seamus swopped his electric guitar for an acoustic, with Kris taking up the lead. Now they were cooking, hitting the crowd with *Back in the USSR* and *Get Back*, a must for Tucson dwellers, then launching into *Jonny Be Good* and *Great Balls Of Fire*, followed by The Stones hits *Jumping Jack Flash* and *Brown Sugar*. Jules was blatantly getting the hump, so a break was called for.

Spencer took up the reins on the CD player and in no time at all, Chester was juggling a honey on each arm, one blonde and a brunette.

Tom approached them beer in hand, all smiles. "Chester man, man Chester."

"Tom, this is Stephanie," he urged the blonde forward. If there were a cheerleader chart list, this girl would have occupied the number one slot for weeks, she was jaw droppingly beautiful.

"She would totally love some of your Britishness poured all over her." He nonchalantly jettisoned the girl like she was an unwanted birthday gift, and then melted into the swathe with the brunette.

Suddenly astonishingly venerated, Tom adopted the most cultivated accent he could muster, "Good evening Stephanie, I'm very pleased to make your acquaintance." He may as well been speaking Urdu. She looked through him like he was the plate glass of an empty shop, appeared lost, then walked away in search of her sole crusade, bedding the drummer. How rude, he thought; stiff fanny.

In the kitchen he found his friends nursing the drinks table; Kate Norton was entertaining a guy he'd never laid eyes on before.

"Tom, I'd like you to meet Omar, he's gonna to be taking Chad's room when he ups sticks."

A whack of sadness hit Tom in the chest at the reminder of Chad's imminent departure; it took his breath away like the onslaught of asthma.

"Hey, man," Omar offered his hand and blew weed smoke off to the side, Popeye style, through his Mexican moustache.

Tom took the warm mitt, "Omar, that's Arabic isn't it?"

"Ah my name's Jim, Jim Days, but everyone calls me Omar, have done since 'Nam."

"Why?"

Everybody laughed. "Omar days," they said in unison.

The band's second set was mostly original numbers in which Jules showed off, back to his over-playing, complicating ways, and Chester losing time more than a sundial on a cloudy day. Chad was coerced back behind the kit, putting Chester's nose right out of joint, but instantly it felt justified, like a jigsaw puzzle piece being righted after a long time upside down.

They cruised through *Be Mine*, *Believe It All* and *Rosa* before Chad decided he was taking liberties, much to the disappointment of some of the guests. A young black dude, a friend of Chester's, was itching to play bass; Seamus switched to drums and Tom took the guitar. It was now a free for all jam of James Brown's *I Feel Good*, with various partygoers getting up to sing the verses; carnage.

Tom couldn't help notice Poppy giving him approving looks. This could be interesting, he thought. Handing the guitar over to Kris at the end of the song he wandered her way emboldened by drink, and over the intro of Free's, *Alright Now*, said "'ello, Poppy isn't it?"

She was swaying from the hips up and sucking something orange through a straw from a fluted glass. Petite, no taller than 5ft with long, curly, ebony hair and molten Bourneville chocolate pools where eyes should have been, she answered his question with a question. "Have we met before, or are you just a really good at guessing?"

Tom smirked, "We've never been introduced, but we 'ave been in the same room at the same time."

She wrinkled her brow.

Tom said, "I used to share a 'ouse with Natty Dread and I've played with Carl a few times."

"Oh you're the English guys," she flourished.

"Yep," he pointed a thumb back over his shoulder, "famous Seamus and Tom two."

"Tom cat more like." She gave him a knowing probing stare, boring into his psyche.

He resisted the urge to meow, instead he changed tack. "So 'ow come you know Chester then."

"Oh, we used to date; now I just cut his hair, I work at a salon in the Tucson Mall, you should come by some time, I'll give you a discount."

Tom fingered his locks, suddenly conscious that he might look like he'd been dragged through a hedge backwards.

She riffled through her purse then handed him a card.

"Hair Today," he read.

"Gone tomorrow," she answered on cue. "Call me." Sucking up another straw length of amber liquid, her eyes narrowed as the cold elixir hit the roof of her mouth, and with that she swaggered off towards the kitchen.

Tom followed her with his eyes admiring perfect pins below her tight fitting black mini skirt, and thinking they would complement his ears exquisitely.

Rachael appeared from out of nowhere, "Hey, wanna grab a beer?"

You wait all day for a brunette, he thought, and then two come at once. "Why not, the night is still young, lead on dear girl."

They strolled to the keg out by the pool where the noise from the band was less intrusive, quelled by patio glass and the still air.

Occupying rattan wicker pool chairs he sunk into his white cushions while she sat on the rim of another nursing a plastic pint glass like it was a sacred golden orb. The talk was of Chester, how they'd gone to school together and been friends since junior high. They'd never really dated but they had made out in the past, now they were just friends.

Tom found out that she worked at La Paloma, a resort in the foothills not too far from where they were, behind the bar, sometimes as a waitress. The money sucked but the music was good. "You should come over one night; I'll get you free drinks," she offered.

"We probably will." Tom gazed into her beautiful soft brown eyes. She was very pretty, chiselled, sultry, moustachioed. He couldn't; she wanted him to, he could tell, all he had to do was reach out and touch her and she would fall into his lap like wind blown chiffon, a delicate scented blossom eager to wrap herself around him with swirls of halcyon limbs and raspberry flavoured kisses. He'd have to let her down.

"D' ya' know what, I love talkin' to ya', but I've gotta go back in there and do some more yelling; we'll do this again sometime though." He got up lazily.

She stared into her beer, it had lost some of its effervescence. She pulled a half smile and nodded like it was a familiar story.

Tom couldn't believe what he was doing, growing some morality perhaps, or maybe she just didn't do it for him; was he going to regret this decision?

The party dissipated in the wee hours, after Chester had retreated into his man cave with his chosen bride, and the congregation had withered to just the family and a couple of incomprehensible drunks. The gear could be retrieved tomorrow; Tom still had the resolve to drive home, and Seamus appeared unaffected by the liberal amount of toxins he had ingested. He did the usual and left with Caryn bidding Chester senior an eventful long life and everyone a bon soirée. Sunday would be a large day of rest for all who had attended.

***

Thanksgiving was a new occasion for the boys, a slap up meal at Kate Norton's much like a Christmas dinner but with exotic trimmings like sweet potatoes, oyster stew, red pepper and avocado salad, green beans with bacon, and a pumpkin pie with a walnut crust, followed by pecan pie with whipped cream for dessert. They felt like stuffed Kings.

"Praise be to the Wampanoag people," said Seamus lifting a huge glass of champagne as they sat glutted around the extended dinner table.

"I hear that," agreed Kate mimicking Seamus' salute.

"Cheers," they all said in unison.

Tom wondered where on earth Seamus had gleaned that bit of information from, but went along with the pantomime all the same. "To Squanto," he added.

"To Squanto," they repeated.

"Whoever he is," announced Seamus.

Kate laughed, Holly giggled, Buster squawked, and Chad gave his lopsided grin. It was his last supper and although it was a glorious meal, a Herculean effort from the girls, he was obviously suffering.

Dawn brought with it a light mizzle, as if their spirits weren't dampened enough, a shroud of grey vapour was determined to wash the colour out of their lives as Chad's yellow camper van kicked up a surface spray cortege, misting the view of a dissolving friendship down South Mission Road. He was gone and with him, they felt, a glimmer of success.

18
X

Within a few days Omar had hauled his arse into Chad's old room and with it, the beer sales at the Circle K down the block took an upturn. Mr Days was a firm believer in chemical enhancement to help fog his reality; alcohol was just one ingredient of a concoction of mind-bending necessities, and pot was a constant.

He made it quite plain, Omar no longer gave a fuck; the war in Vietnam had bashed all the fuck's out of him and now he wasn't conforming to anyone's standards least of all 'The Man'. So his waking hours were spent in relaxed mode, taking care of just the bare essentials.

He told tales of dubious authenticity in his slow gurgling baritone drawl that were both silencing and spellbinding. Like the time he was on patrol, with his platoon, wading shin deep through rice paddy fields in the Red River Delta. In the distance they became aware of a low rumbling, like the sound of approaching diesel engines, only there were no roads out there, just dense jungle, paddy fields and thin trails used by skinny farmers wearing conical hats.

Thirty-nine soldiers hit the deck, crouching into the stinking water, soaking what little dry uniform remained. Omar just had time to pull his rubber coated poncho over his head, covering himself with a Heath Robinson force field, before a dense black cloud of mosquitoes descended upon him, hitting the poncho like a myriad of tiny darts, pip, pip, pip, pip, pip. His right arm however wasn't fully covered and succumbed to a hundred blood sucking beasts, affecting it to swell up like an elephant's trunk, itch maddeningly and infect him with malaria, of which he was lucky to survive because the chloroquine was having little or no effect on the troops by then.

Tom walked away from that fable amused, but questioning whether mosquitoes attacked in droves; he'd always thought them to be quite solitary.

Omar was great company, his dry wit a scream, but he wasn't ready to leave the confines of the hacienda just yet; he needed some time to adjust to his new environment.

Later Tom and Seamus found themselves seated unsteadily on two bar stools staring intently at a large TV screen in the meagrely populated Wild Cat House, insisting on wrestling with the Karaoke machine. Even for a Wednesday night the 'punter' count was abysmal. Their mistake was first to get blindingly drunk, and second to pick Paul McCartney and Stevie Wonder's classic duet *Ebony & Ivory*. This song has a vast vocal range and should not be attempted by anyone who does not, especially if they are seeing double. The harmonies were excruciating and the high notes akin to a squirrel being wound through a mangle tail first. Embarrassed, the boys slouched out of the subdued bar room and the silent 8 person press, and headed for the exit door.

"That needed tweaking a little," Tom slurred in the foyer.

"It needed Stevie and Paul," advised Seamus.

***

Chester's debut gig with the band was upon them, a Friday night at Gracious Bob's. What the lad lacked in drumming prowess, he encouragingly made up with a large following. Enticing at least 20 girls to the venue, plus his family and some college friends.

Tom and Seamus had only managed to persuade Omar to come along, Caryn and Bom were there as standard, and Jules had brought Diane.

The expectancy from rent a crowd was high. The band had been practicing 4 nights a week to get Chester up to speed; they'd learnt some new numbers, Bob Marley's *I don't Wanna Wait in Vain*, and Maxi Priest's version of *Some Guys Have all the Luck*. Any reggae song was a dead cert to get a Tucson throng up and dancing, they'd also learnt *She Drives me Crazy* by The Fine Young Cannibals.

Tom only ever enjoyed himself on stage when the band was tight and impressive. Mistakes and sloppy playing hindered him and marred the whole experience, even if the audience appeared to be having a good time.

Seamus just loved to play, a chance to entertain, to have a laugh, but it was pretty obvious to Tom, his mate was getting frustrated with the performance this band was giving; it was limping along with a stone in its shoe.

The crowd didn't seem to notice, some sat at the bar drinking, some ate at tables, the dance floor was inhabited all the time, and they were applauded. Yet it wasn't right, it was uncomfortable. In the break, after the handshakes and accolades from Chester's contingent, Tom sought out Omar at the bar, who was pouring beer from a bottle into his scooped right palm.

"What ya' doing, man?" asked the curious Englishman.

"Oh just getting my date drunk," drawled the old soldier.

Tom belly laughed. "What d' ya' think, man?"

"It ain't no rhythm and blues brother." The Viet-vet spoke the truth.

"I expected withering boos," Tom said cynically. They were going to have to do better than this to create a buzz around town.

"Ah don't be so hard on ya' self man, they seem to like it." He said tilting his beer bottle towards the crowd.

"But not your cup of tea?"

Omar half smiled at the English phrase, "No it ain't my cuppa tea, I'm more of a Deadhead/Lynyrd Skynyrd type of guy, you got Sweet Home Alabama up y'sleeve?"

"Nope."

"Pity, I would have got up for that."

Rachael cruised over to join them.

"Hey Rachael, glad you could make it. This is Omar, 'e's living at the 'ouse with us now."

The denim clad ex-serviceman exhaled a burst of Malborough exhaust through his new goatee before extending a paw. "A pleasure to meet you, Ma'am," he drawled.

She took his hand, "Nice to meet you too." She was sweet and demure like a handmade chocolate truffle you couldn't afford, unless your name was Tom. She looked around the room, impressed by how busy Bob's was this evening. "How's it going?"

Tom gave her a reasonable nod. "They're dancing, would ya' like a drink?"

"I'll have a Michelob, if that's okay."

"Of course, we've got a tab. Omar?"

"Another Heineken please buddy."

"Ah, a connoisseur eh?"

"Better than our weak ass-piss water."

"Back 'ome, Heineken is a really cheap beer," Tom informed him.

"Costs as much as gold here."

"Seems like it. Hey, what are you guys doing later?"

Rachael shrugged her shoulders.

"Whatever comes naturally." Omar skewed his lips and blew smoke out sideways through his hairy parting.

"We're 'ouse sitting for our friend Macy over the weekend, d' ya' wanna hang out?"

"Sure man. I've got 'shrooms." Omar's eyebrows rose over his spectacles.

Rachael looked like Tom had asked her to marry her.

"Brilliant, we'll 'ave a giggle." Tom leaned into the bar to order the next round.

The gig finished with disappointment for Tom, the groove was groove-less and the timing in parts, was like a mantelpiece clock with a fading battery. Seamus and Jules were obviously frustrated. José, hard to tell as he was neither here nor there; non-committal would be the word.

Chester on the other hand was jubilant, forever the optimist, he thought the performance was "Totally awesome." His entourage seemed to agree, so at least one aspect was covered. If you can please just one person in the room, Tom thought, then you are doing your job right. Trouble was they needed to please the management also.

The till receipts were good, the manager was happy; perhaps that's all that matters; dollars in the till.

Macy had taken her children off to see her Sister in Kentucky, and left the run of her house in the capable hands of two Herberts. She obviously didn't know them well enough.

The party of four landed on the drive after midnight and went through the house heading for the back garden and repose in cushioned pool furniture under the veranda.

Omar produced a baggy of 'shrooms with heads the size old British pennies. "These babies are psychedelic man, far out, better just a half each."

Tom took one, bit it in two and gave one half to Rachael.

Seamus did likewise with Omar.

The night was tranquil, the air was languid, Seamus retrieved some bottles of Michelob from the fridge and dolled them out.

Omar took the floor. "Have you ever heard of a Basenji?"

Seamus was rolling a single skinner, "A basengee, wos' that, some kind of Vietnamese Kung Fu assassin?"

Omar spat smoke though his pursed lips. "The Basenji is an Egyptian animal, a cross between a dog and a cat; it doesn't bark, only gives this blood curdling yodel that makes your skin creep."

"A barkless dog?" Tom was sceptical.

"A barkless cat-dog," corrected Omar. "It's a small, smooth haired, almond eyed pooch with those pointy upright ears that Egyptian dogs have."

"Like Doberman Pincers?" asked Rachael.

"Exactly, and just as ferocious. A friend of mine, Slope, had one in his apartment, a bitch that had given birth to a litter of pups; man was she protective of those guys. One night, Slope threw a party—"

Seamus butted in. "Slope, was that 'is real name?"

"His name was Dan Hill, but everybody called him Slope." Omar continued while the boys nodded knowingly. "It was a small affair, just a few friends for a smoke and a drink. He made a specific point that no one should go into the bedroom where his Basenji had been stowed away from all the noise."

The other three were intrigued now, silently listening to Omar's provocative parable.

"Well this one guy was persistent about seeing this fabled dog cat cross with no bark, but Slope warned him not to go in there for his own safety…."

The psilocin was starting to kick in, Tom's face was heating up and Omar's moustache was taking on an Old Yosemite Sam approach.

"… The guy took no notice and after some time got up to use the bathroom. On his way back, when no one was paying him much attention he snuck into the bedroom to satisfy his curiosity…."

The three of them were captivated.

"… The guy wandered back into the living room, like he'd just witnessed a massacre, with two perfectly shaped half moon cuts, one under each eye, blood still trickling down his cheeks. Every guest watched him as he sat back down with a thousand yard stare, a ghost of his former self."

"The dog bit him?" deduced Seamus.

"She followed him out into the living room with a measured waddle like motion, and stopped about six-feet from the sofa, glaring at him with her head bowed low, giving him a look that said 'Don't fuck with me!', before casually returning to her litter."

The image of a little dog with too many teeth to pronounce the words properly, took Tom over the edge and he burst out laughing.

Seamus too, visualising a cannabis infused outtake from Lady and the Tramp where the Basenji character strode off satisfied with her handiwork to the sound of silence behind her.

He too lost control of his giggle suppressor, which had a domino effect on the other two.

The four of them in fits, scarlet, rose, cerise and burgundy; four giant tulips planted in concrete, their petal heads like open mouths with stamen tongues bobbing rhythmically. This wasn't funny, yet it was, and the fact that it wasn't funny was funnier still.

"What 'appened to the dude?" Tom managed to gab.

"Slope had no sympathy for him, he told him not to go in there. The guy left a short time after and went and shot himself."

"What?" Tom squeaked.

"Only kidding … fucked if I know, but he should have done, just for being an asshole."

They laughed even more.

"I'm thirsty," blurted Tulip Seamus, bolting upright before leaping into the pool fully clothed, sending a splashback that reached Tom's feet.

Not to be outdone, Omar reacted with a handstand on the margins that flourished with a Cormorant-like entry through the choppy surface.

Tom was keen to get involved, but a little less audacious; he at least emptied his pockets and kicked off his sandals before joining his mates with a running bomb.

Rachael's reserve was spellbinding, and it caused a halt to the boys' frivolous pool slapping; they could only stare in wonderment as she stoically removed her T-shirt, cascading her long, dark locks in slow motion down her back, then unbuttoned and wriggled out of her tight jeans before folding her clothes and laying them neatly on a chair.

She then, purposely, gracefully floated towards the pools steps in her matching red underwear, climbing down a step at a time, her hand slipping delicately over the stainless steel rail as she disappeared beneath the water like a sun-kissed ocean siren.

Tom blinked, and in that moment a familiar warm feeling expanded in his chest. Tulip Rachael had taken on a different form; she was now a juicy ripe cherry and perfectly ready to eat.

Some time passed before Seamus and Omar climbed out of the pool, squelching as they walked over to their cigarettes. The hour was right, the three quarter moon high in the sky, the pool water rising off the surface like smoke from burning desire.

Rachael was crucified to the margins in the shallow end, arms outstretched caressing concrete, her back to the wall. The stare she fixed Tom with was enough, purposefully alluring, she smouldered; she knew exactly what she was doing.

He swam to her slowly, breaststroke, eyes locked onto hers, blowing little bubbles of air through pursed lips, till he reached her and in a single silky movement they became one, hot skin on scorching flesh, soft lips on wet Turkish Delight and pink candy tongues probing and penetrating, wrestling like inquisitive little limbs in the dark.

Her skin felt incredible, as though he was touching another human for the first time, the minutiae of her fabric exquisite, electrified. He pressed harder into her, threatening to meld her within the solid ceramic walls; their groins enlarged, pulsating with a surge in blood flow, locked together as if magnetised.

Omar indicated to Seamus with an incline of his head. "They're gonna fall in love," he said sagely.

Seamus, dripping on a lounger, exhaled a rhythmic 4 line beat of little smoke exhausts, half laughter, and half acknowledgment. "They're gonna set fire to the water in a minute." He imagined the pool surface ablaze with him and Omar trying to beat it out with wet shirts from the sides.

The pair of them erupted with a fit of the giggles which sent Omar into an asthmatic coughing fit that Seamus couldn't help him with because it was so funny he was in tears.

The kissing couple emerged from the water oblivious to the hyenas on the furniture and Tom unperturbed by the massive bulge in his jeans pointing the way. They headed hand in hand towards the patio doors. They slip-slopped along the cold tiled floor towards Macy's bedroom, where Tom was camped, on

Macy's orders, for the weekend; each step a giddy prospect on a toboggan run.

Suddenly there was carpet underfoot, Tom could feel every fibre in the pile sensually arousing his erogenous response and ranging up through his toes like twill blades of grass. On 'shrooms his senses were super-exaggerated, he felt totally alive for the first time in years; he could hear both their heartbeats, he could smell her sex, he wanted to taste it. He turned to kiss her, her long black sodden hair fell against his smouldering brown arms wrapped around her back like a cool flannel on a feverish brow, as she yielded to his embrace. Locating her bra hook he deftly undid it with one hand while the other put pressure in the small of her back, pressing her closer to him.

Releasing his grip allowed her bra to fall to the floor, revealing the most pert buoyant breasts you could imagine, perfectly formed with muddy pink bullet-hard nipples, swollen with desire. Tom, vanquished by the psychedelics, believed them to be raspberry jellies, desperate to be devoured. He lowered his head to feast on one, causing Rachael to throw her head back with the touch on her aching bosom, inhaling like it was her newborn breath. The ceiling spiralled above her dizzy form, till it and the roof blew away by a pixelated whirlwind, revealing the black velvet firmament peppered with twinkling diamonds; this business had been a long time coming.

With one hand still on her back, the other was free to go a wandering. He caressed a bum cheek, kneading it gently, tentatively probing his fingers between her legs. Then down the back of a silken thigh, around to her knee, and then softly, barely touching, he brushed up the inside of her thigh and came to rest his cupped palm on the warmth of her firm satin mound. Her body tightened as electricity surged through her system sending blue sparks crackling from her extremities, shrouding them in a perfect azure hue.

His hand slid up to her belly, he registered each tiny filament of baby hair on her abdomen. They acted like triggers of impending bliss as his fingers crossed the frontier of her panties and traversed the velvety down of her pubis till they reached the sodden delicate elasticity that his cock was yearning for. She was wetter than she had been in the pool, but she wasn't surrendering just yet.

After a breathtaking minute of almost climatic clitoral stimulation, she found the strength to push him away and back onto the bed. She wanted to taste him first, wanted to feel the expanse of pulsating muscle on her tongue, the roof of her mouth and down the back of her throat. She wanted to suck him dry, feel the ejaculate erupt and swallow it all. He was quite prepared to let her, sinking into the giant mattress like a stuntman's air cushion breaking his fall, he was almost consumed. His soaking jeans combined with his underpants, were proving hard to prise off, even with his backside arched off the bed, but eventually she rolled them inside-out past his feet. They flopped on the carpet like a shed exoskeleton, the lower half of a man, crumpled and discarded.

He laid there smiling in the half-light, his miniature totem pole leaning at a jaunty angle, but iron poker stiff.

Rachael wasted no time. She set to it with both hands like she was turning a clay pot, his pre-ejaculate juices just enough to stop the inexperience being painful.

Tom raised his head to look down on her curiously, she seemed mesmerised, hypnotized by the one-eyed trouser-snake, throttling and pulling at it like she was trying to kill it.

He grabbed her hands, "Easy," he said gently, "kiss it."

She paused, examining her meal like she was calculating whether it was edible, then ran her tongue up the length of the shaft from root to tip, before rolling her soft warm mouth over the purple throbbing head and then going at it like an otter on an eel.

Once more Tom had to intervene, correcting her inexperience, encouraging her to just use her lips and tongue, "Imagine it's the best tasting ice-pop you ever had."

And hey presto it was, but this ice lolly wasn't going to melt away to a puddle; this popsicle was everlasting, well at least for an hour or so, and its flavour was intense.

He put his clasped hands behind his head, closed his eyes and inhaled contently, this could just be Elysium, he thought, as a hot wet pocket enveloped the centre of his universe, stimulating every nerve ending with slithering suction, he dreamed of immortality. Tom could never cum by blow job alone, no matter how expert, it usually took a hand to get involved, but preferably, a nice tight pussy, and fortunately this is what Rachael possessed.

Her own desires had overwhelmed her, the longing for something solid and muscular deep inside her soaking tunnel was too powerful to carry on slurping this candy; she couldn't bear it any longer. Crawling up to him in slow motion, pecking at his belly and chest as she curled a leg either side of him, resting on her knees, vaginal juices from her dripping labia poised above his penis. She rubbed herself along it and shuddered, her long black hair dangled into Tom's face, her sighs long and breathy. At long last her right hand reached down and took hold of him, guiding the sticky rod of iron to her sodden opening, and plunging down upon it. A pitiful little moan erupted from her throat as her sensory cortex released oxytocin, creating a kaleidoscope of florescent fractals in her mind.

Tom raised his pelvis to meet her, thrusting his cock as far into her as it would go, threatening to lose it altogether.

Her pelvic thrusts were rapid, her lithe young body easily coping with the mechanics and the exertion submitted, sitting down on his balls and riding him like she was on a runaway colt at full gallop.

He almost shouted "Yee-haw!" as her Stetson flew off in the slipstream. Tom was reaching the point of no return, a volcano of white hot lava was pondering eruption from his thermal vent; he had to swerve it momentarily until she came. He reached forward putting the flat of his hand on her tummy allowing his thumb to work on her clitoris.

She immediately flinched, the pleasure endorphins doubling, inducing short melodic moans in the key of A, with each forward lunge. Her stomach muscles visibly tightened, taut caramel skin glistening in the low light, a strangled cry emitted as dopamine flooded her entire system sending her logical reasoning on vacation and the psilocybin to re-imagine herself launched into the air ahead of an elaborate water jet gushing at her crotch, suspending her unyielding pleasure.

Tom's ejaculate was that fountain, like a bunch of fire hoses released in unison, he'd pinned her to the ceiling with a colossal blast of muscle milk he was unable to shut off. It was by far the most intense mindblowing orgasm he'd ever experienced, every sinew in his body had contorted; breathing had ceased, his brain squeezed like a grey sponge, clamped by oversized hands, causing splintered neon colours to fracture behind tightly clenched eyelids.

She eventually landed with a splat reminiscent of a large specimen whacked onto a fishmonger's slab. They lay there, two steaming masses, a cowgirl and the fireman completely spent.

Minutes passed, Tom regained some humour as he pictured Rachael holding her own, keeping in the saddle, riding an unbroken horse. He chuckled.

"What?" she said raising her head from his chest.

"Your first Rodeo?"

She smiled, "Hopefully not my last, Mr Mustang."

"All you wanna do is ride around Rachael, ride Rachael ride." He half sang, half giggled.

"Oh yeah," she affirmed flirtatiously, reaching down towards his cock and feeling the blood already beginning to surge back into the beast. Round two was imminent.

In the morning, in that foggy period between waking and getting up, they played that game in which neither one of them wanted to admit that actual sex had taken place last night at all.

Tom was frail, dehydrated and sleep deprived. He pulled on his damp jeans, left Rachael in bed, and courteously went looking for her clothes and a gallon of water to throw down his neck.

Seamus was nowhere to be found, but Omar was blissfully asleep in a splayed out compromising position on a sunlounger, fully exposed to the sun and the rising temperature. He's gonna wake up hurt, concluded Tom.

Rachael's clothes had been staged on a chair to look like she was still in attendance. The boys had been entertaining themselves, so it seemed. He gathered the clothes, located a couple of pint jars, half-filled them with ice from the fridges nifty push-lever ice-dispenser on the door, then topped them with water before heading back to the bedroom.

"Yambozie!" rumbled Seamus from some unseen position down the corridor.

Tom replied with a deep croaky "Rasta!" He followed the noise down to Kimberly's room where he found the horizontal one naked, all but a twisted bedsheet wound round him; his usual reluctant toga.

Seamus spoke in hushed tones. "'ow d'ya' get on?"

Tom produced an assured grin. "I fully endorse sex on mushrooms." He smiled radiating like a torch.

"Yes I!" expressed Seamus artfully

Tom moved on, he'd fill in the details with his buddy later.

Rachael, already clad in her underwear when Tom returned, sipped at the water graciously.

Tom climbed back onto the bed and sat up against the headboard glass in hand, whilst she dressed in silence. He observed her intently, entertained by the reverse striptease. Her demeanour was as if she was embarrassed to be there, ashamed maybe at having let herself be ravaged so, but it was a two way thing, Tom hadn't taken advantage of her. They were both as fucked-up as each other last night, and they'd both shared a mind blowing experience.

He figured that in the sober light of day she might be feeling a little slutty, like she'd lowered her standards or something. Her participating in 'shrooms was definitely out of character, maybe she'd never done drugs before, perhaps she was suffering a guilty come down; she obviously didn't feel like talking.

He'd let her go, unhindered by any obligated ties, and see what transpired over time.

"I'll see ya' soon," he spoke as she opened the door to leave.

"Ah ha," was all she replied.

Tom slithered down the bedsheets and rolled onto his front, he'd deal with tidying the house later, now was time for some much needed shut eye.

***

Rachael didn't put in an appearance for the rest of the year; Tom supposed he must have upset her in some way. Seamus suggested that she had just checked 'fuck an Englishman' off her bucket list and done the off. It was conceivable.

In December the days were noticeably colder, but the temperature hardly dropped below a mild 50°F. It had in fact snowed the previous winter, just a ground covering, a dusting of icing sugar that melted to nothing after one sensationally rare cold spell. This Christmas, however, it rained all day, which felt perfectly normal.

Greeting cards came from home, warm messages and miss-yous, but little in the way of gifts. Holly was thoughtful though and had bought Tom a new guitar strap and some strings. Kate gave them a big bag of weed and Seamus got a blue and white tie-dye T-shirt from Caryn, which suited him. He wore it for dinner, another roast turkey spread at Kate's, but scaled down from the huge Thanksgiving meal last month.

On Boxing Day, they decided to buy each other a gift, so drove up to the Tucson Mall on Oracle where they purchased a couple of thick sweatshirts from a sports store. Seamus' was an official Chicago Bears number in navy and orange, while Tom got the New York Giants, sky blue with red writing. The tops weren't particularly rock 'n roll, but they were warm and they would be grateful of them in the months to come.

The last night of the year looked promising. Kate Norton, KP and Glen had all been invited to a party in the foothills at a house belonging to a bloke esoterically known as X. A mystique semblance, a manufactured persona symbolised by a single letter, formally known as Xavier Dina.

He was also went by the name 'The Meteorite Man' on account that he travelled the globe collecting fallen meteorites, paying local farmers a pittance for them and selling the rocks, or their content of gemstones, on the open market for thousands. Another exotic, unique and highly profitable enterprise this astute, wealthy individual developed a few years prior, was the invention of the 'Space Passport', a spoof document that allowed Earth's citizens to travel anywhere in the galaxy, had they the means. It had made him a packet.

The boys were paper-clipped onto the invite and set to leave at around 9:00 that evening, so there was plenty of time to get dressed up and drive to a local cowboy bar for a few liveners before they set off. And dress up they did, in matching cream chinos, white shirts, blue blazers and red cravats, an absurd impression of a couple of 'Dirty Rotten Scoundrels'.

The haunt, one of which they hadn't frequented before, was fronted by rugged aged timber and hard to distinguish against the night sky, save for bright neon tube advertising, promising Miller beer and Bud Lite, dished out to heavy drinkers. Inside, it was liberally sprinkled with ranch-hand types, hicks and rednecks, either occupying the vast array of red baize pool tables, or propping up the bar.

The piano playing literally stopped as they entered the smouldering room, all eyes gazing upon the two sore thumbs as they ventured to the bar, creaking the wooden floorboards and chafing their chinos as they trod. They may as well have painted targets on their chests. But if the cow-folk actually felt any disdain, none of them vocalised it, which was somewhat anti-climactic.

Seamus and Tom slid onto bar stools and ordered a couple of long necks, at which point the brief temporal distortion ceased to be, the sound system slurred back into life with a Def

Leppard tune and the patrons around them returned to their beer swilling, normal business restored.

A pair of baseball-cap wearing dudes closest to the boys, showed some interest. One, wearing a white cap-sleeved T-shirt, had a cigarette pack tucked up underneath a sleeve on his left shoulder. He must have seen it in a movie and thought it to be really cool; it wasn't. The other had on a brown and beige plaid fleeced jacket, giving the impression that he worked with trees, but this may have been paraded as fashion in these parts, for there were other men in the bar similarly attired and they couldn't all be arborists. White T-shirt dude spoke up first. His probing impish half smile gave away an insecure meddlesome nature. These two newcomers had disrupted the equilibrium somewhat, and he was intrigued.

"Where y'all from?" was all he could muster.

Tom, tired of the question, and without too much thought, simply replied, "Norway."

The dude appeared blown away by the revelation. Exotics, in his local. The only non-Americans he'd probably ever met before would have been Mexican, which was hardly surprising.

Plaid jacket leaned in, his limp blond hair languished on the bar surface mopping up spillage. "And what's a couple of fuckin' Vikings doing in a Tucson bar. You over here a rapin' and a pillagin'?"

White shirt laughed showing some missing teeth.

Tom decided to educate them, hoping that he was right, "Actually, Viking *is* a Norwegian word, but most of the pillagers back in the day were Danes, or Swedes, we Norwegians tended to be more civilized, preferring to explore or trade around the world."

"And shag!" said Seamus.

"And shag," agreed Tom.

This really baffled the American duo; they hadn't come out for a history lesson.

"What y'all doing here in town?" inquired plaid.

Seamus rose to the occasion. "Allow me to introduce us." He feigned a slight Scandinavian accent, "I am Sven and this is Tomas…"

"Deke," said white shirt raising two fingers to his chest.

"Clovis," said the other one, gripping the peak of his cap.

Seamus continued. "We are here making a movie—"

"I fuckin' knew you guys was actors, the fuckin' minute you walked in," Deke sat back in his bar stool, assured of his intuition. "Nobody wears shit like that in these parts!"

Tom's face was twitching, trying to hold in the mirth.

Seamus simulated aghast, "Shit like that? I'll have you know that this cravat is made of the finest Tibetan silk. And this blazer belonged to my father; it's an honour to wear it." His accent was slipping into French.

Clovis offered an olive branch. "What's the movie about anyways?"

Tom took up the mantle. "Sid Salter."

Everyone else was none the wiser.

"Sid Salter, the famous diamond thief of London town. In 1961 he was the United Kingdom's most wanted man, when after a raid on a jewel merchant's basement, where an assistant got killed, he went on the run with his male lover and they ended up here in Tucson, holed up in the El Presidio hotel, up on campus."

Clovis screwed up his forehead. "What happened to 'em?"

"You will have to watch the movie to find out my friend."

"Ah, you can tell us, we won't let on n'all," pleaded Deke.

"We are bound by contract I'm afraid," piped Seamus, "it's all very hush-hush." He tapped the side of his nose like he was David Niven.

Deke, possibly the more naïve of the two, had taken the tale all in good faith, "So what's the movie called then?"

"Diamonds are for Trevor," replied Tom.

Two hours later, three people were crammed into the El Camino laughing their heads off. Kate Norton at the wheel and her two English boys squashed in the passenger seat, like overdressed pilchards. They'd dropped some mushrooms before departing the hacienda and the effects were kicking in with magnitude.

X's house clung to a hillside like it had subsided fortuitously during a landslide; its three stories of pristine white clapperboard siding brilliantly illuminated by strategically placed spotlights under the eaves and amongst the rocks in the garden.

Tom may have been heavily under exotic influences, but it looked like the coolest pad on the planet, an intergalactic ship disguised as a swanky foothills home, and if they didn't climb aboard right now it might just take off on a trip around the cosmos without them. It was difficult to locate somewhere safe to leave the car, there were dozens of vehicles on the drive and roadside, some big vans too, catering trucks and people carriers, the house was going to be rammed.

Inside the property, the colour scheme was entirely black and white, things were either black or white, and some were a mixture of the two. The floor was a diagonal chess board, and on it, in the spacious living room, a stage crammed with band equipment, a decent-sized PA system and a lighting rig had been set up. The foundations were in for a test tonight.

X, welcoming guests in the foyer, lit up when he spotted Kate enter. He bundled over, head to toe in a white suit and shirt, his black curly hair greasing his shoulders. "Kate," he wrapped his arms around her, "great that you've made it, and sober too."

Kate hissed out her husky laugh, "I wouldn't say that man, I dropped a big old boomer before we left; it's making itself known now."

"Well you're in the right place to let your hair down right, anything goes."

His eyes flicked at the two identically dressed lawn bowls dudes.

Kate loquaciously introduced her boys.

"And where on asteroid Earth have you guys emerged from?"

Seamus stepped up, "Tom's from a little place called Watford in Hertfordshire, and so am I."

"Is that near London?"

Tom joined in, "Just next door, within the M25 orbit."

Their host looked slightly puzzled, not quite bamboozled, but curious. "Why are you guys dressed the same?"

"We are twin Saguaros, wrenched from the desert dust, with a thirst to quench," said Seamus, "but sometimes we are one."

X's brow crinkled slightly.

"Well, everyone's welcome here, including Watfordarians. Help yourselves to food and drink, there's a huge spread out the back; the band starts at ten, fireworks at midnight. " His eyes widened. "Enjoy," he said, before whooshing off to greet another newcomer.

X came across as a unique mixture of laidback exuberance, confidence, and pleasing openness. They liked open; they had a free pass to go explore. Down a flight of stairs at the back of the house, the opportunity for a banister ride was irresistible. The landing however wasn't as deft as they'd hoped, as they both crashed into a wall on the stairways return, ending up in a hysterical crumpled heap. Kate took the formal route, one step at a time, gurgling laughter in their wake.

Before them, in a room fronted with an enormous plate glass window offering an all-encompassing view of the obsidian Sonoran plateau, groaned several tables laden with exquisite delights. Every spirit you could name, and some you couldn't. A banquet of luxurious party food, canapés, crostini, Satay chicken skewers, lobster tails and charcuterie boards; the caterers had been enthusiastic, not a vol-au-vent or sausage roll in sight. Even the sandwiches looked like the work of an artisan, sculptured arrangements on tiered silver cake stands, it seemed criminal to disturb it all, but ruder not to.

"What the fuck is this man?" questioned Tom aloud.

X had followed them down the stairs and was closing in, "That's baby red potatoes topped with crème fresh dill and Caspian Sea red caviar."

"Thought as much," concurred Seamus.

"And what's this white stuff on top of the fish cakes?"

X was pretentiously amused, he snorted, "They're crab cakes topped with sweet chilli sauce and white caviar."

"White caviar?"

"Yes, snail's eggs."

Tom grimaced, "I think I'll give them a swerve, who thought that was a good idea?"

"The snail that deposited them I should imagine." Kate chuckled at her own wisecrack.

But Tom was now imagining giant snails had crawled across the spread, trailing their slimy train. It didn't deter him though, he was ravenous.

"Drink anyone?" proffered Seamus.

"D' ya' 'ave any champagne X?" verbalised Tom, chewing on a chunk of tortilla wrap containing something orange and spicy.

"Verve Clicquot okay?"

"Just the ticket."

X pulled a bottle from a cooler box beside the tables, skinned the foil and metal cage, then wrestled with the cork, turning his thumbs white with the effort till the resistance finally conceded with a large pop, sending spume arcing across the room like an albino rainbow.

Seamus overplayed the excitement for the opening of a bottle, with an exaggerated "Wuh, huh, huh, huh, hoo!" which helped the bonding process with their host, but raised one of Tom's eyebrows.

They all partook in emptying the bottle.

X must have been charmed by the company. "Who'd like to see my latest acquisitions?" He was wide eyed, waiting for a response.

"Is it more exotic eggs?" asked Tom.

"Kind of." He was charged now, buzzing. "This way to the bat cave!" He marched off with a quick step that was impossible not to emulate.

Through a door at the back of the room, was another chamber which must have been carved out of sheer rock.

Diamond white light ignited automatically as they entered, revealing a white rectangle lobby with a huge stainless steel vault door opposite.

"Look away," commanded the meteorite man. They performed as he bid to the sound of whirring and clicking behind them, as X dialled the combination on the lock, followed by a whoosh as he pulled back the 12 in thick metal door.

More blinding lights blinked on as the trio turned in concert to gaze upon a repository of riches, a box room 4 yds square, racked to the ceiling with stainless steel shelving, laden with sparkling gemstones, lattice crystals of every shape and colour, geodes sliced and halved, and of course, meteorites of various size and aspect. The three guests were stupefied, and, mostly due to the influence of the 'shrooms, extensively mind-blown.

Prisms of light, diagonal rainbows, crisscrossed the room, reflected and counter reflected as the people moved into the space; it was like stepping onto the dance floor of the world's greatest silent disco. Sparks ignited, bounced and flashed in front of their eyes from the polished surfaces of octahedrons, hexagons and trigonal covalents; it was dazzling.

"Wow, that's some glitter ball man," concluded Seamus.

"Yeah, it's funky alright," said X. "Take a look at this." He reached to a top shelf and pulled down an olive wood box with a carved relief of Monument Valley around it. Inside cushioned on black velvet, was a hunk of sandy rock, encrusted round a red candy apple hexagonal mass of crystals, whose luminescence was magnificent.

"That sure is preddy," drawled Kate.

"Looks like rhubarb crumble," said Tom. "Is it worth a few quid?"

"This, my friends is Red Beryl ...."

A picture of the actress Beryl Reed flashed into Tom's mind.

"...one of the rarest crystals on Earth. It came out of the Wah Wah Mountains, Beaver County, Utah, and it cost me a packet."

Seamus had gone into earnest mode. "'ow many of them 'ave been dug up then mate?"

X had taken the gem out of its box and was holding it aloft 6 in from his eyes, losing himself in its lustrousness. "For every hundred and fifty thousand diamonds that are found, you'll find one of these," he said hypnotised by its beauty.

"Expensive then?"

"Oh, about ten thousand dollars per carat."

"And 'ow many carats is that one?" enquired Tom naively.

"More than Bugs Bunny could eat in a year."

Tom's brain was too spangled to attempt to work out value on the stone, besides; he had no idea how big a carat was.

Seamus was eyeing up some smooth black lozenge shaped stones that had vibrant flecks of red, green, yellow and blue within their make up.

"What are these X?"

"Black Opals, they're only found in one small town in South West Australia, a place called Lightning Ridge, so they are incredibly rare also."

The cave was starting to appear like a candy store; Tom had visions of stuffing his face with some of the crystalline delights. He fixed on a clear disc of a gem shaped like a fifty pence piece. It had a pinkish hue around its outer edge and contained drifts of silver and amber suspended in time. It was presented on a tiny wooden easel.

"An excellent eye my friend," noted X. "The rarest crystal of 'em all, Taafeite, there are only fifty known specimens in the world. And I have one of them," he boasted. "A mineral composition of Beryillium, Magnesium and Aluminium, they come out of Sri Lanka and Tanzania, very reluctantly."

"Valuable then?"

"Not as valuable as you might think, they're not as prized as the Red Beryl. Shall we go upstairs? The music will be starting soon; I don't want to miss out." He ushered them to vacate and swiftly locked up his stash behind them. "Grab a bottle do." He said bounding up the white steps two at a time; I can't be late, no, no, not at all."

He had turned into the White Rabbit from Alice in Wonderland.

Tom turned to Kate, "Come on Dinah, curiosity often leads to trouble."

They followed Mr X up the stairs to the sound of the band striking up with INXS' *Devil Inside*. Seamus brought up the rear with a bottle of bubbly under each arm and a pre-made spliff between his lips, "Trouble on," he commanded.

The empty hall at the top of the stairs was also a shiny chessboard tiled floor, perfect for Hopscotch, Leapfrog and the 'dancing on a single coloured square only' game.

To the groove of Stevie Wonder's *Do I Do*, Seamus and Tom performed an exhausting rendition, to anyone who happened to pass by the door, of their legendary Blues Brothers routine; Seamus on white squares, Tom on black. They received some analytical looks, bizarre stares; a few inquisitive minds even stayed for a while, until the boys went into Russian dancing mode and inevitably fell over each other laughing uncontrollably.

Kate wobbled off gripping her champagne glass like she was about to break it, chortling her toothy howl. It was an effort for the lads to get back on their feet.

Evidently the band had both male and female singers, because they next hit the crowd with Miami Sound Machine's *1-2-3*, which got the boys' attention. The musicians were competent and versatile, and the singers excellent. They stopped fooling around in the hall and squeezed into the sweaty living room. The female vocalist was amazing, pint-sized, with a mass of crimped, flame coloured hair. She had on a black, lacy, fairy dress and black, diamond fishnet stockings, finished off with four inch stiletto ankle boots.

"She looks just like the girl from T'Pau," Tom shouted at Seamus.

"Carol Decker? That can't be 'er mate," his buddy hollered back, "She wouldn't be doing this."

'Spose, thought Tom, but it really did look like her. He spotted KP and Glen with Kate Norton, swaying to the Latin vibe. He staggered over and spoke into KP's ear. "Don't ya' think that singer looks like the girl from T'Pau?"

KP gave him a searching look. "Who?" she said.

"Carol Decker, the singer."

"I don't know who that is Tom."

He couldn't comprehend that KP didn't know the singer of *China in your Hand*.

"Really?" he slurred perplexed. "Hmm."

The next song set upon by the band was Belinda Carlisle's, *Heaven is a Place on Earth*; it lit up the room. Amongst the cavorting throng, Tom spotted Seamus talking to some dude dressed as Beetlejuice with a Wynona Ryder lookalike on his arm, in a red wedding dress and veil. She appeared aflame; Tom thought it only proper to inform her of her predicament.

He surfed over on an invisible hover-board. "Your dress is on fire!" he cautioned.

"And so it should be," she replied completely unfazed, "I'm hotter than Hell." She was, but unfortunately shackled to a ghost.

"Tom Bongo," he said, "at your service." He offered a chivalrous bow.

She grinned, and presented a lacy-armed, fragile, porcelain paw, palm down. "Amy, Amy Zing, and I don't need servicing." She waited for a response.

Tom took her hand gently, it was as cold as steel, for now she was a finely-tuned, mirror shiny Ferrari, ultra responsive and dangerous to the unfamiliar.

"Ah, but 'ow are your treads?" he queried, "can ya' 'andle an 'airpin bend, Cavillina?"

"If it's a cocktail I'll take two," she decreed.

"Thirsty eh? I'll see if I can muster up a couple of gallons." And with that, he floated off in the hope of finding someone a little less presumptuous and more available. There were none; no single girls, or groups of girls even, just trendy couples, nomadic odd looking blokes and old hippies.

X took to the microphone; it was almost midnight. "My friends, are you enjoying the party?" A cheer went up. "1988 is coming to a close, a new year awaits just past the hour. A new dawn, new romance, new love, new opportunities, and lets hope some fantastic new finds." Another cheer reverberated around the cavorted ceiling. "We're having a short interlude in the music Ladies and Gents, while we witness an awesome spectacle in the heavens; to the rear balcony folks, for the countdown to the New Year and some formidable fireworks!" The room erupted and a tide of bodies snaked out back.

You'd be excused for thinking that an invasion was taking place by the enormity of gunpowder exploding in the air above the house. Night became day in a psychedelic aerial display that illuminated a square block of Sonoran desert like a landing strip. It was phenomenal, exhilarating, and deafening. The whooshes, pops and bangs greeted with whoops, woos and squealing, plus exaggerated smiles that threatened to split faces. Dazzling magic, heat, light, sound, kinetic energy, missiles, screaming Banshees, the smells of gunpowder, Saltpeter, sulphur and Thermite, laced the air in ghostly wisps that swirled and danced to nothing.

In Tom's 'shroomed-out mind the metal salts exploding, fizzing and crackling, in a conservation of momentum, looked like massive flower heads. Copper blue and Barium Allium blooms, inflating, nodding and freefalling to earth. Sodium Dandelion Pappus expanding from a single bright point to a huge balloon then blinking out like it was never really there. Sparking orange rocket trails of Potassium Nitrate thumping into bold red Dahlia orbs of burning Strontium that wiggled like erratic worm embers enjoying a last hurrah.

X knew how to throw a party; he literally had money to burn. The show finale was an enormous white sky breaker which sent a shockwave back to the ground so fierce, that it took the wind out of you. The boys stood transfixed like they'd just witnessed an atomic bomb test. After ten seconds of silence they both said in unison "Again!"

Back inside the house, the band was obviously on a break; because a skinny dude sporting a long black mullet was manning a couple of turntables, head down concentrating on the faders. The Cure's classic hit *Boys Don't Cry* was fuelling some weird gyrations on the dance floor and flying the flag for Brit pop, which made a refreshing change from the Americana played eternally on all the radio stations.

Through his beer goggles, Tom spotted her poised on the edge of a white leather couch, legs crossed, fingers tapping rhythmically on her knee; Carol Decker. She obviously needed company; why else would she be alone? He plonked himself down on the empty cushion beside her, so lumbering he almost evicted her.

Uncomfortable, she quarter-turned so that her back addressed him.

"You look just like the girl from T'Pau?" he slurred.

She didn't respond; she couldn't have heard him above the music, he tried again.

Leaning into her nest of ginger curls he could smell the hairspray. "Excuse me," he sounded just like Arthur, "'as anyone ever told you, ya' look jus' like the girl from T'Pau?" Nothing, a complete blank. He couldn't fathom why she was ignoring him. He gave it another shot. "'ello! You look jus'—"

She stood up, brushing his floppy face with the harsh ruffles of her tutu, and walked away, leaving Tom doubting his existence.

"How rude," he said to himself watching her sashay away and meld into the late night revelling. His dejection was interrupted suddenly with a bark from Seamus, "Ras'."

Tom jerked upright and twisted his position round on the couch.

His buddy clutched two flutes of bubbly in one hand a bottle of Tattinger in the other. "We 'aven't toasted the New Year in yet, 'er y'are." He handed Tom a glass.

Bongo got to his feet unsteadily and swayed like he was out at sea. "To money, music and minge," he decreed. "Not necessarily in that order."

Seamus laughed, clinked Tom's crystal and said, "I hear that."

By 2:00 a.m. the party had thinned considerably, the music was at a minimum, X was nowhere to be seen and the boys were atrociously drunk. Luckily Kate had remained relatively sober, and was sensibly calling time on the evening. Trying to prize Seamus away from a situation, especially when he was inebriated, was like trying to remove a Velcro ball from a Velcro wall, wearing boxing gloves; difficult and frustrating. Just when you think you've got him unstuck, he sticks somewhere else.

Muttering incoherently to a Dutch couple decked out as Adam and Eve, Seamus was baffling the ivy strewn pair with an explanation of the differing frequencies of light in a rainbow. In his altered state it all made perfect sense, but the first man and woman were stupefied, yet too polite to tell the Englishman it was time to fuck off.

Tom wasn't so gracious, "Ras', come on, let's do the Frank Bough."

Seamus slowly turned to Tom; his eyes were half closed and glassy. "I was jus' telling Bart and Nadya 'ere about the electromagnetic spectrum, an' that we can only see a part of it, between 400 and 700 nanometres, infrared to ultra violet, but there's so much more—"

"Everyone knows that, you're boring them; come on, it's 'ome time."

"'ang on, 'ang on ...." Seamus paused to gather his thoughts. "Why is the sky blue? Because clean air scatters blue light more than red—"

Tom joined in, "Why is the sea blue?"

"'cause it's reflecting the sky."

"No, because water *is* blue. Now come on, let's get going."

"Yeah but what about microwaves, x-rays and gamma-rays, they're passing through us all the time, and what damage are they doing?"

"Fuck knows."

Kate interrupted, "The only colours I can see around you two right now are a dirty greyish white, which means you're both gonna be ill in the morning. Now get your shit together and let's get going."

"Yes Mom." They both obeyed.

Finding the El Camino wasn't hard, there weren't too many vehicles left at the scene, most sensible people had long since gone home but not these three gluttons for punishment. Once shoe-horned back into the seats, which was a task, they decided that breakfast was in order, and a stop at Denny's on the way home a necessity.

Kate managed to exit the car with a decent enough manoeuvre, but the boys were stuck, rammed against the door panel and disabled by the drink. Tom was functionless and fathomless, which is a good title for a Rod Stewart song. Their chauffeur had to walk round and extricate them. Popping the door handle caused Tom to suddenly expand sideways and flop into the car park unceremoniously, swiftly followed by the chortling Seamus.

Tom, on his back laughing, was unable to get up; Kate, croaking huskily, couldn't lift him, and Seamus was redundant, laughing at the two of them. An upturned turtle and a helpless mother hen. Somehow, between the three of them, Tom was righted, brushed free of grit and guided towards the restaurant.

For this time of the morning, trade was fairly brisk. It was mostly truckers, but with it being New Year's Day, there were still some residue from the night before. Their waitress, way too cheery for this hour of the day, was labelled Nancy. She was short, possibly Hispanic, and gave the impression she'd seen everything there was possible to see before.

They ordered tea, coffee, a pitcher of water, orange juice and three Grand-slam breakfasts, two without meat, Kate also added a side order of pancakes. The drinks came over swiftly and were hastily delved into. The tea was piss-weak, even after several minutes of dunking the Lipton's bag into the barely boiled water.

"They got this fuckin' water out of the 'ot tap," garbled Tom.

Kate guffawed, "Yeah, probably man."

He took some orange juice and necked the whole glass. The room was brightly illuminated, the yellow and red décor a blurry eyesore. Tom's lids were weighing heavily, the conversation around him fading; he was heading for night-nights prematurely.

At the precise moment that Nancy returned with the mountain of food, Tom keeled over into the aisle, headbutting her in the stomach and launching her and the food in three different directions. The clamour caused the entire restaurant to stand up and take note; staff rushed over to see what was afoot.

Nancy sat on her arse winded, with legs akimbo, whilst eggs, hash browns and sausages slowly slipped off the static furniture.

Seamus couldn't contain himself and was laughing uncontrollably.

Kate, utterly embarrassed, had a hand to her mouth to smother her mirth.

Tom assumed the foetal position on the aisle carpet, in his blazer, chinos, white shirt and red cravat, surround by pancakes, bacon, toast and maple syrup.

"We'll take that to go," said Seamus.

To be continued ....

Thank you for reading my book. I hope you enjoyed the story and will be tempted to buy another of my books. I would be grateful if you would take the time to write a short review, and post it on either Amazon or Goodreads. Reviews benefit potential readers and assist me as a writer.

Other Titles by Anthony Randall

With Doug Goddard
The English Sombrero (Nothing to do but run)
http://www.amazon.com/The-English-Sombrero-Nothing-but-ebook/dp/B00IHH209W

The English Sombrero (The little white ball)
http://www.amazon.co.uk/The-English-Sombrero-Little-White-ebook/dp/B00KC5DBWM

Short story

Colin and Sandy
Contained in the anthology: You're Not Alone
http://www.amazon.co.uk/Youre-Not-Alone-Author-Anthology-ebook/dp/B00Y5RCOOE

About the author

Anthony Randall was born in 1961 in King Street, Watford, Hertfordshire. He has resided in Tucson, Arizona, and in Bourlens, France, but now lives in sunny Dorset on the south coast of England close to the sea. He has been a singer/songwriter for thirty-years, recording and performing pop songs all over the world. He wrote and published his first novel The English Sombrero (Nothing to do but run), with his co-author Doug Goddard back in 2005, the first of a four part saga about the trials tribulations of Don Simmons, an extravagant millionaire who lends himself to some outrageous adventures and sticky situations. Book two, The English Sombrero (The little white ball), see's Don further his journey of enlightenment. Both books are available as e-books and paperbacks. Anthony and Doug are currently working on three more novels. Anthony has a short story published in the You're Not Alone' anthology called Colin And Sandy, has published many articles and short stories in the on-line magazine Mom's Favorite Reads, and is hard at work writing volume two of Tales of Tucson.

www.ingramcontent.com/pod-product-compliance
Lightning Source LLC
Chambersburg PA
CBHW021239200726
48288CB00014B/70